BROKEN

SINS OF OUR FATHERS
BOOK ONE

EMMA LUNA

COPYRIGHT

Copyright © 2020 by Emma Luna

All rights reserved. No part of this publication may be reproduced, stored or transmitted in any form or by any means, electronic, mechanical, photocopying, recording, scanning, or otherwise without written permission from the publisher. It is illegal to copy this book, post it to a website, or distribute it by any other means without permission.

This novel is entirely a work of fiction. The names, characters, and incidents portrayed in it are the work of the author's imagination. Any resemblance to actual persons, living or dead, events, or localities is entirely coincidental.

Emma Luna asserts the moral right to be identified as the author of this work.

Emma Luna has no responsibility for the persistence or accuracy of URLs for external or third-party Internet Websites referred to in this publication and does not guarantee that any content on such Websites is, or will remain, accurate or appropriate.

Designations used by companies to distinguish their products are often claimed as trademarks. All brand names and product names used in this book and on its cover are trade names, service marks, trademarks, and registered trademarks of their respective owners. The publishers and the book are not associated with any product or vendor mentioned in this book. None of the companies referenced within the book have endorsed the book.

First edition

Editing: Emma Luna at Moonlight Editing

BROKEN

SINS OF OUR FATHERS BOOK ONE

EMMA LUNA

Proofreader: Dani Black at Black Lotus Editing

Cover Design: Raven Designs

DEDICATION

*To my Dad and Grandad,
for showing me exactly what
a male role model should be like.*

*The person I am today is all because
of how you raised me
and I am so proud to call you my family.*

AUTHOR NOTE

Thank you for taking the time to read this book, I really do hope you enjoy it. However, this book does contain scenes that may be a trigger for some people. It also contains scenes that are only suitable for those aged over eighteen. So please, only read on if you are a lover of dark romance.

I am an English author and this book is set in London, England. Therefore, I use English spelling and phrases, so please, take that into account when reading.

PROLOGUE

History says that the son shall not pay for the sins of the father, and yet, that is exactly what has happened my entire life. I have been moulded in his image, paying for his crimes since I was born. Now, it's my turn to get revenge. It's time for the father to pay for the sins of the son. Once upon a time, in London, there was a man. A violent, sick man. This is his son's story of revenge.

CHAPTER ONE
GRANT

"Morning, family, so lovely to see you all. Looks like it is going to be nice weather today," my father sings as he practically skipped into the breakfast room. Myself and my step-witch are already seated at the table, just like we are every morning waiting on Father.

This jolly, middle-aged man with short, salt and pepper hair looks and sounds so friendly, but you could not be more wrong. The tight smile on my stepmother's lips as she quickly looks around to make sure everything is just as he likes it, shows another side to him. The house staff who rush around quickly but efficiently, never making eye contact or speaking, tells you everything you need to know. To the outside world, Alan Blakeman is a billionaire businessman, loving family man, and humanitarian. But behind closed doors, he runs an illegal enterprise of money laundering, drug smuggling, human trafficking, and racketeering. He is also a stone cold son of a bitch who likes to rule his family with an iron fist and is happy to kill anyone who crosses him. The people who matter know he is the biggest crime lord in all of London and that he rules the streets, but still, he wants to come across as the family man. All part of his sick image. If any gangs are operating in London, they are doing it with his permission. He owns this city and everyone in it, including most of the law and politicians. The Blakeman Family is a name that strikes fear into the hearts of anyone who hears it and has done so for generations. As long as a Blakeman rules, nobody will challenge the organisation and my father will continue to rule with no remorse.

I am heir to his empire, it's something he has been training me for my entire life. I have never known anything else, have never even been allowed to think for myself. He has predetermined every step in my future journey, and he fully intends to control me until the day he dies.

"Good morning, darling. We are all fine today, as always, aren't we, son?" screeches the woman to my side who now calls me her son. What's really ironic is that the dumb, blonde bimbo, with giant fake tits, courtesy of her very own Daddy Moneybags is actually four years younger than me, at twenty-three. My mother died when I was just four years old and I've had more 'mothers' than I can count since then. This is just the latest one. She, just like all the rest, is terrified of my father and does everything just to make him happy.

Having spent years learning exactly how to interact with

my father, I know that it is in everybody's best interest not to piss him off at any time, but it is almost a cardinal sin to do it before he's had his morning coffee. I even have a very small scar on my forehead from where a teacup hit me when I was twelve. So while Barbie chooses to be far too bright and energetic even for me, I just mumble in agreement to her question. Barbie's real name is Mindy, but they never stick around long enough for me to bother learning their real names, plus she looks far too much like a Barbie doll for me to call her anything else. She can fuck right off if she thinks I will ever call her Mum.

"That's fantastic. I actually have a job for you today, Grant. I want you to take Ryder and Victor with you." I roll my eyes at that, he adds it on everytime, but like I would go anywhere without them. Vic is my muscle and driver; he's the guy you want next to you in a fight because he isn't afraid to dive right in. I know he would take a bullet for me because he has. Vic is the type of bodyguard that is always around but you never see or hear him, he never really talks and he never questions an order, he just does as he's told. Ryder, on the other hand, is the complete opposite. He is my head of security. He's the one who thinks of all the possible scenarios beforehand to make sure a fight never even occurs. He is chatty, opinionated, and never does as he is fucking told without a good reason. But, he's also the closest thing I have to a friend. They both are fantastic at their jobs and that is the only reason I didn't get rid of them like I did all of my other employees who were hired by my father. I prefer to choose my own employees, to know that who I work with won't be reporting back to him. I trust Vic and Ryder with my life.

"You will take them both and find Manuel Delgado. The football game he placed a bet on last night sadly did not go his way and his debt is just racking up. He has missed the last three payments, he now owes forty thousand pounds. I want you to go there and stress to him no more bets. We are going to need some form of agreement to pay, even if it is just a little. I don't think he has anything but take anything you see of value, just nothing sentimental. Remind him you don't renege on a deal with Alan Blakeman. This is my honour and our family name you are defending, but remember, Grant, dead men cannot pay," says Father with his usual cocky, superior tone that insinuates I will mess this job up in some way. What he doesn't realise is that this is the job I have been waiting for. This isn't the first time Manny's name has flagged up, but it is the first time we have acted on it. I know there have been grumblings within the employees, questioning how this person keeps getting let off so easy and until I looked into it, I had no idea the extent of it. Father has obviously heard the grumblings now and decided he has to appear to be acting, but the consequences he is asking me to dole out do not fit the situation. Father is hiding something, but now he has passed the job over to me and I intend to make sure that my family name is given the recognition it deserves.

After leaving the breakfast table, I head towards my room

in the big family house that we all live in. This is where I am expected to stay the majority of my time, but it is not where I live. I have my own home and I plan on spending a lot more time there. Reaching my room, I take out my mobile and call Vic. I skip any pleasantries and get right to business.

"Prepare my countryside residence, I am coming home. I want a full perimeter with armed security and someone manning the CCTV at all times. I want it minimally staffed and fully stocked by this afternoon. I will send you a list of specifics. Have Ryder prepare the car and both of you meet me out front in one hour. We have a job from Alan." I reel the information off down the phone at quick speed, but I know Victor has everything and I know he will delegate appropriately to ensure it is completed on time. I then text him with a list of female home comforts and clothes I want stocked in the house. He doesn't ask any questions, which is what I like about him. A small smile crosses my lips as I prepare to head out and all I can think is that I cannot wait for this job.

Sitting outside Manny Delgado's shitty excuse for a house and scoping it out before we make our move to go inside, I feel a sense of anticipation as I work the plan over in my head as I have multiple times before. We are in one of the poorer neighbourhoods in the city and just being here makes my skin crawl. My expensive Mercedes Benz S Class sticks out like a sore thumb. My nerves prickle as I cast my eyes around to make sure there is nothing that is a danger to me here. There are what looks to be a couple of gangbangers on the far side of the street, but I know Ryder will have already seen and taken care of them. His eyes dart around at a speed that would make me dizzy and his fingers type on his phone with a rapid yet confident dexterity. Most likely, he has just informed their boss who we are and now we have an extra set of eyes making sure no damage comes to my car. Still, when we get out I listen for the tell tale beep that lets me know Vic has activated the alarm on my baby. I don't want any of these opportunistic poor fucks thinking they can make some quick cash by stealing from me.

As we reach the white plastic-looking door, I nod for Victor to knock and let Manny know we are here. His knock reverberates loudly around the small, shitty looking house and the door shakes like it might fall off its hinges. The sound of footsteps walking towards the door has my heart racing, but I try to squash it down and look disinterested, I cannot seem anxious. This is just any other job.

Manuel 'Manny' Delgado opens the door and his face shifts from one of curiosity, to one of fear and he looks as though he has just aged ten years. Manny took the death of his wife Marianna hard. She died from ovarian cancer fifteen years ago and ever since her diagnosis, Manny had struggled, only for it to worsen when she passed. He has trouble holding down a job, he drinks far too much, and has a penchant for gambling, something he is not at all good at. If what Eli, my hacker, tells me is correct, he has gambled away more money than is even possible. Well, he did until I put a stop to it and now he has slowly gambled away all of his wife's life insurance, even the part left to his daughter. The bet he placed last night used the last of it and his lack of money to make repayments is what flagged up to the family accountants. Father always had it sorted so money made it into Manny's account before it got this bad, until I interfered. Once he flags to the accountants, the muscle gets called in, no matter what. But still Father meddled and I need to know why.

Manny is not a large man and as he invites us into the house, he seems a lot smaller next to my six foot frame. I am not a big muscular guy like Vic is. Vic looks like he used to be a bodybuilder, and I wouldn't be surprised if he dabbled with anabolic steroids to help get ripped. My body is more like Ryder's. We are lean but all muscle that we earned through hard work in the gym. Ryder does it so he can be strong and he runs daily to improve his cardio, whereas I go to the gym simply for vanity reasons. I know I'm hot, people say with my sandy blonde hair and crystal blue eyes, I look like the typical high school jock in movies who everybody loves, which is exactly what I was. I look like a perfect boy next door because that is how I am expected to look, but looks can be deceiving. Manny, on the other hand, looks like your typical middle aged Mexican man with greying black hair and a wrinkled face, which now seems to have acquired more stress lines as he stares at the three of us making ourselves comfortable.

I sit in what is clearly Manny's chair and the boys take the sofa, leaving Manny with the other smaller chair. While we are sitting comfortably, lounging back as much as we can on this shit excuse for furniture, Manny is perched on the edge of his chair with his back straight. His eyes are darting across each of us but also towards the hallway, which tells me everything I need to know. Someone else is in the house. But I already knew that.

"Hello, Manny. Thank you for allowing us into your home. I trust you know why we are here?" I ask in my sickly sweet voice, the one I use when I want to lure people into a false sense of security. I know it's important for me to look like a nice guy, so I play on that regularly. I even manage to force out a smile that I hope looks genuine.

"Yes sir, I do. I'm really sorry the game didn't go my way. I don't… erm have… erm the money today. I had to pay the rent. But-but… I can get it," Manny says, fumbling the words as he spits them out as quickly as he can.

"I hear you, Manny, and I believe you, but my father says you have missed several payments and you are continuing to bet. This means, not only are you losing more money which is increasing your debt, you have interest which is banging it up too, and to top it all off, you aren't paying anything. Do you see where that figure is going? Not the direction we usually like. My father is concerned you cannot pay, which is why he sent me here to discuss it with you personally." I know mentioning Father will set him even further on edge and I can see him visibly gulping when I speak.

" I.. I.. I promise you, I can pay," stutters Manny, clearly looking for leniency from me, and by the way he is eyeballing Ryder and Vic, he is hoping to remain alive.

"I'm sure that is true, Manny, but I need to go back to Father with more than just your word. I need some assurance you can pay off the debt, otherwise I fear he may want to visit himself," I say, continuing to sound sweet right up until the end. Everybody knows that if my father visits, it is to watch you die. He's a sick bastard who loves that type of thing and so when I add that in, I know Manny can hear the threat in my voice. There is no way he wants Father anywhere near his house.

"No!" he shouts before remembering who he is talking to and looks at me apologetically, before checking that Ryder and Vic are not about to attack. I can see Vic has placed his hand on his weapon, just in case. He knows I don't like to be spoken back to.

"I'm sorry for my outburst, but there is no need to trouble your father. He's a busy man. I am sure you and I can come to an arrangement that will satisfy everyone," mumbles Manny with fear, causing his voice to shake.

Soft footsteps alert us to a person walking down the stairs and entering the small living room, and now my heart really starts to beat faster. As she walks through the door, I feel my palms start to sweat and all my nerve endings feel like I am on fire. Standing before us now, looking at her father with concern is Ava Delgado, and not only is she more beautiful than I had imagined, just the very sight of her causes my temper to flare and I know that no matter what, I need her. She is going to be mine.

Ava is petite at around five foot four and has the most

gorgeous curves. Her complexion makes her look like she has a natural light tan and her skin almost glistens as it is so smooth. Her long, black, wavy hair flows down her back and shapes her perfect face. But it is her chocolate brown eyes that are her biggest selling point. Sadly, she has ruined her perfectly good image with the way she dresses. She is wearing ripped jeans, an old rock band t-shirt, and scuffed trainers that have seen better days. She has what people would call an edgy style, but I will be changing that. She will need to be demure if she is going to cut it in my world.

Ava looks around, taking in the scene before her and once her eyes land on Ryder and Vic, I can see the look of terror spread across her face. She looks at me and I give her one of my heartbreaking smiles and I see it soften her face slightly. Then she turns to her father with concern.

"Papa, who are these people? I heard shouting and got worried." When Ava talks, it's so smooth and sexy, I'm sure it would make most guys' dicks twitch in appreciation, but I am not most guys. My desire to own her has nothing at all to do with her sex appeal.

"No, Ava, everything is fine. Please go back to your room," Manny replies, almost pleading with Ava to leave, but now that she is right where I need her to be, that will not be happening. I can see she wants to disagree with him and so I speak up on her behalf, oh, and mine, of course.

"That's ok, Manny. Your beautiful daughter, Ava, is more than welcome to join us. She looks like she is an incredibly smart young lady who might be able to help us solve this little problem," I say sweetly, staring straight at Ava. She doesn't even acknowledge I have spoken or thank me for my supportive words. This just reinforces the type of girl I was expecting to be dealing with. A bitch.

"Papa, I'm staying!" Ava states firmly before perching her tight round ass on the edge of her father's armchair next to him. In what I am assuming is an attempt to appear tough in front of us, Ava crosses her arms and looks straight at me with her molten eyes. The problem is that when she crosses her arms, it pushes her average sized tits up, making them, and her cleavage, look so succulent, even my dick starts to spring into action. I might think she is a bitch, but I am still a man who can appreciate a nice rack.

"That's great, the more minds the better. So do you want to update Ava on where we are at or shall I?" I ask Manny with a condescending tone. I don't need to play nice with him anymore. I already know the outcome of this visit, he just needs to learn what will happen if he doesn't get on board.

"Erm... Well... I," stumbles Manny and I can't help but huff out an exacerbated breath; we will be here all day at this rate. It's clear he doesn't want to tell his daughter the truth, but I don't give a shit about what he wants, so I jump right in.

"Manny here likes to gamble, but the problem is that he's not very good at it. He owes my father over forty thousand pounds. Not only has he missed several payments, resulting in severe interest being added, but he has continued to place bets and lost again last night. Father is very displeased and has sent me to arrange a suitable payment plan. However, all your father is able to offer me is his word and sadly, at this point, that doesn't mean anything." I watch her beautiful face distort into pain and can't help the little twinge of joy that attacks my chest. She looks so hurt and I can see tears filling her eyes but she tries to hold them back. Manny is looking at the floor in shame and cannot bring himself to look his daughter in the eyes. Fucking coward.

"Papa, is this true?" she mumbles and I hear her voice start to crack at the end, like she might actually cry. I know I should feel bad for causing her hurt like this, but I don't. This is just a means to an end.

I hear him croak out, "yes," and her breath hitches. Then her back straightens, clearly she has found some inner strength and she turns to address me.

"What do we need to do, Mr..." She fades out, having realised she doesn't know my name. Ava maintains eye contact with me to show she is being strong for her father, but she is nibbling on her lower lip, an obvious indicator of her anxiety.

"Blakeman. Grant Blakeman, but you can call me Grant. Unfortunately, Ava, your father has become unreliable in the eyes of *my* father. So, we will need some collateral to act as an initiative for him to get the money," I say this just as smoothly as I practiced. Out of the corner of my eye, I notice Ryder start to fidget because he is worried I have gone off-book. This is not what Father ordered or what we planned.

Well actually, this is not what we planned with my father. I, on the other hand, have always had a different plan.

"But we do not have anything of value you could take as collateral. We do not even own this house, Sir. I'm sorry, I don't know what we can give. But now that I know, I can take on extra shifts. I will get a second job if I need to, and after we pay our rent and buy a little food, the rest of the money will go to you every week," says Ava with conviction in her voice. She must really love her father if she is willing to work herself to the bone for him. I look at Manny, expecting him to say he can't let her do that, or that he will be the one to work instead, but, of course, he doesn't, which is exactly what I was hoping for.

"Ava, this is not your debt. You should not have to work yourself to death to pay it off," I say sweetly, trying to show her how much I care about her, but that just causes her to look confused.

"It may not be my debt, but he is my papa and I will do whatever I can to help him. If that means working two, even three jobs, then that's what I will do. That is what you do for family," she states with conviction in her voice and I am almost jealous with how much she clearly loves her father. It is an alien concept to me given that my father is an evil bastard who has tortured me my entire life. Manny looks like her speech might have been enough to spur him into saying something, but him talking will ruin my plan, so I cut him off.

"Well, Manny here may be willing to let you run yourself

into the ground for his debt, but I am not. So, I will offer you both a one time only deal, if you are interested?" I ask as my vision flits between them both before landing on Ryder, who has on his normal worried frown. Ryder is my security manager and his job is to assess risk. The best way for him to do this is to have as much information as possible. Right now, he has no idea what is going on and his posture and face show that.

"I'm listening," says Ava as casually as she can, but I can see the hope glistening in her eyes. She is naturally apprehensive, not an approach that is shared by her desperate father.

"Yes, please. We are so grateful to you for offering us a deal," shouts Manny, with no idea what my offer is.

Ava subtly shakes her head, trying to tell him they need to hear me out first, which is a wise move. But what Ava clearly has not grasped, that Manny has, is that they are in no position to negotiate.

"I am willing to offer Ava a position in my countryside home. It will be working as house staff, helping in the kitchen, cleaning, and so on. It will be a live-in position as the house needs to be cared for when I'm staying at my father's house in the city. I will give you an above average wage and you can keep a small percentage to live on, then the rest will go towards the debt. The wage itself will be more than working three jobs combined and you will not need to exhaust yourself. All of my staff live in comfort and are treated well. Once the debt is paid off, you will be given the option to stay on staff or leave, but you may not quit until the debt is paid off. If you do, all of the money on the debt will be reinstated. That will be written very clearly into your contract. Manny can continue paying off the debt with any money he has available also, to help it get paid faster, and of course, he will be prevented from placing any further bets with our business until the debt is paid." I present my case softly, as though it is a perfectly legit business transaction. It is not.

I see Ava's shoulders drop when she realises this really is the only option they have of ever getting the debt paid off. But she has no idea how long she will be gone and I can see her internal struggle with that. Watching as her face morphs into a look of humiliation and fear as she silently communicates with her father and realises he is more than happy to sell his daughter to pay off his debt. That's when her face hardens like stone and she turns to me sternly.

"I'm happy to work for you, Sir. But I will not move into your home," she says fervently, clearly thinking this is a negotiation. It is not. I get what I want. Manny, obviously latching onto some of his daughter's courage, begins to speak.

"Could we not come to some agreement that does not involve my daughter moving away from me, please?" he asks shakily, clearly not as tough as his daughter. I look at him with an air of disappointment so he knows I'm not happy he has even *tried* to negotiate. His face morphs into one of fear.

"Unfortunately, no. All of my contracts are the same and

require a live-in position. Mine and my father's business is very important and we require a lot of trust from our employees. But, I am willing to pay Ava more than is standard for this job role. I anticipate that, even without any contribution from you, she will have the debt paid off in under six months." Manny starts to cough and choke as Ava's eyes open in shock. If my proposition was genuine, I would be severely overpaying Ava and they both know it, the question is; does it matter? They can obviously tell there will be more to the job if I am paying so much more but they seem to ignore that part. Well, Manny does. Ava still remains a little untrusting and she is right to be.

"I'm sorry, Sir, but I'm still not sure if I want to move away from Papa," Ava explains and I smile sweetly like I understand what she means. I don't. Every night I am forced to spend in the big house under the same roof as my father provokes fury and disgust. Even being in a different wing of the house is too close to him for my liking, which is why I bought my house in the country. But, Ava doesn't need to know any of this. I just have to say what is necessary to get her to the house. The rest will go from there.

"Oh, Ava. I completely understand that. I will give special permission to your father so he can visit the house. Before you decide, why don't you come with us and let me show you the house? I can introduce you to Hilda, who will be your boss. She runs the house for me as I'm hardly there. You can meet the other staff and hear what it is like to work there and I will show you what would be your room and the facilities you will have access to when you are not working. I hope that will be enough to reassure you this is a legit offer, Ava," I say sweetly, trying to reel her in. All I need to do is get her into my house and I can take care of the rest. If she continues to say no, I will be forced to kidnap her. And I really don't want to have to. It's messy and gets things off to a bad start. So, bribery seems like the best way to get her on board. For now.

Ava looks at her father and I can see the pleading in his pathetic eyes. He knows his daughter is the only way to get him out of this shit hole that he's dug for himself. She obviously sees the look of desperation in his eyes too because I see her take a deep inhale of breath as she resigns herself to her fate. Yet, she still tries to maintain some of her tough girl exterior.

"Fine. But if I'm not sold after the tour, can we discuss another deal?" she asks, sounding a little hopeful. That tough girl act is the first thing I need to get rid of when I get her home. She will need to learn to be obedient, quickly. But for now, I just need to get her there. I know I have no intention of negotiating with her and that the offer is irrelevant anyway, but she doesn't need to know that. So, I agree.

I explain we will need to leave straight away as I have further business later, but Ryder will be able to drive Ava home after the tour. Ryder looks at me with a curious look and I just smile. He knows I'm lying and he is trying to figure out what is going on. There's no denying that Ryder has one of those trusting faces, which is why I suggested he would be the one to get her home safely. Ava seems happy with this and goes to get her bag and jacket.

Whilst Ava is not in the room, I decide to let Manny know there can be some leeway with his ability to place bets once he starts paying his debt off, if he wants, we just won't tell his daughter. This causes his face to light up before realising that placing more bets could result in his daughter staying in my employment for longer. However, Manny is a true gambling addict and I see the look of hope on his face that his next bet will be the one where he wins big and can pay it all off and free her. He's right, it might be, but we all know that rather than pay off his debt, Manny will place it on a bigger bet to win even more, until he finally loses it all. But I don't give a shit what he does. As far as I am concerned, the minute Ava's round juicy ass hits my expensive leather car seats, she is mine.

CHAPTER TWO
GRANT

Ryder holds the back passenger side door open for Ava and she slides in, before he takes the passenger seat in the front of the car. I slide into the back and I'm instantly hit by her sweet, floral scent as it fills the small space of the car. I notice she sits as far away from me as she can with her tiny little body curled up against the door. I love the fact she instantly knows that she should fear me because fear makes people obey, which is exactly what I want from her. She will be mine and everyone will know it. I will take pride in bending her to my will.

I smile sweetly towards Ava and tell her she looks beautiful today, but all I get is a small smile in response. I need to start a conversation with her to make her feel more comfortable, but it's difficult when I already know everything I need to know about her. She is a means to an end, nothing more.

But she has the look of a scared animal about to bolt and I can't have that, so I turn on my best sociable personality.

"What job do you currently do, Ava? It is obviously important for me to know some of your work history if I am to be your employer," I say despite the fact I already know the answer, but this is just the first step to getting inside her head.

"Oh, yes, of course. Well, erm, I currently work at a diner in the city called Regina's. I'm a waitress and have been since I was sixteen. I'm sure my boss would be more than happy to give you a reference, if you need one," Ava fumbles over her words as though she is nervous. Good.

"That won't be necessary. I'm sure you are fantastic at your job and that the customers love you," I say and I can see her blush slightly at the compliment.

"I hope this doesn't come across as rude, Ava, but you seem like such a smart girl, what are you doing working in a diner?" I ask and watch as her back straightens like she is offended but then her shoulders slump and her head dips down. She doesn't seem too happy with my line of questioning, not that I care.

"You have no idea how smart I am. You know nothing about my life," she snaps at me with venom in her voice and I am not happy with her snarky attitude. Normally, I would make her pay for speaking to me with that level of disrespect, but I need to win her over first and so I take some deep breaths and remind myself I am supposed to be charming.

"That is true, Ava, but that doesn't mean I don't wanna know. Not just because you will be working for me but because I am genuinely curious. So, please believe me when I say I didn't mean to offend you," I state as sweetly as I can manage while throwing in a charming smile at the same time. I can see Ryder looking at me in the vanity mirror on the sun visor and he has a slight smirk on his face, I don't think he has ever seen me apologise before. He thinks I'm doing it because I want in her pants. I give him a cocky wink without Ava seeing and let him think that, for now.

"I'm sorry. I didn't mean to snap at you. I was going to the local college and studying to be a teacher but we struggled with the payments for my tuition. Then Papa lost his job after he hurt his back and I needed to go to work full-time so we could afford the rent. That was almost a year ago and I haven't been able to go back yet, instead I have been picking up more shifts," she sighs, looking out of the car window wistfully as she answers me. Clearly, my question hit too close to home. She had to give up her dream because of that low life sack of shit Manny. Obviously, I already knew all of this, but it doesn't hurt to hit home about how shit her father is.

"Why would you do that?" I ask incredulously. With that, she swings around to face me with a look of fire in her chocolate eyes.

"Do what?" she spits, clearly on edge as she feels like I am attacking her and her father. I'm not, I just don't understand.

"Why would you give up your dream for Manny? You

could have used the money you earn at your job to pay for your tuition, just worked less and carried on with school. But you gave it all up for him, why?" I ask, genuinely confused as to why she would do something like that. Manny is clearly a dead weight that is bringing her down and she should have cut him loose a long time ago but for some reason she hasn't.

"Are you serious?" she asks me with the same genuine confusion in her voice that I have in mine.

"Of course, I am. Why would I be joking?" I ask her. We have both turned in the car to face each other now. Clearly, we both have something to learn from the other.

"I would do anything for him, he is my papa," says Ava, like it is the most obvious answer in the world. I am not stupid, I know that factually he is her father and that you should support family, but he is doing nothing to support her. It seems to be a one way relationship where she gives and he takes. That shit is unhealthy and needs to be cut off, I know because I have a similar situation myself.

"But he is using you. He is taking all the money you worked hard for and pissing it up the wall with stupid bets. How can you not be angry at him?" I say and she may not have any anger towards Manny, but she sure as hell has some towards me right now.

"He has an addiction and he needs my help, so I help him. I would never abandon him. If you and your fucking father stopped letting him place bets then he would never have got into this situation," Ava shouts and now I am fucking fuming.

Her father is a degenerate gambler who makes her give up her dream, work all hours of the day, then takes all her money and I am the fucking bad guy. I think it's time to teach her smart mouth to show me a bit of respect. Before I am able to, we turn off the small country road that we had been driving down, past a large growth of trees and then make a slight turn down an almost hidden gravel road that is actually a long driveway.

"Sorry to interrupt, but just letting you know that we have arrived," Ryder says with a cocky smirk aimed directly at me. Damn, that observant asshole really does not miss anything. He knew I was planning on teaching her a lesson and this is his way of stopping me from messing it up by acting in anger. I should have known the animosity I feel towards this girl would affect my ability to act rational. I need to keep a check on it, but times like this, I'm glad I have Ryder. This is why I keep him around!

Ava turns to look out of the window as Victor drives the car down the long bumpy road that leads to the main house. Just visible in the distance is a big set of intricately carved wooden gates that sit in between matching rows of beautiful green conifer trees. To the outside world, this appears to be a beautiful countryside estate, but on closer inspection, there is so much more than the eye can see.

Behind the immaculately manicured trees that act as a perimeter for the property, is a live electric fence that is ten feet high. The other side of the gates are fully lined with metal that makes them impenetrable and bullet proof. What looks to be a perfectly normal yet old fashioned gate house actually houses a state of the art computer system that runs a license plate check through the police database on any car that turns onto the road. We know who the car belongs to before it even hits the gates. There are over fifty hidden security cameras placed all around the outside of the property, not to mention how many are inside, and they are manned by security guards at all times. Finally, every security guard that can be seen, or more importantly that cannot, is carrying at least two guns and a hidden blade. This place is built like a fortress. Nobody can get in but more importantly right now, nobody can get out either.

CHAPTER THREE
GRANT

Ava's face has been a mixture of both shock and awe since we pulled up to the gates of the house. Her eyes are wide as saucers as she climbs out of the car and walks towards the house. It's like she can't believe where we are. I can imagine that compared to the shitty little house I just rescued her from, this looks like a palace, but for me, I have lived in places that outshine this by miles. Yet, I am a big believer in the age old saying, 'there's no place like home' and for me, this is my sanctuary and there is no place better.

My country estate is a two story, old mansion made of white stone and has two big pillars on either side of the door. Ryder always says it looks like a smaller version of the house from the Fresh Prince of Bel Air and I can see that. I didn't buy it for how it looks, I bought it because it is in the middle of nowhere. The nearest neighbour is a twenty minute drive away. We are surrounded by acres and acres of fields, that I have made sure I now own. I grew up surrounded by people, in the heart of London and I hated every minute of it. Silence is bliss.

Ava turns towards me with a look of pure wonderment on her face and I swear that for just one second, I saw reflected on her face all the joy I get out of this place and it makes me feel a weird kind of connection with her. She has been raised in less than ideal surroundings because of her father and his choices, we have that in common, and yet, I'm not looking to find anything in common with her. In fact, I don't care about who Ava was at all. All I care about is who I am going to make her.

"Wow. This place is phenomenal. I can't believe you actually live here!" she screeches and you can hear her excitement buzzing. This is exactly what I want. I need her to be comfortable and happy here. It is her home now, after all.

"Well, technically, I don't live here all the time. Sometimes I live in the big house in the city centre, with my father, but I am trying to do that less and less," I explain.

"Oh, ok. So if you aren't here, who lives here then?" she asks suspiciously.

"Well, at the moment, nobody technically lives here full time, but as I said, I plan on changing that. I plan on being here at least three or four nights a week, if not more. I also have a cleaning team who comes in daily to ensure it is well looked after. A chef, who lives close by, is on stand-by for when I need her. I have one live-in house maid who oversees everything and does the majority of the face to face work with me. There's a building out on the land that houses the majority of my security staff, only Ryder sleeps in the main house. That's it really," I explain, trying my hardest to read her facial expressions and determine what she's thinking.

"So, if you have all that set up, then why do you need someone like me to live in it?" she asks, with confusion in her voice. I try my best to look sheepish so she will believe I am giving her an honest answer. I can tell she is beginning to think my reason for getting her here is bullshit, and really, it doesn't matter now that we are here, but I don't want to shatter her illusion just yet.

"Honestly, I don't need anyone to be here full time. But your father owes a lot of money and given the way he is gambling, that debt will only get bigger. I didn't want you to get sucked into his hole. So I said you could come here to work off his debt, which I stick by, but at the same time, I want you to complete online classes to get the qualifications you need to go to college. By agreeing to live here, not only do you pay off the debt for your father quicker, but you also have somewhere to live whilst you study. I am sorry I wasn't honest with you before, but you were so angry at me, I didn't think you would have listened. The debt belongs to my father and I cannot wipe it completely, but I can do this so you have the means to pay it. This is the only way I could think of to keep you safe, Ava," I declare with so much passion, I almost start to believe my own bullshit.

"Why me? I'm guessing you don't do this for everyone

who owes you money, so why me?" she whispers. She has so much insecurity in her voice, it makes me smile. Her eyes are downcast and she is slumped in a way that a girl as beautiful as her should never be. I walk towards her very slowly, trying to gauge her reaction. It reminds me of those damn nature shows Father likes to watch. I am the predator and I am slowly stalking towards my prey. I make myself look as non-threatening as possible and use no sudden movements to spook the prey. Then once I'm within striking distance, the prey is mine.

I move towards Ava and I see her eyes lift slightly to see me coming towards her and her chocolate eyes start to sparkle. When I am finally within touching distance, she stands tall and finally looks me in the eye, clearly her armour is back in place. I will make sure it's gone before she even realises it. I give her one of my famous boy next door, soft smiles and I cannot resist touching her. She is my enigma and I have to know what is so special about her. I raise my hand slowly and gently cup her cheek. As I touch her, she breathes out a little sigh and then moves slightly into my touch. Her skin is soft and smooth, like holding pure silk. I cannot resist touching more and so I begin rubbing the pad of my thumb slowly across her face in a soothing gesture. I see the edges to her plump red lips turn up into a small smile and despite all of my efforts to the contrary, my dick responds. I am imagining ruining these plump, succulent lips by ramming my cock as far down her throat as I can. I then picture, instead of gently stroking her cheek as I am now, I would grab her throat, hold her tightly where I want her. Show her who's boss. If I want to take away her air, I will. This is unexpected, I never planned on using sex to manipulate her to get what I want, but with the way she is leaning into me, I think that the whore might quite like it.

I am so absorbed in my fantasy, thinking about how I will make it a reality, I don't even realise Ava is still waiting for me to answer her question. It's only when Ryder subtly coughs from by the door, gesturing for us to go inside when we are ready, that I truly get pulled back to the present.

Obviously, I don't want to let Ava know why I just spaced out for a short amount of time, I'm supposed to be winning her over, not scaring her off. So, I decide to use this to my advantage once again and turn on the charm.

"I'm sorry, princess, it's just that you are so beautiful and I couldn't help myself. The answer to your question, Ava, whether you believe it or not, is that I chose you because I think you are worth it." I say it with such conviction, but in my mind I am trying to hold back the disgust I feel at saying that she is in any way special. She has done nothing to deserve being put on a pedestal and I will make sure she comes as far down as she can fall.

She is clearly shocked by my 'candid' reply and before she gets a chance to overthink the situation or my words, I need to get her inside. "Shall we?" I ask as I gesture towards the door where Ryder is standing. I'm hoping she will make the decision to enter the house willingly because if I have to drag her inside, it will severely ruin the plan, forcing me to implement plan B.

Luckily for everyone, she heads towards the door. I stay back to ensure the perimeter security is all in place and to give my security manager the go ahead to indicate we are in lock down. I need her to be fully inside the house before I can do that. As she walks up the steps, I see her taking everything in and she looks to be assessing the whole situation. Then her eyes reach Ryder and I watch as she stares at him for longer than anything else. Initially, I think nothing of it because he is a good-looking guy with that tall, dark, and handsome look he's perfected, of course women give him a second glance. This would not be the first time, or the last. Then I realise the way Ava is looking at Ryder is more than that. She is actually checking him out and with the way she is fluttering her eyelashes, I think she is flirting. I cannot believe the fucking bitch has the nerve to practically eye fuck my friend right in front of me. Then again, I already knew she was a slut. Given the area she is from, it's just a given. Still, she will be punished for that.

I look over at Ryder to see if he is in any way leading Ava on. Thankfully, he looks the same as he always does. He is assessing the scene around him and only glancing occasionally at Ava to determine if she is a threat. I have seen him do it a thousand times. He is protecting me, not betraying me. He has no idea who Ava is or what my intentions towards her are and until he does find out, he will always be suspicious. That is how he is trained. I should have known he would never flirt with someone on the job. Ryder is as loyal as they come. Ava, on the other hand, will need to be taught that her wandering eye will get her into trouble. The only man she needs to look at from now on is me. She may not be actively seeing anyone at the moment, but women like Ava are all the same. They use men and aren't afraid of who gets hurt in the meantime.

Ava is completely oblivious to everything that has just gone on in my head, and realising Ryder is not interested in her whoring ways, she casts her eyes away and into the house before willingly moving inside. Just like I wanted her to do. The predator just caught his prey. I signal to my security manager to begin the procedure I have been training them for since I first came up with the plan. From the minute I step inside the building, we will be on lock down. Nobody is getting in or out of the building without my consent. The staff have had the training. I made sure I selected some of my very best employees, ones who have worked for me for a very long time and know exactly how much I require my privacy. They were trained for a situation where I needed to stay here and be guarded, a potential situation given the lifestyle I lead. What they didn't realise is that their practise was always going to become reality. I never told anyone about my plans for Ava. Ryder designed all of this for a 'what if' situation, but I had something different in mind all along.

CHAPTER FOUR
AVA

As I walk into the biggest, most beautiful place I have ever seen, I can't truly take in all of its beauty because I am so on edge. I don't know what to make of Grant or his far too generous offer. There is no denying he is smoking hot. He looks like the guy in all the movies who plays the typical captain of the football team, he's the popular jock in high school who would have totally ignored me. He has sandy blonde hair that is just long enough for you to run your fingers through it, but not so long that it looks messy. Short on the sides and long up the top, like he isn't quite sure what he should do with it, or maybe he knows and he isn't allowed. Everything about this guy screams serious. He looks so pristine, I am frightened I might wrinkle his immaculately straight polo shirt, just by being near. His shirt, combined with the black slacks and perfectly polished shoes make him look smart, professional, and I am guessing older than he actually is. There are times when he smiles or when I catch him looking at me when I think I can't see the boy behind the uniform. I think this is the armour he wears when he becomes his father's son and he puts on the costume to go out and do his job. At least, that is what I hope. I really want there to be a fun-loving, carefree, young guy underneath. But, I don't know why I want that. Maybe it's because I feel sorry for him, who knows.

When Grant touched my cheek, I can't deny I felt a flutter in my stomach I have not felt in a while, but I also felt something else I didn't like. There is something about Grant which screams danger to me. He is one of those things that looks perfectly safe and innocent, but in reality, it's all an act. Whilst there is a part of me that wants his real personality to be the gorgeous boy next door, deep down I know that's not the case. This guy is trouble. I felt it from the moment I met him, the hairs on my arms went up and I was on full alert. Almost like I am prey and I can sense that there is a predator nearby. I have caught his face changing a few times when he thinks I am not looking. He has dropped his mask and his real face of anger and superiority are immediately visible. It is clear this little rich boy thinks the world should bow down to him and I am determined not to. The only problem is that I would do anything for Papa. I need him to be safe, which is why I am willingly walking into the lion's den.

Grant is the kind of guy who makes you feel constantly on edge, preparing for whatever move he has planned next and hoping you can get through it. All of that causes my stomach to churn with anxiety and worry. I wish I could stand here and tell you the somersaults I'm feeling in my stomach and the sensation of electricity running through my body is only caused by being on alert from Grant, but it isn't My body started to spread with heat from the moment I laid eyes on Grant's gorgeous bodyguard.

I'm sure I heard Grant call him Ryder when we were back at my house. I cannot help being drawn to him. He is absolutely gorgeous. Standing next to his partner, who I think they called Vic, he looks almost small, but that is simply because Vic is unnaturally large. At about six foot six, Vic makes me look like I am an oompa loompa from the chocolate factory. It's not just his height that is imposing, it's also his muscles. I have never seen arms as large as his. They are literally so big, the short sleeves of his t-shirt slightly indent into the muscle because they are stretched too tight. I am sure he has ripped his fair share of t-shirts. Large, angry blue veins can be seen running over the sinew of the muscle and that sight makes my stomach turn. Nothing more unattractive on men than bulging veins. His arm muscles are big and they stretch up the back of his neck, giving the appearance that this large man doesn't even have a neck as it has been consumed by skin and muscle. He looks like an extreme body building body guard and it is clear, between the two of them, which is the brawn of the operation. So, that means that gorgeous Ryder is the brains of their team, and right now as I'm perusing his impressive body, I would love to know what he is thinking. I know I'm hoping Grant goes back to his family home and Ryder stays here for some holiday time. Then he can fuck me in every room of this massive house. But my spidey senses are tingling again, telling me the chances of that happening are slim to none, and since I don't like that thought, I go back to listening to a different kind of tingle, this time the one in my pussy that is getting wetter the more I think about Ryder.

As I ascend the steps to the house, I subtly sniff the air. The closer I get to him, the more I can smell him. I am instantly addicted to his smell, which is a mixture of peppermint, a woodsy grass-like smell, and something that is just Ryder. I really wish they could bottle it so I can spray it on all future men in my life, because I'm sure nobody will smell as perfect as him. God, when did I start to sound like this much of a girl? I don't think this kind of shit normally, but clearly, this situation is truly messing with my brain.

Still, I can't stop my wandering eyes. Trying to be coy about it, I rake my eyes over his toned, ripped body. The black t-shirt he wears is strained against what I am sure are rock hard abs and pecs. Not strained like Vic in an abnormal way, this is the perfect amount so I can see the contours. He is wearing perfectly sculpted dark denim jeans that I am sure if he turns around, will cling to his arse in just the right way. I make a mental note to confirm my theory as soon as possible.

While his body is everything that women look for in a man, it is his face that really wins me over. He has the most glistening emerald green eyes that so beautifully match the forest scent that is all him. His jet black hair is short at the sides but the top is long and unruly in your typical fauxhawk style that is usually only pulled off this well by male models. It's long enough for you to grab onto as you scream his name, but not too long that it looks wrong. Everything about Ryder seems perfect, especially his gorgeous face. He looks so kind and caring, despite the brooding expression he wears continuously.

When we were back at the house and Grant was throwing accusations at Papa, I kept looking at the bodyguards to see how much trouble we were in. There's no doubt that Vic would have shot us both right there and buried our bodies somewhere we would never be found if Grant had asked him to. The same could not be said for Ryder. Just from the fleeting glances I saw him give Grant, it's clear he has his own mind because he is constantly evaluating the situation and trying to guess every possible situation so he can be prepared. However, there were times when he didn't know I was looking and I caught him staring at me with a strange look. It was one of sorrow and fear; clearly, he felt sorry for me and my situation. However, I also saw flashes of lust in his eyes and I could have sworn he wanted me as much as I wanted him. But as quick as those thoughts appeared on his face, the next second they would be gone. Replaced with the mask of professionalism he wears all the time, coupled with the brooding look I cannot help but be attracted to.

There's something about Ryder that I'm drawn to and I can't deny it. He is gorgeous, intense, and yet his eyes have a kindness about them that suggests he has another side to him and that intrigues me. I can't for the life of me work out why someone who appears to be so quintessentially good would work for someone like Grant. I know I'm making assumptions based solely off my gut reactions, but it has always led me right in the past. There's something about Ryder that makes me believe he's good and that I can trust him. The same cannot be said for his partner, Vic. It is clear he is Grant's guy through and through, he will do anything that is asked of him with no questions. Vic has a vacant expression and his hand is always far too near to his weapons for me to ever trust or feel safe around him.

Grant is more difficult to read but I feel like he does that on purpose. He wants me to trust him so I will stay here, but I still don't know what his motives are and that scares me. I can't deny that what he is offering me will change my life, but I have been raised to know that you never get anything for free in this life. Which tells me he wants something. But, he's not the first guy to have lied to me to get what he wants. I just need to be smart, stay on my toes, work out what he wants, and see if I can use him before he does me. So when Grant walks up behind me and wraps his arms with mine to link them before throwing his fake as fuck charming smile at me, I match his grin with one of my own. I know I need to play my part, not just if I want to get the information I need, but also to ensure I get out of this shitstorm in one piece. I am dealing with London's biggest crime family after all.

"What do you think, Ava? It really is beautiful, isn't it?" he asks, as he spins me in a circle to look all around at the elaborate entrance way. There's no denying that it is a stunning property. White marble is everywhere, all up the walls and on the floors, making it seem so shiny. Directly in front of me is a big staircase that goes up to the first floor before splitting off into a balcony that stretches to both sides of the house. The stairs are so grand and elegant. In fact, every bit of this place has exactly the type of finishing touches I would choose if I was ever decorating a house like this. I can't help being in awe of how stunning this place is.

"It's really amazing, Grant. If I owned this property, I would live in it all the time. I don't know how you can stand to be away," I say with a wistful edge to my voice. Girls who come from the side of town that I'm from don't end up in houses like this, unless it's to clean them or steal from them.

"One day you will have a house just like this one. I am sure of it," he says with such conviction that for a split second, I almost believe him. Then I remember who I am and why I'm here. The absurdity of his comment has me laughing, but not just a cute little giggle. No, the craziness of the situation has caused my whole body to shake and fall into a proper belly laugh.

My eyes are streaming with tears of laughter and my stomach is cramped from laughing so much when I finally calm down. Wiping away the tears from my eyes, I look over at the three men in the room with me. Grant is looking at me with a mixture of confusion and revulsion that causes insecurity to ripple across my skin and I shrink back. Vic is looking at me like I am a mental patient and I realise his hand is poised a little nearer to his gun as though in this manic state I might become more of a threat. But it's Ryder's beaming smile that catches me off guard the most. He is the only one who understood why I was laughing and he is looking at me like seeing me laugh genuinely made him happy. I tell my brain to ignore the butterflies that begin to flutter in my stomach because nothing can ever happen. But the fact that Ryder knew why Grant's words were a joke to me, tells me he knows what it's like to live on the other side of town. To be raised with nothing and to do what is expected of you, even if it's not your dream. Maybe that explains why a guy like Ryder is doing a job like this.

"What's so funny?" Grant asks through gritted teeth, pulling me out of my thoughts. Clearly he doesn't like to not be included in the joke, or maybe he doesn't like girls laughing at him.

"Girls like me, who come from my neighborhood, don't get to live in houses like this, Grant. That's just not in our futures and I'm okay with that," I explain and it's true. To some people, it may look like I live in a shit house, but to others it looks like a castle. To me, it's a modest sized house. I have my own space and it is well loved. It's my family home, where I grew up and made memories. Every part of my mum is in that house and that makes it better than any mansion. Yes, I would love to have a bigger house, one a bit less run down in a better part of town, but to me, family is more important. I would rather spend any money I make ensuring I give my future husband and kids a happy home where we create memories.

"Don't ever compare yourself to the girls in your neighbourhood. You are a princess next to them and I don't want to hear any more about it. I have a very good feeling that you will be living in a house like this sooner than you realise," he says with a hard edge to his voice that he has been careful not to let slip before now. I don't like the demanding tone and although everything screams at me to be cautious around this guy, I'm not good with guys trying to control me. Obviously, he sees the urge to argue back with him flare in my eyes because he stops me.

"Come, let me show you what will be your room," he says to me, again leaving no room for argument. Before I know it, his arm that is currently linked with mine, slides down and captures my hand. He laces his fingers through mine and clasps our hands together. He gives my hand a little squeeze. I'm not sure if it's supposed to be a comforting gesture or his way of asserting control by telling me he isn't letting go. Either way, my skin prickles and my stomach starts to flip. Being this close to him sets me on edge, but I don't know how to get away.

CHAPTER FIVE
GRANT

Touching Ava and holding her hand in mine make it easy to feel the goosebumps that spread across her skin. She fears me and she is right to do so. What she doesn't know is touching her in this way, or any way, is the last thing I want to be doing. The feel of her skin against mine repulses me, but I can't let her know I feel that way. I need her to believe I like her and I desperately want to help her. It's harder to see what's really going on when you don't suspect them.

I pull her along behind me as I travel up the stairs and through the house. I can feel her try to gently slip her hand out of mine, but I won't be having any of that. Squeezing her hand gently, I try to show her she has nothing to fear from me and that her hand in mine can feel nice, but I also ensure there's a bite to the squeeze, letting her know she can let go when I tell her she can.

I feel her stalling and trying to look into each room as I call out the names. The library particularly seemed to call to her as it took a good pull and a stern look to get her moving away from there. But if I thought the library drew her attention, that was nothing compared to her reaction to the media room. The door had been left open so she could see the giant cinema style screen and the mixture of recliner and loveseat type leather sofas that make it look like an actual cinema, only comfier. I would put good money on it being Ryder who left the door open. He is always in this damn room when he isn't at work, feeding his addiction for movies of any kind. He constantly tries to get me to join him to watch a movie, but it's just not really for me. I can't sit still for that long and not do anything. I mean, don't get me wrong, I have been to the cinema or watched movies in the past, but usually I am with an incredibly hot girl and she is playing with my cock to help hold my interest.

I allow her a moment to look and admire what could one day be hers if she behaves. I want her to see that she will have everything she will ever need. Given the look of awe on her face as she glances around the room, I can see this one has won her over already. She has a slight shy smile on her face as she turns towards me.

"Are staff allowed to use this room?" says Ava with a wistful tone to her voice. "Of course. It's Ryder's favourite room. You like movies?" I ask, but not only do I already know the answer, I also don't give a shit.

"Absolutely. I'm a massive film addict. I love any kind of movie, but mostly horrors or classic chick flicks." Ava is beaming as she talks about movies. She is reeling off her favourite films and I have no idea what she is talking about. I have heard of some of the bigger titles but only ones that are in the news or that I've heard Ryder talking about. She is so animated, her face lights up as she talks and it makes her eyes sparkle. There really is no denying that Ava Delgado is a beautiful woman and that thought makes me sick. I hate the fact that she looks so perfect and has one of those personas that is adored by everyone, but not me. I am going to take great pleasure in corrupting her.

"Sorry, Grant, you must be so busy and here I am, boring you stupid talking about movies," she says with genuine embarrassment in her voice. Fuck, because of the look of disdain I had on my face she has misread it as boredom and now has gone back to seeing me as her potential boss. I definitely can't be having that and I need to think on my feet quick if I'm going to get this back on track.

"Oh no, Ava, please don't think that. I was actually chastising myself because I couldn't remember the name of the new movie coming out next week that I have been so desperate to see. You know what it's like when your mind just goes blank, and I can't for the life of me remember. Then I started to get embarrassed in front of such a beautiful girl who loves movies as much as me, but it hardly looks that way if I can't even remember the name!" I say that all with such a fake sadness to my voice, I honestly think I should be nominated for an Oscar. Not only was that some amazingly quick thinking on my part, but I also got to throw in a compliment and make myself look vulnerable because that's, apparently, what women love. Naturally, it's all absolute bullshit. I can't remember the last time I went to the cinema. I have no intention of going and sitting on some filthy, cum soaked chairs in a room full of teenagers and poor people to watch a film I care nothing about. I am better than that. But I need to get Ava to like me, not think I'm a dick, so I play the part.

With Ava, she already knows the public persona side of me. Everyone has heard of Grant Blakeman, son of Alan Blakeman, heir to the biggest criminal family in London. But Ava is feisty, independent, and rebellious. No matter how much I present this kind, wholesome side of myself, it's clear there's mistrust still there. I'm actually quite shocked because I expected her to be the kind of whore who forgets what she sees as long as there's money involved, but that doesn't seem to be the case. But it's starting to dawn on me that my plan to gain her trust is going to take a lot longer than I thought and I am not a very patient person. I don't have time for her to piss about, she will be mine and soon. So either she comes to that realisation on her own or we can do it the hard way.

My vulnerable reply seems to have really thrown Ava as she is staring at me like I am a puzzle she just can't work out.

She is scrutinising me with her gaze and I do everything in my power to keep my smile in place.

"Come, let me show you to your room," I say, as I pull her further down the hall, but she stops me. She cocks her hip and puts her free hand on it to pull off a very sexy pose. She is glaring at me with a question in her eyes and she is clearly trying to look rebellious and independent. If she doesn't uncock that hip soon, I will have to punish her.

"You do mean *if* I agree to move into here, I'm assuming," says Ava, clearly trying to remind me she has yet to agree to living here. What she doesn't realise is that from the minute she stepped over the threshold, she made that choice. There is no getting out now.

"Ava, princess, I can assure you as soon as you see the bedroom, you will be begging me to let you stay. You were close with the library and media room. I haven't even shown you the indoor pool, spa, and gym in the other wing, but I know you will love them," I reply confidently. Her eyes light up like it's Christmas morning and I can't help but smirk.

"Hold up, you have a pool in your house?" Ava splutters incredulously. After doing some research into Ava and her life, I know that she loves to swim. It is her form of stress relief and whenever she can, she goes to the public pool and swims lengths. I followed her there once but when I saw how vile and disgusting the place was, I left quickly. I was in the men's changing room and all of a sudden this old dude came walking towards me with his wrinkled cock and saggy bollocks flapping about in front of my face. Apparently, poor people have to change in front of each other. I was genuinely worried one of these poor bastards would realise that the shoes I was wearing cost more than some of these hobos make in a month and they would be gone. There is no way I was letting them get their hands on my stuff, so I got out of there as quickly as I could. I had all the information I needed anyway.

"Yes, I do. A full sized heated pool. I will show you it later, but it's getting late and dinner will be ready soon. Let me show you to your room so you can get cleaned up," I say, clearly refusing to allow any room for discussion over whether she is staying or not. It is not up for discussion and given the way her back becomes straight and her body tense, she now knows that too.

Gripping her hand tighter, I pull her to the end of the corridor and open the door to her 'bedroom'. The best thing to do when you want to keep someone caged is to not let them realise it is a cage. So, as Ava walks into the room, I know she will be stunned by how perfectly designed the room is. I have used the extensive knowledge I've collected about her to create her perfect room. Her eyes take in the gorgeous king-size bed, covered in purple fluffy cushions, her favourite colour. The magnolia walls are adorned with paintings by her favourite local artist, that to me personally look like shit and cost far too much money, but she sees it as art.

Attached to the bedroom is a giant en-suite with a walk in shower big enough for two. But it is the giant jacuzzi tub that captures Ava's attention and she looks at me, questioning whether the giant porcelain corner bath really is a jacuzzi. The look in her eyes makes me wonder whether she has ever even been in one.

"You like?" I ask with a smirk because the answer is written all over her face and she knows it.

"Obviously. This bathroom is bigger than my living room at home. Is that a jacuzzi bath?" she asks, with big doe eyes that she clearly is used to using to get guys to do what she wants.

"It is. Have you been in one before?" I ask, trying not to make it sound as though I'm asking because she is poor as shit and obviously can't afford to own one. That is exactly what is going through my mind, but we are not showing her the real Grant yet, so I bite my lip.

"I have once when my friend took me to a spa day for my birthday. It was amazing. So relaxing and soothing. I used all the equipment and had my first and only hot stones massage. The way they manipulated my muscles with the hot stones felt amazing. I was so relaxed and my body felt incredible. I am sure you have massages all the time. I know I would if I had your money," she replies before gulping and looking sheepish at her comments. Clearly, she hadn't meant for all of that to come spilling out of her mouth.

"I don't actually get massages all that often but I probably should. I will make sure that someone comes here once a week to give you the best full body massage," I say as I bring my lips up into my charming smile. She thinks I'm being kind and I know she doesn't trust my motives, but she still hasn't worked out there is no fucking way I will be treating her like a princess. Other men may choose to, but I know she definitely doesn't deserve it.

"Oh wow, you don't have to do that. I, er, I'm not sure, erm, even on a better salary, I wouldn't be able to afford that, Grant. I'm sorry, but thank you for the thoughtful gesture," says Ava with an embarrassed look on her face.

"Babe, I never said you would have to pay for it. Call it a perk of the job," I explain and see her eyebrows shoot up at my casual use of the nickname 'babe', but she lets it slide. She's clearly picking her battles, which is good because that means she is learning I always win.

"No, it's too much. It can't be a perk of employment unless it is offered to everyone you employ," she says and it makes me laugh.

"Fine then, I will offer it to Ryder and Vic too. That poncy twat, Ryder, will probably take me up on it, he pampers himself like a girl." I enjoy seeing the way her face scrunches like she doesn't know what to make of my offer.

As I am explaining to Ava how much of a girl Ryder can be at times, with his love of chick flicks and the excessive amount of time he spends on his hair, I hear her start to giggle. I am sure Ryder is lurking somewhere, cursing me out, but I had to find some way to win her over. Apparently, she finds me funny, who knew?

"So, we have about an hour before dinner will be served. Do

you want to wash up and get changed, then you can meet me in the dining room around six? Does that sound ok?" I enquire, making sure she knows there's no real choice available to her. She will do as I instruct. I also know she is going to have at least one issue and now is the time to show how thoughtful I am.

"Erm, I guess so. But I don't have anything to wear other than these clothes," she says shyly whilst looking down over her very casual attire. Most definitely an outfit that is not suitable for the grand dining room I showed her downstairs and she knows it.

"That's ok, princess. On our way over here, I texted my personal shopper. She has kitted you out with things you should need in that closet over there. Also, in the bathroom you should find some supplies. So, you have nothing to worry about. I will leave you to it and see you at six," I say, letting my generous gesture sink in. I decide it's best to walk away before she over thinks things, like she is prone to, and then she will start asking questions. I want her to think I have done a nice thing, not to know I have studied her for a long time. I give her a big smile and turn to leave the room. But it's not soon enough. She pulls me back and uses her tiny hand to grip my wrist. I quickly remove her hand with more force than I should given how her gaze snaps up to mine. I cover by taking her hand into mine again, making it look like a sweet gesture.

"How the hell do you know my size?" she screeches at me and I resist the urge to laugh at her stupidity. As if I would get into this unprepared. Instead, I just smile sweetly as I reply.

"My personal shopper called to your house as soon as we left to see your old clothes and take some measurements. I want to make sure you have everything you need. Just a nice gesture, nothing more," I reply gently.

Before I let go of her hand, I gave it a small squeeze to say goodbye. Flashing her my best smile, I'm delighted to see that she smiles back. Her gorgeous eyes glow as they stare into mine. We're standing so close together, I can feel the electricity rippling between our bodies. I don't want to touch her, but I know that getting her to like me is part of the plan and so I lean in slowly, giving her time to prepare. I'm aiming for her plump red lips and she can see that. It's almost like I can see the cogs turning in her brain as she considers what to do next. To my wonderment, she does not pull away. Instead, she turns her head to the side. I plant a tender kiss on her soft, delicate cheek and I try to ignore the wave of nausea that rolls over me. It's not that she isn't gorgeous, but she doesn't need any more members of her fan club. But that's exactly what I pretend I want to join. So, I smile at her and show that I'm not bothered by her actions, which gives me a small twitch from her lips as they transform into a minute smile. I turn to walk away, but give her a little cocky wink as I turn, just so that she truly starts to think I'm funny and playful.

As I'm leaving, I discreetly look around and check that the room meets my requirements. While it may seem superficially perfect to Ava, I have a slightly higher specification that goes beyond decor. The walls are both padded and soundproofed to ensure she cannot hurt herself or be heard. The windows are one way glass, so she can see out but nobody can see in. They are also bullet proof and cannot be broken. They can't be opened either. The paintings that adorn the walls hide cameras with in-depth imaging and microphone capabilities. Her every movement in the large room and bathroom will be monitored. The deluxe king-size bed has hidden restraints and handcuffs on all four corners. Ryder has taught me to be a planner and I would be stupid to think that she is going to bend to my will easily. There are going to be times where I need to teach Ava a lesson and restraints will most likely be necessary. I just hope she is a fast learner so we can really move the plan forward.

As I am walking out of the room, I close the door and press the button in my trouser pocket. This activates the lock on Ava's door. Unless she tries the door, she will never know that I can lock it, but there may come a time when I need to use it. It may look like Ava is in a cell, but it will not be for forever. She has all the comforts that she needs and as soon as she agrees to my demands, it will all change.

CHAPTER SIX
AVA

"Oh God, Oh God." I keep repeating those words to myself in a really quiet, whispered hush as I pace around this gorgeous excuse for a room. It feels like an absolute palace in just this one room and I cannot get over it. There's a part of me that is freaking out about even being in a house as ornate and valuable as this. I suspect the amazing bathroom I have just been ogling is worth more money than my entire house, and probably Mrs. Santiago's place next door, too. I mean, this room is just so perfect. If I had been allowed to design my dream room, I think this one would fall pretty close.

I know that doesn't sound like a bad thing. If I am going to be living here for six months, at least I know I will be living in luxury. Shit, it's more than luxury, this is so out of luxury's league and that's what is creating the feeling of unease deep within my stomach.

I know the rumours about Grant Blakeman. I know who his father is and the type of business that they run. No, I don't mean the legal business that they present to the world, but the criminal underground business which deals in guns, drugs, and girls. Where I live, all you hear is street talk, and believe me, the Blakeman family doesn't even try to hide their business. They don't need to when they own the entire city. Knowing Grant is part of that kind of business is enough for me to already have feelings of disgust towards him, but I didn't miss the thinly veiled threats that he threw towards my papa. It may not have been a direct threat, he may not have said the words, but I saw the way Vic had his hand against his gun the entire time he sat in my house. I feel sure that had Grant given the nod, he would have used it. So, when I first met him, my opinion of him couldn't get any lower, but then he made me the offer.

I know that his offer is not a regular way of dealing with people in their debt. They are a business that deals in cash. One where if you don't pay, they provide you with a lot of incentive to go out to find it, and quickly. I'm not stupid, I have seen my papa gambling and coming home with unexplained cuts and bruises. I've also overheard rumours at the diner. So, I did my research to find out who exactly Papa is in debt with. I found anything about the Blakeman family I could. About how Alan rules with an iron fist, but that he always keeps people alive. Apparently, his motto is that 'dead men can't pay'. But that is the only way he draws the line, everything else is allowed. From what I have heard, I hope I never meet this disgusting excuse for a human being.

Whilst researching, I did find another strange anomaly which I have never been able to explain and no matter how many times I ask Papa, he just tells me not to meddle. But from what I can tell with his gambling habits, we should have been in this shit years ago. There's more money coming into our bank than is even possible and more going out than I can even comprehend. The money doesn't add up and it makes me suspicious of my father's involvement with the Blakemans. Add these feelings together, combined with my skepticism over Grant's offer, it all leaves me feeling incredibly on edge. I cannot get rid of the nagging feeling that this is too good to be true. Why me?

Grant says this offer is all about helping me out, but guys like him don't do that. He thinks I can't see the way he looks at me when he thinks I am not looking. I don't even need to be looking to know when his eyes are gazing over my body. I feel the most disgusting shiver go down my spine. My gut is telling me Grant is not the man he appears to be and his motives are not as honourable as he suggests. If this is the case, I need to think seriously about how far I am prepared to go to fix Papa's debt. First, I need to go have dinner with the devil in disguise and find out what he really wants from me.

Walking back into the bathroom that I would take home with me if I could, is such an amazing experience. I know it's only a bathroom, but I seriously notice new little features every time I am in here. On the wall there is a heated towel rail with the towels all ready for me. There is even a gorgeous fluffy bathrobe waiting for when I get out. I decide to take advantage before I begin getting ready for dinner. I strip out of my clothes, ready for the shower. Looking into the mirror when I am fully naked always makes me smile. Don't get the wrong idea about me and think that I'm vain and love my body because honestly, I have the same insecurities every other woman has. I may be petite but I can see my curves; boobs that are a bit too big for my frame, patches of cellulite across my thighs and an arse that has got a bit more of a curve than it should. Even though I dance, run, or swim to keep fit, I like to eat. My papa is Mexican and they love their food. I have always been brought up the same way. So I have curves and sometimes I do feel insecure, but that is not why I admire my naked body. I smile because I have something that is just for me.

When I was seventeen, I realised that no matter how hard I worked, my life was never going to take the direction I wanted, and for a time, I resented my papa. I had always dreamed of following in my mum's footsteps and becoming a teacher, but that dream is a long way off. I realised that I had to do what was necessary, not what I wanted. There was a strange part of me that felt like my life would always be that way and I hated it. I wanted something for me that nobody could ever take away, something that when I looked at it, it would always remind me of my power and my independence.

So looking in the mirror now, I smile at the gorgeous, intricate tribal style tattoo that curves all the way around the right hand side of my body. It starts just above my right breast and curls around it before travelling over my rib cage and down past my hip to my upper thigh. Most people would not associate such a dark tribal tattoo with a woman, but for me, they would be wrong. I love it. When I went to the tattoo parlour, I wanted something that showed strength and the warrior who was hidden beneath my skin. It's symbolic for me, I guess. I have always had to be strong since my mum passed, but there are a lot of times when I don't feel it. So seeing the ink on my side reminds me I am strong enough. I'm a warrior who can cope with anything. I love the fact that it is just for me. To the outside world, I just look like me. Unless they were to see me in my underwear or when I swim, they wouldn't know. That's why I swim at a pool outside of town because I don't want people I know to see it. I know that sounds kinda stupid, but my papa would definitely want to kill me. He made it very clear since I started asking in my early teens, that tattoos are forbidden in his house. So, I obey by keeping it covered. I will tell him one day I'm sure, but right now, he doesn't need to know.

When I have stopped ogling myself in the mirror, in a completely not big headed kinda way, I slip into the shower. It is the most amazing shower I have ever been in, with its rainfall style feature. It is big enough for a whole group of people and has so many buttons, it would take me hours to play with all the gadgets properly. I make a mental note to come and press all the buttons to find out what they do when I have the time. No point having a shower this amazing and not using it to its full capability.

As I am washing my hair and lathering up my long black strands with the shampoo that was left for me on the side of the cubicle, I can't help but notice the gorgeous vanilla pod fragrance. It smells amazing and I can feel that smell trying to trigger a memory in the back of my mind. It's so bloody annoying when you know, but just can't remember. Putting it to the back of my mind, I finish rinsing off the shampoo suds from my hair and make sure that it is completely clean, then reach down for the bottle that I didn't pay too much attention to before. The bottle is for a very expensive brand of shampoo that you typically only get in hairdressers. That's when the memory comes flooding back. Last Christmas, Papa gave me a voucher for a cut and blow dry at a world famous salon. They have an exclusive waiting list and their prices are so expensive, they don't even advertise them. The salon is run by a world famous hairdresser who works primarily with celebrities. I was blown away when Papa presented me with the voucher. He said he won it in a bet and made sure he went for it, just for me. I remember going in and feeling like such an outsider. I mean, I don't exactly look like a troll, but I felt like one surrounded by so much beauty and wealth. The woman who did my hair, Lolita, was lovely, and never made me feel like an outsider, and oh my

God, can that woman do hair. I look after my hair, it's kind of like my baby, but she made it so silky and smooth, I wanted to hug her. I think I even said that to her because I couldn't get over the shine. She said it was the shampoo that did it and she showed me the exact bottle I have in my hand. I smelt it and I remember the same vanilla pod scent infusing in my nose and I was addicted. I loved that it made my hair smell the same. I almost didn't want to wash my hair after because the smell would go away. Lolita offered me a discount on the bottle of shampoo, but when she told me the price, I almost fainted. A thousand pounds for a bottle of shampoo is excessive, no matter what the contents are, or who designed it. So, I politely declined, as I figured it was more important that me and Papa have a roof over our head than my hair smelling like vanilla. Obviously, Grant doesn't have that problem. I don't know why it bothers me so much that he bought me such an expensive shampoo, but it does. I have a weird feeling in my gut that something's not right. I know there is no way he could possibly know that this is my dream shampoo, but combined with all the other little things in the room, I can't help the weird feeling. He only met me a couple of hours ago, his personal shopper could have got some of the clothes in that time, but could he have got all the other stuff too? I have a really bad feeling that Grant is lying to me and he knows a lot more about me from before we even met. Now I just need to find out why.

After drying, I get wrapped up in the most gorgeous soft robe that I wish I could stay in all night. But now I have a mission. I need to find out what Grant's real agenda is because he is definitely not being open and honest with me. Dinner is the ideal place to do that, which is how I find myself standing in front of a wardrobe looking at clothes that would easily pay off all of my papa's debt and more if they were sold. The names on some of the tags are brands I have only ever dreamed of wearing. I'm not a massive fashion fan, and I most definitely am not a girly girl, but even I know these brands. I love my jeans and tees with comfy converse, but sometimes I like to put on a bit of make-up, wear a dress, and look nice. This, however, goes so far beyond that, it's unreal. As I am stroking the different fabrics and freaking out over which one I am going to wear, I see a note attached to one of the hangers. It reads 'I picked this out special. Wear it tonight. Grant x'.

I'm trying not to read too much into the note, but I get this weird creepy shiver going down my spine. I think this is supposed to be a kind gesture, but that's not how it comes across. Does he think this is a date? I start to wonder if maybe he thinks I will sleep with him to clear my papa's debt. Would I? I want to keep my papa safe, but I think that might be a line I just cannot cross.

I pull the hanger out and looking down I see the most beautiful silk red dress. This is not the sort of dress you wear for a business dinner to discuss the terms of your agreement, as we said it would be. This is the sort of dress I would wear if I was trying to get laid. This is the dress you wear when you want a guy's eyes to pop when they see you and to imagine peeling it off you. If Grant wanted me to imagine his reaction to me in this dress, he really missed the mark because my thoughts are nowhere near him. Ryder, on the other hand, is standing front and centre in my imagination. I know my little crush is silly and nothing can ever happen, given he works for Grant and will soon be my colleague. That doesn't stop my mind from wandering and I feel sure that he will be in my thoughts the next time I alleviate the tingling he has caused between my legs.

Clearly being led by a different body part than my head, I give myself a mental shake because I need to get my head fully in the game if I am going to find out what Grant's plan is. I'm guessing he is not going to come out and tell me straight away, so I will need to work for it. My number one aim is to pay off my papa's debt, but I also need to make sure I'm safe. I don't know if I'm capable of selling my body to pay off the debt, so I try not to think about what that would mean. After applying some make-up and doing my hair in a light curl, I finally go to get dressed. I look in the drawers for some underwear to wear underneath it and there is nothing like what I have ever worn before. My go to is normally boy shorts with a novelty picture on them. Today, I have on the most amazing pair of Harry Potter panties, but I took them off with my jeans. I could put them back on but given the silk material of this dress, I would have some major panty lines, which nobody wants. So instead, I pick up the tiniest, red thong that I know will match this dress so well. I decide not to wear a bra. I am lucky enough that the girls are not too big that they need to be controlled, and not too small that I don't have a cleavage. They are just right for this, and given the plunge in the neckline, there is no way a bra can be worn. When I slip the silk dress over my skin, I realise I have never felt so sexy. Then when I add the matching Louboutin heels, I'm in Heaven. I love this dress and I look so sensuous, it feels like such a shame to waste this on a dinner with Grant. But, maybe I can use it to my advantage, to get him to be honest with me. We will see. I just hope I get to see Ryder, then I won't have to imagine his reaction.

CHAPTER SEVEN
RYDER

I'm sitting downstairs like a fucking muppet just waiting for the penis to come back down from his tour of the house with Ava. I know he's up to something and I have no idea what it is, which scares me. Grant always discusses his plans with me because he isn't smart enough to come up with them by himself. Well, technically he can, I just make sure they aren't insane and that nobody is likely to die. But really, the more I have gotten to know him, the more I have come to realise that it's all an act, a persona he presents. The boss only trusts him with shitty little jobs because he thinks he is unpredictable, but I've realised that is far from the case. That is why I keep my eye on Grant, because he is more clever than he lets on and nobody knows the real him.

The boss assigned me this job two years ago to stay close to Grant because he is being trained to take over the company when the old man has had enough. The Blakeman crime family has ruled London for generations and the only reason nobody has ever challenged their rule is because everyone is scared of the Blakemans. So while one sits on the throne, they will have power. The problem is that Grant is the last descendant and he wouldn't be anyone's first choice. Personally, I don't think the old man will ever leave, he loves it too much. But more than that, he doesn't trust handing everything over to his son. However, it would be a massive show of weakness and disrespect not to hand over the reigns to Grant. It is important that rivals do not see any cracks in our operation. So I have my orders and I've managed to calm Grant down, keep him in line, and ensure he follows the boss's orders, until today.

When we were sitting in Manny Delgado's house this morning, I had no idea how many things were going to go to shit. We were supposed to threaten him, ban him from gambling, and move on. Personally, I think the boss has a bit of a soft spot for Manny. They have some sort of a history, they knew each other a long time ago and Manny changed when he lost his wife to cancer. From then on, he has pissed his life and inheritance up the wall. Now, I know he has no way to pay back the massive debt that he owes, because our hacker Eli says he's blown all his cash.

Eli is our early-twenty year old hacker who we pay to do all our online dirty work. If you want to find something out, Eli is your guy. The kid has been working for Grant since he was only seventeen, but he is a whiz with a computer and I have seen him hack things that top level hackers can't even do. He makes my life easy so I love having him around, but at the same time, there's a part of me that feels sorry for him being stuck working for this business at such a young age. His skills are invaluable and he is most definitely irreplaceable, which makes him a very valuable asset. That means Eli is part of the firm until he gets nicked or he dies, a bit like me, I guess.

When the order came through to just warn Manny, I was shocked. Usually when Eli tells us they can't pay, there is no use for them. Like I said, I think the boss has a soft spot for Manny, but it can't be that big a spot because he isn't wiping the debt completely and we all know Manny will never be able to pay it off. Eventually, the order will come through that someone has to hurt Manny to let him know we don't take kindly to deals being broken. That person is Vic. He is one sadistic bastard and has no problem beating the shit out of someone or just shooting them. He is like a machine. If the order comes through, he doesn't question it, he just does it. He doesn't need to know why or what the person has done wrong. That is where we are very different. I will not get my hands dirty if I can help it. My main aim is to encourage Grant not to use violence and to be smart with his plans. Sitting in that room with Manny, I thought we had a plan. Then Ava came into the room.

Fuck, I had never seen anything so beautiful. In walked this tiny little fireball with curves in all the right places. Her long shiny black hair almost glistened a bluey colour in the light. When she cocked her hip to put her hand on it, trying to look fierce, all it did was make her tight little arse stand out and my jeans got a bit tighter. Then there is her tight old band t-shirt that is clinging to her chest in a way that I could only ever dream about. I know some guys like big tits, but they're not for me. I like a more natural look. As my mates say, a handful is just enough for me and by the looks of her stretched fabric, she has slightly more than a handful. It made my mouth water. What really tipped me over the edge is when I looked at her face. She seems like a bit of rock chick to her and I love that. I cannot stand high maintenance girls. If it takes an hour to put your face on, I'm not interested. Ava looks like she hardly has any make-up on and when I looked into her beautiful chocolate brown eyes, I can see why. She doesn't need anything. Her eyes shine all on their own and honestly, they light up her face. But the way she looked at Grant put the most sexy fire in her eyes and turned them almost black. It made me wonder if they turn black when she gets all hot and bothered too. Could I make them go completely black when she cums? Woah, can't be thinking those sorts of things while I'm trying to work. Definitely don't want my dick on show when I'm sitting next to Vic, who I'm pretty sure was fondling his gun and wondering if he should be shooting Ava. Or anyone for that matter, he really doesn't care who. Then there's also my boss and her dad, two people who you most definitely do not want to be getting a hard on in front of. So, I casually adjusted myself and tried to remain as neutral as I could. But when I looked over at Grant, he seemed to have noticed the same things about Ava that I have and it makes my skin crawl. The thought of that slimy piece of shit even looking or thinking about someone as perfect as Ava is disgusting. She may be a lower socio-economic class than him, but my God, herbeauty is so far out of his league, they are not even playing the same sport.

I looked over at Ava and noticed her surveying the room, trying to take in the situation, but if she was scared, she didn't show it. She tried to look tough and it was actually pretty adorable. There's no way anyone like her would need to look tough because people should always protect beauties like her. I know I would protect her. I watched as her gaze travelled over Vic and I knew she could see him caressing the edge of his gun and her breath seemed to catch. Now she realises the gravity of the situation. She took a subtle step towards her dad and amazed me even further. This tiny excuse for a girl was willing to throw herself into a potentially deadly situation just to save her father. What she didn't know is that I would never let that happen. We were there as a threat and nothing more. Given that Manny was sitting there with a terrified grimace on his face and shuffling on the seat like he was about to piss himself, I think we have achieved our goal. Grant just needed to lock the deal up with one last warning and we could get the hell out of there.

For some strange reason, I felt like I had to get us out of the house and as far away from Ava as possible. I feel this protective urge over her, which is crazy because I hadn't even spoken to her, and given the way she was shooting death glares at Grant, she didn't look like she needed my protection. But I wanted to and that thought made me laugh. Some fucking mobster bodyguard I am! I don't let my mind go down that route. I am what I am and I can't fucking change it. So we needed to make the best of a bad situation and get the fuck out of the house, and far away from the beautiful siren that made me think strange thoughts.

I looked over at Grant to give him the nod, signalling that it's time to wrap things up. We had done what we set out to do, so let's go. We have a routine and we do it this way every time. When I'm sure the target is adequately informed of the situation and understands the gravity of the shit hole they have got themselves in, I signal for us to leave. Sometimes I have to wait until Vic has done a little roughing up, but we all know that isn't happening with Manny. He's scared shitless of us, the problem is that his addiction overpowers his fear.

I gave the signal but realised I may as well not have bothered because I don't think Grant was aware anyone else was in the room other than Ava. He was looking at her like she's a shiny new toy and I cannot stand it. I know that shitty little weasel too well and I could see the cogs going over in his head. He was planning something and that's bad. Normally, Grant acts impulsively and irrationally out of anger or greed. It's normally something that he has not given any real thought to and once he calms down, I'm able to talk him out of doing something stupid. This time, I don't think that's going to help. He is plotting something to do with Ava and I can feel my blood start to boil and my pulse race. I have to stop him, but I don't know how. He is my boss and I have no choice, I had to be here.

Watching him convince Ava to come to his country residence to be the live-in cleaner was soul destroying. I wanted to warn this beauty that she needs to run away. She's walking into the lion's den and she will never be able to get out. I know his place because I practically live here. Whenever Grant is at the big house, the boss' security team takes over, I'm only called in if needed. So I live in the country house the majority of the time and I've noticed over the last month, he has been doing renovations but when I asked him about it, he just said he was giving the place a face-lift. I left him to it, I didn't even look at what they were doing. As long as it didn't affect my room or the movie room, I was fine. Then he installed a massive indoor swimming pool that I was able to use and I couldn't have been happier, I love to swim. However, that feeling of suspicion never went away. Particularly when he increased the security team and made the perimeter fencing more secure. I thought he was paranoid about people getting in, but as I watched Vic drive the car in through the gates, I looked in the sun visor mirror and Grant's smile changed to a shit eating smirk, I realised he was never planning to keep people out. He was planning to keep Ava in. The worrying thing is that I thought he only met Ava for the first time today, but these renovations have been going on for around six weeks.

How the fuck did I not realise he had created a special room just for a woman? My job is to see things, to be observant, and to monitor what the fuck is going on in this place and I failed. I got distracted by the work the boss asked me to do, but now Ava's life could be on the line. I have to protect her.

After well over an hour, Grant comes strolling into the living room looking like the cat who got the cream. He slumps himself down onto the comfy chair that he always uses and drapes his arm across the back, like he is king of the world. I am suddenly filled with a rage I have never felt before and I feel like my skin is prickling as my blood boils. All I can think about is the idea that he might have put his filthy psychopathic hands on that beauty. Fuck, there's no way I am jealous. I never get jealous. But right now, I am, that's the effect the little fireball has on me. I need to put that out of my mind. I'm here to do a job and that is what I am going to do. I may not like the job and I may lie awake at night thinking of different ways that I could inflict pain on the dickhead that is Grant, but truthfully, I work for Alan, the big boss. He is the one who recruited and hired me. I originally worked his security detail for a short time until he saw I managed to get on with his son. This was something the majority of other security staff hadn't been able to do. They all hated Grant and the way he treated people, but mostly, it was his unpredictability they hated. It's hard to keep a man safe when you have no idea what he is going to do. There have been numerous times I've ended up bloodied and bruised because that bastard had started on the wrong people and then just expected us to pick up the pieces. For some reason, he is different with me. Grant sees me almost like the friend he's never had. He talks to me about what's on his mind and he actually asks my opinion on things. Since I am quite fond of living, I play along in an effort to get him to trust me enough to share any crazy ideas he has, which is why I'm so fuming right now.

"What the fuck is going on, Grant?" I yell at him, while he just sits there lazily. I can feel myself getting more and more worked up.

"What do you mean?" he asks cockily, and I literally have to take some deep breaths because I can feel my hands balling up into fists, ready to pound his stupid head.

"You know exactly what I mean. What the hell is she doing here and how long have you been planning this?" I screech in a tone that is definitely not something you should hear out of a man's voice. That is literally how perplexed I am by this shithead.

"Listen, Ryder. I am your boss. I am the one who makes the decisions and you go along with them. What I have planned for Ava is none of your concern. You do what you are told, like my father pays you to do. Understood?" He really is peacocking at this moment, with his chest puffed out to reiterate the fact he is the boss. But I can't just accept that. Not where Ava is concerned. I need to try a new tactic.

"I understand, boss, but I was talking to you as a friend. You have never been like this over a woman before, why is she different?" As I talk to Grant through gritted teeth, I am trying to sound respectful and like I genuinely care about him. Whereas in my head, I am picturing whipping my gun out of its holster and shooting him in the face. Daydreaming about that has become a regular pastime and helps me deal with being near Grant.

"Sorry. I guess I'm just temperamental when it comes to talking about her. I know you will be on my side, but I know my father will not approve. I disobeyed his orders and I guess, I was just thinking you were going to report back to him," Grant explains. It's actually quite laughable that this grown man who is being groomed to take over one of the largest criminal enterprises in the world is still afraid of his father. I mean, I have met the guy since he is my boss and I am not going to lie, he's a scary dude. I guess, I stupidly thought that since Grant is actually rebelling against his father's wishes, for the first time ever, he'd actually grown some balls and was not afraid of the consequences. Turns out, he is afraid and this makes me happy. It means the old man will not be happy about this and will shut it down. Hopefully, I can have Ava home safe in a few hours because I know some of the other staff work for the old man and get paid extra to keep him informed of Grant's stupidity. So chances are, he already knows.

"Come on, G, you know I'm always on your side. Yes, your father pays my wages and hired me, but that doesn't mean I'm not loyal to you. However, I can't say the same for everyone on staff. You are obviously going against the old man for a reason, why is she so important?" I ask, hoping I can pry the information out of him. The more I know, the easier it will be to keep Ava safe.

"It's hard to explain, without sounding strange. Just trust me when I say I need Ava. I'm gonna ask her to do things she won't want to do but she will. My father will be unhappy, but that's the plan. I can't tell you more than that, I'm sorry." His statement causes me to falter and makes me even more anxious. He knows what he is doing will piss off a whole bunch of people, yet he is doing it anyway and he doesn't want to discuss his reason with his only friend… I smell trouble with a capital T.

"Sounds like you have it all planned out. So what's your plan to win her over?" I ask, hoping I will be able to help him not make a cock up of this.

"Well, we are having dinner soon. I am hoping that she will be able to see how much I have to offer her, but I'm going to make it very clear to her that when she agrees to my deal, I will not only wipe off Manny's debt but I will also buy that shithole they call a house. I might even sweeten the deal by agreeing to give Manny a monthly payment that he can gamble and piss up the wall. All she has to do in return is marry me and be the good little wife I need her to be. You don't need to know why it has to be Ava, but just know that it does." Fuck, did he just say marriage? He actually does have it well thought out and there's no way Ava can say no to that. She is all about caring for her father and doing everything she can to look after him. But will she give up her own life and happiness, just to protect him?

I mumble out congratulations to Grant and tell him that it's a good plan, but really my heart is racing and my head is spinning. I know he said there was a very good reason why he chose Ava, but I have to know what it was. As my head is spinning, Grant stands to take his leave.

"I need to go and get ready for dinner. I trust this information will remain just with you, as always," he states, like he always does. He's paranoid that people are reporting back to his father about him, which I am sure that they are.

After Grant has gone, I use the time I have to scout out the house again, armed with the knowledge I now have, I need to find out what secrets he has been keeping from me.

CHAPTER EIGHT
GRANT

As I leave Ryder in the living room, I feel a lot more confident now that he knows my plan. He's always the sensible one, the planner, and so if he thinks a plan is good then it's because there is no better one. Just as I am about to head out of the room, I remember what he said about my father. I can't believe I ever had the nerve to suggest Ryder isn't loyal to me, I know he is. But it's important for me to keep all of my employees on their toes, including my best friend. He did tell me that even if he doesn't report this back to Father, someone else might and I need to know who. So I turned back to face him.

"Ryder, before I go, you mentioned that there are people who will be quick to report my actions to Father. Do you know who these people are?" I ask him as casually as I can but inside, I'm seething. I handpicked and hired every person who works in this building. They work for me and have nothing to do with Father or his business. So, he obviously has approached someone in my employment and has turned them into his spy. I need to find out who they are so I can get rid of them. I don't need him ruining my plans before they have really even begun.

"Not for sure, no. But I know what your father is like, he will have eyes and ears inside this place for sure," Ryder replies.

"Yeah, well, I can't have him knowing my business. I want you and Vic to interrogate every person I have on staff and have Eli perform deep dives on their bank accounts. I need to know if any of them have any contact with my father or any of his known associates. When you find out who it is, I want to speak to them. Ok?" As I am passing on the instructions to Ryder, I feel a vibration as my phone goes off in my pocket, indicating a message. Reading the message causes my heart to race and it feels as though my stomach has sank. He knows.

"Put a rush on that, Ryder. Someone has already informed Father. He is requesting our company at the big house tomorrow morning at ten. He says to ensure you are there as he wants to discuss bringing us both onboard for the next shipment." I can see Ryder's eyes go wide on hearing this. While my father has been saying for a while that he is training me to take over from him and that he wants Ryder trained as my right hand man, he has never made good on this promise. He has never included us in any major plans, only low level shit. Well, not since I fucked up the last piece of training he took us to. So this is big. I am just worried that the only reason he is saying I can be a part of a shipment is because he wants to have something to barter with. It's like hanging a carrot in front of me and saying that I can have it as long as I give Ava back.

"Fuck, G, that's big news. Being involved in a shipment and getting more access into how the business runs is what you have been working towards, well, what we both have. This is a big day, man. Why don't you look happy?" Ryder asks with an obviously fake, forced smile on his face.

"Come on, Ryder. You and I both know my father does not do anything as a nice gesture, particularly after I have disobeyed his orders. I went against his instructions by bringing Ava here and I knew he would not be happy. I expected he would call me in for a bollocking, but this is a whole new level of mind play. I have no idea what's on his fucking mind. We have to be ready for anything and everything tomorrow, Ryder. You prepare and I am going to win over the girl. I won't need you until the morning. See you then," I say as I walk away. Using the fancy app Eli set up on my phone, I make sure that the door to Ava's room unlocks so she can come down as instructed. I have security everywhere, so if she even *thinks* about trying to run, I'll know. That's why I can confidently sit here and wait, knowing she will be here soon.

My staff have done a fantastic job of getting the dining room prepared. The long mahogany table that runs along the centre of the room has just two places set, one at the head of the table and one directly to the left. All of the finest silver and china crockery have been set to make the table look as beautiful as can be. Personally, I do not care for all the fancy shit, particularly the elaborate gold candelabra that sits in the centre of the table. That cost over fifty thousand pounds and all you do is set it on fire, madness to me. But there is a reason behind all this dressage. I want Ava to see what her life could be like if she agrees to a life with me. I want to show her the luxury she has never known.

I have been sitting here for a lot longer than I should have been, just messing about reading the enormous levels of emails that I have to go through. I keep seeing the maid pop her head around the alcove into the dining room to see if it is time for her to bring the drinks. I demanded it be ready on time and since Ava is now ten minutes late, I'm sure the kitchen staff are worrying about the food getting cold. We may have had an exchange of words on a previous occasion that resulted in the death of a very rude chef. Normally, I wouldn't have given a shit, but Father was in attendance and he expects certain behavior. The chef actually had the nerve to answer me back and say it was my fault the food was cold for not being there on time. Even if that was true, and it was, that's irrelevant because I expect my staff to meet my every need. If I'm not there on time, find a way to keep the food heated. He started going on about chicken and salmonella, but he had the nerve to do it in front of all the other members of the kitchen staff, some house maids, and Father himself. I couldn't have that kind of insubordination in front of Father, he expects me to behave a certain way and if I don't, it's me he would punish. So I made the only choice I could; I picked up the nearest large chef's knife and I plunged all eight inches of the glistening, stainless steel blade into his neck, severing his carotid artery. He fell to the floor and blood spurted out of the wound covering all of the kitchen, the staff, and myself. How my father acted so proud of my behaviour and the praise I received did nothing to quell the darkness that I felt absorbing into my soul.

After that, I promoted one of the other kitchen workers to senior chef because I knew after seeing that, he would never disobey me. All of my staff have been extremely efficient since then. I, on the other hand, have felt like I am on a slippery slope into despair, following my father down a rabbit hole I'm not sure I will ever be able to climb out of and even if I do, I'm not sure my soul will be intact.

I'm pulled out of my daydream by a very small squeak from the door as the old hinges creak when they open. Ava opens the door just enough for me to see her face and she has truly worked wonders with the expensive make-up kit that I left in her room. I have always known Ava is beautiful, even if she makes my skin crawl, but seeing her all dressed up in the things I picked out for her, makes me smile. It's just the beginning of me moulding her into exactly who I want her to be and making it look to the outside world like she is a lady who is worthy of standing on the arm of one of the city's most eligible bachelors. Fuck that, I'm THE most eligible bachelor in the city, and once I take over my father's enterprise, I will be one of the most powerful men in the world. For that role, appearances are everything.

As she glides into the room, my eyes slide over the sexy red cocktail dress that I purchased for her. It fits her curvy body like a glove, almost appearing to ripple down her body like a waterfall of blood. She moves with a grace I am shocked that someone of her upbringing is capable of, particularly in the four inch heels I picked for her. I smile at her to show my appreciation for not only how she is dressed, but also the fact she agreed to wear the clothes I picked out for her. It's the first sign she's given me that she can be moulded into the wife I need.

I rise and quickly stride over to meet her at the door. Taking her by the hand, I led her into the grand dining room. I use my arm to indicate all the finery that has been set up, just for her. Then I move closer to her body, so close I can feel her body warmth. Her lavender and vanilla scent radiates off her, but all it does is cause my nose to wrinkle. Time to put on the show though.

"Ava, darling, I'm so glad you agreed to join me for dinner. I thought the staff had done a marvellous job in setting up the dining room, but all of that paled when you walked into the room. You look absolutely gorgeous. That dress is just perfect on you." Blush creeps up her cheeks with the compliment and I cannot stand the way the words taste in my mouth. Quickly, before she even realises what my intentions are, I gently place my lips against her cheek. I let my lips rest against the blush I saw fill her cheeks and it feels so delicate. She almost feels like she is breakable, which I very much hope she is. I count down the seconds my lips are pressed to her skin, trying to think of anything but the act itself. This is purely to win her over.

"Erm, thank you." Ava looks very unsure, either about my comment or about the kiss. She is refusing to make eye contact with me and she is stroking the fabric of the dress as if she doesn't quite feel comfortable in it. She looks almost like a rabbit caught in headlights, like she is unsure what I plan on doing next. So before she gets even more skittish, I decide that maybe a bit of wine and food will make her more pliable.

"You should accept the compliment for what it is, Ava. You are a very beautiful woman and that dress only enhances the natural beauty you have. But, we didn't come here for me to shower you with compliments, though I will if you want me to." I give her a sexy wink and a crooked smile that always wins over the girls. "Let's sit down, shall we? That way we can enjoy some wine and the chefs can begin bringing out the food." Her returning smile is timid but certainly brighter than before. Hopefully, my charms are working and she is coming around.

Still holding her hand, I lead her over to the dining table and show her to her seat. Before she has even sat down, the hovering maid is next to us, holding out the chilled bottle of Dom Perignon White Gold Brut I had already selected for us. It will go perfectly with the butter poached lobster I've had the chef prepare.

As soon as we are seated, the busty blonde maid picks up my crystal champagne glass and gently pours a small tasting sample of the champagne. This is one thing I was taught by my father, how to appreciate good wine. Ryder is always trying to get me to try a bottle of beer or lager, but he is never successful. My father instilled very early on that the Blakeman family only does luxury. I slowly sip the fruity drink and admit that it does taste delicious, but for the price, it should.

"Excellent. Ava, would you like a glass?" I nod to the blonde maid to ensure that she serves her first, but when I look over at Ava, she looks a little intimidated and confused.

CHAPTER NINE
AVA

I feel like I have entered a parallel fucking universe. I'm sitting here in a dress that I'm pretty sure could easily pay off my papa's debt, and then the shoes could pay off our mortgage. Upstairs, in the solitude of the bedroom, the dress had felt so beautiful on me. The way the satin silk flowed over my body had made me feel so incredibly sexy. I literally look the best I ever have and probably will ever look. Then I walked into the ornate dining room and met Grant. I have never felt so out of place in my life. You can dress me up in fancy shit but it doesn't change who I am, and what I want to know is why Grant clearly wants to change me. Why did he bring me here, under the pretence of a job, when he has more staff here than he needs? I am unsure of his motives and that's making my hands sweat, I'm so nervous.

When he opened the door to meet me, I have to admit I

was taken back by how good he looked. I would have to be blind not to see that Grant is a good looking guy. Then add in his expensive suit, his obvious rock hard abs the white shirt is clinging to, and his signature smirk, and I'm sure he has women queuing up to be with him. But he doesn't do it for me. When I look into his eyes, I see a darkness, one that is not there through lust. Even though he has been nothing but nice to me, there is a part of me that thinks Grant is capable of causing a lot of harm. And not just to me, but to anyone he comes in contact with. So when he kisses me on my cheek as a greeting, the tingle that I feel rippling down my spine is not one of lust, but instead, one of unease. His closeness makes me nervous and the fact I can clearly see a gun outline on his waistband does not help. I try to push my worry to the side and just get on with the evening. The last thing I want is for him to see my fear.

Before we are even seated, a blonde house worker enters the dining room and she only has eyes for Grant. She is wearing a short black skirt that barely passes the middle of her thighs and a white shirt so tight, the middle buttons are almost bursting open. Now, I know this woman has clearly got some artificially enhanced tits going on, given their size, but just give the girl a bigger sized top. Then we wouldn't need to see the lacy black bra she is wearing under her white shirt. If I do end up working here, there's no fucking way I will be dressed like this. I have seen hookers on my block wearing more clothes.

If it's even possible, when she presents the champagne to

Grant for inspection, she thrusts her tits out towards him even further. If he turns around to face her, he will definitely end up with a nipple taking his eye out. But for some reason, he's barely even acknowledging she's in the room. His eyes never leave me and that starts to freak me out. I mean, this girl is clearly very beautiful and she is obviously more than willing, so why is he ignoring her? He either thinks so little of her because she is essentially his servant that he wouldn't stoop to that level, or he has already fucked her and he doesn't do returns. I don't know why I am trying so hard to work this out because it's not like I'm jealous, but it does kinda look like we are on a date and you don't do that. I'm a waitress, so I know, you never hit on the guys who are on dates. I feel like this whole fucked up situation is starting to go to my head and I most definitely need some of that champagne that is on offer.

The blonde pours me a glass and then tops up Grant's glass for him, before he dismisses her. I take a large gulp of the bubbly drink in the hope that the alcohol will hit me quickly and help to quell my nerves.

"Stop! You do not drink champagne like that," shouts Grant as I down half the glass in one mouth full. I look over at him in shock, not understanding why he raised his voice at me. So far, he's been calm and, well, nice, but now there's a flash of anger marring his features. His hands are balled up into fists and he appears to be taking deep breaths as if to calm himself down. Wow, whatever I did really pissed him off!

"Erm... sorry? What did I do wrong?" I know I'm not from his upper class society and wasn't raised all high and mighty like he was, but I'm fairly sure that champagne goes down the same way as cheap prosecco and I'm an expert with that shit.

"The drink you have in front of you is a Dom Perignon White Gold Brut from 1995. It is one of the finest champagnes in the world. Each bottle sells for around three thousand pounds and I own several crates as it's my personal favourite. I like to use it for special occasions, such as this. But it is a drink to be tasted, savoured, and enjoyed, which means drinking it slowly. Allow the bubbles to burst against your lips and the fruity grape flavour to absorb on your tongue. You cannot do that if you are chugging it down like you're at a frat party." Initially the way he talks about tasting the wine is slow and has a sensualising hypnotism to it. I'm genuinely entranced and want him to show me how to taste this ridiculously expensive drink in a way that it deserves. But the moment is completely ruined when he chastises me like I'm a child. He is about to learn that I do not deal very well with being told off or being told what to do in a condescending manner.

"Well, if I am not drinking it to your standards then perhaps you had better finish this expensive glass and I will just have some water," I say with as much fake sweetness as I can manage through gritted teeth as I push the glass towards him.

"There is no need for that, Ava. You just need to learn to

drink like a lady, that's all." He takes another stupidly tiny sip of his champagne and now I'm really annoyed. He basically just called me trash. Well, I will show him how girls from my neighbourhood do things. I take what's left of my stupidly expensive drink and swallow the entire contents of my glass. I have to admit that the drink does taste good but wow, does that alcohol hit my system quick. I start to feel a little woozy and I'm instantly regretting my plan. Maybe I should have eaten something before drinking like this. I can't afford to lose my faculties in front of this guy and it's clear he knows how to wind me up as it is.

"I'm not interested, thank you. There's not much call for ladies in the bars I go to and I certainly won't be buying this fancy stuff myself, so why do I need to learn how to drink it properly?" I ask, hoping his answer will shed some light on why I am really here. But before he gets a chance to reply, Tits walks in, holding our meals.

She places a plate down in front of me and it is covered with the silver cloches that you see in fancy restaurants, or on the TV food shows I love watching, like Masterchef. When she places Grant's plate down in front of him, she waits for him to gesture she has his consent to remove the lids. Underneath, sits a giant red lobster, dripping in this light yellow sauce. There are three small stems of asparagus, all of the exact same length, placed on the plate together. Opposite them sits four identically sized baby new potatoes, each drizzled with some of the same sauce that adorns the lobster. I had no idea you could even *get* new potatoes that are all the same size. How the other half live!

Staring at the lobster on my plate, I have to admit that the whole meal both looks and smells delicious. I have never eaten lobster before and am sitting, questioning how I actually do go about eating it. I am most definitely a cheeseburger type of girl. I pick up a fork and prod around a little, feeling for an area that is not shell because everyone knows you can't eat the shell. I stick my fork in the baby potato instead, deciding that's the safer option. Just as I open my mouth to try the butter soaked potato, I feel that telltale wary tingle over my skin. I look up to find Grant staring at me with his baby blue eyes. He looks like he's mesmerised by my facial expressions as I contemplated the lobster and he almost seems pleased at my discomfort, or like he is happy that I don't know how to eat the damn lobster. But why would I? This food probably costs more than Papa and I spend on our weekly food budget. When he looks at me in that way and my skin starts to crawl, it almost feels like he has a deep hatred for me, but that can't be possible as I've never met him before today.

"I'm sorry, Ava. It never occurred to me that you wouldn't know how to de-shell a lobster," he says in what is clearly a condescending tone before raising his voice. "Can I have the chef in here now?"

Within about a minute, there is a rapid knock on the door and after Grant signals permission to enter, in rushes a middle aged gentleman dressed in chef whites and a matching chef's hat. Given that the hat and apron do not have a spec of dirt on them, compared to his chef top and trousers that are clearly marked with the days preparation work, it's obvious he has tidied up his appearance specially for this.

Once he reaches the space directly at the end of the table opposite Grant, he stands bolt upright like he is in the army, or someone has shoved a rod up his arse. His eyes seem to be flitting around; firstly looking at myself and Grant, and then looking at each of our dishes, he is clearly trying to assess what is wrong. He looks incredibly shifty, like he's nervous and beads of sweat are starting to appear across his brow. But still he says nothing, like a good servant, he waits to be spoken to first. Given the way his eyes are darting around and he is fidgeting, it's unclear if he's just uncomfortable or if he's genuinely scared of Grant. I have seen this behaviour before, he looks like my papa did just this morning. He looks like he knows exactly what Grant is capable of and I feel like a bucket of cold water has been thrown over me. It quickly reminds me that Grant is dangerous and this is not a game.

"Ah, Chef. Ava here is a lobster virgin and I am taking her cherry. If you could de-shell it to make the experience easier for her, and be quick because I want to start eating," he states, with no please or thank you. No manners at all, just the ridiculous sexual entendre. The chef clearly looks startled by his instructions and looks to be contemplating if he should do it table side, which would be quicker, or taking it back to the kitchen where he has tools to make it easier. I try to help him by making the decision for him. I take hold of my plate and pass it towards him.

"Thank you so much for this. If it's easier for you to take it to the kitchen to prepare it properly, Chef, then that is good with me. It looks so delicious and I want to be able to taste the meal properly without any bits of shell that might end up on my plate if you had to rush doing it here with the wrong tools." I smile at him sweetly, trying to make his life a lot easier and given the barrage of thank you's that leaves his mouth in a rush, I can tell he's grateful. His eyes remain downcast as he walks towards me and then he finally looks up to take the plate. His wrinkled eyes sparkle as he takes in my appearance for the first time. Why he looks so shocked I don't understand because I'm sure Grant is surrounded by girls much prettier than me on a regular basis. I put it down to the gorgeous dress and the way the chef's eyes peruse my body seems to confirm that. Before I have a chance to feel uncomfortable at the staring, we are all startled by Grant's bellow.

"GO NOW!" Chef snatches the plate off me and literally runs out of the room. I am in total shock that he would treat a member of his staff in that way. Before I can ask him, he starts to chuckle. A look of disbelief crosses my face. Why is he laughing at scaring the shit out of a middle aged man just trying to do his job?

"I'm sorry about Chef just then, Ava. It would appear your beauty is so bewitching, it makes my staff forget themselves. Don't worry, he will be suitably punished," Grant states. I can't help the way that I'm now glaring at Grant like he is a fucking alien. Why the hell would he think I want him punished for looking at me? The chef didn't look at me any differently than Grant has done all night. In fact, Grant's leer feels worse.

"What?" I ask with disbelief. "Are you serious? He didn't do anything wrong or act in any way that was inappropriate."

Grant huffs and raises his glass for another ridiculously small sip. "Chef knows that you are my guest. That means the social order should be respected and he should not have looked at you or behaved in that way."

Now it's my turn to laugh. He really does believe in the whole upper class, lower class divide. So why is he behaving so nicely to me? I sure as hell fall right at the bottom of the pile. It just reminds me how much I fucking hate people who behave this way.

"As far as I am concerned, Grant, the only person behaving inappropriately is you," I state with venom in my voice that comes from years of having people look down their noses and me and Papa because of the area we live in or the fact we live from one pay cheque to the next. It's not the greatest, but I know my papa did the best he could for me after Mum died. So having anyone look down their noses at us for that is a big hate of mine. Grant looks shocked that I would have the nerve to talk to him like that.

"How was I inappropriate?" he asks. He really has no idea that the way he behaved is totally unacceptable. It's almost like dealing with a child who doesn't know any better. But instead, he's a grown man who should know better. If this is behaviour that he has learnt from his parents, I don't ever want to meet them.

"Grant, you cannot talk to people in that way. Yes, he works for you but that does not mean you are better than him," I explain. He looks baffled and I cannot believe what I'm seeing.

"Ava, he is the hired help. He makes a decent wage and I pay him more than most other places would. In exchange for that, his job is to do as I tell him to. It's obvious that the people he cooks for are out of his league and once he took one look at you, he should have known that. But instead, despite knowing you are here with me, he forgot his place and leered over you. So, yes, he will be punished." Now I really am pissed. Who the hell does this guy think he is?

"Actually, Grant, he is nearer to my league than you are. Just because I agreed to this meal with you does not mean that I'm here with you. You make it sound as though I'm on a fucking date with you," I shout at him, losing my cool at this whole situation. I look up to see how he has taken my words, as I wasn't quite brave enough to look at him during my rant, and the look of disdain mars his normally pretty face. He looks genuinely disgusted at me right now and I can't help but lower my eyes, not wanting to see the look in his eyes any more.

Unfortunately, Chef chooses that very inappropriate moment to return with my lobster. He walks in with his head down, moving so quickly, he manages to reach my side and place the plate down before Grant even realises he is in the room, but when he does, he explodes.

"OUT. Get the fuck out now!" As he shouts, his pale white skin begins to turn a ruby red colour as he heats with rage. Chef makes a quick exit towards the door and just before he can reach for the door handle, Grant releases the crystal champagne glass that he had in his hand. He launches it straight at Chef's head. Luckily, it misses by the narrowest of margins and instead, smashes into the wall next to the door. The crystal shatters on impact and the sound can be heard all around the room as the remaining liquid splashes up the wall and the tiny glass pieces spread across the floor. Chef's scream is so high pitched, he sounds like a girl, but he doesn't slow down. He is straight out of the door, ignoring the mess around him like he is used to this sort of behaviour, but I'm not. As the glass hits the wall, a small shriek leaves my lips and I quickly push back my chair and move to the far corner of the room, as far away from Grant as is possible in this space. In my neighbourhood, you learn fast to get as far away from the drama as you physically can. I risk a look over at Grant and his eyes are shining with rage and what looks like lust. He looks like he is getting turned on by either his display of angry violence, or my fear. Neither of those are things a guy should be getting turned on by. I'm starting to worry about being in the room alone with Grant in this state, but before I know it, Ryder comes bursting through the door the chef just closed as he left.

Ryder storms the room looking like a sexy fallen angel, his hair is flopping from side to side as his head moves to assess the room for any danger. He looks just like pure sex on legs and with his body so ridgid from the tension and apprehension of an unknown situation, his muscles are all coiled tight, which just enhances them. He's not the usual body type you would expect to see in a bodyguard, instead he's more lean, like a runner. But his stance right now exudes power.

Ryder sees me cowering in the corner and before he has even looked over to see if his boss is ok, he runs into the room and puts his hard body between mine and any possible danger. Little does he know the danger is actually his boss.

All I can see is Ryder's muscular back rippling under the tight black t-shirt he is wearing as he breathes heavy with the adrenaline of the situation. Even though I can't see where he is looking, I can feel his eyes assessing the room. I'm sure by now, he has seen the crystal glass on the floor, as I heard his feet crunch it when he ran over it to get into the room. He also must be able to see the psycho standing at the other side of the room, looking like he is coming down after going full blown Hulk on a fucking chef. I need to get the hell out of here, but Ryder is blocking anyone from getting to me so well, it also means I cannot get past.

CHAPTER TEN
RYDER

As soon as I heard the crash of what sounded like glass shattering, I was running towards that dining room like split shit. I'm not ashamed to admit I have patrolled the corridors around that room repeatedly since the moment Ava stepped foot into it. Not because I have to protect my boss, fuck no. I don't think Ava is capable of hurting anyone. Grant, on the other hand, has the potential to destroy the poor girl before she even realises it's happening.

I knew something was going down when I heard Trixie come running out of the room shouting for Bobbie, the Chef, to come into the room. The shrill tone she was using could be heard through these heavy reinforced walls, which was not a good sign. Bobbie looks terrified, which is not surprising given that he was there to witness when Grant last used his own initiative and made an example of the previous Chef, Fernando, who was Bobbie's mentor. He was there that day, in fact, it was his knife that Grant used to plunge into Fernando's neck. All because Fernando tried to tell Grant that if he requests food at a certain time, that should be the time it is served because his food will spoil and not taste as good, and he doesn't want to put out inferior products. He also mentioned the dangers of bacteria and reheating or warming food, but I could tell Grant wasn't listening. All he cared about was that Fernando had challenged him in front of his father and other members of staff. Whenever his father visits, Grant becomes so much worse than normal, and I often wonder if he's acting more evil and violent because that is what his father expects of him. He was certainly at his most brutal when both Trixie and Bobbie stood there alongside myself, Vic, and Alan, as he sprayed us all with Fernando's blood. To say that the staff have been on edge since that incident would be an understatement.

Before I started stalking the corridors around the dining room like a crazed man, I did first go on patrol around the house. I wanted to look at the design through fresh eyes now that I know some of what Grant has planned for this girl. I wanted to look and see what I missed before, because I never miss anything when performing tactical risk assessments. As I walk and look at things in the new way he described them, I see he has very cleverly designed it with security in mind. There are locks in the right places, lights and cameras in hidden areas, and more guards patrolling than I knew we had on shift. There's no way that dumb fuck did this without help. I bet Eli found him someone, which means I need to know who it is. If there are hidden rooms or traps in this building that I don't know about, well, that makes me real fucking nervous. The fact I am supposed to be the security manager and yet he hired security staff that I don't even know about pisses me off. Obviously, my role is ensuring his protection and I have team leaders that manage other areas. We meet occasionally and they voice any concerns to me. The leader of perimeter security, Marco, never said a fucking word. But the one thing I will say is that they are fucking well trained because without really looking for them and studying their movements, I wouldn't have been able to work out how many there were or where they are based.

That small piece of good in a surrounding pile of shit is not enough to keep my frustrations at bay. Grant might feel happy being the only one who knows the set up of the house and security, but that is not how it works. I get paid to keep his dumb arse alive, sadly, so I need to know. I cannot do my job accurately without it. At least, this is what I tell myself for a good half an hour before my feet lead me to outside the dining room. Why can't I get the beauty out of my head? It's not healthy to think of her. Grant has set his sights on her, he has a plan, and the spoilt little fucker always gets what he wants.

As Chef Bobbie wobbles into the room, holding his rather large belly and breathing incredibly quickly. He has run all the way from the kitchen and given his size, I don't think Bobbie has ever run before. As he enters, he closes the door behind him and I try to hear what is going on. Trixie chooses that moment to slide along the wall, placing herself in between me and the door I was trying to listen through.

"Hey, sexy, don't you have the night off? Usually you do when the boss has one of his whores over." Trixie has one of those incredibly nasal voices that seems to whistle through your ear drum and starts to grate on you after about one sentence. So, she just reached her quota with me. Sadly, Trixie doesn't take no for an answer. I know she's only trying it on with me because she wants sex, everyone knows the reason she is here is because she wants Grant. She has this stupid fairy tale dream in her head that she will be able to seduce Grant and become his trophy wife. But she made one very big mistake, she opened her legs for him on the first day she got here. He's never looked at her again, but she has never stopped trying. Personally, I think they are made for each other because I saw how turned on the crazy bitch got when she was covered in Fernando's blood.

"Hey, Trixie. You know me, I'm always working," I say as I back away from her advances. She's stalking towards me like a lion tracking its prey. But what she doesn't realise is that I'm leading her exactly where I want her. I need to move her out of the way and once she has advanced fully into the corridor, placing both hands gently on her shoulders, I see her breath hitch like she genuinely expects me to make a move. Instead, I turn her and gently push her in the direction of the kitchen.

"So, go back to the kitchen and let me do my job." She

huffs as I go back towards the door, trying to hear what is going on. But before I get a chance to listen, it opens. I step back defensively, making sure Trixie is covered in the event of any danger. I may not like her, but I don't want her dying. The next thing I know, Chef Bobbie comes wobbling out of the room holding a plate with what looks like lobster on it. He is mumbling something about needing to de-shell a lobster for the pretty girl as he runs towards the kitchen. I stay back to make sure there is no chance of danger and Trixie moves to the door to see if her assistance is needed. When she sees it isn't, she closes the door and releases a little laugh. I look at her with my eyebrow raised, silently asking what she finds funny.

"Stupid bitch doesn't even know how to de-shell a lobster. What the hell is he doing with someone like her? Seriously, Ryder, he always says that he needs to be with a woman of standing because his father will not allow anything else. Well, he can dress her up in as much designer clothes and expensive make-up as he wants, but the minute she opens her mouth, it's obvious she's a poor girl from the wrong side of the tracks," Trixie spits out with disgust. I had no idea that Grant had even spoken to her about his father's requirements for any future wife. As much as I hate to hear those vile insults spill from Trixie's lips, I also know that what she says is very true. If Grant thinks he can fool the old man in some way or even change his mind, he's an idiot. Everyone knows that when Alan Blakeman issues an instruction, that is what he expects to happen. Alan is very traditional and he believes in the social hierarchy and where he stands within the community. He stands on top of anyone else and so does Grant. That means, whoever he brings with him to the top, will have to be just as worth it.

After a rare night of drinking a couple of months ago, Grant divulged all about how the old man informed him that he only has a few more years and then he is expected to settle down and marry before he turns thirty. He is to choose a woman from a respectable family, the higher up in society the better. At twenty-seven, the years are closing in on him and Alan is excited about the prospect of being able to pick for his son if he leaves things until it's too late. If he is not married by the time he turns thirty, then he will be disinherited. It's a Blakeman family rule that has been passed down for generations. The same will happen if he marries someone that the leader of the family doesn't approve of. This is a rule that everyone who works for the family must abide by. Alan has final say over who is let into the fold and if he says you can't marry someone, then you don't. Unless, of course, you both want to spend your honeymoon swimming with the fishes. So, if Grant really does want to marry Ava, he will need to do a lot of convincing and there's a part of me that is very excited when I allow myself to imagine Alan's reaction. There's no way he will agree to this and a smile crosses my lips at the idea that Ava could be free. A small, yet annoying, cough pulls me out of my trip down memory lane and I remember I was talking.

"Trixie, they are just having dinner together. There's

nothing romantic going on. So put your bitchy claws away and don't get them out around me again. Now, get back to work." I use my authoritative voice that I don't often use around here. I may be the most senior employee around here, but that isn't something I like to remind them off. I find it is easier to speak to them on the same level if they don't see me as being different.

CRASH!

The sound of glass shattering pulls me out of my thoughts and snaps me into action. I see Chef come racing out of the dining room, still holding the plate from before, but I ignore him and head towards the possible danger. Before Trixie has even made it back to the kitchen, the dining room door slams shut, and he overtakes her in his fright, making sure the kitchen door shuts firmly behind them both. Grant has an obsessive need to make sure that all doors are closed whenever anyone comes in or out. He says it's because he can never be taken by surprise if someone enters the room that way because he will always hear the door open. I know this is a trait that he shares and probably learnt from his father. Since he grew up surrounded by violence and killers, not to mention his psychotic father, it's not surprising he's wary.

Racing into the room as quickly as I can, my eyes gaze around the room to do a general threat assessment. I was next to the main door, so I know nobody entered through there, but there is still the servant's door, which the house girls sometimes enter from when they are bringing in the food or drink. There are also three large windows overlooking the back of the property. After glancing over and seeing that the service entrance is secure, my next assessment is the windows. Having heard glass shatter, these are my main suspects for if a threat is entering the building. But before I can fully assess the windows to ensure they are all still intact or even identify any possible threat, my eyes catch a flash of red backed into the corner of the room. Ava has her back flat against the far wall and her beautiful face has all the colour drained from it. Despite obviously being terrified, she has a resilient look on her face and her stance is one of someone who is getting ready to fight if they really have to. Her tiny little hands are balled up into fists as though they are going to protect her. Not on my watch. Before I've even completed a threat assessment, my feet are moving of their own accord. I'm very aware I'm breaking protocol and acting in a reckless way that could potentially be putting my life in danger, but my brain is telling me I have to protect this girl. So I run until my body is right in front of hers and then I quickly finish the threat assessment.

Only a couple of seconds have passed since I first entered the room, but it feels like so much longer. I'm trained to evaluate the threat level and then react in an extraordinarily quick time. Any delays or reckless behaviour on my part could get everyone killed. That is why I have a plan and I always stick to it. I assess the room, I identify the threat, I track every individual in sight to make sure they are all safe, and then I plan how I will neutralize the danger whilst keeping everybody safe. When I was first assigned to work with Grant, I was told I would need to ensure that his safety was my number one priority and that is always in the back of my mind. But I don't risk my life or anyone else's safety for his, I just make it look like I do. I have never, in all of my years of doing this job, broken protocol and dove in before I even assessed what the risk was. But the minute I saw Ava cowered in the corner, looking scared, my brain changed perspective. It stopped assessing and all I could think about was protecting her. So I ran and put my body flat up against hers to make sure she is protected. Then, as I complete my assessment, I see the only threat in the room is Grant.

Grant is at the opposite end of the large dining table and, to an everyday observer, he looks cool, calm, and collected. Like he threw the crystal champagne glass, that's probably worth around five thousand pounds, against the wall just as a casual pastime. But from the placement of the shards of crystal glass all over the floor, it looks as though Grant either threw the glass at Bobby as he was running out the door and it missed, crashing into the back wall. Or he threw it at Ava, who was standing near the back wall and she moved to the corner as a way to keep safe. Either way, the bastard got a little too close to Ava for my liking and I want to know why.

"What the fuck is going on in here?" I ask once I've got my breathing somewhat under control. I can feel Ava's tiny hand pressing against my back and it is sending tingles through my body. I don't know if she is trying to tell me something or just reaching out for support, but I move my back slightly against her hand to let her know that I'm not going anywhere until I know she is safe.

"We are all fine in here, Ryder. Tell the blonde she can clean the glass up after we have finished our meal. Don't want to waste good lobster, now do we? So come along, Ava. Sit down and enjoy," Grant says casually as he goes to sit down in his chair at the head of the table. He may look calm, but I know him and I have spent years scrutinising the behaviour of Grant Blakeman.

I know I should move out of the way to let Ava get to her seat, but I still have yet to decide if Grant is a threat to her or not. He said he intends to make her his wife, and Grant always gets what he wants. So, I'm worried about what he might do when this feisty vixen turns him down, because she will. I hope. I can feel her hand still touching my back, my skin prickles like it's coming alive and my heart races. I'm worried that it's her way of trying to hold onto me and telling me not to move. But at the same time, I can see the look of disapproval in Grant's eyes that I haven't moved to the side after he gave an order. I do work for the dick, after all. So, I decide to meet them both halfway, I step slightly to the side. It's just enough so Ava can go and sit back down if she wants, but close enough that if Grant tries something again, I can protect her. Ava peers around my back and with the sexiest look of determination I have seen and a cock of her hip to support it, she goes to town on Grant.

"I don't know what the fuck is going on right now, but there's no way I am having dinner with you. I want to go home. I don't know why you really brought me here. It's clear you lied about offering me a job. So whatever disgusting thing you have in mind for me to do to pay off my papa's debt that requires me getting dressed up like this, I can tell you now, it's a no. Thank you for the offer, but me and my papa will sort out our own way to pay you back. So, I am going to go home, if you let me know where we are so I can get an Uber, please," Ava says with a confidence I did not expect given I can feel her physically shaking.

Now Grant looks pissed. I see the anger flash across his face and his eyes darken to almost black. I know Ava has seen it too because I feel her body tense against mine, where our arms touch. I have a feeling shit is about to get a lot worse.

"You are right, Ava. I didn't bring you here to offer you a job. But unfortunately, your father's debt is far too serious for me to just let you leave without us sorting out a way for my father to get his money back. Even if I were to ask Father to pause the interest, at great risk to myself, it would not help. You simply cannot pay back the loan and continue paying your bills and mortgage with the income you make from that shitty diner. Manny doesn't bring in any consistent money and that makes you unreliable. Therefore, we have to come to some arrangement, or Father will be forced to send his employees to take care of Manny permanently. Just to show others you cannot steal from Alan Blakeman."

Holy shit, Grant really is spewing some shit to this girl. Everyone knows the old man's motto is 'dead men can't pay'.

So he doesn't kill people who owe money very often. Plus, he has a soft spot for Manny. He stopped the interest on Manny's loan years ago and there is no way he would ever sign off on anyone taking him out. Nobody really knows why they get special treatment, but I'm guessing Grant does and he isn't happy about it. But I know that Ava doesn't know any of this and there's no way I can tell her right now. I can't risk my job for this girl, there is too much at stake. Luckily for me, it sounds as though the feisty girl behind me doesn't like to be threatened either.

"Don't you dare fucking threaten my papa. We have some savings and I will get it to you. It's not enough to pay the whole debt, but it's a start. I will work as many jobs as I have to. It's better than fucking you for money. I'm not a whore," Ava spits venom as she shouts at Grant. She has obviously misunderstood his proposal and thinks that he just wants sex. I'm guessing when she finds out what he really wants, she might explode.

I can't help but feel a strange overwhelming sense of satisfaction at the fact she is standing up to this lunatic when everyone else gives in to his every whim. I knew from the moment I met her that she had fight in her, I just hope it doesn't get her into too much trouble. Grant, obviously, is less impressed with her fighting spirit because he starts to laugh.

"Oh, Ava, don't be so naive. You have no money left. We have hackers who follow the finances of everyone we lend money to. It's our way of tracking if they can actually pay us back or not. Manny blew the last of your mother's inheritance last week. He also has four maxed out credit cards and a substantial bank loan you don't know about, plus the three credit cards he has taken and maxed out in your name. You owe the banks a lot of money and that is on top of the money you owe *me*. I brought you here to make you an offer to solve all of your problems, but it's nothing as perverted as prostitution. Look at me. I don't need to pay for sex," he says like the cock twat he is. I can't help the eye roll and I think Ava has a matching reaction. Sadly, he is right. I have seen him pick up girls who have no idea who he really is and that always shocks me. I figured the girls he fucks are usually doing it because they know who he is, who his father is and more importantly, how much they are worth. But I have seen him pull girls just on his looks and fake charm alone, and it is fake. If Grant is being nice and pleasant with you, or if he is smiling at you, it is because he wants something from you. I spend enough time with him, as a friend, to know he is devious and manipulative and his everyday tone is neutral. It's like he is void of emotions when he is just being himself and it's fucking chilling to witness. Ava is stuck between a rock and a hard place here because Grant is not going to let her go easily. He will give her an out, he always does, but I can tell you now, choosing to be his wife will be the better option by a long shot. For some reason, the idea of Ava agreeing to marry this dick makes me feel very nauseous and angry.

"So, if it isn't for sex, then what did you bring me here

for?" Ava tentatively asks. I notice she still has not stepped out from behind me fully and her hand is now gripping my t-shirt like she is holding on to her lifeline. Grant sits back down and gestures for Ava to take a seat at the opposite end of the table.

"I had planned to discuss this in a slightly better setting, Ava, after we had got to know each other a little better. So the least we can do is make it civilised while we talk. So please, have a seat. Ryder, you may leave us." Grant makes it sound as though he is offering Ava a choice, but I can hear the undertone of an order. Fuck, I'm torn because I have to listen to the arsehole, I can't risk my job, but I really don't want to leave her. Given the way her fist clenches my t-shirt tighter, I think she feels the same way. Thank fuck, he can't see her touching me, even just touching my t-shirt would put both our lives in danger. When Grant has decided something is his property, that is that. No discussions, no negotiations, and absolutely no sharing. I'm debating what to do and obviously Ava senses my indecision, so she takes the decision away.

"I will sit down and talk with you, Grant, but only if I am allowed to have Ryder sit next to me. I need to know I am safe." I see the look of disgust and rage on Grant's face, but there is also a flash of something I rarely see marr his face, jealousy. He is jealous Ava feels comfortable and safe with me. Shit, that is really not a good thing, but if it allows me to stay in this room, then I'm all in.

"Fine, but just so you know, Ava, Ryder here may look

kind, but he works for me for a reason. He is good at his job and he follows orders. If I asked him to shoot you in the head, he would because he knows what happens to my employees who cross me. Now, please sit down." That was quite impressive. Not only did he manage to destroy any trust Ava might have in me and my ability to protect her, but he was also able to get an underhand threat in there for me about what happens to his employees that let him down. But he doesn't need to threaten me. I know exactly why I am doing this and we both know that no matter what the order, unless there was a genuine threat to life, I wouldn't shoot anyone.

With Grant's suggestion that I am the dangerous one in the room, I expect Ava to move away from me, but she doesn't. Her grip remains strong until she has to let go and take her seat. Grant is sitting at one end of the long dining table and he motions for Ava to take a seat at the other end. There are chairs lining both sides of the table and I look them over while deciding where I should sit. My instinct is to sit in the chair Ava is heading for and pull her onto my knee to keep her safe, but, fuck, I can't be thinking like that. I should take the seat next to Grant, that is where he expects me to sit to show I will always be on his side, but that's too far away from Ava if anything were to happen. So I eye up the middle seat, hoping that neutral territory won't get me into any trouble. But once again, it's like Ava is in tune with my feelings and she pulls the chair out on her right and drags it as close to her side as she can get.

"You can sit here please, Ryder," she says to me with the sweetest voice that almost made me forget where we are. I look over to Grant to see how he feels about Ava's suggestion. It really is a good idea not piss him off any further. I raise my eyebrows in a casual way, making it look like I think Ava is just being melodramatic. I am saying exactly what Grant wants me to. He thinks she is being unreasonable and stupid. He can't understand that in her eyes, he has essentially kidnapped her and is now gonna propose. I am going to say it again, this is mental!

Grant gives me a slight nod of the head to give me consent to sit next to Ava. I'm glad I was able to convince him because I was tempted to sit there without his permission. As I go to sit down, I feel Ava lightly trail her fingers over my arm. To a casual observer, it appears that her hand collided with my arm by accident, but if the very slight, yet bright smile is anything to go by, it was not an accident. Her touch sends electricity sparking over my skin and it heats up my whole body. My heart rate increases and all the blood must be pumping south because I feel my dick start to harden against my jeans. She obviously felt the electricity between us too because she pulled her arm away. I give her a cheeky wink to let her know I have got her back before taking the seat she offered me.

CHAPTER ELEVEN
AVA

When my hand brushed against Ryder's arm, I felt a sensation that I have never felt before. It's like the tips of my fingers were pulsating with electricity and it lit up my whole body. I knew I was attracted to this man, but, fuck, my body clearly reacts to his. When Grant casually reminded me Ryder works for him and not only does he follow instruction, he has also done unspeakable things, my stomach knotted with a sense of unease. I'm not stupid. I can see the gun Ryder wears and the respect that all the security, house staff, and even Vic, show him. Ryder is obviously high up in Grant's organisation and you don't get into that position by following the law. It hurts my head and my heart to think that Ryder is capable of hurting or killing anyone. He looks so beautiful, but his eyes seem so very kind, like this kind of life just isn't for him. I know men shouldn't look beautiful, they should be handsome or sexy and rugged, and there's no denying Ryder is all of those things, but there is a beauty to his face that I have never seen on any man before. I think it is the way he looks at me, like I'm the most beautiful girl in the world, that causes it. So, while I know Ryder is very much a threat and not someone to be messed with, I truly believe that, even if instructed to do so by Grant, he wouldn't hurt me. He threw himself into the room to protect me, not his boss. He put his body in front of mine and that tells me everything I need to know about the man. So, when Grant told him to leave so he could discuss his proposal, the real reason he brought me here, there was no way I was staying in a room with him alone. Even though I knew asking could potentially put both of our lives in danger, I have to take that risk. I need him, he gives me the strength I know I'm going to need to get through this conversation and save my papa.

As soon as we are both seated, I tell Grant to get on with it, I want to know why I'm here and more importantly, how the fuck I get out. Even though I am still sitting here, dressed up like I am going to a movie premiere, this no longer feels like a date. Now, it feels more like a business meeting. Grant is sitting opposite me with his back ramrod straight and he is glaring at me. I know it's because I am challenging him. Guys like him expect everyone, particularly women, to fall at their feet. Well, he has picked the wrong girl if that is what he's after. So, I relax back into the chair and give him my own cocky grin, just to let him know the power has shifted. I'm no longer going along with this little charade. I want answers and more importantly, I want the fuck out of this house and to never see this douchenozzle again.

"So, you were telling me you have a proposal for me," I sweetly enquire and before I have even got the words out, Ryder starts to choke. Almost like he's choking just on air. It's not like I said anything particularly shocking. Maybe he's just surprised I have the nerves to stand up to his boss.

"You most definitely could say that, Ava." Grant chuckles, like he is in on a joke and I am not. It's clear he likes to play games and manipulate people. Well, he is not playing that shit with me.

"Look, dickhead, either get on and tell me what is going on or I will pick up my phone and call the cops. I'm sure they would be very interested to hear that the son of a crime lord has kidnapped a woman from the other side of town." I know this is an empty threat, but hopefully, he doesn't. I would have to be stupid to call the cops on Grant. Everyone knows the cops are all in Alan Blakeman's pocket. Everyone also knows that despite his son regularly getting himself into trouble, he has never been arrested, not once. It is also very well known what happens to snitches. We all heard about the witness who was planning to testify against Alan's right hand man for some flimsy armed robbery charge; he mysteriously disappeared and the charges were dropped. Alan went to all that trouble for someone who wasn't even his heir, so imagine what he would do to me or my papa. I realise by the smirk on Grant's face, he knows I'm bluffing.

"Really, Ava? You're a smart girl. You know how that would play out and whatever happens, it wouldn't be a good ending for you. But you are right, it is time we discuss your predicament." Grant smirks at me as he talks and it just pisses me off. I glare at him, wishing I could shoot deadly lasers out of my eyes and kill this fucker for good. I hate when people speak to me in a condescending manner or question my intelligence. Grant clearly thinks he is the most intelligent person in every room and I hate that. All I see in front of me is an ugly, bitter, entitled child.

"What predicament would that be then?" I reply lazily, trying to hold my emotions back. Keeping my emotions and my intentions hidden is essential. The only way I can beat him is if I play my cards close to my chest.

"Ava, you are broke and I mean, you are in serious financial trouble. Not just with us but with the banks too. You are around two weeks away from the bank foreclosing on your house and then you and your father will be homeless. I also know that Manny made a bet this morning after we left with a rival firm, after my father cut him off from all of our bookies. He only managed to get one bet on before we found out and cut him off, but he now owes the West 49 crew £10,000. That, plus what he owes us, and what he owes the bank, is racking up fast, Ava. Like I said, we have been lenient because you've had your mother's inheritance and your college fund to fall back on if you couldn't make the monthly payments. But Manny spent some of it on the bet with the 49er's. We thought he had already spent it, but he must have had some stashed away. He's in some serious shit, Ava. Your house, your college fund, it is all gone and you have nothing. Do you understand that?" he asks, just like this was a business meeting and he was telling me the most mundane information. Instead, he has just brought down my whole world. I can see and feel it crumbling to small pieces and they are scattering all around me. I really have no idea what we are going to do. I cannot be homeless. And all my college tuition, how could Papa do this to me? He promised me that money was safe. I feel so dejected and I can feel the tears start to swell behind my eyes. I remember my plan, to keep my emotions guarded, to give him less ammunition, but I'm in so much pain, I just don't know how to do that.

I feel as though I'm slowly sinking in a pit of despair at the thought of what my life has become and what it is going to be like. I fear the tears I am desperately trying to fight are going to fall anyway. Until I feel a very gentle touch on my knee. I realise that very subtly Ryder has moved his hand over and is currently resting it lightly against the red satin dress that is covering my leg. In that moment, all thoughts of tears vanish and I wish there wasn't a piece of fabric separating us. I want to feel what his rough, calloused hands feel like against my soft skin. He slides his hand up slightly and gives my thigh a light squeeze. I realise what he's doing, he's giving me the strength I just lost. He's showing me I can handle this. I have no idea how he's capable of doing it by just one touch of my thigh and he reminds me of the feisty girl I have always been and still am.

"I understand. I'm guessing you have a suggestion to help me with this?" I ask with a lot more confidence than I truly have. But the constant heat from Ryder's hand spreads around my body and I can feel it start to pool at my core. Now I'm wishing Grant would fuck off and Ryder would move his hand a little higher. I have to mentally give myself a slap to bring me out of the day dream. I have never had this kind of instant attraction to a guy before. Leave it to me to have a real crush for the first time on the bodyguard of a violent, psychopathic heir to a crime enterprise. I just don't know if it is possible for him to do the things he does, and see the things he sees, without becoming a bad guy. He might look amazing, well actually, I don't think there is a word to describe how fucking hot he is, but I know nothing about him or his personality. He could be as nutty and dangerous as his boss, except he's more clever at hiding it. I really hope that's not the case, but let's be realistic right now. There is no way after everything I just learnt that I'm going to be capable of dating anyone, let alone him, if he even wanted to. Fuck, I never even considered that he is just being nice. Right now though, his strength is the only thing keeping me going as I wait with bated breath for his response.

"You have to listen to the full suggestion before you interrupt. A girl in your situation needs to hear all the facts before you get ahead of yourself and ruin what might be your only good option. Ok?" Grant asks with his shit eating grin again and this time, I openly look towards Ryder to see what he's thinking. Instead of the neutral body guard expression I was expecting, he's glaring at his boss. He's staring in a way that looks like he's throwing daggers with his eyes. To a casual observer looking in on this 'meeting', it looks like Ryder is on my side. Like I'm his boss and he would be willing to go against Grant if things go sideways, or I ask him to. But before I have a chance to dwell too long on his expression, or before Grant has a chance to see, Ryder changes his expression back to one of boredom. Except the squeeze of his hand on my thigh which reminds me he is giving me the strength I need. So, I nod my head, confirming that I agree to remain silent whilst he talks. Then I bite down on my bottom lip to grip it and stop myself from talking because I have a sneaky suspicion that I'm going to want to talk.

"You already know how much trouble you are in financially, so I won't go over that again, but I will tell you that what I'm offering you will take away your family's financial issues for life. Not only will I pay off your debts with us, the 49er's, and the bank, I will also buy your house for you. This means your father will have somewhere to live for the rest of his life and it will cost him nothing. I will also spread the word to every crew in London that he is not to be given any betting status. He will be blacklisted from everywhere. If he needs help with his addiction, we can get him that too. Also, as an added extra bit of kindness to show you how nice I really am, I will return the entirety of your mother's inheritance and I will give your father a weekly wage to help him get by. How does that sound?" he asks but I don't say a word, I just stare at him. I promised not to talk until he was finished and I know that what he said is not the end. There is no way he is going to do all of that out of the goodness of his own fucking heart. But fuck, does this offer sound tempting. Not only will my papa finally get the help he needs, that I cannot provide for him, but all of our financial problems would be sorted for life. Now, I just need to know what it is that he's not telling me. I'm sure it's fine to break his rule if he asked me a direct question.

"What's the catch?" I ask suspiciously, searching Grant's face for any clues as to what he might say. But the truth is, his face still looks the same as before. He has this fake looking smile that doesn't lift the corners of his mouth properly, but it's his eyes that tell the true story. When you look in Grant's eyes, they are blank and expressionless. They are as dark as his soul. Now, I need to know what deal I'm going to be making with the Devil.

"What I ask for in return is an easy one, Ava. All I want is you. I want you as my wife." The words come flowing out of Grant's mouth like he is telling me about the weather. I feel as though the floor is dropping out from under me. It's like the room is spinning and my brain is trying to process what he said in slow motion. My thoughts keep focussing on the word 'wife' like it's a big red neon sign hanging above my head. Why the hell does he want me to be his wife? We are nothing alike. He needs a high society piece of arm candy who will agree with his every word and obey him. I am most certainly not that girl.

I am literally sitting stiff as a board and speechless. Out of all the things I was expecting Grant to say to me, that was not even on the list. I was sure he wanted to fuck me. I was convinced he was going to ask me to be his sex toy, someone to bang whenever he's bored, and I have to admit, after hearing how much shit we are in, I was considering it. But this is something totally different. I believe in the sanctity of marriage. My parents were married for only eight years when my mum passed, but I truly believe they would still be together now. It's not that my family is overly religious or anything like that, we just don't really believe in divorce. Marriage is hard work, it isn't easy, and it's something that needs to be worked at every day. That's what Mum always told me. She said that if you love someone enough then you fight to be with them, even during the times when you can't stand them. I always remember her telling me that when I meet the man who is supposed to be my other half, I would know because my body would tell me. I would finally feel like I'm alive. What Grant is asking is if I'm prepared to give up the chance of finding that, of finding my other half, of marrying for love. I can't give that up.

I realise I'm still sitting there with my mouth open slightly, just gawking at Grant like he speaks a foreign language. I finally snap myself out of the trance I had been in and realise that Ryder's grip on my leg has become a lot harder. His fingers are clutching in a way that will most likely leave a mark and I feel a little disappointment that it hasn't happened through a more fun activity. I risk a glance over at Ryder's face and he doesn't look surprised by Grant's announcement, just angry. I discreetly lay my hand over his to let him know I appreciate the anger he has about the situation. As my soft hand touches his larger rough one, I feel a tingle rush right up my arm and down my spine. I feel like just the touch of my skin against his is lighting up my whole body. That's when I start to realise the irony of the situation. The guy opposite, who makes my skin crawl, is the one who is asking to marry me, yet the man next to me, who sets my body on fire, will never be able to act on it.

Freaked out by the sensations my body is feeling and the situation in general causes my stomach to churn. I pull my hand away from him, pushing his off my thigh at the same time. I lift my head up and smile sweetly at Grant, finally ready to give him the answer he has been waiting patiently for, while I was having my momentary freak out.

"No. I'm sorry, Grant. But marriage means something to me and my family. If I ever do get married, it will be for love." I hold my head up high to make it clear my decision is final. We will just have to work out another way for me to pay back all of the bills. It will all work out. I hear Grant start to chuckle and I'm confused as to why he finds my rejection so amusing. I look over at him with a raised eyebrow, clearly indicating I want to know what it is about my statement he finds funny.

"Oh, Ava, life isn't a Disney movie. Love is a luxury you cannot afford. Luckily for you, I'm a great catch," says Grant with the biggest, most smug smile on his face. I literally can feel that I am having to hold myself back from smacking that dickhead right in the nose. I may be dirt fucking poor, but I sure as hell can still find love.

"Oh, Grant, that's where you're wrong. You don't need money to fall in love and I will wait as long as it takes for Mr. Right. If he never comes, then that's fine because at least I tried. I refuse to settle for anything less and that is exactly what I would be doing with you. No matter how great a catch you are or how amazing your kind offer is, what you are asking me to give up is too great. Don't you want to find a girl you love?" I ask in a pleading tone. I know it's a long shot trying to pull on his heart strings because I'm not entirely sure that he has any, but I am running out of options.

"I don't believe in all that love at first sight bullshit. My father says that when you meet a woman you are attracted to more than others, you should choose her, make her yours. That is when you mould her to fit with your ideal woman. After that, love will come. It's something that you have to work at and put effort into, a bit like organising a business deal, but once it's finished, everyone gets to reap the rewards." Listening to him speak, I actually start to feel sorry for him because it's clear he genuinely believes what his father has told him. That there is no such thing as love until you make it for yourself. That is so warped and then to pass that onto his son, no wonder he's a bit fucked up.

"Grant, hasn't your father been married four times and had multiple different mistresses throughout his marriages?" I ask calmly, hoping this question alone will be enough for him to see that his father might not be the best person to give relationship advice. Grant acknowledges my question and confirms I'm correct but he looks more confused by my question than anything else.

"I don't mean this disrespectfully, but I don't think with a romantic history like I mentioned, that your father is the greatest person to be giving people relationship or love advice. You cannot *make* someone love you. It happens naturally. You're right that it might not happen instantly, love at first sight might not be a real thing, but it's something you build on together. You should never have to force the other person to change. Like with us, you might be attracted to me, but there is probably a lot that you would change. I would need to change how I look, how I behave, and who I am to fit in with the idea that you have in your head for a wife. Once I have done all that, I would be your wife, but I wouldn't be me anymore. You would have stripped away everything that makes me who I am, leaving just the shell you found attractive in the first place. That's not love," I explain and I realise that my hands are flapping all over the place as I gesture and talk using my hands. It's a nervous habit I have been doing since I was a kid. When I am passionate about something, really want someone to hear what I have to say, or when I'm nervous about what the person will say, they all cause the hands to come out.

"I do see what you are saying, Ava, but I think you are wrong. I know you are the woman I want to spend the rest of my life with, that has been decided. Now, I just need to get you accustomed to being a woman who is married to a man of importance, status, and power. You will have a reputation to uphold that reflects on me, so you will have to learn to stick to it. Once I have shown you what this life can be like and all the things that me and my lifestyle can offer you, I think you will be very happy here. If other women are anything to go by, you will be in love with me after our first night together," he replies with that cocky smirk again. My brain feels like it is about to explode and there is a ringing in my ears. He sounds as though the decision has been made. He can fuck right off if he thinks I am just going to fall in line and do as I am told. I need to wipe that cocky smirk off his face once and for all.

"Look, all of this is irrelevant because I have said no. I don't want to marry you, I don't want to date you, and I definitely do not want to stay in this house any longer," I shout, releasing the anger that has been building since he said he wanted to marry me. Ryder tries to calm me down by placing his hand on my thigh again, but I know what he is doing now. He is obviously trying to stop me from causing too much trouble for his boss. I don't need his false sympathy and so I shove his hand away and try to ignore the look of pain that flashes across his face.

"Maybe I didn't put my proposal across as well as I could have since you clearly think you have a choice." Grant sneers at me as he speaks and there is a flicker in his eye that tells me he has more to say. As if what he has already said didn't pull my world to pieces, he thinks he has another ace up his sleeve. But he is right because I'm not sure if I can take any more heartbreak.

"What are you talking about? Look, I know we owe you a lot of money and I am prepared to speak with your father personally about that, to come up with some form of repayment plan. I will work as many jobs as I have to in order to make the payments. I know you don't think I can do it, but I'm determined. I will find the money somehow, but I can't trade my hand in marriage for my papa's debt. It's just too high a price." I beg with Grant and I know he can hear the desperation and the pleading in my voice. The more I beg, the more I can see his eyes light up and a little smile creep up his lips. This guy is getting off on watching me humiliate myself. I would bet any amount of money, if I actually had some, that his cock is straining in his pants as we speak. He can fuck off if he thinks I'm giving him exactly what his sick brain craves. Time for less begging and more fighting.

"Ava, as much as I'm sure that we could arrange some kind of payment plan for you, it most certainly will not be achievable. But the money you owe me is not what I was referring to. The 49's have access to the same financial information that we have. They know just how broke you are and that you have no prospect of paying them back. Problem is, they aren't as forgiving as us. There's a reason they are known as the most brutal street gang in London. If they know you can't pay, they will make an example out of you. First is the beating that will get progressively more brutal, then they cut off one of your fingers. It's quite clever really, it's their signature move to let people know you have pissed off their crew and if it happens again, you are marked for death. When the finger has been removed, they make you hold up one hand to show you have 4 fingers, then add in the other and you have 9. Permanently maimed by the West 49er's and marked for death. It's creative, that's for sure. But it's all for show. They make you think they give you another chance. Allow you to wander around with their mark to let people see how serious they are and not to be messed with, then when you least expect it, they will kill you. That is a mark for death, a way of placing a hit. Your papa has made their list and was scheduled to be marked tonight. I have paid for the hit to be held off temporarily, so he is safe for now, but that will only last so long. They made it perfectly clear that if full payment is not made within the next couple of days, then he will be marked and executed." I can't help the gasp that comes out of my mouth. Not only does someone want to torture my papa, they want to kill him. My gut begins to churn violently, and I can feel the contents of my stomach trying to work their way up my throat. Controlling my breathing, feeling each breath slowly move inside and then back out, is the only way I can stop myself from vomiting all over the table. A wave of sadness passes over me and I wonder how my poor sweet papa got involved with these people and why anyone would want to kill him. My heart sinks as the realisation hits me, he's the only family that I have left.

My mind is whirling and I clutch my stomach in pain.

Blood is pumping so quickly through my body, thanks to my elevated heart rate, I can feel the whooshing as it passes through my head. The noise fills my ears and drowns out the room as I try my best not to hyperventilate. I feel like the room is spinning, but I am sitting still.

Grant's words echo and repeat through my numb mind as I try to consider every possible option, but that's the problem. There are no options. I really don't have a choice here. If I want Papa to live, I have to sacrifice my happiness. I will never find love and will have to live under the thumb of the monster sitting before me. I will have to bend to his every whim and become the perfect wife he expects. But he is in for a shock because I will only agree to this kicking and screaming. I will not bend, I will not change, I will *not* become his perfect little wife. He can make me say yes to marriage, but he can't make me change who I am. That's when I decide I need to try pushing my luck, just a little, to see how flexible he can be, although I suspect I already know the answer.

"So, I really do have no choice but to marry you. That's what you are saying? But even if I do agree to it, why do I have to change who I am to become this arm candy, this blow up doll for you to parade around? If you want to marry me, surely it is the real me that you want by your side. I have to give up so much already to agree to do this, but you are asking me to give up who I am, to become a completely different person and I don't know if I can do that," I politely explain, very aware of how volatile he can be and not wanting to irritate him any further.

"Ava, princess, don't see it as you giving anything up, because you will never be without. I will take care of you and give you everything you could ever need. I will have the real you by my side, but you have yet to discover who that is. Don't you see, Ava, you have been raised in poverty, you don't really know how to live amongst people that matter. That is what you will learn when you are with me. You will become the Ava you were meant to be if you weren't born into nothing." Grant is talking as calmly as I have ever heard him and I really don't think he has any idea how many discriminatory and derogatory comments he made in one statement just then. Talking about my childhood and how I was raised infuriates me. I was raised by two parents in a loving home and I had an amazing childhood. Even after Mum passed, Papa still did everything he could to remain close to me and show me that I was loved. It didn't require any money, but my favourite thing was to go to the park with him and have him pitch to me so I could practice my baseball swing. Papa would have loved a boy who could play sports with him, but sadly, because of Mum's illness, another baby was not in the cards for them. Luckily for Papa, he got a girl who has more interest in playing sports than she does talking about shoes and wearing make-up. I mean, I'm still a girl, so of course I can appreciate all that stuff. But I also love to throw my Converse on and hit the batting cages. I have so many happy memories of childhood that it breaks my heart hearing Grant dismiss those just because of where I grew up. I feel my blood start to boil and red flushes my cheeks as rage takes over my body.

"Fuck you! I was not raised in nothing. I was raised in a loving home with parents who loved and cared for me. We may not have had a lot of money, but that didn't matter. I was still raised right and you can fuck off if you think you are going to say any different," I shout, feeling the anger bubbling up under my skin. I can see Grant is getting ready to argue back because his cheeks have started to flare red. Before he gets a chance to say anything, I hear simultaneous loud pings coming from both Grant and Ryder. They both reach into their pockets to pull out their mobile phones. Grant flicks it open and smiles, whereas Ryder releases a small groan. I wonder what that is all about.

"Right, princess, we are going to have to pick this up tomorrow. I will call someone to show you to your room for the evening. You will have access to anything on that floor, but that is it. We need to finalise our arrangement before I allow you full access. I have... erm... work that I need to attend to now. You will meet me in the conservatory at nine sharp in the morning for breakfast. Someone will arrive five minutes before to escort you as you will not know the way. Then we will need to prepare ourselves because my father has informed us that he will be joining us for afternoon tea to discuss our engagement." Grant talks in his usual posh monotonous voice and it's as though my previous outburst didn't happen at all. Not only does it appear that I am engaged, but he also seems to have given me the most annoying fucking nickname in the whole world. If he calls me princess one more time, I will have to stab him, just fair warning.

I can feel all the annoyance I have towards Grant, for blatantly ignoring me, bubbling up inside and I'm getting more angry. Grant, however, is clearly finished with the conversation. In his mind, he's dismissed me and now is rising, ready to leave. I'm just about to lose my shit with him when Ryder takes hold of my arm to get me to stand up, in doing so, his touch seems to pull me out of the red mist that had ensnared me.

"Ava, go and wait outside that door for one moment, please," Ryder says, pointing at the opposite door to the one Grant is heading for. He has a stern look on his face, but his glistening blue eyes are what captures my attention because I can see he is pleading with me to do as he asks. I feel all the tension and anger in my body melt away as I look into his sea coloured orbs. I give him a small half smile and a nod as I make my way towards the door. I don't look back at Grant as I leave.

CHAPTER TWELVE
RYDER

Sitting in that room and just letting that prick destroy Ava's life is the hardest thing I've ever had to do in my life. There were moments where she just looked so dejected and I hated seeing her like that. I don't know what it is with this woman, but I feel a connection with her that I have never had with anyone else. When her little hand touches mine, it electrifies my whole body rather than just perking up my cock like most girls do. With her, it's so much more and I have no idea why, which is what scares me. I live this life because I have no choice, I do my job because I want to work my way up right to the top and nothing has ever stood in my way before. I have done some very questionable things and I have stood by while either Vic or Grant do some very illegal things, but that's the choice I made. I'm actually quite lucky I was identified early on as the brains, the planner, rather than the muscle. So, I plan all the jobs and come up with contingency plans to get us out of the shit when Grant inevitably doesn't follow the original plan. That is my job and I made it clear that I'm happy to do that and use my power or weapon in defense, but I will never execute or kill anyone for no reason. I know it happens. Hell, I'm usually there for it, but I'm no killer. I do wonder if just standing there and thinking of the safest escape route makes me just as guilty as the person pulling the trigger. But these are dangerous men and if I start talking soft then it will be me staring down the barrel of the gun.

I have been in a lot of dangerous and illegal situations that haunt my dreams at night, but I know that this night will top out as one of the worst. I don't know what it is about Ava, but I feel like it's my job to protect her. The only problem is that to protect her, I would have to go against Grant and there's no way will I be doing that. He has set his sights on Ava and she will have to go along with his plan until he gets bored. That is exactly where my plan comes in.

The text both myself and Grant received was orchestrated by me the moment Grant told me he wanted to marry Ava. He has never wanted to marry before. Whenever his father has mentioned getting married, he has always said he doesn't want to be tied down to one woman his entire life, and he plans on dating as many women as he can. The old man suggested that he marry anyway and keep his mistresses on the side, just as he does, but given the look of disgust on Grant's face at the mention of behaving like his father, it became very clear to me that he wants his marriage to mean something. If it ever happened, there would be no women on the side. This thought is exactly what I wanted to remind him of. I wanted to show Grant that if he marries Ava, he will either have to settle down just with her, or he will have to have mistresses and be like his father.

The text was an alert from the front gate to let us know Katyia is here to meet with Grant. She often comes around unannounced for casual sex, but Grant never brings her into the house. He always gets in the car and goes off with her alone. He has security guarding Katyia anyway and they take over his protection. But whenever he returns, it's blatantly obvious that Grant really gets off on whatever it is that she offers. So, I may have discreetly arranged for her to show up unannounced and offer Grant the night of his life. I know he would then have a choice to make; does he spend the night getting to know Ava and decide if they truly should get married or does he go and fuck Katyia? I honestly thought it would have been a harder decision to make, but no, the minute he saw the text, Ava was dismissed. But I don't like the idea of her going off and being locked into the far corner of the building and just being able to access that corridor. So I ask Ava to wait outside beause a fucking stupid plan is forming in my dick and coming out of my mouth. I really should use my brain to come up with ideas.

"Katyia is here, looks like you are in for a very good night, my friend." I speak as friendly as I can, slapping him on the back like we are old friends. "I know you probably want me to escort you to her apartment, but I think I would be better off staying here. Vic can do the sweep." I can see his eyebrow pop up in confusion because we have a routine. Whenever Katyia calls, Grant goes back to her apartment and I go with him. I complete a sweep and ensure that Katyia's security is competent and then I leave. It makes him feel better knowing I have checked that he is safe. The look of confusion on his face is because I have never broken protocol.

"I'm just thinking about when your father calls tomorrow. I want to make sure that everything is prepared. I also want to educate Ava on what will be expected of her once you present her as your wife. It's not exactly going to be a fun afternoon tea and we can't have her walking in there blind. We don't want to give the old man any extra excuses to be pissed or to take away the amazing opportunity he has promised us. So, tomorrow we can talk with your father about the job, but to do that, we have to make sure that we keep Ava in line," I say confidently, hoping he will see this plan genuinely is in everyone's best interest. I'm not even lying when I say I need to prepare Ava for meeting Alan Blakeman. He is one unpredictable, evil fucker and she will be walking straight into the lion's den.

Of all the responses I was contemplating, Grant genuinely smiling before starting to chuckle, is the last thing I expected.

"You really do think of everything, Ryder. She does need to be prepared before he comes, even if we have to bribe her with something. Tell her that if she behaves and acts like a wife should in front of my father, I will confirm to him there and then, in front of her, that Manny's debt is paid off. Obviously, all of her other issues like the bank, the house, and the 49's will have to be earned, but this will be a good start. Are you ok staying here to babysit her? You know I can never turn down some time with Katyia." I expect his smile to be slimy when he says that, but it isn't. I think this is one of the most genuine happy smiles I have ever seen on Grant's face. The edges are curved up into cheek dimples that I have never seen before. His angular jaw seems softer almost, like he is no longer holding his face tense and rigid. His eyes are what give the game away because they sparkle and shine with longing. I have known how he feels about this girl from the moment he first laid eyes on her, but seeing it with my own two eyes completely throws me off. If he likes Katyia so much, why is he doing this with Ava?

"Of course, I don't mind. You know me, I like to make sure there isn't going to be any surprises and Ava certainly is a wild card. It's hard to plan when I don't know how she is going to behave. Your kindness with Manny should go a long way in securing her compliance and hopefully, I can talk the rest into her tonight. I would never want to pull you away from the lovely Katyia. Will this be your last time together?" I know that asking this question might be pushing him a little, but sometimes with Grant, you have to push him into seeing what you need him to. I can see the cogs turning in his brain as a frown crosses his face. He looks genuinely upset. Honestly, it still surprises me that Grant is capable of caring for another person, but the look on his face right now confirms it. But, their meeting didn't exactly happen in the greatest way and her background is even worse than Ava's. There's no way in this world Grant would ever get permission to allow Katyia to become Mrs. Blakeman.

Katyia is a twenty year old Russian girl who has been through more in her young life than most people have in a lifetime. She was trafficked here when she was just eighteen years old. She was brought across in one of Blakeman's containers from Russia. Her sister travelled with her, but sadly, did not survive the trip. The barbarians who bring the girls over here make no effort to care for them during the journey. In fact, they know that they are going to be sold as sex slaves, so they take some of them for a test drive right there in the container, infront of all the other girls.

During Katyia's journey, one of the men decided they wanted her, however she had been marked as a virgin and was not to be touched, but he tried anyway. Katyia's sister stood up for her and the two men raped and beat her to death as punishment. Katyia was there the whole time and was made to watch, along with all of the other girls.

When Katyia's transport finally arrived at the dock, the Blakeman's ground crew were there waiting to transport them all to the warehouse. Alan does this so only a very few select crew members know who is involved in every aspect of the business. The person who finds the girls in Russia only meets the crate transporters, the crate transport only meets the lorry driver who picks up the crate, and most of the time, he has no idea what he's even delivering. These girls are transported for weeks at a time in the same container with no cleaning or toilet facilities. The food and water that is packed in with them has to be made to last between them all. When they arrive, they are a mess, so obviously, they are cleaned and made to look 'pretty' before they are sold.

Most of the time, the girls are kept in a facility, taught what to expect from the life they are about to enter, and educated on what it means to obey. Really, they are just waiting for the next auction to be arranged. Katyia's auction was the first time that Grant and I had been asked to attend with his father, to see the process of how the girls are dealt with. Stage one out of three for learning everything there is to know about the business. I still remember it like it was yesterday because even though, at this point, I had worked with the family and Grant for almost a year, and I had seen some pretty nasty, depraved things, I had never seen anything as heartbreaking as watching those girls hopes for a better life get dashed.

THE CAR PULLS UP, VIC REMAINS INSIDE, BUT ME AND GRANT *climb out. I know Grant is excited because I can feel the anticipation humming off him like a ten year old boy about to attend his own birthday party. I, on the other hand, am a bit more dubious because we are walking into the unknown and that is not something I like to do. The old man gave us absolutely no information* about this job. All we know is that Grant is going to learn how a major part of the family business works tonight and if he proves himself, he can slowly be introduced to all the others. This is obviously what we have both been waiting for, the big leagues. The Blakeman family deals in three things; drugs, guns, and girls. So we know in this warehouse we will learn more about how one of these works.

The idea of us becoming more involved with the dealings is amazing. I didn't get into this business just to deal in the small stuff. I want to get the most knowledge that I can and that means getting involved in the main things. The old man meets us as we round the car and the small smile he gives us both is the only sign of affection I ever see him show his son. Standing next to him is Johnny DiMarco, or as he is more commonly known, Bullet. I will give you one guess as to why he is called that. He's the family enforcer and the most psychopathic man I have ever met. He barely talks, he shows no emotion, and he kills without hesitancy or reason. He works for Alan Blakeman because he pays him the most money, but he has no allegiance to this family. He will double cross them all in a heartbeat if it benefitted him somehow. So far, nobody has found anything to tempt him away and people have stopped trying. Mainly because if he turns down your deal, he kills you for wasting his time. He is by far the most dangerous person that I have ever met in my life and I dread to think how many people he's murdered. Just being around him makes my skin crawl.

"Father, thank you very much once again for inviting myself and Ryder along tonight. The opportunity to learn from you is fantastic and I can assure you, we will soak up every ounce of knowledge you give us." I literally have to bite my tongue to stop myself from laughing at how far up Alan's arse Grant is right now. He always sounds like a posh twat but when he's talking to his father, he's so desperate for his approval, he turns on the extra large twat sign.

"Yes, well, I do hope you will behave in a manner befitting our name, Grant. No showboating. Remember, you are here to observe and learn. That does not require you to speak. If you are to take over from me, Grant, you have to learn how things work, but you will also learn tonight the importance of having the right people at your side," says Alan, as he glances over at me before a big smile crosses his face. I feel Grant stiffen at the side of me, clearly unhappy with the attention that his father gives me as opposed to him. Ever since he discovered my ability for puzzle solving and risk assessment, he said he saw something in me. That's why he put me as his son's head of security, with the unofficial task of keeping the crazy in line. When I agreed, I would have done anything to please the old man. You just don't say no to him. Plus, if he supports you then you can go all the way in this line of work, and the higher up you go, the more knowledge and more money. I need to work my way as high up as I can and this is how I plan on doing it. I'm going to ride Grant's posh coat tails all the way there.

"Ryder, my boy, so glad you could make it. You will learn a lot about a main part of my business today. As you will see, it's something that very few people are privy to. Come, stick by me and I will show you how everything operates." He clasps his arm around my shoulders and pulls me along with him. I can almost sense the hiss that comes out of Grant's mouth and I can clearly hear his knuckles cracking as he clenches and unclenches them into fists. That's his tell for when he is considering reaching for his weapon, which he knows is a dumbass move with Bullet standing guard, but it makes me wonder who it is in his crazy little head that is taking the bullet; me or his father. Knowing Grant, he's probably killed us all in his head at one time or another. I don't risk looking back because I need Grant to think I'm going along with this out of respect for the old man, that my loyalty will always be with Grant. Everyone knows that's bullshit, we are all loyal to the old man, but only because he's the one who controls our futures. It's his enterprise and he runs it extremely close to the belt. I want to know how it ticks, and how he operates, the ins and the outs.

We are at an old industrial site that I have never seen before, far on the outskirts of inner city London. We are off the beaten track that nobody would suspect led to this place and there's a reason that this place is so far out, it's not exactly the type of place they want you to stumble across. But if anyone ever did, the old man has that covered too. This large warehouse and several smaller ones surrounding it are all painted and decorated to make it look like they are actual warehouses. Vanilla Sweets 'n' Treats is colourfully displayed across all the walls and on the welcome signs. How ironic that the sweets and treats behind these doors are anything but vanilla, and you can fuck right off if you think they are made here in the UK. Obviously, it's a shadow company of the Blakemans and doesn't really exist. It's just another legal way for him to go about laundering money and having places where he can run the different aspects of his business. I know he has a different venue for all three branches, so the Vanilla Sweets 'n' Treats *company must be responsible for one of them. I would guess either drugs or girls fits more with the name, but I'm sure it won't be very long till I find out.*

Although, there are a lot of things that make this place look convincing as an active operating warehouse, there are a lot more that don't. A distinct lack of lorries and product movement for one. In fact, there will have only been one lorry enter today and he will have left already. No others will enter or exit because this warehouse doesn't distribute to shops, they get the very select clients to come to them. That brings me onto the next abnormal feature. Whilst it can be perfectly normal for warehouses to have electric fences to keep potential thieves out and even the odd security guard patrolling the lot ensuring that everything is in order, with support from the CCTV, this place has all of that and more. The fence surrounding the perimeter has two layers and given the humming from it, there is a seriously high voltage being emitted. But if some super hero somehow lives after touching the electric part of the fence, they then have to get over the rolls of what look to be illegally scaled barbed wire, so sharp it could flay a person's skin off with just a mild catch. Guarding the perimeter is no rent-a-cop security guard, these are highly trained ex-military personnel if the way they operate in formation, march, and hold the weapon by their side is anything to go by. These guns are more than just your standard security job issue 38 caliber revolver. These are high grade, fast, automatic weapons that are designed to cause maximum impact with even the lowest level of training. So fuck knows how much damage these groups of trained killers could accomplish. I sure as hell do not want to be around to find out. Then, on top of all that, there is the technology on site. What looks like ordinary security cameras are so much more. These are top of the range and I know my favourite little hacker Eli would be impressed, but the cocky little shit would still claim he could do better. Alan knows nothing about Eli, he works specifically for Grant only. I am the only other employee that knows about him. Grant needs a hacker that isn't connected to his father and although it is my job to report everything to Alan, I don't. In this case, I never will. It's bad enough that Eli is involved with Grant and his drama, there's no way I want the kid stuck working for the Blakeman's the rest of his life. He can do so much better!

Eli is the reason I even know what some of this technology is. Not only do the cameras record your movements, they also perform a full body x-ray so that it's very clear if you are armed and where. There is also facial recognition software built-in to make sure that the people who come to the warehouse are only those that have been invited. The best part is that they have managed to include all that and make it look like a shitty fifty quid camera that looks like it's probably not even working and is going to fall off the wall any moment. This is Alan Blakeman's planning, he needs to have the upper hand over everyone who is stepping into that room in case there's any potential for things to go down. The security x-ray scan also looks for police wires so they can make sure there's no narcs amongst the visitors. The room also has a signal blocker, so no mobile phone tracker or call can be reached here. The old man hasn't been in this business for as long as he has by not taking every precaution that he possibly can. There will be no way to tie him to a single person in the warehouse, let alone any illegal activity. He will also have someone who owes him, ready to take the fall and say that they sent him in there and he knew nothing. Not that it would matter because I'm fairly sure the Blakemans have several cops and judges on the take. He runs this town and everyone in it is just along for the ride.

Having performed as much of a risk assessment as I could before walking into the unknown, I was shocked when we walked from the side of the building to the front and as we rounded the corner there were several super cars all lined up. I'm talking; Jaguar, Lamborghini, Rolls Royce, Porsche, Ferrari, Hummer, even a limousine. The combined total of the cars in this car park must be around ten million. My mouth drops open and I'm sure a little bit of drool leaks out of the corner. If it hadn't been for Alan pulling me along with him to the entrance, I think I would have been quite happy to spend the next couple of hours staring at these cars. I mean, holy shit, they are things of beauty. I bet they would purr if I got them underneath me. A slight giggling from next to me is enough to break me out of my car related trance.

"Like what you see?" asks the old man whilst scanning an arm to show me the cars. He looks like the world's fucking poshest car salesman on the world's poshest car lot. I have only ever seen these cars on TV and in my dreams. It's kind of a stupid question. I like the look of these cars better than probably half of the women I have slept with.

"They are amazing. I think just one of those supercars costs more than my whole apartment," I say, slightly embarrassed having admitted I live in a glorified shit hole. But it is really just a place to store all of my shit. Most of the time, I stay at Grant's house. It has a cinema room, gym, and a sauna. It's better than most luxury hotels and when I started working for Grant, he made it clear he would prefer his staff to be close. However, I'm the only one he has actually invited to stay in the main house, everyone else lives in the staff house. Vic doesn't stay on site, nobody really knows why and given his constantly angry as fuck face, I'm not asking him! The staff house is a small building at the back of the main house. It's basically an old garage space that has been expanded and made into a staff area. There are small single bed rooms, a large communal area, a male and female bathroom and a small kitchen. Staff are permitted to eat in the house when all their jobs are complete, but they are not allowed to use any other areas of the house. I expected to be joining them and missing out on the luxury, but Grant told me he wanted me in the main house. He says he sees me as a friend, which is great. I want him to trust me because then I might be able to work out how the fucking lunatic thinks.

I hear a throat clearing next to me that brings me out of my day dream. Then I remember I basically told the richest man I have ever met that I'm dirt poor. I risk a look over at his face and instead of the sympathy or disgust I usually get from people, instead he has a gleam in his eye. Alan Blakeman has built his empire by finding weaknesses in others and exploiting it. I can tell that he knows he has just discovered my weakness, what drives me, but he is wrong. I am fine with him thinking that is my weakness because now he will stop looking and he won't find my real weakness.

"Oh, I wouldn't worry too much about that now, son. After

tonight, if all goes without a hitch, I will make sure you not only get a substantial pay rise, but also a nice bonus for helping with this event. I may even let you pick which of these you would prefer." Alan is smiling at me as he makes his proposition, but I can hear what he's really saying. The thinly veiled threat rings loud to me. I am responsible for Grant and I have to make sure he doens't fuck today up in anyway.

"Thank you, Sir. That would be very much appreciated. I will do my best to make sure things remain under control." Even though it's obvious he is referring to his son, the old man never says his name in situations like this. It is always covert, suggestive words that still make his feelings perfectly clear. I think that he just doesn't want to admit that his only heir is a loose cannon because then he would have to consider that he isn't suitable to run his business for him, which would be a fucking disaster. No Blakeman in control means there will be an all out power struggle for the chance to rule and nobody wants that.

The old man nods his head at me to show that he understood what I was referring to and then he nods his head towards the entrance to the warehouse. He walks ahead with Bullet and I fall back to enter with Grant. He seems to be in a bad mood. His face is all scrunched up and his eyebrows are drawn together in a frown. He looks like a teenager who is sulking, and I need to get him in a better mood if he's going to be well behaved tonight. So, I switch on my ultra friendly persona.

"Everything alright, mate?" I ask with a supportive smile to show him I actually care about the answer. The thing with Grant is that he has never been raised with anyone who actually cares for him. So the only time these sort of questions are asked is by work associates who have absolutely no interest at all in the answer. Since I met him, I have been trying to show him I can be trusted and that I genuinely care about him, like a friend would. I have spent the past few months working on it, and since he let me move into the house about two months ago it has been working. I mean, we are like chalk and cheese, and the majority of the time I am putting on an act, but it's starting to work. The more I have gotten to know Grant and have seen how seriously deprived of any kind of love or affection he has been for most of his life, I actually feel an overwhelming sadness for him.

"Why does he do that, everytime? It's like he doesn't give a shit about who I am or that I'm here. He's only interested in you. He even calls you fucking son!" He's seething. His voice is both angry and only a whisper because he knows better than to cause a scene in front of his father's associates.

I remember one time when I'd only been working with Grant about a month and he was so unpredictable, basically a mess. He started on a waiter who served the woman he was with before him. Etiquette says it is always the most important man who should be served first, which was his father. Then his key associates, followed by their women and then everyone else. The waiter had presented the food to Grant's date before him, on instructions from the old man. I think it was a way to test him and, boy, did he fail. Grant was punished for bringing shame and humiliation to his family name at a public event. I was made to stand by and watch as Alan rained blow after blow down on Grant's body, sometimes even using his belt. I was also casually informed that this was a warning *for me too. I was employed to control Grant and I had to get my ass in gear. That's when I started the friend approach, but it was obvious that the beating I witnessed was not the first. Grant had built some very large walls that I needed to get through.*

"Grant, mate, you know he does it to wind you up. This is his way of testing you. He's trying to make sure you have learnt how to behave. That's exactly why we need to go into that room together and you have to be in control of yourself the whole night. No kicking off or doing something your father wouldn't approve of. Just watch and learn how the business, that you will one day soon be running, operates. The more information we gather, the more we have to give to Eli and you know that is essential. Your father is a tough man and he is making sure you can follow his instructions. So can you? Can you go in there, sit down, behave, and just watch and learn?" *I ask and I can see his face relax as he identifies with what I have said. He knows that this is the type of tactic his father would normally use.*

"Fuck, of course, you are right. I can do this. Let's go and see what lesson number one is about. With the mood I'm in right now, I really hope it's not fucking guns. The temptation to use one would be great," *he says with a light chuckle.*

We walk into the warehouse and I'm shocked to find that the inside looks nothing at all like an industrial building. It has been sectioned off with walls to create different rooms and the main one we are standing in at the moment is decorated as though it is an elaborate gentlemen's club. I am suddenly wishing I had worn a tie with my shirt. The walls are draped with velvet curtains and the floor is an ornate hardwood floor. Over to the side is a large mahogany bar that appears to be fully stocked. Dotted around the room, there are large circular tables surrounded by plush velvet seats. On each of the tables is a small lamp and they are providing the majority of the light for the dimly lit room. The tables are all filled with men who are dressed in expensive or extravagant suits, and they all have a drink in their hand. There are a couple of waiters dressed in pressed black dress pants and a white jacket, but I can only see two and the barman. They appear to be moving with not only great speed but efficiency also. I guess the more people the boss hires to work the bar, the more people who are exposed to his business. It is the barman who stops what he is doing and escorts the old man, Grant, Bullet, and myself over to the empty table at the very front that was reserved for us. It appears that we are the last to arrive. Directly in front of us is a large stage with spotlights shining down onto it. It doesn't take a genius to add together a room full of males and a stage, it's obvious today's lesson is girls.

Before I have a chance to say anything to Grant, as it's always best to warn him, even though I'm sure he's worked it out for himself, the lights in the room dim and a short man with a large round belly and a bald head waddles onto the stage. He's holding a microphone in his hand and introduces us to this month's auction. He explains that the boss will always be given the first pick of any girl that he wants to keep and if he declines then the auction begins. I can feel the bile begin to rise at the situation that I'm taking part in. When I signed up for this job, I knew that the old man had a female trafficking ring running and that I would most likely have to take part in it if I wanted to learn the business. But knowing that they are auctioned off to these disgusting rich men like they are slaves affects me in an awful way. Actually seeing it in the flesh is something so much worse, you can't even begin to create it in your imagination. My nausea worsens when ten young girls walk out onto the stage.

The girls have obviously been made up by a specialist because their hair is washed, styled, and set perfectly. They have make-up splashed across their faces and their nails are just as false as the smiles they are being made to present. They are all wearing stiletto heels and various different styles of sexy lingerie. I'm sure all the men surrounding me in this room think they look like beautiful women desperate for sex and ready for buying, but I can see the truth. They all have a look of sheer terror in their eyes. Their faces, below the make-up, look gaunt and if the colour of their body is any indication, they are also very pale. Their bodies may look sexy to these perverts, but to me, I can see their ribs protruding, and they don't have any meat on their bones the way they should. These girls have probably been kept in captivity with very little food and drink for a long time to get their bodies to look like this. No matter how mature the make-up makes them look, some of these are young girls. If I had to guess, I would say there were a couple around the fourteen to sixteen year old mark. The knowledge in itself not only makes me sick but it also makes me angry. I hate the idea that these perverted men are going to buy these scared little girls and use them most likely as sex slaves. This is no life for these broken young girls. That's when I realised that this is the life that they agreed to and so did I. I wanted to learn the Blakeman family business and this is it, so I better shut up and do my job because now I have learnt the first of the three trades, I know too much to ever get out of this job alive.

The auction begins when one of the older girls, I would guess around nineteen or twenty years old, steps forward into the spotlight. She has long red hair and the same makeup and smile that all the other girls are wearing. They have obviously been trained very well. She is wearing a padded jade green bra and matching panty set that very much compliments her hair colour. I can tell straight away that the bra must be padded because she barely has an ounce of meat on her bones, she has no real female curves and so there is no way she has what looks like a good handful of tits. The fat compere announces her as Leyla and she is made to twirl and bend to give the men behind a good view of the produce. Once she is back facing us, I can see the flush in her cheeks, clearly embarrassed about the fact she had to present her ass to this large group of men. First, the compere looks over at Alan and when he shakes his head to indicate that he doesn't want her, the bidding begins. She is clearly very popular and sells for sixty thousand pounds. She's then escorted off the stage and taken to a room in the back. Alan informs me that all of the winners collect their prizes at the end, only after they have paid. I turn to face the man who won the auction and see that he has Mr Timpson, or Timmy, as everyone calls him standing beside him taking down some details. Timmy is the Blakeman family accountant and the person who is responsible for making all the money earnt tonight look legal.

I am still looking over at Timmy, trying to work out how he gets the money and what he does with it when I hear the next auction begin. I'm pulled back to the attention in the room when I *feel Grant, who is sitting at my side, sit up straight and a small groan leaves his lips. I look up onto the stage and there is a small girl with white blonde hair cut just level with her shoulders. Her pale skin and ruby red lips made her seem almost ghostly. Although she is clearly as emaciated as the other girls, she has still managed to keep some of her curves, probably natural. She has a plump ass and decent sized breasts that are made to stand out even more by the red lace bra and thong set that she is wearing. It's very clear she is beautiful, and when, or should I say if, she is healthy and cared for she will look even more stunning, but she looks young. The announcer puts her at eighteen, which is not much younger than us, but her short height has her looking so much smaller. It's obvious Grant is attracted to this girl because, not only has he sat bolt upright to pay attention, he's also casually adjusting his trousers, clearly turned on. Then the announcer makes things even worse by announcing that the girl, Katyia, is in fact a virgin. I hear the small groan he releases and within seconds he is leaning over me to plead with his father to keep her for him. I could see the genuine desire and want in Grant's eyes, but Alan just waves him off, dismissing him like he should never have even spoken. He signals to the compere to commence the auction and that is when all Hell breaks out.*

The bidding gets up to one hundred thousand pounds and I can see that Grant almost has steam shooting out of his ears. He's biting his lip and a little drop of blood appears on his lip. I see him look over at the current highest bidder, the same guy who has been consistently bidding from the beginning. He looks to be only a couple of years older than us and when the light hits his face, I realise he's famous in our world. He runs a local thug gang and has a thing for destroying young virgins before putting them to work in his brothel. Grant must see who the bidder is too and I see him look around the room with a pained expression. I know that he wants Katyia, but he also knows his father has forbidden him from speaking at this event. If he speaks up for her, he risks a severe punishment and so do I. At the same time, we both look up to Katyia and see the fear in her eyes, she appears to be trembling. Grant looks over at me, knowing that our fates are both intermingled and thinking that we have this new comradery, he is asking for my permission to go against his father, to risk everything for this girl. Normally, I would disagree and be fighting him at every turn, but not this time. This is different. This is the first time I have watched him assess the room, look at all possible scenarios, and ask me for permission. This is not a reckless decision made to punish his father and cause a scene. For the first time since I have known him, Grant is doing something for someone other than himself. He wants to rescue Katyia and I let him.

The compere is getting ready to sell to the gang leader for a hundred thousand when Grant calls out in a loud and firm voice, "Half a million." There are gasps of shock from around the room. Not just at the extraordinarily high price, but at the fact the boss' son just bid on a whore. I can feel the rage radiating off the old man from where I'm sitting. The compere looks over at the gang leader to see if he can top the offer and he shakes his head to decline. The offer is put out to anyone else in the room but the air remains silent. Then the fat man looks over at Alan, just to double *check that he has permission to complete the sale and I see him give a very stiff nod.*

The beating Grant got for saving Katyia was horrendous. I have never seen a guy take so many lashes across his bare back with a belt. He was then punched and kicked repeatedly by Bullet until his face was so swollen, he was barely recognisable. I was told that if I took him to the hospital, the same would happen to me. So I took him back to the house, along with Katyia. I called a doctor to check them both over as I was worried Grant might have internal injuries. The doctor came regularly to administer painkillers and tend to his wounds. He mostly stayed asleep because of the heavy pain meds that he was given. Katyia visited him every day. She sat by his side, just being there with him. Once, I even walked in and caught her holding his hand. She looked embarrassed, but I smiled. I don't think he has ever had anyone love or take care of him, maybe Katyia will be good for him. At her request, the doctor taught her how to change the dressings and how to sterilise his wounds. During the times he was awake, I know they talked and grew close. But once he was healed, he was summoned to a meeting with Alan. At that meeting, he was told he could keep Katyia as a whore and only a whore. She was not to live with him, date him, and certainly not marry him. She is a dirty, poor, little Russian whore, according to the old man, and that makes her nowhere near good enough to marry a Blakeman. He said that if Grant did not follow these rules, he would take his little Russian toy away for good. The next day Grant bought Katyia a beautiful penthouse that she chose, in a nice area of London. He said that she could go anywhere but she wanted to be near him. I know Grant did even-

tually take Katyia's virginity but not because she's his whore. They fell in love and I knew how much it pained Grant to be seperated from her. It hurt even more when Alan insisted that he find a suitable girl to marry, or he will choose for him.

My stroll down memory lane is cut short when I realise Grant is talking to me. He is also waving his hand in front of my face because I had checked out mentally whilst I visited the past. Before my space out, he had looked totally relaxed, but now I can see the pain in his eyes. He is thinking about the question I just asked him. Will this be the last time he sees Katyia? I want him to go to her thinking that. I want him to realise he cannot give her up. Then I'm hoping that his disgust at not wanting to be like his father will be so great, he will not want to have a wife *and* a mistress. When this happens, he will have to let Ava go because in the last two years that I have known Grant, I have rarely seen him say no to Katyia. He gives her all the things that she asks for and more, except for the one thing that she wants the most, him. With all of that information flying around his head, Grant heads out of the front door and I see Vic in the car waiting outside. As he gets into the car, I close the door and head towards the room I left Ava in.

CHAPTER THIRTEEN
AVA

To say that my head feels like it is about to explode would be a massive fucking understatement. I look around and absorb the surrealness of the situation I find myself in. I am standing in the most elaborate, entrance hall that I have ever stepped foot into. There's a fucking chandelier above my head, dripping with crystals that would probably pay my way through school. I'm wearing a gorgeous red dress that clings to my body in such a way, even I think it looks sexy. Then you add in these hot stiletto heels that give me so much boost, it shapes and plumps out my arse as well as making my normally short legs look a bit longer. But my surroundings are not the most bizarre, my mind is whirling at the idea that I have just been proposed to. Well, actually if we are being technical, I was just blackmailed, informed I have no choice but to get married, and then my apparent fiancé decided that he needed to leave as he has something more important to do. What I'm really struggling with is how Papa could have gotten us in this much trouble. He always promised me that he only gambled with the Blakemans. I have never found out how they know each other, but Mr. Blakeman has always shown my papa kindness where his debts are concerned. He has even helped him on some occasions by banning him from certain gambling events when they knew he couldn't pay. I also know now that he's responsible for the ban the other gangs have on doing business with him. So, why now have the 49er's allowed him to gamble? Now his life is in danger and if I want to save it, I have to give up my own.

 Suddenly, I feel very claustrophobic despite being in this massive room. The dress feels too tight and it's as though the whole world is closing in on me. I start to pace, but doing that just increases my breathing. I can feel my heart starting to race and the whooshing of my blood and the beat of my heart is rushing through my head. I feel like I can literally hear my heartbeat racing in my head. It speeds up as my breathing has now turned into hyperventilation. Gasping for breath, my stomach pulls in as far as it goes to allow the much needed air to get into my lungs. Before I have a chance to fully inflate my lungs, my brain is telling me to breathe again. The more rapidly I inhale, the less oxygen I'm getting in, but my brain doesn't register that. All I can feel is panic. How the hell am I getting out of this situation? I feel so trapped and I don't know what to do. These thoughts race through my mind on a continuous loop and the panicking gets worse.

Spots of black start to appear in my vision, a side effect of my lack of oxygen most likely. The whooshing and beating of my heart is still audible in my head but in addition to the new black spots, I start to feel as though the whole room is spinning. I'm standing under the chandelier and it feels like I'm on a merry-go-round being spun around as fast as it can go. My stomach starts to flip and all the expensive champagne I had earlier starts to slosh around. It now feels like a competition to see whether I will pass out or vomit first. At this stage, I'm not sure which I would put my money on.

I close my eyes in an attempt to slow down the dizziness, in hopes that will stop the urge to throw up on this fancy floor. Then I realise I would have to throw up on the expensive floor or maybe in a nearby vase because I have no idea where the nearest bathroom is. I'm not even sure I can get back to the room I was given. Having my eyes closed really doesn't help because I can feel myself swaying even more, but thankfully the urge to vomit is reducing. I think I can hear something over the pounding in my head, but I'm not sure. A few seconds later, I feel my legs give way beneath me, but instead of hitting the floor, I feel myself being lifted and cuddled up against a strong hard chest. The smell of peppermint, a woodsy-scent, and something I know I have smelt before, drifts into my airway as my face is pressed against a wall of muscles. Strong arms are supporting me around my back and under my legs. I'm being carried like a bride would be carried over the threshold. Typical me, even in a moment of crisis I turn to romance.

Laying my head against the warm chest feels oddly reassuring and it doesn't even occur to me that I have no idea whose arms are surrounding me. For some strange reason, I feel safe, which is insane because I have essentially been kidnapped by a crime family. I'm most definitely not safe and probably never will be again. But instead of freaking me out even more, I feel the beat of his heart against my face. The soft gentle rhythm is soothing and I know my own breathing and pulse are slowing down to match his. It's like a hypnotic spell that drifts through my ear and over my body, causing our hearts to beat together in tandem. It should be a weird sensation, knowing that my heart beat matches anothers, but instead, it feels oddly perfect.

Without opening my eyes and just focusing on the sensations around me, I'm aware that we are travelling fairly quickly up some stairs. It feels like we turn a few bends and go through a closed door before I finally feel my arse land on something so amazingly soft. It's such a weird contrast to feel half of my body sitting on something so soft and inviting, yet the rest of me continues to cling to the hard body as though it is my lifeline. I need the heart rate and the heat to stop me from losing it. I feel him start to pull away and as my head leaves his chest and I can no longer hear the calming song coming from his heart, I start to panic again. For the first time since being swooped into his arms, I hear his voice.

"Breath, Ava. It's me, Ryder. You are safe with me. I've

brought you upstairs to my bedroom just until you calm down. Mine is on the same floor as yours, but I wasn't sure if you wanted to go to your room just yet." I hear the gentle tone of his voice and my heart starts to speed up, but this time it's not out of panic. I'm shocked that this beautiful guy, who doesn't even know me, would know that I didn't want to go back to that room. I'm not ready to have anything labelled as mine in this house.

Ryder must feel my heart start to race and thinks I'm panicking again. He begins to stroke his hand through my long silky hair. Even though I may not have the greatest self esteem in the world, I know I am not ugly. The part of me that I'm most proud of has always been my long, thick, raven black locks that sweep down my back, almost touching the crack of my arse. I spend time washing and conditioning it to ensure that it looks shiny. I know it probably sounds stupid, but it is my way of making myself feel good. I don't mess about with make-up or getting dressed up, and even though my hair is usually in the easiest style I can be bothered to do that day, I still take immense care with it. So having someone run their fingers across my scalp and down my long hair, brushing gently against my arm on its travels, sends a shiver down my spine. Heat floods through my body and I can feel it pool in my sex. Obviously, Ryder is not aware of this, but what he is doing right now is one of my biggest turn ons.

I know I have to get him to stop because the last thing I need is to be sitting on his bed feeling so horny, I do something stupid, right after being proposed to by his boss. Oh fuck, this is a bad situation and even though my mind is very aware of this, my body appears to be crawling further into his arms and almost mewling like a cat. Traitor!

As his hand makes another journey down to the ends of my hair, I finally open my eyes and risk a glance up to meet his. The glistening emerald orbs that are staring back at me have a heat in them that rivals my own, but there is also sadness there. It looks like maybe Ryder is battling the same feelings I am. The fight over what our bodies feel and what our brains know we can't have. I have to keep my arms clasped around his neck because the temptation to touch him anywhere else is too great. I know once I lay my hands on his rugged skin, I won't be able to stop. I give him a small smile to let him know that I am fine now. Any problems I had with my heart racing and my breathing panting is now no longer caused by panic. It's now accompanied by a wet red silk thong and nipples that could cut glass. In fact, I'm clinging onto him so tight, it's a miracle they haven't drawn blood yet. He registers my little smile and in turn, gives me the sexiest, cocky one-sided smirk that I have ever seen. As just the right side of his mouth curves up, he looks like a sex god who is about to wink at me and make me pass out.

"You doing ok there, little vixen?" he asks whilst staring into my eyes. The nickname he uses for me does wicked things to my body. How just the use of one little nickname can make me feel so powerful and sexy is amazing. It's something I have never felt before and the fire in his eyes as he gazes over my face causes a blush to appear in my cheeks. Most guys would look at my breasts, my arse, or my body in general, but Ryder seems mesmerised by just my face. My brain tries to remind me he's a bodyguard for one of the most powerful crime families in the world. He has probably done illegal and unspeakable things, but that seems like a completely different Ryder than the one I'm looking at right now. This Ryder is kind, caring, and considerate. He put me before his boss, which doesn't scream the world's greatest bodyguard. But mostly, and I know that this will sound beyond stupid, I just feel totally safe with him. That he will protect me and I have an awful feeling that being married to Grant means I'm going to need protecting.

My brains well timed reminder that I may technically be engaged to Ryder's lunatic boss is like throwing a bucket of cold water over me and I let my arms drop from around his neck. What am I thinking? Ryder is more off limits than anyone ever could be and yet I am still sitting on his knee with my body crushed against his. Pulling back, I see the pain flash across Ryder's face at my necessary rejection. But I have to back away. I can already feel the desire I have for this gorgeous Adonis and it could be dangerous to us both if we were to act on it.

Sitting on the bed next to him, I look down and realise I'm still wearing this ridiculously tight dress. It feels as though it's closing in on me, despite the soft flowy material. I think it's just a physical reminder of everything that happened with Grant and the reminder my papa's life is in danger. I always thought that whatever proposition Grant put my way when I walked into this house, I would have a choice of whether to accept it or not. Even when my stupid brain genuinely thought he might be offering me a job. But now I know the whole choice aspect was an illusion. I played right into his hand because he knew that all he needed to do was to get me here and I was trapped. This dress is just acting as a reminder for how truly trapped I am.

"Ryder, I need to get out of this dress." I see his eyebrow raise up at my statement and when I play it back in my head I can hear what he heard. I roll my eyes to let him know that ship has sadly sunk. I can't say it sailed away because then the temptation to sail it right back into his gorgeous arms would be too great. So, I bombed the fucking thing to remove temptation. Then I hear him let out the most gorgeous little chuckle I have ever heard. How is it possible for a chuckle to be sexy?

"Do you now?" he replies using a silky smooth voice that quickly makes my panties even wetter. Damn him, I'm trying so hard and he is not making it easy with his sexy innuendos. But right now, I just need to get out of this dress and if he doesn't help me, I will drop it right here where I stand. I might die of embarrassment standing in front of Ryder in just some sexy lingerie bought for me by another man, but it will be worth it to get out of this dress vice. As I'm having that thought about my embarrassment, all it manages to do is remind me that the underwear belongs to Grant too. That's when I started to panic. I stand up and feel soft carpet under my feet as I realise Ryder must have removed those deadly stilettos sometime during my earlier meltdown and I'm only just realising now.

I let the soft carpet squash under my feet as I pace up and down one small area of the room like a caged animal. I realise then that I hadn't really even looked at the room before, I was too busy focusing on Ryder. It's a massive bedroom, very similar in design to mine. Except, instead of the ridiculously large walk in closet that I have, Ryder appears to have turned his into a sitting room and a gym. It has a little sofa, big TV, and a treadmill. Seriously, his little man room that acts as a closet in my room is the size of my living room back home. I realise that while the room that has been allocated to me has been decorated with feminine touches, this room has not. It's clear that Ryder lives in this room because the smell that is all him envelopes the entire room. His clothes are scattered all around. There's also a Kindle on his bedside table that shocks me and makes me want to discover what his reading habits are. In a house where I feel completely smothered, this room makes me feel safe.

"Ryder, I'm not pissing about here. I feel like this dress is suffocating me, but the only clothes I have are the ones Grant has bought me. They were in the room when I got here. All my size, none my style. By the way, it's still fucking creepy he knows my size. Seriously though, all of the clothes in there are what he wants me to wear, to turn me into this idea that he has of his perfect wife. I can't do it right now. I feel like I can't breathe," I explain to Ryder whilst I continue to pace around on his ridiculously soft carpet. I can tell by the sexy little smirk on his face that he probably thinks that I am overreacting, but when I stop and stare at him, I realise he does get it. He must be able to see the pain and fear in my eyes because I can see them reflected in his gorgeous emerald eyes. He feels my pain and I think he might even feel more for me, which is incredibly dangerous.

"I get it, Ava, and I'm sorry. Eventually, you will have to go into that room and become the wife Grant wants you to be. But maybe for tonight, I can help you out a bit." As he speaks, he walks towards the chest of drawers in the corner of the room and he pulls out an old Metallica band t-shirt. He walks over and hands it to me. As I go to take it from him, our hands touch briefly and the bolt of electricity that flies up my arm shocks me so much, I sharply inhale. Knowing Ryder obviously heard how much the mere touch of his fingers affected me, I shyly look up at his tall figure. He is so close to me, I really notice how tall he is for the first time. He is about a full head taller than me, putting my head level with his rock hard pecs; which, let's be honest, is not exactly a bad sight. However, nothing really compares to his face and as I gaze up at him, I realise he also felt the same connection I did. The colour in his eyes has darkened so much because his pupils have dilated, his breathing seems to have picked up and he looks almost feral, but not in a bad way. He is full of lust and desire and right now, it is all aimed at me.

My brain is telling me this is a bad idea, but right now, all the blood is flowing much further south and she is calling all the shots. I take a step closer to him bringing us impossibly close. The only thing separating us is our hands that are both still holding onto the t-shirt and each other. I don't break eye contact and I'm hoping that he can see how much I want this. I move one of my hands further up his fingers, gently tracing his skin as I go, moving right up his forearm. His skin feels so amazing and as my fingers glide across it, goosebumps start to grow. I go as slowly as I can, tracing the path of his veins up his arm and onto his bicep. When my hand reaches the cotton of his t-shirt, I make my intentions perfectly clear by pushing my hand under his sleeve and running my fingernails lightly across his bulging muscles. The deep groan I hear coming from his lips causes a heat to pool in my stomach and rush downwards, heating and moistening my core.

Feeling even more empowered by the sexy noise I have dragged out of this gorgeous creature with just the touch of my hands, I feel a confidence I don't normally have. I drop the t-shirt from my other hand and take a hold of the side of his jeans, hooking my fingers through the belt loop to help me pull him towards me. He lets go of the t-shirt and as it falls between our feet, his hands snake around my hips. Together, we both pull each other impossibly closer and my whole body is pressed up against his. I can feel the attraction that he has for me growing harder against my stomach, separated only by a thin layer of satin and his jeans. Right now, that feels like far too many layers. My body is burning up with want, my heart is racing, and my pussy is clenching, desperate to be filled by him.

The grip he has on my hips is firm but perfect. It feels as though he is holding on tight, in case I disappear. Little does he know that not only is this the most turned on I have ever been with a guy, but it is also the most I have ever felt for one too. He makes me feel sexy and alive, like I can do whatever I want and take on the world. Right now, the only thing I want to do is feel his soft lips press against mine. Obviously, I want to feel his lips in a whole host of other places too, but you have to start somewhere. The thought of his lips touching and kissing me all over has me even more turned on and despite the fact that all he is doing is rubbing circles into my hips with his thumbs, I release a guttural groan. My body is aching and more than ready for this gorgeous man. I move my eyes from looking at his tempting mouth up to his eyes and find that he is staring at my lips. Without even thinking about it, I bite one corner of my lip and if the sexy moan that left his mouth wasn't an indicator that my actions turn him on, then the increasing pressure from his long rock hard shaft pressing forcefully against my stomach is a dead giveaway.

I rise up onto my tiptoes slightly to make myself a little taller and, most importantly, make his lips more accessible. Ryder remains fixated on my lips and I move my hands up to run my fingers through his hair. The silky brown strands of hair glide through my fingers as they lightly trace across his scalp, eliciting moans from both of us. I feel as though my body is humming in tune with his and even though we are as close as can be, I need more. I need to feel his skin against mine, his calloused hands touching my bare skin. I want to peel his trousers off to reveal the hardness that is currently begging for release. I want to feel him touch my most intimate places, put his tongue against my nub and make me beg for more. As these thoughts race through my mind, my hands have a mind of their own and they grip tightly to his hair. Not enough to hurt him but enough to cause the sharp sting that causes pleasure. Then I use the hold I have on his head to pull him those last couple of inches towards me. I feel his breath fan across my lips and my toes push up even higher, desperate to feel the soft touch of his lips against mine.

Before I can feel the touch of his lips against mine, he pulls away and a small groan escapes my lips. I don't even have time to ask what he is doing when his hands suddenly move to the side slit of my dress. Taking hold of each side, in one rapid movement he rips the satin fabric and the slit that once came just above my knee now reaches my hip. The edge of my red satin thong is almost exposed and I realise Ryder didn't pull away because he didn't want this to happen, he pulled away so he could get better access. Just as I'm about to tell him that he can take the entire dress off, he grabs hold of me like he wants to possess me. His hands rake down my back and over the curve of my arse until they reach the top of my thighs. In the next second, Ryder has lifted me up into the air, wrapped my legs tightly around his hips, and walked me backwards until I am clamped between the wall and his hard body. He ruts his hips slightly and I feel his denim covered shaft press against my now exposed lace thong. I moan loudly and tighten my legs around his back, caging him in to make sure he doesn't leave here ever. Tucked tightly in Ryder's arms feels exactly like where I should be.

"Are you sure you want to do this, little vixen?" Ryder asks, as he gently strokes the hair out of my eyes with one hand before tucking it behind my ear. It doesn't escape my attention that this guy is managing to hold my weight up with just one hand while his hips are pressing me into the wall. However, it doesn't hold my attention for long as he repeats the incredibly sweet gesture and caresses my face at the same time. My heart is racing and I start to realise it's not just my lady parts that are feeling things for this guy, my heart is starting to as well. But I know that is ludicrous because I have only known him a few hours and I know absolutely nothing about him; however, my heart is not listening at all. Right now, it's my lady parts that are shouting the loudest right now, they are becoming frustrated and want to know why Ryder isn't giving them the attention they deserve. Hussies!

"Why wouldn't I be?" I ask with a smile, as I tilt my pelvis, allowing his denim covered penis to press against my aching clit. A spark of electricity shoots through my body and I push my now erect nipples hard into his chest as another loud moan escapes my lips. The answering groan that leaves his mouth tells me he was just as affected by that move as I was. He is probably in more pain because his hard penis is straining to get free from its denim cage. I want to be the one to free it, but as I look up at Ryder, I can see his serious face has returned.

"You know why, Ava. This shouldn't happen and if we do this, it has to be a one off or both of our lives could be in danger," Ryder says in a serious tone. I know he is probably trying to ruin the mood, to make me remember why I am really here and what I have waiting for me in the other room, but I don't want to remember any of that. I know that whatever happens tonight with Ryder may very well be a one time thing, it may cause me physical pain when I have to see him every day and not be near him, but I don't care. If I have to live a life that I did not choose and give up my chance of ever being happy and of ever finding love, then I am sure as hell going to have one last good fuck before that happens. Even if I know Ryder is so much more than that, I know I have to have him at least once. I have to feel his passion and the desire that he has when he looks at me. I have a feeling I am going to need to hold onto these memories to get me through.

"I don't care, Ryder. If I can only have one night with you, then I will take that. I will use the memories you give me tonight to help me get through the loneliness of the rest of my life. You will show me what it feels like to be worshipped and adored and my body will remember that through all the times to come. But, in spite of all the reasons you can come up with for us not to do this and all the reasons I can come up with as to why we should, they are all irrelevant. What it boils down to is that I want you and you want me. So, shut up and kiss me," I say with as much passion as I can muster. I know that whatever words I used to answer his statement would be the turning point in this evening. Ryder is either going to push me away or he is going to kiss me and as I look into his eyes, I see the war he is fighting. The war between doing his job and not betraying his boss, or following his heart's desire and taking me. Right now, I'm not entirely sure which he will choose, but fuck, do I hope he kisses me.

CHAPTER FOURTEEN
RYDER

'So, shut up and kiss me.' The words that have just fallen from her sexy plump lips are flying around and around in my brain. I feel like I am being pulled apart in two different directions. Doing this with Ava could risk everything I have worked for over the last two years. For the past two years, I haven't even been with a woman because my job is my life. But just the slightest touch of Ava's tender silk fingers makes me forget all about that. I begin thinking with a very different head. One that is currently swollen, leaking, and straining to escape from my jeans and get closer to her thong covered pussy. Even through the denim, I can tell that she is wet and ready for me, but I just don't know if I can risk everything for one night of hot sex. My body calls out to Ava and hers calls to mine, I'm not going to ignore her pleas any longer. I smile down at her with the cocky smirk I know she loves so much. She currently is wearing a mask of indifference on her face, her way of telling me she isn't bothered if I walk away. But I can see the fragility in her eyes, the insecurity that I might not want her. How can a girl this beautiful ever think she wouldn't be wanted?

"It would be my pleasure, little vixen." As soon as the words leave my lips, her eyes that had become downcast, fly up to meet mine and they shine so bright. The smile that beams on her lips is the most beautiful thing I have ever seen. So, despite all the reasons why I shouldn't and everything I am putting at risk, I close my mind off to those thoughts and do what I have wanted to do since the moment I met Ava. I close the minute gap between us and press my lips against hers. Her lips are soft and tender, she feels so fragile, almost breakable. As our lips press further together, I feel a heat spread through my body and my cock reacts even more. I feel like a teenager again, leaking pre-cum at the most chaste of kisses. Ava obviously felt the wave of heat too because her hands fist in my hair and she smashes our lips back together with a passion. They collide and it feels so much more intense than the little kiss that started it. I need more of her, so I run my tongue across her lower lip, begging for entry. The desire to taste her is driving me crazy. Her mouth opens instantly and our tongues meet. As they touch and we both finally get a taste of each other, our moans fill the room simultaneously. Ava responds by bucking her hips upwards, causing her clit to rub against my dick again. I'm so hard and the throbbing is so intense, it almost feels painful.

If she feels this good against my cock when there are clothes separating us, I have no chance of lasting when there is nothing between us. Her responding moans are like nothing I have ever heard before. She sounds so beautiful and it is amazingly hot to know it is all for me. There's nothing fake or pretend about the noises she makes, like some of the women I have been with who have clearly watched too much porn. Ava is all natural and that is what has me close to blowing my load over a kiss.

Our tongues continue to twist and taste each other, fighting for dominance but also to consume the other in the best possible way. Ava's hands leave my head and she starts trailing them all over my body, down my back, across my neck, around my biceps. When her fingers reach the bottom of my t-shirt and the exposed skin of my lower back, she trails her nails across it, teasingly pulling the hem up slightly to expose more skin for her to torture and I feel a shiver move through my body. Her touch feels amazing and has me panting into her mouth, but if she wants to tease me then two can play that game.

I push my cock forcefully against her panty-covered core, feeling as it hits her most sensitive spot. Ava cries out with the most beautiful combination of lust and need. I keep my dick pressed hard against the little nub and every movement that she makes trailing her hands across my back, or as she tilts her head to allow my tongue better access, causes my dick to rub against her. Her moans are becoming wanton and I love that she is so free with me.

The pressure against Ava's clit is obviously working because she stops kissing me to catch her breath. She is panting and moaning with every movement, but I am not letting up. I start trailing little kisses across her lips and then her jaw before I pepper them down her neck. The moment I reach her pulse spot, I place a harder kiss against it and I can feel her heartbeat against my lips. My already aching cock starts to pulsate even more at the feeling of how much I am affecting her, her heart is racing like the flutter of a butterfly's wings. I have never felt a pulse so fast and her panting breaths are like music to my ears. She obviously feels as my head swells impossibly bigger because it presses further against her already dripping pussy. She screams and I take advantage of that by starting to suck on her pressure points. This drives Ava crazy with lust and her hips buck against my cock and now she is rubbing herself against me with the sole intention of getting herself off. Her hands that were once teasing the hem of my shirt are no longer in a teasing mood, they are now clawing at my t-shirt, trying to get it over my head.

I stop sucking on Ava's neck to help her to take off my t-shirt and as I move back slightly, I'm no longer putting as much pressure on her clit. As she pulls the shirt from my body, I take advantage of our small break to look at her. She looks even more beautiful. Her hair is messy from my hand and being squashed against the wall. Her face is flush with colour and her lips are so red and swollen, making them look gorgeously plump and inviting. But it is the twinkle in her eyes that really wins me over. Her brown eyes look to be glistening and shining brighter than the dark colour should be capable of. Instead of meeting my gaze, Ava is instead staring at my naked chest. Specifically, she is looking at the tattoo that I have covering my stomach and my back. I am not completely covered but I have different images that appear to all be completely unrelated to each other but to me signify something. I have always needed to keep my tattoos under wraps, they were never allowed to be visible. Obviously, this is not the first time that they have been seen, but the way Ava is staring at them makes me feel as though she can see into my soul. Everyone else would look at the tattoo and see a random collection of animals, ancient symbols, phrases and flowers, but the way Ava's eyes move over each individual piece, it feels like she can see so much more than what is on the surface. She has a quirky grin on her face, showing that clearly she likes what she sees, but then she lets out a little giggle. Not exactly what a guy wants to happen when he takes his clothes off in front of a girl for the first time. I've never had a complaint before, but it has been a while, so I raise my eyebrow at Ava to query her laugh.

Looking deep into my eyes, Ava gives me the sexiest wink and then begins to shuffle in my hold again. This time she is not trying to grind harder against my cock, sadly. No, she is trying to get free but she is caged in between my body and the wall. My brain is screaming at me to not let her go. It is racing a mile a minute wondering what she could have possibly seen on my body that offends her or turns her off enough to walk away from what is quite possibly one of the hottest moments of my life. Despite what my brain and cock think, I can't keep her trapped there, although I am enjoying the feeling of her sliding along my shaft as she tries to wiggle free. I move my hips back slightly and steady her with my arm, I allow her to slide down the wall and back onto her own feet. She must see the flash of disappointment that quickly slips into view because she chuckles again. Then she gives me a seductive smile and pushes me onto the bed. I'm still holding her hand and I try to pull her down onto the bed with me, but the little vixen pulls away. She shakes her head at me as she takes a step further back. I feel like I am getting whiplash with all this girl's teasing. My cock is strained so hard against my jeans, I think there's a good chance it's either going to rip it's way out, like the Hulk fighting to be free, or it will be really fucking bruised tomorrow. I know which one I want to happen, but I'm no longer sure what Ava wants to happen. She obviously wants to have some control over this thing and given everything going on in her life right now, I think the least she deserves is that.

Standing in front of me with a sultry gaze that is staring directly into my own, Ava slowly starts to move her hips. Although there is no music playing, I am almost sure I can hear the song that is obviously playing in her head, just by the way she sways her hips. Ava slowly runs her hands all over her body and her hips continue to grind along to the silence. As she reaches the top half of her body I watch as her hand drifts across her breasts and when a sharp intake of breath fills the room, I can see that she is using her thumb and finger to tweak her nipples through the fabric of her dress. Her head rolls back and she releases a soft moan as she gently tugs on the nipples, adding in just a little pain with the pleasure. It's obvious that she is loving doing this sexy little show and I'm getting off seeing just how hot she looks with this confidence that is sweeping over her body. But at the same time, I am having to shout at myself to remain on the bed, to let her have this power. What I really want to do is be the one teasing her nipples and giving her pain. In fact, I might have to give her a gentle punishment for teasing me so much.

Once her hands leave her nipples, they travel behind her back and I hear her pull the zip down on the dress. Sweeping across her collarbone on each side, she allows the straps on her dress to fall to her waist revealing her beautiful breasts. I am instantly transfixed and they are all I can see. Some men like their boobs big and fake, I am not some man. Ava's breasts are round, supple and the perfect size for her slender figure. I can't even begin to understand women's bra sizes, but to me, if the girl has a nice handful, that's perfect. Ava's look like they would be a very nice big handful and that is more than enough for me. I cannot wait to caress her silky soft skin and suckle on her perky brown nipples. I am so engrossed staring at her tits that she has to cough a little to bring my attention to the dress that is now sitting low on her hips. So low that the top of her thong is just peaking over the ruffled fabric. She begins to sexily sway her hips again, but this time it is to allow the dress to cascade and fall to the floor. It is at that moment I see it and feel like I could hit myself for being so caught up with her breasts that I missed one of the most beautiful things I have ever seen.

"You're not the only one with a secret tattoo," says Ava in a cheeky tone. She is standing in front of me, wearing just her lace red silk thong and whilst it is undoubtedly easy to admire her body, it is the art adorning her skin that makes her truly unique. All along one side of her silky soft skin is a beautiful array of swirling lines and unique intricate designs that all look like they have a significance, the same way that my tattoos mean something to me.

I look up at Ava's face, planning to let her see just how beautiful I truly believe she is, but she isn't looking at my face for approval. She is looking down at the tattoo and her eyes are clouded as though she is a little unsure and then I see the confidence that was previously glowing on her face begin to ebb away. She picks her arms up and slowly wraps them around her body, trying to cover up as much of herself as she can, while also trying to appear very small. That moment right there will be etched in my mind as one of the saddest things that I have ever seen, and no matter what happens after tonight, I know that I will never allow this girl to look that insecure again.

I rush off the bed and stand before her as fast as I possibly can. I take hold of each of her hands and slowly pull them down to her side, making sure she is comfortable with what I am doing at the same time. When her arms are by her side and still firmly in my grasp, I pull her forward so our naked chests are touching. The feel of her silky skin against my chest is amazing. I lean down and place soft kisses around her neck before gently whispering in her ear.

"Ava, never hide yourself. You are the most beautiful woman I have ever seen and that's not just because of your tattoos. They may add to it, but it is you that lights up the room. Don't ever forget that."

I can tell that as I am speaking, my breath is hitting her ear and causing her to tremble. I continue peppering her with kisses and take her nipple in my hand. I slowly rub and pull on her hard peak before replacing my fingers with my mouth. I lick my tongue around her nipple and graze my teeth across the tip before sucking it into my mouth. The moans coming from Ava's tiny, beautiful body are enough to spur me on even further. Not that I needed any spurring because right now, my cock is painfully trapped in my tight jeans and I know if I ever want to have children in the future, I need to rectify the situation. So, I quickly pick Ava up and throw her down onto the bed so she is laying backwards on it. Before she even has time to realise what is going on, my jeans have been removed and I am standing before her in just black boxers. She bites her lip and it's very clear from the glint in her eye that she can see the outline of my cock much better in these. I stalk towards her, desperate to feel all of her.

CHAPTER FIFTEEN
AVA

After I was clearly possessed by a sex demon who convinced me to do a sexy strip tease for Ryder before standing in front of him almost completely naked, I was sure I was going to die of embarassment. I literally have no idea what came over me, but seeing his tattoos and realising he has this whole secret side he keeps from the world just resonated with me. I realised he had obviously trusted me enough to let me see this side of him and I wanted to return the favour. I knew they were not gang tattoos or anything that could be associated with his work because they were beautiful. Each one looked individual, like it might have its own meaning, but they still all fit together like they were designed as one big piece. Very similar to mine. But once I had my tattoo out in the open, along with my breasts may I add, I suddenly started to feel weird. All these thoughts were running around my head. What if he doesn't like them? What if he's not attracted to me without clothes on? What if I'm not his type? All of these levels of insanity were swirling through my brain and then he was standing in front of me. I held my breath, waiting to see what he was going to say, and let me tell you, I wasn't disappointed. Not only does he look at me like he has never seen a sexier woman in his life, but he makes me feel it.

Now, I'm laying on Ryder's bed, faced with the very large erection outline in his boxers and trying so hard not to stare at his cock. Trying and failing miserably. So instead, I visualise what it would look like if I removed his boxers and took his giant dick into my mouth. Just the mere thought of this has me biting down on my lip to stop myself from going to him, but as I do it, I hear a sexy little growl come from Ryder's throat and I know he knew what I was thinking. Obviously, he was a fan because in the next second he is on top of me kissing me. He tortures me by kissing and nipping his way down my body, across my already painfully hard nipples and down past my belly button. He reaches the waist of my red silk panties and before I have a chance to raise my arse in the air slightly to help him get them off, he literally growls like a caveman as he rips the fabric at both sides of the strappy thong before pulling it away from my body and throwing it over his shoulder. Fuck, that is literally the hottest thing that has ever happened to me and I can feel myself panting, desperately gasping for air, but he gives me no reprieve. His kisses continue, but this time, he peppers them up my legs, starting from my ankles and all the way up to my thigh before breathing softly just next to the area where I am craving him the most.

I'm lying before him, completely naked, but all feelings of self-consciousness left along with the ripped thong. He is looking at my shaven pussy like it is the water in the desert that he has been hunting for days. His eyes are firmly gripped on me and he looks like a starved man. Slowly, he hooks his arms under my legs and spreads them wide before throwing them over his shoulders. I am laying completely bare in front of him and I know for sure, he can see moisture glistening from the effect he has been having on me. I feel as he takes his finger and gently runs it from the top of my folds down to the bottom and back up again. He is gently spreading the moisture around and torturing me at the same time. Everytime he reaches the top of my mound, I feel his fingertip brush across my clit and electricity shoots through me. I raise my arse off the bed, desperate to get closer to his touch, needing more, but he holds my stomach down with his other hand. Clearly, he loves to torture me. I'm just about to start begging when I feel his tongue touch my lips instead of his finger. The sensation is warm and wet but incredibly sexy and when he circles his tongue around my clit, I can't help the moan that leaves my mouth. I have goosebumps all over my body. He continues tracing his tongue around my clit at a lazy pace until I am almost frantic with need and breathing so fast, I'm starting to see spots in front of my eyes.

"Ryder, please. More," I moan in between pants of breath, desperate to let him know I want to feel more of him. Each time I ask for more, he sucks on my clit just a little bit harder until I feel like I might be starting that journey to breaking point and then he pulls back. He is driving me fucking mad. So, the next time when I tell him I want more, I don't beg, I demand and it comes out as a breathy shout. "Stop fucking around, Ryder, and put your cock in me. I need your cock inside me right now!"

The cocky bastard actually stops what he is doing completely then, but keeps hold of me so I cannot move. He is smirking at me like he knows how incredibly crazy he is driving me and I actually pout at him because my brain is sex starved and I'm not thinking of anything but his cock right now.

"You want my cock, do you, little vixen?" he asks me in his cocky yet deep voice. I can tell how much he is affected by this too, no matter how well he tries to hide it. As he is asking me, I feel his finger has taken the place of his tongue and it is continuing its slow lazy path up and down my soaking wet folds.

"Yes," I breathe out.

"Are you sure that you are ready for me, baby?" He gently places the tip of his finger inside my pussy as he asks me that and the resulting moan and affirmative are all rolled into one. The cocky git actually chuckles before punching his finger all the way inside. This time when I moan, I hear his moan alongside it.

"Fuck, your pussy is so tight," he says as he starts moving his finger in and out my tight, wet hole. "You are so wet, baby. Is all of this for me?" As he asks me, he takes his finger from my pussy, leaving me feeling indescribably empty and desperate for more, but then he surprises me further by placing his finger onto his lips. He then sucks his finger into his mouth and starts licking it like it's the world's best lollipop. The groan that vibrates from his throat as he tastes me on his finger is so hot, I'm sure I can feel myself gushing even further. Then he adds a second finger to his mouth and before I know what he is doing, he pushes both fingers into my tiny wet hole.

"Fuck. Oh fuck, Ryder. That feels so good." My brain has lost the ability to think in anything other than curse words and all I can think or feel is the sensation of his fingers as they are moving in and out of my pussy. I can feel my vaginal walls start to clamp around his fingers and Ryder moans. I see that his other hand has disappeared into his boxer shorts and he's making movements that make me think he is stroking himself in pleasure. I couldn't see even if I wanted to because the steady rhythm that his fingers are making is causing me to beg unashamedly for more.

I can feel my muscles start to tighten and the electricity starting to shoot around all over my back. The warmth is pooling in my body and my lower stomach, a clear indication I am getting close. In between panting and incoherent mumbles of how good Ryder's fingers feel, I manage to let him know I am close. I really didn't need to tell him because if he couldn't work it out just from looking or listening to me, then I'm sure he can feel the way my pussy walls are clamping down on his fingers like a vice. Just as I'm about to tip over the edge, I feel his fingers retreat and I'm left feeling so empty, but in the next second, I realise why.

Ryder has removed his boxers and is standing before me with his cock in his hand. He is gently stroking it from the shaft up to the tip and when the tip is reached, I notice a drop of pre-cum sitting on the end of his enlarged, angry looking head. He gently massages the pre-cum into the purple swollen head before moving his hands down the shaft to begin the process again. I sit there transfixed and the pulsating need that I feel in my pussy is growing stronger. I didn't think it would be possible to grow even wetter, but just the sight of what quite possibly could be the largest yet sexiest penis I have ever seen, has me doing just that. Ryder sees me staring and gives me his sexy little smirk.

"See something you like, little vixen?" he says, moving even closer. I know he is tormenting me and so I decide to play him at his own game. I let my legs fall open and for a moment, I can't believe that I'm displaying myself so openly in front of a guy I barely know. This is really not me. I can count on one hand the amount of guys I have had sex with and even with my long term boyfriend that I lost my virginity to and thought I was in love with, I never felt like this. I've never acted so brazenly, like the vixen Ryder says I am. It's just, there is something about him and the way his gorgeous ember eyes stare at me like he is looking at one of the wonders of the world and he can't quite believe it. That sexy smirk gives me a confidence that I never knew I had. I take my finger and run it gently and slowly up and down the wetness in my folds. I wonder if I should feel embarrassed by the fact I'm almost dripping, but then I remember how close to orgasm I was a few minutes ago and it's not surprising. Just looking at the gorgeous guy standing in front of me does crazy things to my body. An overwhelming desire to drive him as crazy as he drives me takes over. Once my finger is coated in my juices, I make sure that my eyes never leave Ryder's face and I slowly move my finger up to my lips. I start by gently licking the tip of my finger and running my tongue around the top, collecting all of my juices. Keeping our gazes locked, I suck my finger deep in my mouth and I'm sure he knows I'm pretending my finger is his cock. His hand has stopped stroking his growing length, clearly too distracted by my racy display. The deep rumble radiating from him is pure desire and it is almost as though I'm causing him physical pain and fuck, does that feel sexy.

"You know I see something I like, and I know you see something you desperately want. So, why don't you stop jacking yourself off and fuck me?" I answer his question when I finally remember he actually asked me one, before we started teasing each other. As much as I love to tease him and watch him squirm, my pussy is pulsing with need and I can't take any more. I have to have him inside me.

Just as Ryder is about to move forward with intent burning in his eyes, I can see how much he wants to be balls deep inside me too, but then he stops. His face is a picture of despair and he suddenly starts looking around the room like the world might end.

"Ryder, what's the matter?" I start to panic that he is changing his mind. He's running his fingers through his gorgeous chocolate brown hair and sending it flying at all angles. He looks so stressed, like he's trying to solve the world's hardest math problem. Whatever is wrong with him, I want to help. The sooner we sort out his problem, the sooner I can impale myself with that big cock.

"I'm so sorry, Ava. I didn't even think about this when I got things going. I should never have got us both so wound up when we can't go through with anything." Despair fills Ryder's voice as he says the words I had been sure would come since the moment I kissed him. I should have known he would change his mind. But I have to know what made him decide to. He looked so completely sure just a second ago. I quickly close my legs, pull my knees up to cover my breasts and wrap my arms around my legs.

"Why?" I ask in the smallest voice, sounding more sad than I intended. Ryder sits down on the bed next to me, completely unaware that he is stark-bollock naked still and his cock is standing to attention, staring at me as a reminder of what I can't have. Ryder moves from running his fingers through his own hair to mine. He gently places a strand of hair behind my ear and forces me to look up at him.

"Hey, don't ever think this is because of you. I want to fuck you so badly, little vixen. Look at what you do to me!"

Ryder points at his cock that definitely did not need any presentation, it's doing a perfectly good job of making its presence known. I'm trying not to look at it, so I continue staring at Ryder. Hoping that I will be able to magically see the reason for him stopping.

"Babe, I don't have any condoms with me. This is not something I ever do here, so why would I be prepared? I should have remembered that, but you and your sexy little body just drive me so crazy, I seem to lose my mind," says Ryder whilst peppering little kisses over my arms and neck. As soon as the words leave his mouth, I pull away.

"Wait, so the only reason you won't have sex with me is because you don't have a condom? Otherwise you would want to still?" I ask, desperate to try and understand his motives and when he nods his head to confirm, I can't help the little laugh that escapes. Ryder is looking at me like I have lost my mind. So, before he can object, I quickly climb into his lap, pushing him back so he is laying on the bed. Straddling his hips with my thighs pressed tightly against him, I can feel his dick that has started to soften at the idea of no sex is now becoming rock hard again. As it grows, it gently slides next to my folds. I put my hands on Ryder's chest to pin him down and even though he could most likely move me with one hand, he let me do it.

"Ryder, I have the hormone implant in order to prevent pregnancy. The last time I had sex was over a year ago and when I was tested after I dumped that cheating scumbag, I was clean. I have never, and I mean ever, had sex without a condom. I may not get a lot of choices in my future and so I want to make as many of them as I can now. Ryder, if you agree and you are clean, then I choose you to be the first person to be inside me bare," I explain to him, trying not to get melancholy at the part where I may never get to make a choice of my own again after tonight. I look down at him, hoping that he agrees with the proposition.

Before I even have a chance to realise what is happening, I have gone from straddling Ryder's thighs to lying flat on my back with him looming over me. My legs are wrapped around his hips with my feet digging into his arse, trying my hardest to pull him closer. I can feel the tip of his cock touching my outer lips and I moan, hoping this means he agrees. I look into his eyes and I'm floored by the amount of emotion I see. He's looking at me like I have just agreed to give him my virginity, which, in a weird way, I have. He will be the first person to be inside me without a condom, if he agrees. I raise an eyebrow, silently asking him if he is going to answer me.

"I'm clean, haven't had sex in over two years. I've never had sex without a condom either, it's not something I have ever imagined doing unless I was in a serious long term relationship," Ryder explained to me and I felt the breath I had been holding rush out. I don't know why but hearing this makes me inexplicably sad and a wave of despair runs over me. I can feel the tears begin to build in my eyes and I try to pull them back. Who the fuck cries because a guy won't fuck them bareback? I am being unreasonable and I know it, but I can't help it. Before my stupid body has time to gather enough moisture to create enough tears to start flowing, I am pulled away from my sadness by Ryder's breath hitting my ear and his thumb gently wiping across the underside of my eyes.

"Shush, baby, don't be sad. I was about to say that despite always thinking that way, it went out the window the second you asked me to fuck you without a condom. All my brain kept picturing was feeling the warmth of your tight snatch as it grabs hold of my cock and milks every last drop from me. I can feel my body going all caveman as I have the overwhelming urge to claim you with my cum. I want to be the first person to cum inside of you, so you will always remember that, in some way, you will always be mine." As he says the final part about how I will always be his, I feel him push his giant dick past the entrance to my pussy and as deep as he can get. He builds up slowly, gently rocking back and forth, trying to get more of himself in each time. He's so fucking big and I feel like I'm being stretched beyond belief, but it feels so good.

He places his hands under my arse and gently tilts my pelvis upwards more and then pulls my little body towards him as he plunges completely inside me. I feel every inch of his cock. He feels like he's so deep and yet my walls are clamping on desperately to never let him go. Gripping my legs tighter around his arse, I make it known to him I love how full he makes me feel. I know that by not moving, he's giving me a minute to accommodate his length, which is by far the biggest I have ever felt. The feeling of his silky soft skin against the warmth of my body is such a weird yet incredibly satisfying feeling. Once I'm sure I'm comfortable with his size and am desperate for him to move, I nod my head, giving him the go ahead. But instead of starting to pound into me, he leans over and kisses me. It's a rough, passionate kiss with his tongue invading my mouth and massaging against mine, making it clear he owns me right now. I feel his hand move in between our bodies and as his finger presses on my clit, I begin mumbling incoherently. The feeling of his cock deep inside of me and his fingers gently teasing my swollen nub is making me frantic with need.

"I'm going to fuck you so hard now, little vixen. Is that what you want? Do you want me to fuck your tight wet pussy?" Ryder, the cocky twat, taunts me by whispering his dirty words into my ear and making me tingle all over. I don't know how he manages to do it but I can feel him everywhere. It's like every single nerve ending is alive and pulsating with desire, and it's all for Ryder.

When he doesn't move and instead continues whispering dirty promises into my ear, I decide to take matters into my own hands. I start tilting my hips as much as I can when I am trapped beneath his hard body and with his arm blocking the way, but it has the desired effect. Just the slightest movement of his dick inside of me gives me the perfect friction that I am desperate for. The movement also forces Ryder's finger harder against my clit, which sends me crazy. But it's obvious that

Ryder is not too happy at the loss of control because as soon as I start rocking my hips, he pulls his hand away, making me cry out. The next second, I feel a whack as his hand comes down firmly against my arse. I can't believe he just spanked me. But more than that, I can't believe how much I loved it. That bite of pain that reverberated through my nerve endings at the same time as the pleasure was indescribable and my voice makes a high pitched gasping noise followed by a moan. I look up at Ryder and even though his face is wearing that cocky smirk he uses to let me know he's in charge, his eyes are almost black with desire. He was turned on by the spank just as much as I was. Before I have time to say anything about it or beg for him to do it again, he finally gives me what I want.

Ryder begins moving inside of me, gently rocking at first but then as the sensation starts to change, so does his pace. Ryder pulls back until he is almost completely pulled out, leaving me feeling empty and desperate. Except for my entrance that is stretched and feeling a beautiful sting that makes me beg Ryder to get back inside of me. He doesn't disappoint. He slams his cock into my tight wet hole and I feel him hit deep inside as his balls slap against my arsehole. He feels so incredibly deep and the matching groan we both share fills the room. When Ryder hears my moans, he seems to lose all control and he starts pounding into me with great speed. Everytime his balls slap against my arse and the tip of his cock nudges against my sensitive spot, I cry out in beautiful agony. My pussy is getting wetter and my walls are clamping down tightly, desperate to keep him inside me. I can feel the electric sensations building and I know I am getting close again, but this time I am desperate for him to let me finish.

"Fuck... Ryder... I'm gonna cum... please... finish with me. Are you close?" I gasp out the words as best I can in between being impaled on Ryder's cock. He is speeding up now and each thrust is accompanied by a sexy deep grunt. He leans down and takes one of my nipples in his mouth, giving it a sexy nip and the rasp of pain shoots through me, causing me to pant uncontrollably. I can feel myself riding on the edge of bliss and he nips at the other nipple, not wanting it to feel left out, obviously. My body is flooded with even more sensations and I can feel him everywhere. I'm shouting Ryder like he is some kind of God to be worshipped, and at this moment in time, I am completely praising him and his cock.

Ryder has an amazing ability to know exactly when I'm right on the edge because he slows his rhythm down and I can feel my pussy clenching with the desperate need for him to speed back up. He always manages to distract me with kisses or little bites all over my body. Oh fuck, can this guy talk dirty. Hearing him tell me how wet I am just for him and how he loves the feel of my tight pussy gripping his cock, does crazy things for me.

"Do you like that, dirty girl? Fuck, do I love seeing my cock slipping into your tight little hole. Do you want it harder? You have to beg me, little vixen. Tell me who this tight pussy belongs to," he moans, and fuck, do I beg.

I am a panting desperate mess when I finally look up and see he has started to lose control. His pounding is becoming more erratic and his grunts are sounding primal and animalistic. I can feel all of the muscles in my core and stomach begin to tighten and Ryder is finally letting that feeling build up further. I can feel him everywhere and it feels like this is building to be the strongest, most powerful orgasm I've ever had. Ryder also looks like he is about to lose control and it's the sexiest thing. To drive him crazy and get us both there that little bit faster, I tighten my vaginal wall muscles around his cock when he is in to the hilt and it has the desired effect because Ryder groans with need.

"Cum for me, little vixen," he whispers in my ear in a stern commanding voice and my body responds. My body begins to shake and my muscles tighten. I can feel my stomach and pussy tensing as I ride out my orgasm. As soon as Ryder feels me start to cum for him and my pussy clamps around his cock like a vice, it's not long before he is grunting and letting me know he is cumming deep inside me.

When we both come down from the earth shattering orgasms and we have stopped panting enough to breathe normally, Ryder lays down beside me and kisses me so sweetly, I can feel my heart starting to hurt. I don't want to think about what this might mean, I just want to enjoy the here and now.

"That was amazing," I whisper when he finally lets my

mouth go. I feel empty without him in my pussy. His cocky smirk lets me know how pleased he is to hear that. Like he didn't already know. I have just spent the last hour calling out his name like he is the newest deity I worship. Now that is totally a religion I could get behind. When Ryder starts chuckling, I realise that I have just said that entire conversation I thought I was having in my head out loud. Kill me now. But Ryder doesn't seem bothered by my verbal diarrhoea, instead he has the biggest smile on his face. Not like before when I was praising him, although there is still a hint of that cocky bastard. But instead, he looks happy and I don't know what to do with that. There's a part of me that wants to stay curled up in his arms all night, but I know that's far too dangerous. There's no more denying where I am or what my life is about to become. Ryder was an amazing last night of freedom and fuck, do I wish we had met under different circumstances. Maybe we would have stood a chance at having something real, but that was just a pipe dream. Instead, I'm stuck with the reality I need to leave his arms, move into the bedroom down the hall, and agree to marry his psychotic boss. I really don't know which one of those steps is the hardest.

CHAPTER SIXTEEN
RYDER

Leaving Ava last night was quite possibly one of the hardest things I have ever done. After the mind blowing sex, I just remember staring down at her beautiful face and thinking I don't remember ever being so happy. I'm not talking about the post-orgasm high that people get. I'm talking about my heart feeling like it's swelling up and I am actually having feelings for possibly the first time in my life. It's not that I'm closed off emotionally or anything like that. I am capable of falling in love or dating, but work has always come first. My dad worked in the same business I do, but for a different family. He always talked about his desire for me to work my way to the top and to do my family name proud. I was pushed from a very young age to learn this lifestyle and I never really had a choice.

My life isn't exactly stable enough to bring girls into and I don't have time for a regular girlfriend. Hell, I don't even sleep at my own house. I have to be here all the time. If I am to remain on top of everything and to keep Grant under control, I need to be here. I wasn't even slacking off and he was able to plan and essentially kidnap Ava without me having a clue what he was up to. Imagine the devastation he could reek if I wasn't watching his every move.

Thinking about Ava is physically painful. We both just laid there in silence, me stroking her hair and her tracing the intricate lines of the tattoos on my chest. It was peaceful and beautiful. Neither of us wanted to break the moment first, but I knew I had to be the strong one for us both. However, I wasn't that strong because I talked her into having a shower to clean off and naturally I joined her for round two against the shower wall. Fuck, the feel of her silky pussy as it clamps on my cock like a vice is amazing. I have never been inside anyone bare before and it's fucking intense. I'm glad I got to share that with Ava.

After she dried and dressed in the t-shirt of mine I tried to give her way back when the night first started, I told her everything that she will need to know to stay safe while living in this house. I let her know where the cameras are, including the ones in her bedroom. I tell her where the locks are and talk to her about what I have learnt triggers Grant. I hate to talk to her about him, but if I don't, she won't be prepared and that could be dangerous. I let her know I will always be nearby and if she needs me, all she has to do is ask. Wishing I could save her from this shit show of a world that she is about to enter, is the only thing that I can think about, but I know it's pointless. We knew it before our lips even touched. This was a one time deal and my role from now on will simply be to watch her from afar and ensure she is protected at all times.

Grant slamming the front door as he practically sprints into the hallway is enough to bring me out of my memories of last night. He is wearing a fresh new suit, which isn't surprising since he has an entire wardrobe at Katyia's, just as he has here. He probably spends more time there. I inspect his face looking for any sign that he may have changed his mind about this ridiculous plan of his, but if anything, he looks happy. Now I really am confused because the old man will be here soon and that thought never makes Grant happy.

"Morning, Ryder. All good here after I left? No problems with Ava?" Grant asks and initially I wonder if he knows, but there's no way he would. All of the staff were out of the house in the staff quarters, the alarms were set so I would have known had anyone come in. There are no cameras in my room and so he would have no way of finding out. I made sure of that. That's when it clicks that when he left, Ava was a bit worked up and he was probably just wondering if she gave me any trouble. The thought makes me want to laugh. That girl is nothing but trouble, but not in the way he thinks.

"Morning, boss." I start with a suck up comment because he loves it and it softens him up a little for the day ahead. "All was fine here. No problems at all from Ava. I gave her instructions for meeting your father this morning and she should be down soon." As I say those words, I hear the clatter of heels on the staircase before looking up to see Ava making her way down.

I cannot get over how beautiful she looks. She is wearing skinny black jeans that she has clearly ripped holes into on the knees, giving it an old, worn, frayed look. She has paired the jeans with a white vest top that I am fairly sure is supposed to go underneath a shirt. The way the top dips down in a heart shape, along with the push-up bra that she is wearing, shows off her cleavage amazingly. Her hair is down and lightly curled and she is wearing very little make-up because she knows she doesn't need it. She is the most beautiful girl I have ever seen but hearing the annoyed grunt coming from beside me, it's clear Grant is not happy. Ava makes it to the bottom of the stairs and I give her a little smile and a cheeky wink Grant doesn't see. He's too busy staring at her like she has an alien popping out of her head.

"What the fuck are you wearing?" Grant screeches at Ava and I see the little glint of mischief in her eye. Last night, I told her that she would be expected to dress respectfully in front of Grant's father. To be presented to him as Grant's fiancé is a very big deal and the impression she creates will set the tone for how this will go. Clearly, she wants to start as she means to go on, by causing trouble. I almost chuckle because I know that this is her way of saying a massive fuck you to Grant and Alan Blakeman. I think she is hoping that the old man will take one look at her and say Grant can't marry her. I have to admit, I'm kinda hoping the same thing, but I also know Grant very well. He always gets what he wants and for some reason, he wants Ava.

"Morning, honey. You look nice. When will Dad be arriving?" Ava sings in this incredibly sweet yet sarcastic voice. She is clearly taking the piss and, man, do I want to laugh. Grant, on the other hand, does not look like he is trying his hardest not to laugh. His face is turning red and he is practically shaking with anger. What the fuck is she doing? I told her last night not to wind him up because he gets unpredictable and that's when he's at his most dangerous. This would be bad enough on his own, but to embarrass him in front of his father is like a shitshow waiting to happen.

"What the fuck are you playing at, Ava?" Grant screeches as Ava takes her final step and stands before us in the hallway. As this is happening, I get a silent buzz from the pager in my pocket, I know without looking at it that security at the gate is alerting me to the old man's arrival. Now I just need to tell Grant.

"I don't know what you mean, darling." Ava smiles sweetly as she addresses Grant and I can see he is getting more and more angry. But I need to remember I am just a normal bodyguard. I wouldn't interfere with his arguments with Katyia and I can't do it with Ava because he will know.

"Shit, there is no time for your games. My father will be here soon and I cannot present you to him looking like a hobo. Now, get upstairs and change into one of the outfits I bought you that you haven't defaced. I will deal with your behaviour after this is all over. Now go!" Grant screams and I see the smile fall from Ava's lips. When Grant issued the threat of dealing with her later, I know that he means it, and by the look on Ava's face, so does she. But what neither of us know is what that entails and that really fucking bothers me.

Now I'm faced with a big problem because Ava has to go upstairs and change. This meeting has the potential to go very badly if she meets the old man dressed like this, but I also know that he hates tardiness. In fact, I saw him issue the order for a bullet to shoot one of his long term business associates in the head because he arrived for a meeting five minutes late. So, I have to tell Grant he will be here any second and it could potentially mean more trouble for Ava. This whole thing is killing me.

"Sorry to interrupt, Grant, mate, but I got the page your father has passed security. He will be here any minute." I see his eyes go wide as saucers and they start to flit between the front door and Ava. He is clearly torn by which one will cause him the most trouble. Ava has a slight smirk on her face like she planned this scenario exactly. That little vixen is going to be so much trouble, I can tell.

"Fuck, fine, Ava, you stay like that. We will say we have not had a chance for the personal shopper to change your outfit yet. But listen to me, you better be on your best behaviour with my father. I am already planning to punish you for this situation. Believe me when I say you do not want to add to it. Now, come on, baby. Let's go and meet my father." He takes hold of Ava's arm a little rougher than I would have liked and he drags her towards the door. I stay behind in the background like a good bodyguard does. But then Grant stops and turns Ava to face him.

"Shit, nearly forgot. Here, put this on. Can't not give my fiancé a ring now, can I?" Grant says as he shoves a small black velvet ring box into Ava's hand. Not exactly the most romantic of proposals, but then again, this isn't the most romantic of matchings.

Ava opens the box and I can see the massive diamond in the box from across the room. It's huge and probably cost a fortune. Not to mention, it's so big, the glistening that comes from it almost provides its own light source. Ava is looking at it like she cannot quite believe her eyes. Even though I have only known Ava for a very short amount of time, my heart is telling me it isn't the type of ring Ava would pick out if she was getting married under normal circumstances. It's just too showy for her tastes I think, but fuck, what do I know?

"I can't accept this. It looks like it cost a fortune," Ava says, stumbling over her words as she tries to get them out while still staring at the ring.

"It cost just short of two million pounds. No fiancé of mine would be seen in anything less. Now, I don't have time to argue about this, so unless you want to call the whole thing off and you can go and plan your father's funeral instead, then that's fine by me," Grant snaps as he strides closer to the door to await his father's arrival. The harshness of Grant's words seem to resonate with Ava because the look on her face turns extremely sour and her face turns white. The thought of having to plan her father's funeral has literally caused all the colour to run out of Ava's body and she just looks desolate. Silently, she puts the giant rock on her finger and hands the box back to Grant. I don't think he has a chance to notice because she shuts things down as quickly as she can, but I'm certain I saw her eyes mist over with tears as she put the ring on her finger. I hate seeing her like that, but even more so, I hate the feeling I get in my stomach when the ring goes on her finger. I feel like I have been punched, but I have no reason to feel like that. It was one night and that's all it could ever be, we both agreed on that. So, why does it cause me so much pain to see another man's ring on her finger?

Before I have time to even analyse the shit I'm feeling, the doorbell rings and I step forward to answer the door. Not only is that what the hired help does, but it also helps me to complete a thorough assessment before they even step foot in the building. I have to assess how many there are, who they are, do I know them or not. This is particularly important because if I know them, I know their behaviour patterns and I can usually predict how they are going to react. However, if I don't know them, then they are unknowns, and unknowns can be dangerous. If it was any other visitor, I would also need to check whether or not they are armed, but with this particular group, it is a given. The rumour is that the old man is so sure in his staff, he feels no need to arm himself. But the rumour is wrong. I'm sure the old man has a gun strapped to his lower leg and a small dagger up his left sleeve. I have never pointed this out to anyone because I've never needed to. The old man would be right to arm himself, you can't trust anyone in our world.

As I survey the group in front of me, I'm shocked to find it's just the old man and his head of security, Len. I worked with him a bit when I was first hired and he was not happy when I was promoted to Grant's head of security. Apparently, Len had been training his son for the role so they could pass down their family legacies as the family that stood beside the Blakemans. The only issue with his plan is that his son, Kaylan, is a massive idiot. He has no skill when it comes to doing this job, which is why the only promotion he ever got was given by his father. The boss hated him too and he made it clear to Len that Kaylan could work for the family, but in a role of zero importance and with no possibility of promotion. Naturally, Len agreed because nobody disagrees with Alan Blakeman, but it doesn't change the fact that Len blames me. He doesn't even recognise that, at times, Kaylan doesn't know how many weapons he has, let alone the amount that someone else has. All he sees is that I got the job his son should be doing, which explains the giant scowl that is on Len's face when I open the door. However, the fact his hand goes straight to rest on his side piece seems a little on the harsh side. I match his gesture, but since I was the one who was challenged, I decide to go bigger and better by making my position of importance known to Len. Well, that and I subtly hold open my suit jacket to make it clear that I, too, am armed. You did hear me correct when I said suit jacket. Even though when I'm working with Grant, he doesn't care what I wear, or it's more that I don't let him tell me what to wear. But, the old man likes things done a certain way and that means that security staff all wear black suits, including the jacket and a dark shirt. If the way Ava keeps looking at me, with almost blown pupils and eyes filled with desire, is anything to go by, then I think she is a fan of the suit. No more thinking of the words Ava and desire in the same sentence, back to showing Len who is in charge in this house.

"Mr. Blakeman, Sir, welcome. So kind of you to drive all the way out here for a visit. Before I invite you in, it's policy that each of your men confirm they are only carrying one weapon, as agreed, and that only one member of your team will be coming in. Is that ok with you?" I say politely, holding my hand out to the boss. This is where I am showing Len my position because everyone knows you do not extend your hand out to greet him until he has greeted you first. However, the old man made it clear to me a long time ago, he didn't want me to follow the same rules and that I could greet him as an equal. Something that even Len is not allowed to do.

"Enough of the 'Sir' crap, Ryder. You are making me feel old," he jests whilst clasping his slightly wrinkled hand into mine. Despite being in his sixties, the old man is still young for his age and didn't look bad. He is what most of the whores he fucks call a silver fox. So I'm not at all surprised when he matches my firm handshake with one equally rigid.

"I know the rules, Ryder. Len will enter and you have my word he is only armed with the piece he currently has his hand on. The one he is envisaging blowing your brains out with, I'm sure. Now can we come in?" I let out a laugh at the fact the old man literally does not miss anything. I didn't even see him look over in Len's direction, but then again, he knows of his distaste for me. I also know he loves winding people up and looking at the purple shade Len's face has now become, it obviously worked. As soon as I have finished my little chuckle at Len's expense, I formally invite them in and move out of the way for Grant to welcome his father. As I walk into the house, I risk a glance at Ava, who looks like a deer in headlights and I can see her eyes are focused on Len's gun and the one she has just seen in the back of Grant's trousers. Idiot wears it stuffed in the back of his trousers, thinking it makes him more gangster. I'm just waiting for the day he blows another hole in his arse. I try to give Ava a reassuring smile, but she doesn't even notice me. Her gaze is still locked on the weapons and the foreboding presence that is Mr. Blakeman.

Grant looks equally as pissed off to be doing this ridiculous formality of welcoming his own father into his house, but Alan respects tradition. He believes when a guest enters your property, they should be formally announced and when it is someone of higher status, they should be met by the leader of the house. This whole circus pisses Grant off everytime, but this time, I notice he has a slight smirk on his face. That worries me because it means he is planning something. Isn't presenting Ava as his wife enough of a shitshow for one day?

"Father, welcome. How lovely to see you at such short notice, we were not expecting your visit yet. As always, it is a pleasure to welcome you to my home," Grant says in an unusually chipper voice. His thinly veiled dig at his father requesting this meeting at such short notice does not go unnoticed by anyone in the room, but it is unusual for Grant to speak like that to his Father. Normally, he is almost robotic around him, sticking to all the socially acceptable ways to address him and showing the utmost respect. There are times in public when he challenges the system, but as far as I have seen, in a one-on-one situation, he is well behaved. It's almost like the abused and repressed small child appears and behaves exactly as expected. Today is different and I think it's because of Ava. That starts to worry me because if Grant throws off the status quo with Alan, I'm not sure how anyone is going to behave and there is no way Ava is getting hurt on my watch.

"I have a special surprise for you this time, Father. I would like to present to you Ava Delgado, my fiancé." Grant steps back, allowing Alan to get a full look at Ava, who had been subtly hiding behind Grant. Just in case the old man was in any doubt of who Grant was talking about, he makes sure to wave his arm in Ava's direction. It looks like he is presenting a prize horse and she's now about to be assessed.

Alan takes a step closer to Ava and much to my surprise, she doesn't move back. Most people would see the man who is infamously known as the most violent crime boss in the country coming towards them and they would take a step back, but not Ava. I see her pull her shoulders back and take a deep breath, clearly affected by the big statement she just made. Announcing to him that she is not afraid is a big deal, but I can see the real Ava. The look of panic in her eyes, the way she is chewing the inside of her lips and the way she is using her thumb to scrape across the skin on her hand. All classic signs of anxiety and being scared as shit and I do not blame her. What does surprise me is the returning look Alan gives Ava. I watch as he runs his gaze over her body, not in a sexual way, but to take in her very casual appearance. That combined with the blatant disregard of his power when she challenged him by not stepping back would normally make him go a little crazy. I watched him beat the shit out of a guy once for not having his shirt tucked in. Well, he threw the first punch and his men finished the job, but it's the same thing. However, when he looks at Ava, he has a strange combination of emotions on his face that I am struggling to place. He looks pleased to see her standing up for herself, but he also has this sort of wistful, far away glaze over his eyes, like his memory is somewhere far away from here. This is then replaced by a look of sadness before he has time to school his features and put his big boss man mask on that he usually wears. That could possibly be the first time I've ever seen him show so much emotion and I have no idea what Ava had to do with it.

"Hello, Mr. Blakeman, my name is Ava. It's a pleasure to meet you," Ava says chirpily whilst holding out her hand. What the fuck is she doing? Both myself and Grant look at each other with a look of horror on our faces. I told her last night about the rules and the social expectations. It seems like the little vixen has decided to go against every rule I told her and do her own thing. I watch as Len physically takes hold of his gun and I start to reach for my own. No way am I letting that bastard shoot her in front of me. I have been looking for a good excuse to put a bullet in him for a while, but I constantly have to remind myself it would put my job in jeopardy and ruin everything that I have worked towards for the past two years. Yet all of that seems to go out the window at the idea that Ava might be in trouble. Luckily, the old man appears to have had a personality transplant because he laughs and reaches out to take her hand.

"Beautiful Ava, such a pleasure to meet you." It's a short acknowledgement but it's still the strangest thing I have seen in a long time. As soon as he is done saying his quick hello to Ava, he turns to face Grant with a completely different expression on his face. He looks murderously mad and the anger that is radiating off him is all aimed at Grant, who either doesn't realise or he doesn't care.

"Grant, let's go to the living room, we have business to discuss. I will send word for you both to attend my house for a proper meeting. You may leave now, Ava, I'm sure you have plenty of better things to be doing." The old man steps aside to let Ava through and out of the door. It almost feels like he knows she is trapped here and he is helping her out, but that just feels so unlike him. I don't fucking like not knowing what is going on.

Ava makes a brave move for the door, but Grant takes a step forward and grabs hold of her wrist. I can see the pressure he is applying from here and the matching grimace on her face confirms his grip is too tight. So tight, he might even bruise her perfect silky skin. I feel myself clenching my fists to avoid physically acting on the anger that I feel brewing in my stomach.

"Yes, Ava, why don't you go up to your room? It will give you time to settle in and get your wardrobe sorted. That way, when you meet my father next time, you will be dressed appropriately." Grant makes it clear that Ava is to remain in the house, he even partly drags her towards the stairs. She looks over at Alan, giving him a small smile.

"Yes, of course. I apologise if you are deeply offended by my clothes, Sir. I thought you would prefer to meet the real me, rather than the person your son will have me become," Ava says to Alan with an air of sarcasm that I would be proud of if I wasn't so worried about the look of fury on Grant's face. He has turned purple and I can see the large vein that travels up his neck pumping furiously, indicating that his breathing has increased. His anger towards Ava right now is worrying. I am also expecting to find anger on both sides, as I didn't think Alan would like her sarcasm regarding his son. Apparently, I was wrong because Alan is just smiling at Ava like she is the most unique person he has ever met. I know that feeling.

"Yes, well unfortunately, my dear, the family you are marrying into comes with a certain status and we must match that at all times. I am sure you will pick it up quick enough. I will ensure my son helps you to learn our ways. It was nice to meet you, Miss Delgado, and I look forward to talking to you more soon."

I look over at Grant and then at Len, they are both wearing matching expressions that basically say, 'what the fuck?' Not only was he reasonably polite to Ava, he basically implied his son was to blame for the way she was dressed. Then he called her by her name and smiled at her. Even Ava is standing there, looking a tad stunned and by the wince she gives while looking down at her arm, Grant is gripping on even tighter, clearly enraged with the situation. My role here is to plan and interpret the way that situations are going to go, it might be the thing that keeps us all alive. However, even I did not see the old man being nice to Ava like that. Normally, he hates when people don't respect formality, he's very old fashioned in that sense. Plus, for as long as I have known this family, Alan has made it clear Grant has to marry a certain type of woman, and despite the fact Ava is worth a million of whoever he would find, she is not the type of woman who marries into the Blakeman family. No matter how much Grant makes her over. The type of shit that went down today will continue to go down because Ava is a feisty woman who does not like to go down without a fight. The little glances that I catch Alan throwing her way makes me think that he appreciates her tough independent nature almost as much as I do.

Grant, obviously, did not anticipate for things to go down this way and the sneer he now has on his face, distorting his typical boyish charm, makes him look outright scary. I'm sure I can see the skin on Ava's arm changing colour as he cuts the circulation off with his all encompassing grip. One... two... three, I was always told that if I counted to ten, taking deep relaxing breaths in between, it would help with my anger, but right now, I just feel like I am counting down until I punch Grant in the face. Fuck, this was not supposed to happen. This is my job and I need to do it well, which means ignoring how he treats Ava. I'm part of the security team only, a fly on the wall. I do not get to have an opinion and I certainly think my job would be in jeopardy if I punched my boss' son so hard, he needed to eat through a straw for a while. Strangely, just picturing it does make me feel a little better. It's more effective than the damn counting and breathing technique, I will remember that for the future. I'm snapped out of my rather delightful daydream when I hear Grant say my name.

"Ryder, why don't you show my father through into the dining room and have the maid make him a drink? I am going to make sure Ava gets settled in her new room and will be back down shortly. Please bear with me, Father, she is still getting used to such a big house," Grant says, addressing his father after me. Instantly, I want to say no. There's no way I want that smarmy psycho alone with Ava, but I have to get it in my head they are engaged, which usually means alone time. The haunted look in Ava's eyes are directed right at me and feel like a punch in the stomach. I have been given my orders and so I lead Alan and Len into the living room, leaving Grant and Ava in the hallway, his hand still firmly gripping her wrist.

CHAPTER SEVENTEEN
AVA

Meeting *THE* Alan Blakeman was quite an experience, but definitely not the one I spent all night losing sleep over. After the best night of my life with Ryder, I knew I had to get back to reality. If I wanted to keep my papa alive, the only thing to do is to marry Grant. I made my peace with that. The fact I would be marrying into one of the biggest, richest crime families in the country did not even occur to me. The notoriety alone for just being associated with this family gets you a reputation. People who are linked to the family are known all over the city. London belongs to the Blakemans and everyone knows that. On paper, they are a respectable, rich family with very successful businesses, but everyone knows it is just the public image they show. Nobody exactly knows how far their reach goes, but I know that nothing criminal happens in or around

London without Alan Blakeman knowing about it. The idea that I would now be a part of that family and everything they stand for wasn't even something I had even considered until Ryder mentioned it last night. He told me about the rules and how I had to impress Alan, following all of his expectations or he may not consent to the marriage. That is when I saw the plan forming before my very eyes.

The look on both Ryder and Grant's face when I walked down the stairs this morning, wearing my skin tight ripped jeans and a vest that I'm pretty sure is supposed to be worn as lingerie, is fantastic, but both for very different reasons. Ryder's eyes grow wide like saucers and he appears to catch his breath. He's looking at me like he is picturing what I looked like last night when I was wearing nothing at all and he looks like he wants to grab me. The desire in his eyes is obvious and I'm sure I have a matching gaze in mine. Then it's as though we both remember where we are and who is standing with us and we school our faces, leaving Grant to look at. His face is exactly what I was going for. He's furious and his cheeks are red, his eyes bulging. From what I have learnt about Grant over this past day, he clearly likes to be in control and have people do exactly what he tells them to. I have no intention at all of going down without a fight, and this is just the first step.

Meeting Alan Blakeman does not exactly go down the way I thought it would. Ryder had told me stories of how he demanded respect and was a big fan of formality and showing loyalty. So I had not expected to see him be so nice to me, he almost seemed taken by me. But, no matter how much I tried, it was impossible for me to forget that I was standing in front of one of the most deadly, evil men in the world. Honestly, he looks like your average older, gray-haired businessman. I can't deny that he looks good for his age, it's obvious he keeps himself in good shape and he's tall. He's a lot like Grant in shape and I can see some of Grant's facial features. Except with Alan, there is a constant air about him, he almost exudes power and superiority. Even if you wanted to, you could never forget he is the best person in any room because that is just the way he is, his stature and posture make that perfectly clear. When he speaks, it is reinforced even further because his voice takes on a tone that leaves no room for discussion. When he speaks, he does so with power and boldness, ensuring there is no way anyone would dream of disputing what he says.

When he told me I was not needed for this discussion and that I could leave, I have to admit, I was far too quick to make a run for it. A decision I will most likely regret if the bruising grip that Grant has on my wrist is anything to go by. I should have known it wouldn't be that easy. As I watch Ryder lead Alan and his bodyguard away onto the living room, I can't help the sense of foreboding that fills up my abdomen. The way Grant is looking at me with disgust is completely different from the mask he put on for me yesterday when he was trying to win me over. Obviously, now I'm trapped and he no longer feels the need to pretend to be a nice guy. He's no longer looking at me like I'm beautiful, the look he is giving me now is closer to hate. I know my clothing stunt would piss him off, but I had no idea things would go down like this. Although the fear I feel starts to take over my body, raising my heart rate and making the hairs on my arms stand on end, I put it down as best I can. I'm tough and I'm not going to let him push me around.

"Upstairs, now! Do not say a word until we get there," Grant hisses at me, spitting as he gets his point across in as low a volume as possible. His eyes have taken on an almost feral look and as soon as he releases my wrist, I don't give him a chance to change his mind. I start sprinting up the stairs as fast as I can in these stupid heels. I'm trying to remember the way around this ridiculously large house, trying to retrace my steps in my head. That's when I hear Grant's footsteps, walking steadily behind me up the stairs.

I have no idea how I do it, but I make it back to the corridor that my room is on the end of. Right now, I'm standing outside Ryder's room. Not even twelve hours ago, I was pinned against the other side of that door, getting hot and sweaty, having an amazing night. Now, I have to walk past the room and see the man who set my nerve endings on fire, yet I can't even look at him for too long in case anyone figures it out. Ryder said that it would be dangerous for both of us, but until Alan Blakeman arrived and I saw exactly how many guns people are armed with, I didn't fully understand what he meant. Before today, I had never even seen a gun in real life and now everyone surrounding me has one. But most worryingly is that the psychopath who I am engaged to and who I just pissed off royally in front of his family, also carries a gun. Now, I'm really starting to regret my stupidity.

Dawdling in front of Ryder's room gives Grant the chance to catch up with me, but, of course, he was always going to. Where the fuck am I going to go? I'm on the third floor and none of the windows open, even if I did want to risk a jump. The only way down is using the stairs, which would have meant passing him, so of course, Grant felt no need to rush. Making it look like I waited for him to catch up in an attempt to be polite doesn't work. When Grant reaches me, he actually pushes me so hard, I almost fall over and face plant on the floor. He grunts the word, "move," at me and then returns to looking at me like I'm something he wiped off the bottom of his shoe. The shove really threw me off guard. The panicky feeling starts to return as I make my way back into the room that he calls mine.

I enter the room and wait to see what Grant is planning. For some reason, the idea of being stuck in this room with him is making my heart start to race and my eyes flit around looking for something to magically appear. He stalks towards me and once in the room, he gently closes the bedroom door.

CRACK! The sound of flesh against flesh fills the room and it takes me a second to realise the excruciating pain I now have in my right cheek is a result of Grant slapping me. My cheek starts to burn and sting, as well as ache with the aftermath of pain. I'm sure that it will now have a very bright red handprint plastered across it. My eyes start to fill with tears and I instantly bring my hand up to caress my cheek in an attempt to soothe it. I have never been hit, and, I have got to say, it's not something I ever want to repeat.

My brain is yelling obscenities about what type of a mini-dick, cock sucking cuntwaffle of a man actually hits a woman. In my head, I'm yelling all of this outloud at Grant and making my feelings for him very clear, but I'm not as stupid as I was thirty minutes ago. He has made his point real well. I now know he has no problem living up to his psychopathic name and that he really is the type of guy who is not afraid to hit a woman. But the bit that scared me the most is the look I saw in his eyes when he hit me. Obviously, I was startled too much to have missed his initial response, but I know what I saw. He had a look of excitement on his face. Not just that he enjoyed hitting me, or showing me how powerful he is, but it was almost like he got off on making me hurt. I have no intention of letting him hurt me again, even if that means behaving.

"What the fuck, Ava? Did you enjoy that little game that you just played? How fucking dare you dress like a whore in front of my father and then make it sound as though it was my fault. You will be punished for that, is that understood?" He pauses, clearly waiting for me to acknowledge his threat and, of course, I do with a mumbling affirmative. There's not really much more I can say. What I wanted to say included telling him where he could shove his apology and his punishment. But I can't. I'm stuck here and I have no idea what he means by the word punishment, but the sick look of glee that he has plastered on his face is not helping.

"You will stay up here in this room only. I will be locking the door. You will spend the day thinking about how much trouble you caused this morning and how you can make it up to me this evening. I will be having a mini cocktail party for a variety of my friends where I will be announcing my new fiancé to them. This is your chance to make up for what you did today. I will pick what you wear this time, since you clearly cannot be trusted. Be in your best lingerie, looking perfect, like someone who I would consider to be worthy of being my wife, when I come up here at six tonight. Am I making myself perfectly clear?" I can feel shivers crawling all over my skin, not just at the thought of him seeing me in my underwear but also that he is going to see my armour. The tattoo I keep hidden because it is for me, gives me strength and I only share it with people who are special to me. That will be on display for him to see and judge. I know he will not like it, but I do not care. I never have because this tattoo was made specifically for me. I do contemplate telling him, but what the fuck can he do about it other than cover it up and, to be honest, that's how I prefer things. I know I don't have a bad figure and my curves look good, but I'm still not someone who walks around showing off lots of skin. I might let my legs show with a short skirt on a night out, or wear a thin vest top like this, but that's it. I rarely show anyone, and I'm pretty sure that nobody's response will ever top the way Ryder looked at my skin like I was a work of art. His eyes definitely gazed over every section of my skin, taking in not just the tattoo, but me too and he liked what he saw. I've always struggled with my confidence, which was the reason for getting the tattoo in the first place. It's my armour that lets me know that no matter what, I really am beautiful. But last night I didn't need it. Ryder made me feel like the most beautiful girl in the world even before he laid his eyes on me. So it's that feeling and those thoughts are what I am going to have to hold on to later tonight when Grant is the one ogling my body.

"I understand. What exactly do you expect me to do in this room all day? There's no form of entertainment, not even a book. Am I at least allowed down the hall to the TV room?" I ask as politely as I can manage, but even I can hear the hint of sass in my voice as I speak to him. I can't help it, I've spent my entire life being a strong, independent girl and I'm hardly going to fall in line because of one bitch slap. I know he can hear the back talk in my voice too, but what surprises me is the harsh laugh he lets slip out.

"Wow, I knew you were poor, but I had no idea you are thick as pig shit, too." I stand there, open mouthed at the audacity of this prick. I can't believe he is questioning my intelligence.

"Excuse me? How fucking dare you speak to me like that!" I screech at him. No matter how much of a big shot he thinks he is, I can assure him that holds no weight with me. All I see in front of me is a very small man.

CRACK! This time the slap hits my other cheek and a

combination of it being more forceful and catching me off guard results in me losing my balance and falling to the floor in the middle of the room. The pain is radiating through my cheek and my jaw from the force of the contact. As he hit me, the ball of his palm connected with the corner of my lip and caused the flesh to rip open. Beads of blood begin to pool on the corner of my lip and not knowing what else to do, I lick them away, tasting the rich copper taste. My ear is ringing and my head feels a little dizzy from the impact. Obviously, my brain is not too keen on being smacked around even if it is protected by my skull. It's funny like that, isn't it?

My hand repeats the process from earlier by pressing against my cheek in an attempt to soothe the discomfort I am feeling from the slap. My hand is met with moistness at both ends. The blood from my lip on the lower part of my hand and the tears I hadn't even realised were falling on my fingers. I never wanted this prick to ever see me cry but that slap hurt and I couldn't control the way the pain brought tears to my eyes. It suddenly starts to dawn on me exactly what type of a relationship this is going to be. Grant is going to beat the shit out of me until he has turned me into the girl that he sees in that crazy head of his. If he thinks he can break me, he is very fucking mistaken. He has picked the wrong girl.

Before I even have the chance to get my bearings and work out how to get up off the floor and begin pulling myself together, Grant must have sensed the change in my demeanor. It's like he could tell the exact moment I had decided I refused to be a victim because he crouched down in front of me with a sneer on his face. Then, before I even realise what is happening, he has my hair fisted in his hands and he is pulling my head close to his face. He twists his wrist, forcing me to look him in the eye and causing the stinging pain on my scalp to worsen into a pain.

"Listen to me, you little bitch. You have no idea what I have had to give up for you to be my wife. It is a great honour and it is one you will be thankful for. You will do your duty as a wife and you will show me respect. Everytime you don't, when you let me down or anger me in general, you will be punished. Let me be very clear, this is not a punishment. This is merely my way of getting you to hear exactly what I have to say. I am giving you one chance to learn from your mistakes, but rest assured, you will never get another. You have until six tonight to become the wife I expect or you will be severely punished. You will not be allowed to leave this room because I believe you need to be in here, thinking about how you can make me happy and then making it come true. You think you won today by getting my father to take your side, but you are wrong. All you did was make me accountable for your appearance and behaviour. So, if you are a disgrace, it will be me who is punished and let me tell you right now, that will not happen. You will behave and you will show me the respect I deserve because if you don't, I will personally blow a hole in your father's head. Now, do I make myself clear?" I start nodding as quickly as I can, even with his hand still fisted in my hair. I'm not sure if he actually wants me to speak or not. The feeling of dread that filled my stomach at the mention of him shooting my papa was worse than any slap he could have delivered. The pain that I felt at hearing those words is etched into my soul and I know that no matter what, no matter how much it goes against my nature, I have to behave. I have to become the well-behaved, quiet piece of arm candy Grant wants. The thought that this is my life now leaves my body feeling incredibly hollow. It takes me a few minutes after that awful interaction to realise Grant has actually left the room and locked the door, leaving me laying there on the plush carpet. I physically cannot get up. Now that I am alone and I know that he will not be returning, I drop my barrier and allow the pain and despair I am feeling after that encounter consume me. Tears stream from my eyes and sobs wrack my body. I cry, not just from the pain and the threats. I cry for everything I have lost and everything that my life has become.

CHAPTER EIGHTEEN
GRANT

Fuck me, this evening is most definitely not going how I wanted it to go and I really fucking hate when my plans go wrong. First, Ava comes down dressed like a tramp. I mean, there was no denying that she looked amazingly gorgeous, but that is not how I wanted her to meet my father. I wanted to show him she has agreed to be my wife willingly, and that she has changed for me and wants to please me. So when she came down, rebelling against all of that, I saw red, like I could literally hear my heart pulsing in my head. I wanted to ram my fist into her face, but I restrained myself. Then when my father came in and I introduced him to Ava, making sure I announced her surname clear enough for him to know who she is, he didn't flinch. I know my father is an expert at wearing a mask, but this was ridiculous. He has spent years protecting and defending this girl without anyone realising it. I have seen the books, he has paid off Manny's debts when he hasn't been able to afford a payment, multiple times. He protects him from other rival gangs, even coming close to starting a massive brawl over it. Not that we wouldn't have wiped out their whole crew if it had come to it. But I just do not understand what is so special about Manny Delgado. Why is my father protecting him? So, naturally, I figured the best way to find out is through Ava.

Coming up with the plan to marry Ava and find out exactly what the Delgado family meant to my father seemed easy. I had Eli do a deep dive to find me all the information he possibly could on the family. Then I found exactly what I had been looking for and I wished I hadn't. I have always hated my father and I never thought I could think less of him, but I was wrong. That was the moment I decided to step up my plan and make it happen no matter what.

When I introduced Ava to him as my fiancé, I expected a reaction. I know he arranged this meeting yesterday when he found out that she was here. People talk, which is exactly what I wanted, but I suspect Manny was the one who went to him, begging to get Ava back. I knew my father would walk in this building with a plan, I just hadn't expected him to be so nice to her. Especially when she is blatantly flouting all the rules I have taken numerous beatings for throughout my pathetic excuse of a childhood. But no, perfect Ava is far too special to do anything wrong. That was all I kept thinking during that whole fucking interaction. My hands were shaking and I was actually sweating through rage. I was so angry. After getting Ava alone in that room, I just couldn't help myself. The first slap felt so fucking amazing. I needed to show her how much it pissed me off that she was allowed to get away with breaking the rules and how that will not be the case with me. Being my wife means she will obey me and she will fall in line with whatever I expect of her, even if it's not what she wants. The second slap was to ensure she took me seriously. I am not playing around. She has to know I have a plan and if she thinks she is going to ruin it, she is very much mistaken.

Feelings of pleasure are swirling around my body and I have to admit, I am getting hard just thinking back on what happened in the room. I humiliated Ava, made her cry, slapped her, and it felt so fucking good. Normally, I would never hit a woman, not unless she begs for it, but with Ava, a red mist just comes over me. I am reminded of my father and the pain, which makes me take it out on Ava. The plan is to break my father but to do that, I have to break Ava first. Hearing her muffled sobs on the other side of the supposedly soundproof door reminds me that tonight, I have taken a step in the right direction. Just for a second, a small voice whispers in my head telling me maybe this isn't the right way to do things and I shouldn't take the rage I feel towards my father out on Ava, but I quickly quiet this voice. Now is not the time to develop feelings. Now, I have to go down and face my father.

Walking into the living room, I see that my father, Len,

and Ryder are all seated in various seats around the room. My father is typically in the leather armchair he knows is mine. Ryder is on the sofa nearest the door, his usual spot. I know he takes it so that he can monitor the rest of the room, see all entrance and exit points and be closest to the door in case of emergencies. His brain is one of the most organised I have ever seen and when he tried to explain to me on one occasion how he manages risk and assesses situations in the blink of an eye, I was genuinely in awe. When my father paired us together, I resented him. Then when I found out he planned on using Ryder as the leader and me as his puppet, I fucking hated him, but then we bonded. We got to know each other and Ryder is actually a good guy. I have tested him on multiple occasions and I know that he works for me and isn't some spy for my father. It's strange because I don't think he actually wants to run the business. He wants to work his way to the top, but I don't think he wants to rule the way I do, I think he wants to be the top of the security chain. That is why he is sticking with me and working for the old man, so he can learn everything he can to get us to the top. I should hate him, but I don't. He is the one person in this world I actually consider a friend, but even he didn't know about the plan. Maybe I will fill him in and get him to help take my father down with me, but only after I have tried several things myself. I may have said that I trust him, but that doesn't mean I fully trust him. The one thing I learnt from my father; never trust anyone

"You're here at last. Good of you to finally join us, Grant.

Now sit down, we have much to discuss," my father abruptly says the second I enter my own living room. I nod to him and sit down on the same sofa as Ryder, but at the other end, closest to my father.

"Of course. So, what brings you all this way today, Father? A congratulations on your engagement card would have sufficed." The smirk I have on my face at my own sarcasm lets my father know I am not messing with him any longer. I have spent my whole life being afraid of him, but not anymore.

"So, you are serious about being engaged to that girl?" he spits back at me.

"Marriage is hardly something to joke about now is it, Father?" I can see his hands ball up into fists and he begins to grind his teeth, making it very obvious I am affecting him.

"She is not a suitable candidate and you did not seek my permission. That is totally disrespectful," he replies, raising his voice more everytime he speaks. I am enjoying this. It might actually be the first conversation I have ever had with my father that I'm enjoying.

"I never meant any disrespect. We fell in love and it just happened. If we are in love, how can she not be right?" The sing song tone to my voice sounds like something straight out of a rom-com. I think I even hear Ryder try to hold back a giggle.

"You know the rules, Grant. She is not part of our society and will not take the Blakeman name." He actually stamps his foot as though he was standing up and having a tantrum. It looks a lot harder to stamp your foot when you are sitting down. This time, it's my turn to hide the chuckle.

"I know that, Father. But I thought that an exception could be made for love. Besides, you saw her before and you liked her. She is beautiful and with the right clothes and training, she will fit into our society." I make sure to include the subtle dig that earlier he had seemed engrossed by looking at her. Then again, there really is no denying she is a beauty.

"I was being polite. Of course, she is beautiful, but she is not from a good enough background to be part of our family." Bingo, he walked straight into it. Exactly what I wanted him to say.

"How could you possibly know that? You just met Ava five minutes ago. How could you know her family?" I see the red start to creep up his face and this time, I actually hear his knuckles crack as he makes his fists. Normally, my father is very cold and controlled, particularly in front of other people. He loses his shit in front of me all the time, but with Ryder and Len here, this is unexpected. I must have struck a nerve and I can feel my own body humming with excitement.

"Don't piss about this, Grant. We both know that Ava is Manny Delgado's daughter. I sent you there yesterday to do a job. Then I find out that instead of doing the job, you have essentially kidnapped the girl, and are now marrying her. What the fuck do you think you are playing at?" He's up now and pacing the floor in front of me, getting more and more annoyed. Len is looking down at the floor, obviously wishing he was anywhere but here. I cast a glance over at Ryder and he looks nervous. I can almost see the cogs working in his brain as his eyes shift around the room. He is assessing the best way to soothe the problem or to get us both out of here unharmed. But, I'm not worried about that. For the first time, I have the upper hand and I very much plan on using it.

"Love at first sight is a thing, Father. Besides, your dealings are with Manny and not Ava. When we marry, I will allow Ava to pay off her father's debt, so it will all be sorted then," I reply with a smile.

"No, I forbid you to marry this girl," he yells towards me with spittle flying everywhere and a feral look on his face. I've done a lot of shit in my life to piss him off and I can happily report that this is the worst. Wow, he really doesn't want Ava married to me. That is a shame!

"Look, I'm sorry, but I have always followed your rules. I have always done as you have asked, but this time I can't. I love Ava very much and knowing she feels the same way is the most amazing feeling. You said that having a wife by my side when I take over the family business would be beneficial. Ava is ideal for that role. She is beautiful and with a little adjusting, she will be perfect. You have seen her, she follows all of the society rules for women. She takes good care of her body, skin, and hair. She does not smoke or have any ridiculous piercings. She has no tattoos covering her perfect skin. She can be made into a society girl. I know that if she doesn't meet those standards, then I am not allowed to marry her and I would honour that." I begin trying to justify to my father, planting the seed to let him know that I am doing this no matter what he says. As I am explaining the rules I have to follow if Ava is to ever be accepted as a society girl, I am interrupted by Ryder, who begins coughing and spluttering.

"Sorry, water went down the wrong way," he sputters while pointing at the glass of water he just placed on the table. He looks to have an amused smile on his face, but it's being masked by the crimson shade he turned from choking. After I have checked he is fine and breathing normally again, I turn my attention back to my father.

"You will not marry this girl. It does not matter that she meets the standards of a girl who can be trained into our society. That exception has always been for lower class people. I am the boss and I would never degrade myself by dating below my station. As my son, I expect you to do the same." He is standing tall now, trying not to sound like the hypocritical dick that he is. He would fuck a whore off the street if she had a wet pussy and he was nearby. He has no loyalty to his wife or any of his previous wives. I'm not even sure he has ever been in love, so this whole 'stick to your people' rule is bullshit. He makes the rules up to suit him, but not this time.

"I'm sorry if this offends you, Father, but I have already asked Ava, she is wearing my ring, and I will not be taking it back. You cannot change my mind. Love is a powerful thing." I smile at the last part, letting him know the real reason I am doing this. If he is clever, he will be able to work it out, since I have only ever truly loved one person, but that would require him knowing something about his only son.

"You are right, love is a powerful thing. So, on just this one occasion, Grant, I am willing to bend the normal rules. I will let you marry your Russian whore, but not Ava. I know where your heart truly lies." Fuck, I so had not seen this coming. The wanker really does have great timing, given that my 'thing' with Katyia blew up for good last night and I don't see it ever getting fixed when this mess is all over. Every time my memory flashes back to last night, I can feel the knot in my stomach and a sadness I have never felt before envelopes me. Coming from a loveless home, being raised surrounded by violence and subject to emotional and physical abuse my entire life has helped me build up walls of protection to make sure I am as strong as can be and that nobody can hurt us. Katyia burrowed under those walls and made me feel a sadness that, despite my pathetic life, I had never felt. I try to block out the memories, but they keep flooding in.

As I arrive at the apartment I bought for Katyia, I begin to feel the butterflies I feel in my stomach every time I come to visit her. From the very moment I saw her face, stood up on the stage for everyone to gawk at, looking like the saddest angel I have ever seen, I felt an immediate connection with her. Something that had never happened before and has never happened again since. It was her pain I connected to. Looking at her, I could see she had been through more than any young girl ever should. Her gaze was full of despair and that was what my soul recognised. Like for like, we have both experienced pain.

Rescuing her from being sold to my father's disgusting acquaintance was one of the riskiest things I have ever done. I still have the scars on my back from where the buckle of his belt caught into the skin when he whipped me mercilessly until I was a bleeding heep on the floor. Ryder called the doctor and helped to get me healed the best that he could. He helped me get Katyia set up with her own apartment and got her checked over to make sure she was well. It took time for her to trust me. We started as friends just talking, or me helping her go back to school, generally just trying to help her make the most of her life here. I never wanted her to feel like I own her. So we took things slow and things developed naturally. Without sounding like a pussy from some romance book, the night she gave me her virginity was magical. I never knew I could enjoy slow, sensual sex so much. Normally, I like it rough and dirty, but I didn't want that for Katyia's first time. But since that day, she is all I think about. I only have to hear her name and my dick is hard.

The night Katyia sent a car to collect me, summoning me to see her, was unexpected. I was in the middle of putting my plan with Ava together and I had no intention of backing out. I enjoy being with Katyia and the sex is fucking amazing, but we both know that is all it will ever be. As far as the world is concerned, she is the whore I bought. I hate the fact people see her that way, she is worth so much more. We have been fooling around for over a year and she is amazing. We have fun together, talking, just generally coex-

isting together and those actions are what makes me feel comfortable. I have been surrounded by people my whole life in one form or another. Nannies, servants, bodyguards, work associates, family, the list goes on, but never have I felt comfortable in their company. I have always felt as though I am being watched or judged in some way. That they are reporting back to my father, but with Katyia, I know that isn't true. She hates the dick as much as I do. It's her presence, just being near her soothes me. That's why I still get butterflies everytime I come to visit and why there is always a smile on my face around her. Sadly, I know this visit will be different. Today, I have to tell her that I'm getting married.

Opening the door to Katyia wearing this tiny black lace teddy with matching thong and suspenders, literally floors me. Katyia is five foot seven and with her heels on, she almost reaches my height, which is exactly the way she likes it. The stilettos she is wearing seem to make her legs look like they go on for days and her arse is curved like a beautiful peach I just can't wait to take a bite out of. She doesn't even have time to greet me before I grab her around the neck and push her back into the room, kicking the door shut with my foot. Before she even knows what is happening, I've spun us around and slammed her back up against the door whilst still holding onto her neck. I'm not clamped on hard enough to cut off air completely or leave a bruise, but it is enough to let her know who is in charge. My dick responds appropriately by straining to get out of my trousers.

"Oh, my naughty little angel. I have been thinking about you the whole car ride over here, but you know you're not allowed to answer the door looking this sexy. This is for my eyes only and you know it." I pepper little kisses across her neck and around my hand, in between talking. I look at her and the fire shining in her bright eyes kicks me over the edge. We may have made love slow and sensually for her first time, but since then, I have taught her all about sex and Katyia has a wild side that rivals my own. I lean in to capture her glossy plump lips with my own and as soon as we touch, she nips at my lip, almost drawing blood. The groan that rumbles through my body is powerful and I can tell it ignites the fire in Katyia further. She places her hand on my elbow, gently telling me to bend the arm that is against her neck. She wants to close the distance between us and I am more than happy to do that, but I show her who's boss first by giving her neck a little squeeze and she gasps for breath in the most beautiful way.

As soon as I release my grip and let go of her neck, Katia begins to pant, but not just because she is gasping for air. She cannot get enough of that roughness, and she launches her sexy little body into my waiting arms. Our bodies crash together and our lips are not far behind. She licks my lip that she bit earlier, asking for entry and when I ignore her request, but match it with a lick to her lips to show that I want entry to her mouth instead, she groans. Katyia loves trying to get control over me and I love taking it away from her because I know that is the part of the game that turns her on the most.

Instead of giving me access to her mouth, she releases my lips and begins kissing her way down my neck, sucking on the sensitive parts that make me growl with lust. As she does that, she straddles both her legs to either side of my knee and crashes her panty covered pussy against the leg of my trousers. The more she grinds and bounces on my leg, the more that beautiful friction between her legs and I know those panties will be soaking. Her lust becomes too much and she stops peppering my skin with kisses to just enjoy the sensation on her clit. Just seeing the glow on her face and the tiny little moans that escape her sexy mouth is enough to have my dick rock hard and bursting to get free. Seeing her so wantonly trying to gain her own pleasure against my leg drives me crazy and the animal inside me awakens to show her she doesn't need to find her own pleasure because that job belongs to me.

Gently, I push Katyia off my leg just as I can see that high is getting her to the place she so desperately craves to be. I tut at her, telling her she knows better than to think I would let her cum when I wasn't involved. I tell her to remain firmly against the wall whilst I quickly remove all of my clothing. I have no time for anything else, I have to have this woman right now. I catch her eye when I take my boxers off and it is the same look every time it happens. She looks shocked and scared because my dick is slightly larger than average. So when it was her first time, she was sure I wasn't going to fit or was going to cause her pain. Naturally, that wasn't the case and she soon learnt to take all of me in all her holes, like the good little angel she is. Despite the fact she can take all of me with ease now, she still looks at it with fascination and awe. It most definitely does a lot for a guy's self esteem when I see her drooling, looking at my cock like it's the best thing she has ever seen. Then as she is staring, I see her lick her lips and then bite down on the corner of her lower lip. This is her way of encouraging me because she knows how much it turns me on to see her hot and ready.

A short flash enters my mind and I remember that this is

possibly going to be the last night I have with Katyia and I feel a physical pain swelling in my chest. It's something I have never felt before and I have no intention of wasting time analysing weird feelings when I can be tasting the gorgeous woman standing in front of me, so I stalk towards Katyia with my cock leading the charge. As soon as I reach her, I capture her lips in a bruising kiss, but this time, I give her no choice but to allow me entry. My tongue pushes into her mouth and it becomes a battle as we both take what we can from the other person.

Katyia's arms fly around my body, clawing at the skin on my back and gripping the hair on my head. She knows all of the little things that I love and that are guaranteed to make me moan more. Electricity flies around my body and all my nerve endings feel as though they are on fire. My cock feels like it is swollen to the point the head is painfully engorged and dripping with pre-cum. My hands take on a mind of their own and I have removed her bra in an instant. I use both hands to massage and tweak both nipples at the same time and it drives her mad. I have learnt where her breaking point is, that fine line between pleasure and pain. I always make sure to push her over it just a little because I know that the pain turns her on more than she admits. I release her lips that are now puffy, inflamed, and bruised looking from my assault on them and I know that mine will look the same. We are the perfect match for each other.

Now that my lips are free, I begin my assault with them on her nipples. Taking turns between them, I make sure the other one still gets attention from my hands. I start by gently licking around the nipple and grazing the tip of it with my teeth. I do this while I am *gently squeezing on the opposite nipple before I start massaging it in circular motions. As my mouth begins to suck Katyia's nipple harder into my mouth, she releases a guttural moan and arches her back, begging for more. I can feel my cock pushed against her stomach, desperate for more, but I'm not done teasing my little angel just yet.*

In a flash, I spin Katyia around so her face and tits are pressed up against the door, but I make sure that her back is arched, her arse is stuck out and her legs are apart. This gives me the most perfect view of her pussy and I can see the patch of wetness on her thong. I take a second to look at the gorgeous view I have in front of me. A juicy pussy, plump arse, suspenders that make her legs look like they go on forever, and stilettos finish off the package. Standing in front of me is every guy's wet dream and I intend to make sure she knows that no matter what happens, she is mine.

I stalk towards my prize like a hunter would move towards their prey, and as I do, the animal in me takes over again. With a growl, I rip off the thong that is covering my prize and I crouch down to taste her. I lick from her clit all the way to her arsehole as forcefully as I can, desperate to taste every last drop.

"Oh fuck, baby. You are so wet," *I moan before diving back in to devour every piece of her. My tongue assaults her pussy and Katyia is unable to form any coherent replies. Her moans and gasps for breath fill the room and that just spurs me on. As I circle my tongue around her clit, she starts to whimper and pushes her arse back into my face, desperate for more.*

"Do you like when my tongue touches your clit, angel?" *I ask in between circles that drive her even more crazy every time. Her* pussy is almost grinding on my face now and I am having to use my hands on her arse to stop her from taking too much control, but still she pushes back with a groan.

"More... please... please, babe. I'm so close... argh... yes... God... I need... fuck yes... oh my God... keep going." Her words are panted out in between breaths and I can tell even without her telling me she is close to cumming. Her pussy is dripping wet and when I squeeze a finger into her tight pussy, I can feel her walls clamping down on me. She grinds down onto my face again.

WHACK. I spank her hard on her arse to remind her I'm in charge. She squeals on impact and as I rub the area gently to take away the bite of the sting, she begins to whimper. I see her snake her hand down the front of her body and she sneakily starts to play with her clit. I think about stopping her but the moans she is making are driving me crazy, so I decide to join her. I use my tongue to piston in and out of her pussy, but that is not enough for her. So I add two fingers into her tight wet hole. Her loud moan fills the room and she begs for more and for me to go faster. With each thrust of my fingers deep into her cunt, I make sure to curve them right at the end to make sure I hit that sweet spot that makes her go crazy.

She is panting hard now, babbling incoherently and her pussy walls are starting to tighten. I know it won't be long, she just needs a little something to tip her over the edge. I see the fingers that were circling her clit are now pressing hard and grinding against it to create as much friction as she can. Her hips are now bobbing up and down, shaking her arse and ramming my fingers harder against her core. I take my tongue from her pussy and begin circling it around her arsehole. Her moans become more frenzied and I can see her free hand is clawing at the wall in front of her. I can feel her orgasm approaching and she is building and building, just the way I like. Her body is tense and her moans are uncontrollable, the begging coming out of her mouth is just a sex filled mumble. Just as I feel her pussy begin to spasm with the start of what I'm sure is about to be an earth shattering orgasm, I take my tongue away from her now soaking arsehole and roughly press my finger deep inside. Katyia screams out in pleasure and her whole body begins to quiver. Her pussy walls clamp tightly against my fingers and I can't help but wish it was my dick that was being milked by that tight hole. Whilst she is riding out her orgasm, I continue to gently pump into both her holes with my fingers as she screams at the top of her voice, letting me, and the entire street, know that she is cumming. That alone makes my cock strain even more, I love her wild abandon and the fact she doesn't care who hears the noises she makes when she is turned on. Thinking about that, I look up at her face. Her eyes are crunched tightly closed, her cheeks are a bright shade of crimson and sweat is plastered across her brow. But it is her plump, bruised lips scrunched together in the typical 'O' shape in between her mumbles of profanity, that really causes my heart to start racing. I love the fact I know her body so well, I can play her like a finely tuned instrument and get the same beautiful song every time. These are the thoughts that run through my mind as I pull my fingers out of Katyia's dripping holes.

I give Katyia a couple of seconds to catch her breath and she puts both hands on the wall to steady herself. I make sure my hands are gripping both of her hips because I can see the wobble in her legs. She always gets a bit of a jelly leg and sees stars after an intense orgasm, which is why I give her a few seconds to catch her breath before leaning in for a quick but sensual kiss.

"Did my angel enjoy that?" I ask her with a cocky smile on my face and I love the cute little shy smile she gives in return.

"You know I did," she replies with a tut before returning my kiss. She's still in the same position and I'm leaning over her with my chest touching her back. In this position, my cock is bobbing about, pressing against Katyia's entrance, in urgent need of some relief.

"Well then, what do you say?" I ask her whilst lining up my tip with her clit. I gently rub it over her already sensitive nub and she mewls. She knows the rules and still tries to flout them, but I love to tease her until she remembers them. The yelps that come from her throat every time the tip of my rock hard length presses against her clit forces more precum from the tip. I really hope she replies soon because this is driving me just as crazy as it is her.

"Thank you for making me cum. Happy now, you arsehole? Stop fucking around and put your cock inside me, now!" she screams whilst trying to back her arse up onto my cock. Fuck, does she get me horny when she is all hot and desperate like that. So, with one hand on her hip, I take the other one and fist it in her hair, pulling roughly until her back is arched even further and her tits are squashed against the wall. I gently nudge both her legs wider apart, giving me better access and then, when she least expects it, I plow my cock straight into her pussy, slamming hard until I am balls deep. She cries out at the sudden deep intrusion and I groan loudly in response. I wait just for a second to let her accommodate my size and then I begin to slowly move in and out of her sopping wet snatch. Desperate for me to go quicker, Katyia begins rocking her pelvis to help me to slam into her and at the same time, I feel her clamping down on my dick with her walls. The gutteral sound that erupts from me is almost caveman like and I spank her arse again to remind her who is in charge.

As my hand makes contact with her milky white arsecheek, Katyia yelps out, and as she does that, her pussy walls contract as though they are trying to massage the tip of my dick. It feels so fucking good and I start to speed up, pistoning in and out of her body whilst giving her the occasional spank. Seeing her milky skin turn bright red under my palm, accompanied by her breathy moans and begging for more, drives me crazy. I slam into her hard and each time, I feel my balls slap against her clit, making them squeeze together and my cock swell even more. I can feel my heart racing and my breathing becoming desperate pants. We both are so close to the end, but I want to make sure I take her over the edge with me. So as I'm pistoning rapidly in and out of her pussy, I take a spit covered finger and edge it into her arsehole. Her responding scream fills the room and she pushes back, impaling herself on both my cock and finger. The sensation of feeling my cock moving through her hot arsehole is so bizarre, but I know what my girl likes. So, I alternate strokes, pulling the finger out as I pound my cock further in and then vice versa. This drives her even more crazy than when it was my tongue and I can see her fingers are now playing with her nipples. In between mumbling incoherent words, I hear her calling my name and letting me know she is going to cum and hearing the dirty words coming out of my angel's *voice makes my muscles tense right up. I pound into her again and again before finally, with a deafening roar that fills the entire room, I spurt my hot cum deep into her pussy. Feeling my cock fill her hole is enough to make Katyia's orgasm follow closely behind and as her pussy contracts, it milks the last drops of cum from my cock.*

After we both come down from our earth shattering orgasms, I feel Katyia's legs start to give way, so I pick her up and carry her into the bedroom, pulling her shoes off as we go. We spent the whole evening together talking, laughing, eating, and having more mind blowing sex before falling asleep in the early hours of the morning, only to be woken a couple of hours later by the alarm on my phone. Time to go back to reality.

Laying in bed with Katyia in my arms and her head resting on my chest while I stroke her hair is never a place I ever thought I would be or want to be. I think that this is the closest I have ever been to happiness and I have to ruin it. She knows I am sad and that I'm hiding something from her, she always does. But she knows I will talk to her in my own time. I am not good at talking as it is and it's only ever been her that I feel comfortable with.

"Angel, I am so sorry about everything." I know she can hear the pain in my voice, I just hope she realises I'm apologising for much more than just what I'm about to tell her. My father brought her over here to be a sex slave, he degraded her, and people beat her because of him. He is the reason her only sister is dead and I can't make up for that. I'm also guilty for the fact that there is a tiny part of me that is pleased she had to endure all of that because it brought her to me. That incredibly selfish side needs to apologise

the most. When she looks up at me questioningly with her gorgeous green eyes that glisten like gemstones, I feel a sickness in the pit of my stomach.

"What do you have to be sorry for, Grant?" she asks, her voice husky from lack of sleep, which brings out the twang of her Russian accent more. I have always found her accent and the unique way she says words that she doesn't know or understand fascinating. My brain is screaming at me not to do this, urging me to see I am making a mistake. But even if I am, it's something that I have to do. This plan has been in action for close to two years while I have been bating my father, gathering information, and generally just waiting for the right time to strike. I just never envisaged Katyia would be collateral damage.

"I have something to tell you and you are not going to be happy with me, but please, I want you to just listen to me. I am not doing this to hurt you, believe me it is hurting me just as much. I have a plan and I need to follow it through to the end and I don't know when that will be." I am aware I'm talking incredibly fast and literally just blurting out whatever comes into my head. She gets up from lying on my chest to sit in front of me and I prop myself up so we are facing each other. She looks so confused and I hate that.

"You are not making any sense," Katyia says while taking hold of my hand tightly for support. I can't believe this beautiful, kind woman is actually trying to support me while I break her heart. Fuck, I'm an arsehole.

"Katyia, I'm getting married." As the words fly out of my mouth, I can see the look of pure shock as it rips across her face. She looks as though I have physically slapped her and what little colour she naturally has in her cheeks drains. I feel my stomach flip over and a burst of pain in my chest when she drops my hand like she was holding a hot pan.

"What do you mean? How can you be getting married? Who is she?" Katyia's voice breaks with every question that she asks and I can see her eyes beginning to fill with water and I think for the first time in a very long time, mine may be too.

"She is nobody you know. I am only doing this because I have to. I have a plan, but as part of the marriage agreement I'm not allowed to have a mistress." As soon as the lie leaves my mouth, Katyia's mouth drops open. Her swollen eyes worsen and her tears now flow free. Seeing this tough, feisty girl huddled in a ball, crying because of the things I said to her is awful.

"You don't have to worry about that because you know I would never be your mistress." Katyia wipes at her eyes and tries to look tough when she speaks to me, but I know her too well. I can see her hands are shaking, her eyes are blinking rapidly to try and dab away the tears, and her brow is furrowed in a way that shows me how much pain she really is in. I can't drag this out. I don't want to hurt her any more than I have to.

"I'm sorry, angel. I really don't have a choice." When the words are leaving my mouth, she almost appears to be frozen and then she jumps into action. She leaps off the bed, and despite the fact it is a very inappropriate moment, I cannot help but admire her sexy little naked body. She really is perfect. I watch as her arse sticks out, exposing her swollen pussy lips as she bends over to grab what looks to be one of my old t-shirts from a drawer. I completely buried her and she looks just as sexy wearing my clothes as she did naked. When she turns around, she sees me staring at her with the lust that is always in my eyes, she pauses. Her eyes naturally glance down to my rock hard cock, that is currently pitching a tent under the duvet, out of instinct and then it's like a mask covering her face when she remembers what we are talking about. The blank expression is quickly replaced by one of anger.

"Do not call me that! You have no right to ever call me that again," she screams with tears streaming down her face. As she wipes her face on the back of her hand, she releases a deep breath I hadn't realised she was holding.

"How long do I have before I need to move out? I have a little bit of money stored away and I can quit college and find a job straight away. That will help me find a place. Then I can be out of your hair as quickly as I can." As she is speaking, she is pacing up and down the room, I can see the panic building in her eyes. I can't believe she thinks I would do that to her.

"Absolutely not. You will not quit college. Your school is paid for and there is an account in your name that should see you through until well after university. You don't have to worry about the flat. I put it in your name a few months ago. You own this place not me," I say, confident that I have now sorted out all of her problems. I may not have been pleased by what I was doing, but I'm not a total monster. I care for Katyia, so of course I would always make sure she is safe and taken care off. There have even been times when I wished it was Katyia I would be marrying, but life doesn't work out like that and I try not to dwell on it. I just want to make sure I do right by her. However, given the look of fury that has flashed onto *her face and her balled up fists, it appears Katyia does not share my nice sentiment.*

"Oh great. So I was just your fucking whore," Katyia yells in my face and honestly, she may as well have just slapped me across the face. I have never, in all of our time together, called her a whore or made her feel like one. In fact, I have done my best to try and help her forget that night and how my father made her feel. So, I feel like I have been punched in the gut right now.

"Katyia, you know that you have never been my whore. I would never make you feel like that," I say softly, with an overwhelming sadness in my voice. I try to stand and go to her but she holds her arm out to stop me.

"You just did! I will be in the other room. Get your stuff and get out. I don't ever want to see you again." She turns her back on me and walks out of the room without a backwards glance.

I'M PULLED OUT OF MY MEMORY OF HOW BADLY I HANDLED things with Katyia this morning by the sounds of my father's dulcet tones. My brain is still spinning from the fact he has offered up Katyia, but given the shining look he has in his eye, I don't think he is quite finished.

CHAPTER NINETEEN
RYDER

I have to admit, I'm struggling to hold back my excitement at the way the old man is handling this situation. I have no idea what the situation is between Alan, Manny, and Ava, but right now, I really don't care because it may just be enough to save her. I have to admit, I have speculated for a while now about why Alan gave special treatment to Manny. I heard they knew each other when they were younger, maybe they were even friends, but I find that really hard to believe. Manny Delgado and Alan Blakeman are from very different parts of London and there are no parts that would see their paths crossing, but there must be something. It's obvious that Grant thinks so too and whatever it is that he thinks he knows is why all of this is happening to Ava. There is no reason at all that she should be punished for the sins of her father.

Alan seems more determined than I have ever seen him to make sure Ava does not end up married to Grant, and I couldn't be more grateful. As soon as the offer that Grant can marry Katyia as long as he leaves Ava is spoken, I feel as though I should be jumping for joy. This is a sure thing. I have never seen Grant care about anyone or anything the way he does Katyia. I would probably even go as far as to say that he is in love with her and he doesn't even realise it. But that's not really surprising since I don't think he knows what love is. He hardly has positive role models for this after all.

"Why would I want to marry my whore?" Grant says in a bitter voice. The whole room is a little shocked. I have only heard one person refer to Katyia as Grant's whore and he took his gun and shot him in the head. So, to hear it come from Grant's own lips is very worrying. I wonder if he is lying to throw his father off the scent, but if that's the case, then does he plan to keep seeing both Ava and Kaytia? I'm so fucking confused right now. I see the look of shock and confusion on Alan's face is a duplicate of mine; however, Grant seems to be finding this very amusing. This is the first time I have ever seen him so relaxed in front of his father. I know that he has had a hard life and his father is a complete dick to him. As a result of what I imagine is years of abuse and assault, Grant naturally has a healthy dose of fear where his father is concerned. I have seen him push the old man too far and pay for it, but that has been very rare recently. Since meeting Katyia, he has been almost normal, with the occasional psychotic unpredictable moment that is quintessentially Grant, but otherwise, he has been fine. Yet now, he is slouched back on the sofa with his arm around the back of it and his legs apart like he is snuggling in for a night in front of the TV. He actually looks at ease and that makes me very nervous. Grant has a plan happening right now, that is the only reason I can think of to explain this situation, and I have no idea what is going to happen. My brain is whirling a mile a minute trying to analyse every possible scenario, to work out where Grant is going with this. But more importantly, I need to know why Ava is so important to Alan Blakeman because I think she may be the key.

"You are kidding, right? I know you have been seeing that girl since the moment you paid for her. Setting her up in an apartment, paying her school fees, giving her a monthly allowance. Really, Grant? Once you had fucked her and taken her virginity, you didn't have to keep paying for it. Did nobody ever tell you that? Never stick with the same whore!" Alan sneers at Grant as he speaks and it's obvious he is trying to goad Grant into getting what he wants, but Grant's face remains the picture of calm. I can, however, see the way that his fingers behind the back of the sofa are scraping against his palm. The only visible sign of irritability that I can see.

"Just cleaning up your mess, Father. I made sure she is well and settled here and now she knows I'm engaged. We have agreed not to see each other again because that wouldn't be fair to my beautiful Ava. Besides, that was your condition during the first five years of me learning the company, was it not? To avoid distraction I am only allowed one girlfriend at any one time and if I marry, I may not take a mistress. Very hypocritical of you really, but since I have no desire to be like you, then I am fine with it." The cocky smile Grant tacks on the end is too much for Alan to take, who stands on the spot and faces him with one fist raised and the other hand firmly clutching the butt of his gun. Alan's face is contorted into one of anger and disdain, whilst his body appears to be physically shaking with rage. I risk a slight glance over to Len and see that he too has sat up a little straighter with his muscles poised ready to coil. He looks like he is waiting to pounce and I'm sure I look the same. We both have our hands on our guns, hoping this is not going to escalate any further. I, for one, have no intention of shooting anyone, and no matter how much they may despise each other right now, I can't let father and son shoot at each other.

"Now, you listen here, you cocky little shit. I am your father and your boss. You will show me the respect I deserve. I have never tolerated your back talk and I am not fucking starting now. As your father and the head of this family and business, I forbid you from marrying Ava Delgado." As Alan spits out these words with venom and finality, he makes it very obvious this is the end of any discussion. Everybody knows that when the boss forbids you from doing something, that's it. I can't help the tiny smile that raises in one corner of my lip and the little beat my heart skips when it registers with me that Ava is free and won't be marrying Grant. I have no idea what that means for us, but I want to know. I think this is the first time I have actually allowed myself to think there's a possible future with this girl. That beautiful bubble doesn't last long and is popped by cackling coming from beside me. Why the fuck is Grant laughing? Maybe he finally has gone mad?

"Father, you know I respect you in all of those roles, but you cannot command love. I'm sure that this action will come with consequences and I will accept them fully. I am marrying Ava, no matter what you say." Fuck, it is literally like you can hear a penny drop in the room, as everyone sits or stands there in total silence. I'm not even kidding when I say that nobody in the room expected that. I can see Alan processing how to handle this and for a moment, it appears his shoulders sag as though he is defeated, but it doesn't last long. He pulls his shoulders back and it is almost as though he has done an hour of meditation in his mind because he looks like a completely different guy. His muscles are relaxed, he has stopped pacing, his fists are no longer clenched or holding the gun and his face is back to the serene fake mask we are always used to. The guy who looks like a robot and like nothing at all ever phases him. Come to think of it, I have been in a lot of, shall we say, precarious situations with Alan and think this is the most emotion I have ever seen him show.

"Fine, if that's your decision, I will accept it. However, as you said there will be consequences. I cannot work with someone who has a blatant disregard for me and my word. So, if you do go ahead with your engagement with Miss

Delgado, then I wish you all the luck in the world, but you will not work for my company. I will not train you to replace me as I had planned. I will not give you jobs, or pay your wages in any way. You still have your trust fund that your mother set up for you before her passing, so money should not be an issue. Now, if you decide you would like to honour our family and follow in my footsteps as we always planned, then you have one week to decide. In one month, I'm receiving a large shipment where I will be able to teach you both phase two and three of the operation at the same time. This is a very big business deal, worth millions of pounds and if you are going to take over from me, you need to learn how to deal with the big transactions. So make your choice. You have until Friday to tell me your decision. I will take my leave now." Alan starts heading towards the door before we have had a chance to digest the massive fucking bombshell that he just dropped on us. Even Len looks a little bit shocked and bumbles around, trying to get up to follow Alan out of the room. They have both reached the door and I look at Grant for instructions on what to do next, should I let them go? It appears Grant is just frozen there in complete shock and I don't blame him. This is really fucking bad. Nobody ever suspected he would disown Grant. Family and image mean everything to the Blakeman family and this business has been in their family for generations. Alan is effectively ending his family line within the company and will need a new leader to take over from Grant. This is completely unknown territory because nobody can even speculate who this could be. But as much as I am loyal to Grant, I need to be at that shipment. If I can get him to ditch Ava and go to the shipment, I would be killing two birds with one stone, but I also need to plan for if he doesn't back down. As much as I like Ava and I want to help her, I'm here to do a job and I have to get as far up in the business as I can. Now there's a spot right at the very top and I am going to make sure that it's mine.

"I'm going to walk your father out, I'll be right back," I say to Grant as I spring up off the sofa and stride towards the door and into the hallway after Alan and Len. I don't know why I bothered to say anything because he still appears to be in some kind of trance. I will deal with him when I return. I catch up to them further down the hallway in just a matter of seconds.

"Mr. Blakeman, sorry, please allow me to see you out," I say, trying to be as polite and as professional as I possibly can. Len, being the responsible adult he is, motions from behind Alan to silently refer to me as a kiss ass, but I ignore him. I have a plan and I need it to work.

"Ryder, yes, of course, you may show us out," Alan says as he turns and acknowledges it was me who followed him. Given the look of disappointment on his face, he must have heard my footsteps and assumed it was Grant following him. "I am sorry you had to witness such unpleasantness. I know my son has always had a penchant for pushing boundaries and fighting with me, but I never saw this level of betrayal coming." He looks genuinely sad as the words fall from his lips.

"Sir, forgive me for asking this, I am simply trying to help. If you gave permission for him to marry Katyia, who is very far from being an acceptable part of this world, then I just wondered why you cannot accept Ava?" I ask tentatively, hoping he doesn't take my question the wrong way. I had intended to get straight to talking about business, but once I actually had the chance to talk to him, all I could think about is finding out why Ava is so special to him.

"That's a reasonable question, one I'm sure my son will want to know the answer to when he gets his head from out of his arse. Manny Delgado and I go back many years and I promised to look out for Ava. When Manny came to me yesterday, he asked me to make sure his daughter comes home. He is worried about her safety here with Grant and quite frankly, so am I. I saw the look on your face every time he spoke. Despite being the best risk assessor and behaviour analyst that I have ever worked with, you have no idea what he is doing, do you?" he asks and I can't deny what was already blatantly obvious, so I shake my head in confirmation. Knowing a little more about why Ava means a lot to him set my mind at ease that there's nothing worse going on here that I don't know about. Now, I need to convince him to keep me in the business.

"No, Sir, I didn't see this coming at all and for that, I can only apologise. I will do whatever I can to make Grant see sense and help you honour your promise with the Delgados.

Please do not take this in bad taste, but I have to say something. When I started working with you, I made it very clear I wanted to work right at the very top. I have worked hard and proven myself on many occasions, which is why you promoted me to Grant's head of security, a job that I have done better than anyone else previously. But, if Grant does choose to remain with Ava and to leave the business, I want to make it clear right now that my loyalty is to you and the job. I have never hidden my ambition and I plan on making it to the very top. I want to be at the shipment next month to prove to you I am capable of leading," I say confidently, but trying to remain slightly humble at the same time. I know the old man and he likes people who are confident in their abilities but he hates cocky twats. Finding the fine line is not easy.

"Ryder, I completely agree with you that you have never let me down. You have always put this company and my family first. I am not even sure you have a life outside of this job and your desire to play an important role in this business has been noted. However, I assigned you to look after my son because he is the ultimate challenge. You definitely have done better than everyone else that came before you, but ultimately this is your biggest task and you are failing. My son cannot marry Ava and the only way for you to remain part of the business is by my son's side. Everyone knows that my ultimate plan is for him to be the face of the company but you the brains. You will be the puppet master pulling all the strings, but you come as a package deal. If my son doesn't run this company, neither will you. You can remain his head of security, but given he will play no part in my business, I find it difficult to see why he would need security. That will be his decision. So now you have a choice, Ryder. Get him to break things off with Ava and run my company, or fail. The choice is yours." Hearing the words tumble from his lips leaves me shellshocked. I don't even remember acknowledging him, escorting him out of the building and saying goodbye. Obviously, I must have done it all, but my body is on autopilot, reliving every word he just said to me. I can have everything I have worked for these last two years. The keys to the business and all the inside knowledge that I need, but in order to do that, I have to get Grant to leave Ava. This sounds like a fucking win-win situation for me. I get my girl away from that nutter and I get to achieve my goal. Fuck, did I just think of Ava as *MY* girl? Wow, I really am having a mental moment. Seriously, this sounds like the perfect ending, but the only thing standing in my way is the pig headed idiot who seems determined all of a sudden to rebel against his father. I need to find out why, which is what I'm thinking as I head back into the living room.

Opening the door to the living room, I find Grant in exactly the same position on the couch, only this time he has a glass of scotch on the rocks and appears to be smiling. Sitting down on the sofa as I did earlier, I turn to face Grant and as I'm examining his face, I realise he looks different. The blue bags he normally has under his eyes are reduced, the frown lines that normally scrunch up his brow have lessened, and his hair that is normally perfectly styled with so much gel it never moves, it has no gel in it and has almost taken on a life of its own. The blonde strands are sticking out at different angles, almost like he woke up that way and keeps running his hand through it. He looks so much more relaxed. There is a hardness and a determination in his eyes I haven't seen before. Whatever he has planned has left him feeling relaxed and almost free.

"Well, that was quite a meeting, wasn't it?" I ask Grant with a hint of amusement to my tone to try and lighten the mood more since it seems to be working for him. He chuckles and it is both scary and a relief to hear him laugh. I have worked with him and been some version of a friend to him for two years and I've never really seen him laugh.

"You are right about that. So, what did he say to you when you walked him out? I know he will have issued you with an ultimatum to pressure me into doing what he wants, so I want to know what it is." His eyes are boring into mine, desperate to see if I tell him the truth or not. I have no reason to lie, he didn't tell me anything he hadn't said in here. Well, except for me being Grant's puppet master and being the real one running the company, but I don't see any reason he needs to know about that.

"He basically told me I was failing him. I should have stopped you from doing something he forbade you from doing. Then he told me our outcomes are linked. So, if you decide to marry Ava and abandon the company, then I go with you. I don't think you will have much use for a security team if you are just going to be a regular Joe, but still. However, if you opt for the company, then he will start training us both. You will rule and I will be right by your side, helping you just like I do now, but on a much bigger scale. This is what we have always talked about, isn't it?" I hear my voice start to become more desperate and high pitched towards the end of the speech. Hell, I'm desperate. I need to learn everything about this company and how it runs. It's what I have dedicated every day for the last two years towards.

"You know it is, but, Ryder, this is bigger than all of that. There are things you don't know about, important things I have to keep private. I am on a tight deadline that is getting ever closer. It has taken me a long time to be able to get to the stage where I can challenge my father, but I need to do this. We will still run this company, I promise you. It just might take longer than we initially thought," Grant says, looking as calm as a cucumber and I can feel the anger inside me beginning to bubble away. I can't believe this pompous dick is going to risk everything I have worked for just so he can stand up to his father for the first time.

"Fuck, Grant. Are you really telling me you are risking both of our futures simply so you can finally challenge your dad?" I ask in complete disbelief at what I am hearing.

"You know it's not just that I'm challenging my father, it's bigger than that. It's hard for you to understand without knowing everything, but trust me when I say, this plan ensures we will both end up running his company, a man who has ruined a lot of people's lives will be taken down, and I can finally be free to live my life." The pain I hear as he talks about the damage his father has caused is something I have never heard in Grant's voice before. I have always known that he's had a terrible childhood. But I have never truly known how much he hates his father. Me and my dad don't exactly get along all the time but I couldn't imagine plotting to take away everything he has worked for.

"Grant, I know you had a horrible upbringing with your father. I don't blame you for wanting to get him out of your life, but what you are talking about is a suicide mission. He will never allow you to take him down. And what the hell does Ava have to do with this plan of yours?" I try to casually drop Ava into the conversation because I need to know why he has chosen her. It's obviously not for love or attraction like he said. She is a part of his plan and if it is the suicide mission I think it is, then she could become a casualty. Grant is not bothered by who he hurts in this raging war he has against his father. I'm scared for her and I can feel a physical pain in my chest at the thought I can't help her. I need to be in this company. I have a job to do and the fact I have to choose it over Ava is physically painful.

"Ryder, you know there's a lot more to it than what you are saying and I don't have to talk it through with you. Ava is none of your concern. You are my employee, after all," Grant snaps at me with a finality and I know the conversation is over. I know him well enough to know that if I push him, he will get aggressive and argue back. He is like a caged animal when challenged.

"Ok, if you say so, *boss*," I say with false politeness, making sure I emphasise the ridiculous notion that I would ever see this dick as my boss. What is pissing me off right now though is that I thought I had a handle on things. I thought I knew Grant and his behavioural patterns, but I couldn't have been more fucking wrong. I underestimated him and now my job and Ava are both at risk. I have to fix this, but fuck me if I know how.

"You may go now. But ensure you are in the living room at six this evening as I am having a party to celebrate my beautiful wife-to-be, and I have a feeling it's going to be a blast." The sadistic smile on his face has me walking out of the room with my fists clenched and mentally telling myself all the reasons why it's not a good idea for me to punch him.

I spend the rest of the day loitering between my room and the entertainment room. Normally, I would go to the gym or for a run, something to distract myself and give me time to think, but today, I felt this intense need to be near Ava. I know I cannot contact her or go near her in any way, but being on the same corridor means I can watch out for her. It means I will know if Grant comes near her. This need to protect her is growing with every passing moment and it's crushing me I don't know how to do it.

CHAPTER TWENTY
AVA

Fuck, I hate not knowing what is going on. It's obvious Grant is up to something with his father and he is using me to do it, but I don't know what it is. I had hoped that Alan Blakeman was going to come and shake some sense into his psychotic son and get me the hell out of here, but I heard him leave hours ago and I'm still here.

Alan has always had some weird relationship with my papa for as long as I can remember. It's not like they had dinner or were friends, nothing like that. It's just that I know Alan has been bailing my papa out of shit for years. He thinks I don't know, but I'm not blind. Ever since Mum passed, whenever Papa got in the shit, Alan would bail him out. He doesn't pay off his debts or anything like that, he just makes sure he doesn't get into too much trouble. For some reason, he has always done the same with me, not that I have ever gotten into any real trouble. But, I found out recently that when Papa spent my college fund, Alan paid it back and sealed the account. It was sealed until about a week ago when it went missing again. I assumed Papa had found out how to access it and had spent it, but given that one of the ways Grant lured me here was talk of paying for my college, I'm now thinking maybe he had something to do with it. The thought infuriates me and I realise as I am pacing up and down the bedroom, wearing a hole in the fancy new, incredibly soft carpet, I am going mad overthinking things. What I need to do is go to the source. So, tonight at this party, I will be extra nice and I will make sure my husband-to-be has his glass topped up the entire evening. Then when he is more than a little tipsy at the end of the evening, I will get all the information I need.

The closer it gets to six, the more antsy I'm starting to feel. I have primped, waxed, and beautified myself in every way I know how. My hair is perfectly styled in light curls that are slightly pulled back from my face and secured in a half up, half down style with the most beautiful grip. At first, I thought it was a diamante clip like the ones I have at home, but on closer inspection, I think they might actually be real diamonds. The thought that I'm wearing something in my hair that probably cost more than my car freaked me out for a while, but after several rounds of deep breathing, I moved on.

Putting on the sexiest black lace lingerie that I can find, and the matching lace French style panties makes me feel so incredibly sexy. When I put on the black stilettos I picked out to match, I walk over to the full length mahogany window and I am blown away by what I see. The black in the lace makes my tattoos pop and look even more intricate and beautiful. I feel so unbelievably sexy right now and all I can think about is that I wish it was Ryder who gets to see me wearing this. In a few minutes, it will be Grant who walks through the door and sees me dressed like this and that thought sends a shiver of disgust down my spine. I had almost blocked it out. As I was getting ready, through every little primping and polishing stage, all I could think about was if Ryder would like what he saw. I know he would because when I walked down the stairs today dressed in my homemade grunge outfit, designed specifically to piss off Grant, Ryder looked at me exactly the same way as he did when I stood before him dressed like this only the night before. He looked at me like I was the sexiest girl he had ever seen and my heart melted. There's something about the guy that does it for me, and I missed that he needed to adjust his trousers when he saw me. That thought did wonders for my ego. So, I know if he saw me in this, he would have to have me. That thought brings back the heart wrenching sadness that I have spent the last day trying to avoid.

 I hear Grant's footsteps coming down the hallway and I do one last check of my make-up. Luckily, I was able to apply some foundation and concealer to the bruises Grant caused so nobody would be any the wiser. I didn't do it for him, I covered them for me. I don't want to be reminded of a moment I was weak and allowed him to gain control over me. It will not happen again.

Pulling the silk robe I slipped on to cover my body tighter to make sure Grant doesn't get to see anything he shouldn't, I take some big deep breaths for luck. The door swings open, as if announcing Grant has arrived. He is here, at exactly six, as he said he would be. Initially, when he opened the door his face looked almost focused yet serene, maybe even happy, but that all changed when he caught sight of me and my heart jumped in my chest. My mind is running a mile a minute trying to think through what I could have possibly done to piss him off in under ten seconds. I think that might be a record and I am secretly a little proud of it, no matter how confused I am. I smile at him to try and placate whatever has caused the anger in him, I do after all need him to not suspect anything if I'm going to be able to pull off my plan tonight.

"Why the fuck have you not followed my orders? Was I not clear enough earlier about what I expected?" he snaps at me with the most condescending tone.

"I have followed all of your dictated demands, Grant. So do not talk to me in that tone," I spit back as venomous as I can, letting him know I will not be taking any of his shit. He glides towards me like a predator stalking his prey and the look of repugnance on his face worries me. My palms start to sweat and it's almost as though time stands still. I'm frozen and my brain is overthinking and panicking as I try to contemplate my options. Except none of them come to me and the overwhelming feeling I have no idea what is about to happen, other than it will be bad, makes me feel like I am drowning.

Before I even realise what's happening, Grant is standing in front of me with his hand fisting in my beautifully styled hair. The diamond hair clasp crashes to the floor, I feel a searing pain in my scalp as he tightens his grip and pulls my head back to face him.

"Oh come on, princess, I never had you down as being an idiot. You can follow simple instructions and just in case your poorly educated brain didn't understand before, you will follow my rules. You will do as you are told and if you dare to ever speak to me again in that way, you will regret it. For every disrespectful comment you make, I will punish you five times. Do not test me on this one, princess. Do you understand?" That feeling of being frozen in fear is back and I know when he says that he will punish me, he means it. I have no idea what those punishments will be, but I have no intention of finding out. So, I politely nod in confirmation as best I can with his hand in my hair. The smirk that crosses his lips at my agreement is disgusting and I'm sure I can actually feel my skin start to crawl.

"Good, now on this one occasion, I will remind you of my instructions. I made it very clear you were to be waiting in your nice lingerie and I don't see that, all I see is the robe you are wearing. Now, shall we fix that?" he sneers at me and I reluctantly nod in agreement. Inside, I'm screaming and shouting, I can feel my nerves tingling, begging me to fight him, but I don't want to get hurt. The look in his eye is almost vacant and I can tell he has closed off any emotions he might have had. He is acting out a plan and if I don't follow it exactly, I have no idea what he could do.

As soon as I nod in agreement, I slowly reach up to the robe tie that is holding my silk shield in place, but apparently, my dawdling is not acceptable to Grant. His hand leaves my hair and within seconds, both hands grab hold of the edges of the silk gown and rip it open. The force he pulls with actually does rip the silk completely and the once beautiful garment falls to the floor like a wilted petal. As I watch that beautiful garment fall, I realise my dignity has fallen with it. Now I'm standing here in front of a man I despise in skimpy, lace lingerie and high heels. But the worst part is that he can see my tattoo.

Initially, Grant's eyes are so focused on the round swell of my cleavage, he doesn't notice anything else about my body. I mean, I knew I had a great pair of tits, but I didn't know they were so fascinating. When his mind finally snaps out of my cleavage, he takes a step back, wanting to take in all of me. However, the minute he does that, everything starts to go wrong. I see rage flash through his eyes and he advances towards me quicker than I could imagine.

Everything happened so fast. One second, I was watching Grant prowl towards me and the next, my head is spinning and there is a burst of pain shooting through my nose and face. Out of instinct, I bring my hands up to my nose and they are wet, but because of the black spots dancing around my vision, I'm struggling to see. Then it's like everything catches up with me and crashes over me at once. Grant just punched me in the nose. I have blood pouring out into my hands and tears streaming from my eyes. I had no idea I was crying because my vision is filling with more of the black spots. The ringing in my ears feels deafening and I'm sure if I could see the room, it would be spinning. Nausea fills my stomach and I desperately try gasping for breath through my mouth. All the blood and whatever damage the punch did is preventing me from inhaling through my nose. I know I am starting to hyperventilate and my mind is whirling. It's a mixed up place of pain, confusion, darkness, and panic. My legs begin to feel like they are made of jelly and before I know it, the whole world turns black.

When I finally come around, I find I am propped up on my bed, surrounded by cushions. My nose had stopped bleeding and my eyes were no longer watering. However, my head was still very much banging. In fact, if someone doesn't mind telling the brass band that is currently parading through my skull, that they can fuck right off, that would be great. I can still feel a pulsating pain on my right cheek, spanning below my eye and across my nose. I tentatively try to move my face muscles but that just increases the pain and makes the floaty spots appear in my vision again. So, I guess that is nature's way of telling me not to do that. When I feel the pain in my cheek, it's like a flashback to the fact Grant punched me and I need to find out if he is anywhere near me still. My senses are all over the place and I need to use my eyes.

Peeling my eyes open as gently as I can is easy enough on the left side, but on the right side, no matter how much I try to open my eye fully, only a sliver of light gets through. Obviously, that eye is so swollen, the eyelid is almost shut. Fuck knows how terrible I must look right now and I chase away the sob that is building in my chest. I can feel sorry for myself later, but right now, I need to assess the danger.

It turns out that danger is not too far away. In fact, he is propped up on the bed at the side of me, holding a towel to my nose to ensure the bleeding is stemmed. He isn't pressing too hard, so I'm guessing the majority of the bleeding is over. As I gaze up at him through my good eye, I feel confusion over what I see. He is looking at me with this mix of contempt and disgust, but there is also a little fleck of sadness glistening in his eye. Does he feel bad for what he did? I don't have time to focus on something that I could be misinterpreting. I raise my hand up and take hold of the towel before shuffling as far away from him as I can get on the bed. Admittedly, it is not far, but I don't have the energy to actually get up and I just need this small victory. I hear Grant release a dark and sadistic laugh at my actions, but I ignore him. Slowly, I raise the towel up into my line of sight and see that while there is a lot of blood on it, most of it has now dried and there doesn't appear to be any fresh. To confirm, I raise my hand and gently press around my nose. It causes all kinds of pain, but no more bleeding, which is a bonus. With everything that is going on, I can't help but wonder why Grant is still here. I know he has a big party tonight, that's what I was supposed to be getting ready for. His guests must have arrived, so why isn't he down there with them? I need him to leave this room. Hopefully, when nobody sees me downstairs, Ryder will come looking for me. I need him to come and find me.

"Why aren't you downstairs with your guests?" I snarl, hoping I can get rid of him, but he chuckles.

"Oh, princess, have you forgotten already? This is our engagement party. I can't go down there without you." He practically sings the words and is in complete denial that, who knows how many minutes before, he punched me for no good reason. But he must have had a reason. If I'm going to keep myself safe from this monster, I need to learn everything that triggers him and make sure I avoid those things.

"Grant, why did you punch me? I did everything you told me to do. I followed all of your rules. I'm so confused and I don't know how to be a good wife for you if I don't know what I've done wrong." I try my best to sound genuine, like my main goal in life is to please the sick bastard.

"Why the fuck did you do that to your beautiful body? I always thought that you were so perfect, despite your financial problems. But all this time, you were hiding this shit under your clothes. Why?" he sounds genuinely disgusted as he talks and I can tell that where he would normally be perusing my body, now he can barely stand to look at me. My heart starts to race and I start to feel hope. Maybe now that he has realised I'm not his dream woman, he will let me go. I love the fact that the beautiful art I have always seen as my armour, is actually acting like it right now!

"I have had these tattoos for years, Grant. They are my personal body art and each part symbolises something important. They are a part of who I am and I'm sorry if knowing I have them is off putting for you," I say, as politely as I can manage through gritted teeth.

"Don't worry about it. I made a call while you were sleeping. We have an appointment with a specialist next week. He says it will take time and it will be painful, but he will be able to remove that trash from your body." I just sit there, looking at him, even more dumb founded. He wants to take my armour from me. No fucking way am I letting him do that.

"No! Weren't you listening? These tattoos are important and hold sentimental value to me. Each of them signifies something that happened to me and together it is like the roadmap of my life. I don't want to get rid of it," I shriek. I know I was trying to stay calm, but the idea that some doctor wants to remove my ink has me terrified. I scurry off the bed and begin pacing around the room, trying to ground myself by feeling the softness of the carpet below my bare feet. The movement is too much for my head and the band restarts again, but luckily, at a lower decibel. The black spots are still there in my vision, so I try to reduce my erratic behaviour. I don't ever want to be unconscious near Grant again because I do not trust him. Taking big deep breaths, in and out, helps to calm my dizziness, but my fury at Grant still rages on.

I hear his footfalls crash to the floor and instantly time freezes as he gets up off the bed and stalks towards me. The fact I freeze on the spot makes it easy for him to reach me in next to no time. He gives me the once over with his eyes and I can see the disgust there, but there's something else there too. It's like he wants to hate me, he needs to, but there's a part of him that doesn't. He's so difficult to read and I never know what he is going to do, so I just stay rooted to the same spot.

"This is not up for debate. My father always said when he set out the standards of a woman fit to be my wife, she must have unblemished skin. I have managed to negotiate your unfortunate upbringing and have ensured Father that as far as anyone else knows, you are the perfect wife for me. So, you see those disgusting things have to go." He is talking a mile a minute, and at this point, I'm not sure if he is trying to convince me that it will work, or himself. He knows that even with the tattoos, I will never be good enough to be his wife and fuck, that is fine with me. The sooner he realises that, the better.

"You are right, this is not up for debate. I will not let you remove my tattoos. You can drag me to the hospital, but I will shout and scream. I will fight you on this every step of the way," I say, looking him in the eye and standing as tall and proud as I can. The confidence I feel from my tattoo is helping me to stand up to him. I see he is about to say something back and I'm sure the rage on his face is an indicator it wouldn't have been something good. Luckily, his phone vibrates in his pocket, distracting him, and he takes it out to read the message. As soon as his eyes pass over the words, the look on his face changes back to his blank, unreadable mask. Whatever was in that message may have just saved me today, but I have a feeling it's just delaying things in the long run.

As I'm frozen to the spot waiting for Grant to respond to my very clear violation of his 'obey me' rule, instead of continuing his advancement towards me, he changes course. He puts the phone away and heads over to the wardrobe. After several seconds of looking through the mass of colours that are hanging in there, he settles on a teal coloured knee length wrap dress. It's made out of a beautiful, soft cotton and while there is nothing overly special to look at, it still looks gorgeous. He walks towards me holding the dress out in front of me.

"You have been insolent towards me far too much tonight. This is a matter we will resolve at a later date, but you will no longer keep my guests waiting. You have five minutes to fix your face and put this on, then you will come and meet my friends. But let me be very clear about this, Ava, I will not forget this behaviour. It's not acceptable and you will be punished. I will not tell you what the punishment is or when it will be, but I can assure you that when it is over, you will be desperate for me to remove your tattoos myself." He whispers the part about the punishment quietly and directly into my ear. The feel of his breath and the vibrations of his voice, combined with the anger in his threat, sends shivers down my spine. The little hairs on my arm stand on end and he must see that I visibly start to shake because it makes him laugh. He puts the dress in my hand and pushes me towards the bathroom. His warning that I have exactly five minutes and not a second more, has me trying to frantically apply makeup to my swollen eye. Even with a really good concealer, which this is, you can still tell I have bruises spreading under both eyes and that one is almost swollen shut. But I do my best, which is not easy given my hands are shaking and my brain is whirling. I try to push the threat of punishment out of my mind because I know it's just as much a psychological punishment as it will be a physical one. He wants me worrying and obsessing about when it will be, what it will be, and I have no intention of giving him that satisfaction. Obviously, at this point, I am trying to bullshit my own brain because, of course, I am terrified.

Finally getting the dress wrapped around my body and tied in a secure loop at the side, I look at myself in the mirror. I'm squinting with one eye and the other just looks bruised, but the concealer has done a really good job covering up the majority of it. If it wasn't for the half swollen shut eye, nobody would be any the wiser. Looking down at the dress, I feel a bit confused. From what I have learnt about Grant in the short time that I have known him, he's all about image. I had to wear a frickin cocktail dress to dinner when he was the only one present. Yet, for a party to introduce our engagement, he has me dressed in what I can only describe as a very beautiful, but casual, summer dress. This is the type of dress you would wear to go shopping when it's hot. There's nothing overly flattering about the way it clings to my body. I have tied it in the middle in such a way that it shows off my smaller waist and emphasises my hourglass figure, but that's the most it does. Grant usually enjoys staring at my tits and arse, he loves any opportunity to show them off. The fact he is choosing not to do that tonight has my nerves on edge. Part of my brain is saying that it's probably a smart casual dress code for the party and he doesn't want me to look too sexy when he introduces me to the people in his world. I know again that this is bullshit, but I have to keep telling my brain something or I am going to freak out.

The sound of Grant's fists pounding on the bathroom door and his shouts about time being up and that I need to drag my arse back into the bedroom makes me physically jump. My nerves are already fried and then to be caught off guard like that has me shaking even more. Giving myself a mental pep talk that includes my usual 'calm the fuck down' speech helps slightly, but my nerves are still on edge. My heart is racing and I can feel the pounding in my ears as my shaky hand goes to open the door.

I walk out with a false confidence, but it is irrelevant because I barely register to Grant. He doesn't look me over or ogle my body the way he usually does. Instead, he seems like he is itching to go, and when he looks at me, he has a glint of mischief in his eyes. He takes hold of my hand, and at first, I think he is going to mention the fact that my palms are disgustingly full of sweat but he doesn't. He just smiles his usual manic grin and ushers me through the door. At this point, he is all but dragging me down the corridor and I am just going along with it. As we reach the door for Ryder's bedroom, my heart skips a beat as it does everytime I walk past it. But today, instead of my mind daydreaming about that hot and sexy night that we had together, I'm imagining what Ryder will do when he sees my face.

I know when Ryder and I talked about what would happen after our night together, we said it couldn't change anything. His job is always going to be the most important thing in his life. It's something I really fucking do not understand. I mean, you look at Grant and you can tell he is your typical gangster, crime family, or mafia person, whatever the hell they call themselves. But Ryder could not be further away from what I would associate with those guys. He is not a bad guy. I could never see him hitting a woman or killing someone. I know he said he is here as the brains behind the operation, but if he is that intelligent, he could do anything. Why a life of crime? The Ryder I have in my head, who spent the best night of my life with me, and that I'm pretty sure I'm slowly falling for, he wouldn't hurt anyone.

I must stall slightly outside of Ryder's door as I'm imagining all the ways this could end tonight. I'm not ashamed to admit I have even considered the big extravagant knight in shining armour theory where he rides in on a white horse, scoops me up, and we ride off into the sunset together. Ok, so I know that logistically the majority of that will never happen, but I like the idea behind it. I like it very much. That is playing on replay in my mind constantly on the walk downstairs.

As we reach the first floor, I can hear the party in full swing downstairs. It looks like they are in the living room and dining room. The doors have been left open and people are just milling about throughout the entire ground floor. They are all holding different shaped crystal glasses, depending on what their drink of choice is. There are catering staff in black trousers and white shirts flying around, making sure that everyone has a drink in their hand. There are also some holding silver platters that are filled with different types of vol-au-vents. Everyone seems to be chatting and having a great time, but the one thing I do notice is that they are all in black dress suits and ball gowns. I am severely underdressed to meet all of these people. Is this my punishment? Do I have to meet the high society people dressed as a plain Jane? Because it's not much of a punishment. I don't care what these people think of me, it's only Grant here whose reputation will be smudged. That thought brings me joy and a slight smile crosses my lips.

Just as I'm about to walk down the stairs to face the crowd, Grant pulls my hand into a different direction. Instead of going down the stairs, he pulls me off to the right, along the corridor on the first floor. This is his wing. I was told from day one I wasn't allowed down this part of the house. It's Grant's private section of the house and all I know is that he has a bedroom, bathroom, and what I think may be a private study area. Now my heart really is starting to race. With people, I'm safe. This does not feel safe and so I stop.

"Grant, where are we going? The party sounds like it is going on downstairs," I say as politely as I can. He obviously knows this, but I am trying not to antagonise him.

"We are going to my personal study. I have had Vic bring a few of my close contacts upstairs so I can introduce you to them personally. These men are very important and very powerful, you will do to remember that. With the backing of these men, I do not need that of my father. They are keen to support me and even more excited to meet the woman I have finally decided to settle down with. So, let's not keep them waiting." Grant's practically dragging me towards the room and my heart is racing. This doesn't feel right and I'm not afraid to admit I am freaking the fuck out right now. The idea of being stuck in a small room filled with dangerous men who all support Grant seems like a disaster waiting to happen. If these knobheads think he's a good leader, they have to have something mentally wrong with them and I really don't want to find out what that is. But I also know that pissing Grant off even more could be just as dangerous. So, stuck between a rock and a hard place, I take a big deep breath and walk towards the room.

Grant opens the door and the room is exactly how I pictured it in my head. It is covered in dark mahogany. There is just wood everywhere. On the floor, the ceilings, the walls, and the big desk that sits off to one side is just this massive mahogany monstrosity. It's exactly how you would envisage an old fashioned office to look like. There is nothing modern, spacious, or airy about this place. There is one window on the wall opposite the desk, but it is covered by blinds. There is no personalisation to the room at all. No pictures on the walls, no family heirlooms, only essential items. Other than the desk, which features the usual computer and big leather chair, there are some filing cabinets, a couple of wooden chairs, and on the window side of the room, there are two sofas. I would imagine under normal circumstances this room would be bare and boring. But from the minute I walk in, it's buzzing with excitement.

There are around fifteen men of all ages, races, shapes, and sizes dotted around the room, either seated or standing up. They look like there is nothing in the world that would connect them. On one sofa, there is an old bald man who looks like your typical Daddy Warbucks type rich guy, and he is talking to a thin African man with big afro styled hair. He is covered in tattoos and is wearing the most hideous velvet purple suit I have ever seen. He looks like your stereotypical eighties movie pimp. The idea that the pimp and Daddy Warbucks have anything at all in common to talk about is hilarious. But there are more pairings like this all around the room.

I'm not ashamed to admit that before my eyes fell on all these odd pairings, I did scan the room for Ryder. My heart sank when I saw that he wasn't there. The very small amount of calm I had managed to talk myself into went straight out of the window when I saw he wasn't there. When Grant closes the door behind us and gives me a cocky grin before pulling me close to his side, it finally dawns on me that I'm trapped.

"Gentlemen, welcome! So good that you were all able to make this little last minute gathering. But as I'm sure you can imagine, this is such special news, we just couldn't wait to share it." I cannot believe how much sway Grant obviously has with all the men in this room, because as he speaks, they all stop what they were doing and their eyes fly to meet us. He grins out at his adoring crowd and squeezes my hand, which I'm sure indicates I should be doing the same thing. He is about to carry on with more of what I'm sure is utter bullshit in his speech when the door behind us creaks back open. I turn to look and my heart starts hammering in my chest when I see the person entering the room is Ryder. He has his eyes downcast as though he is trying not to look at me and he is carrying a tray with two glasses of what I'm sure is the most expensive champagne Grant could order.

Walking around us and straight to Grant, Ryder has still managed to look everywhere but at me. So much for my plan that he would see my eye and rescue me. He first holds out the tray to Grant and it gives me time to study him, which is one of my favourite pastimes. Ryder always looks gorgeous, but today is something on a whole new level. I am so used to him being laid back in sweats or jeans, I never thought to imagine him in a suit, but even if I did, my brain couldn't have created this. He is wearing a crisp black suit with a dark grey shirt and they are all nipped and tucked to fit his body perfectly. The trousers hug and show off his arse perfectly without being tight. The shirt stretches across his chest and down over his rippling abs and the fabric is so thin, I can almost see every line. He is mouthwateringly beautiful and as he moves over to hold the tray out to me, I risk a look at his face.

Ryder looks like he's desperately trying to look anywhere but at me and at first, the sinking feeling in my gut makes me feel like maybe I have done something wrong. When I take the glass from him and give a quiet, disheartened, "thanks," I finally see his gaze flick to mine. It's only subtle, out of the corner of his eye and I watch as his face instantly morphs into one of rage. He has clearly seen my eye and is not happy about it. As quickly as I see the look of fury fly across his face, it disappears just as fast and is replaced by a mask of indifference. I realised then why Ryder wasn't looking at me. I'm not his to look at and we can't do anything about that. If he feels even a fraction of the pain I feel at that realisation, then he must be dying inside.

"Ah good, thank you, Ryder. Now that we have the bubbly, we can properly toast. Friends, I would like you all to meet the beautiful Miss Ava Delgado and soon to be Mrs. Grant Blakeman." Grant raises his glass and directs their attention to me like I am a fucking auction prize. Don't even get me started at the wave of vomit that tried to wriggle its way up my throat at the mention of me becoming his wife. But I don't want to give Grant even more reason to be pissed and so I smile and raise my glass before taking a healthy gulp of the champagne to help with my nerves.

"I know you will all be aware of the party going on downstairs and I will let you get back to that very soon, but I wanted you all to meet my fiancé personally first. I'm sure you have worked out we were a bit late to our own party since Ava here, has yet to learn the importance of obedience. All of you work with me in some capacity and I know you all know what I expect from people in regards to loyalty and commitment. You all know how I feel about my instructions being followed, don't you?" Then, like all of the guys in the room belong to some kind of cult, they all begin nodding and shouting confirmation. It's clear Grant has some kind of hold over all of these guys and they do whatever he wants. A wave of shame comes over me at knowing all of these slimy looking men are judging me, knowing I am pushing back against this engagement. I don't understand why he would say it, surely this isn't exactly giving off the perfect image of domesticity he wants everyone to believe.

"I found something out about my beautiful fiancé today and since she will not listen to me about it, I thought I would ask for advice from my most trusted advisors. Are you all happy to help educate Ava?" Grant talks like he is addressing a class full of students and encouraging them to shame the dunce of the class up at the front. I feel so on display right now and I can feel the blush of embarrassment spreading across my cheeks and up to the tips of my ears. The room erupts into cheers of confirmation and I can feel my heart start to race and my palms are sweaty. I am trying not to make eye contact with any one of the numerous eyes that are boring into me right now. Grant breaks me out of my spiraling anxious state by taking hold of my arm as he leans into my cheek. To everyone else in the room, it looks like a sweet gesture, but I can see the glare on his face. His breath on my cheek sends chills down my spine, but not the good kind. No, this is pure fear and I hate that ever since I learnt he was capable of punching me and feeling no guilt, I have felt a horrible sense of foreboding.

"Drink up, princess. You are going to need it," he whispers for only me to hear before guiding my arm so I can swallow the last of the champagne in my glass. It's a wonder I don't choke on it because I'm frozen with fear and yet gulping to not only to try and consume the alcohol that he assures me I need, but also to get in some much needed air. Breathing, panicking, and drinking have never been a good combination and I do start to cough and splutter at the end as Grant takes my glass from me. He chuckles and tells the room how clumsy I am. The rest of the sheeps join in laughing and no matter how much I try to convince myself that these people don't matter and that I am strong, I know I don't feel it. I feel trapped and scared with no way out. I had hoped Ryder was going to be my ally, the person who would stop Grant from taking things too far. But since Ryder can't even look at me, I think it's safe to say his job is the most important thing for him.

Gripping tightly onto my forearm, Grant walks me more

into the centre of the room and I become hyper aware. Something is going to happen, I can feel it, and the smirk on his face is only acting as further confirmation. That's when I noticed his other bodyguard, Vic, slowly moved behind us to stand in front of the door. I don't know whether he is blocking people from getting in or me from getting out. I can feel my heartbeat pounding in my head as the fear of being trapped in a room with this many less than moral men takes over. I risk another look over at Ryder and I finally see his face has come to life. He is no longer wearing the mask of indifference I have seen him with since I arrived. Now, his eyes are scanning every section of the room, the door which Vic now appears to be guarding, the behaviour of the other guys in the room, and most importantly, Grant's behaviour. I can see him doing the risk assessment that he's hired to do and I wished to God I knew what he was thinking. No matter how much I assess, all I can see is danger, everywhere I turn, and with no way out. I have to see how this plays out and hope Ryder has developed a conscience because I can tell by the smarmy looks on everyone else's face, they will not be stopping this shit show.

"Right, let's get this show on the road. As you all know, being my wife comes with certain expectations. She has to fit in at the social events I attend and uphold the Blakeman family name. Now, as I'm sure most of you all know, Ava comes from nothing. In fact, most of you have probably had the pleasure of dealing with her no good, deadbeat, drunk father." Hearing Grant talk about me like I am worthless is embarrassing, but hearing him talk about my papa in that way is infuriating. What right does he have to announce my papa's problems to this room full of people? I feel myself curling my hands into fists as rage races through my veins. Before I even have a chance to say anything, to defend my papa, Grant continues.

"In spite of Ava's less than perfect upbringing, I knew from the moment I met her that she would be perfect for me and the plans I have for the future. Naturally, she jumped at the chance to be my wife, didn't you, princess?" Grant says jovially as he reaches around and squeezes my arse cheek. This results in cheers and cat calls from all the scumbags in the room. Then before I even realise what has happened, Grant pulls me so my body is flush against his. One hand slowly gropes down towards my arse again, and his other hand grips the back of my neck. We are so tightly pressed together, I can feel all of his hard ridges, his chiseled chest is pressed firmly against my breasts. The hand that is resting very low down on my back pulls me in closer as he tilts his hips and I feel the outline of his erection pressing against my body. Disgust fills my body and I'm sure you could probably see shame seeping out of my pores. I can hear the jeers around me and that seems to egg Grant on further.

With my head secured by his hand at the back of my neck, he pulls forward and before I know it, his lips crash against mine. They feel hard and bruised as his lips push against mine. His tongue sweeps over my bottom lip, trying to get access. I'm frozen. Somewhere in my mind, there is a part of me that is shouting and screaming for me to fight this. To push him away. But the other side is terrified of what the repercussions would be if I fight Grant in front of his men.

Even though to the spectators it looks like we are enjoying a sexy kiss, I am holding my ground as much as I can. My arms are firmly by my side with my fists crushing so tight, I can feel the nails digging into the skin on my palms. But where I am fighting the most is my lips, they are crushed as tightly closed as I can possibly get them to ensure the monster currently groping me doesn't get the entry he so desperately craves.

Grant obviously has other ideas because he changes tactics and the hand around my neck starts to grip tightly and his teeth take my bottom lip into theirs. He bites down hard, so hard I fear he might actually draw blood. I try my best not to scream, but the attack does cause me to jolt backwards. As I am firmly in his hold, I have nowhere to go and my mouth opens in fear. He sees this as an opportunity and his tongue snakes its way into my mouth. I try to move my tongue away but he seems to find it and it feels as though we are in battle. Normally, in a kiss, it's a battle for dominance over who can give the most pleasure and who can take charge sexually, but this is different. This is completely about Grant exerting his power and authority over me. He is showing me he always gets what he wants and I am his. So by moving my tongue out of the way, by fighting back in any way I can, that is my way of taking back what little control I can in this situation.

Since this isn't a fairytale romantic kiss, I don't have my eyes closed and I'm not stuck in the moment squirming over how amazing the kiss is. Instead, my eyes are taking in everything around me. I can hear the catcalls and the shouts for more like we are a live porn show. Over in the corner is a young sleazy looking guy with hair that is slicked back, not by gel but by grease from the looks of things. I can see him staring at me, licking his lips and groping his dick with his hand in his trouser pocket. He looks like the type of pervert that has the pocket cut out so he can reach in and play with himself whenever the need arises, and apparently, given the stroking motions he is currently making, the need has arisen right now. The repugnance I feel at the situation has just been heightened even further and I can feel the nausea growing.

My slight reprieve comes when Grant pulls away and I am forced to stand there while everybody claps for me. Grant smirks, but I know from the look on his face that he isn't done and now I really start to panic. I don't want to look because I'm scared of what I will find, but I have to see Ryder. I have to make him see how scared I am. When I look over at him, my heart breaks just a little bit more when I see that instead of looking at me and the shit show in front of him, he's totally engrossed in the bottle of beer he's holding. I watch him gaze into it like it's the most fascinating thing he has ever seen before he then takes a swig and repeats the process. The devastation I feel is heartbreaking. Why did I ever think that one night with him might have been enough for him to choose me?

"Right, so we can all agree that Ava is a beautiful woman and exactly what society expects from my wife. So, you can imagine my complete surprise when I finally got Ava naked, I discovered she was, in fact, not as gorgeous as I had hoped. She had defiled her body and lowered herself to the point that she may as well have written 'I'm a whore' on her body." Grant is practically foaming at the mouth as he describes my tattoo to a complete group of strangers. The one part of my body that I keep hidden because it is just for me is being discussed with a group of strangers and I feel like my world is spinning. My tattoo has always been my shield and I have always seen it as something beautiful and unique, but Grant is talking about it like it makes me a slut to have it. The humiliation I feel starts to consume me and the more the room jeers and hisses, the more I can feel tears start to fill my eyes. *Ava, you will not let them see you cry.* I mentally repeat this to myself over and over again, trying to block out the room.

"Now, I have offered to have her whore mark removed so she can put her slutty past behind her and move forward. I think this is a more than fair offer, yet Ava has declined. She is insisting she keeps the tattoo. What do you think she should do?" he shouts the question to the room like he is a pop star at a concert, shouting to his adoring fans, and, of course, they reply exactly how he wants them to. He wouldn't have asked the question if he didn't know they would agree with him. But still, the calls of 'slut', 'remove the whore mark', and 'tramp', chip away at a piece of my soul. I can count on one hand the amount of guys I have been with and the amount that have seen my tattoo is surprisingly even less. I have only ever had one, one night stand and that just so happens to be with the one person I would give anything to have more with. The same person standing on the other side of the room like a statue, staring into his beer. I really need him to teach me whatever technique he is using to block out the whole fucking thing because he is doing a bang up job, whereas I am snowballing.

"Oh, stupid me. You can't make an accurate judgement without seeing the monstrosity, can you?" Before he has even had a chance to finish his sentence and for it to fully register in my brain, Grant is ripping open the ties on my dress and pulling it off me. In a matter of seconds, I'm standing there in a room full of disgusting men, in just the skimpy lace lingerie Grant forced me to wear. Not only is my tattoo on display completely to the entire room, but so is the rest of my body. The bra is the type that pushes you up, giving you an enhanced cleavage, yet the cups themselves are thin and next to nothing. You can almost see my nipples through the fabric and given that this room is freezing and I am terrified, it won't be long until my nipples are hard enough to cut glass. I really don't want that to happen because these perverts will think I am getting turned on. The worst part is the barely there French knickers that are scarcely covering my arse cheeks.

I literally do not know what to do. I wish I had a shit load more hands so I can cover my body with them. Instead, I have two and I have no idea which are the most important areas to cover, but that seems irrelevant right now because I am frozen. I'm not sure if it's fear or just sheer fucking disbelief that this is happening. I feel heat rising up my body and inflaming my cheeks with embarrassment. My eyes remain firmly on the floor before I squeeze them tightly closed. I know it sounds stupid, but remember when you were a kid and you played hide and seek, but couldn't think of anywhere good to hide, so you closed your eyes really tight, hoping that made you invisible? Well, I am trying that technique right now because it's the only one I have left.

I don't know if it's because of the fact my eyes are closed and my other senses are picking up more, but all of a sudden it dawns on me that the catcalls and jeering about my tattoo, from before he took my dress off, have all stopped. In fact, it's so silent in this room, you could hear a fucking pin drop. Tentatively, I open my eyes to see what is going on and I'm stunned by what I see. The room full of disgusting men that were looking at me like a cheap nasty whore when I had my dress on, are now looking at me with a mixture of awe and desire. I can hear mutterings of the words 'beautiful' and 'gorgeous'. This gives me confidence to lift my head and try to glance over at Grant whilst remaining inconspicuous. He looks absolutely fuming; his fists are clenched so tightly, they are going white, his teeth are grinding in such a way, it makes his face look misshapen, and his skin is tinged an angry purple colour. Initially, I think his behaviour is a bit over the top. I mean, of course, a room full of men are going to like seeing a lady in lingerie, but then I see there's more to it. These are the men he selected because he knows they follow him no matter what, they are his sheep. Except right now, instead of following his lead and insisting my tattoos are trashy and need to be removed, they see the beauty I have always seen. Not in me, but in the tattoos.

After much avoidance, I risk a look over at Ryder, although I have no idea why I'm torturing myself with this. He hasn't given a shit all evening, no matter what they have said or done to me, so why should he care now? I think there is also a secret part of me that wants to see the fire in his eyes, the same as everyone else's. I want him to look at me like all of these disgusting excuses for men are. I know that when they see me, even though their opinions have changed to a more positive one, they still only see me as a sexual object, but Ryder has never made me feel like that. As I finally find him, and our eyes meet, the sinking feeling in my gut becomes heavier. He isn't looking at me with the same lust from the other night, instead he looks to be almost disgusted and a little pissed. Is he pissed off at me? Like it is my fault I ended up half naked in front of a room full of slime balls. My anger starts to rise and thankfully, it starts to overtake the sinking feeling I had been allowing to consume me. I don't need that dickhead to save me, I can do it myself.

Grant is obviously not happy with the fact his cronies are not joining in with his plans as expected, they should be telling me to get my tattoo removed, but instead, most of them are pitching tents in their trousers, and the rest are fantasising about what I would look like without the underwear. But it's not until he notices the change in my demeanor, the way I stand tall again and allow my gaze to reach anyone who challenges me, that's when he realises his plan has failed. He wanted to crush me and break me, for whatever reason, but I will not let him. No matter what he does, no matter how long it takes me to get there, I will always fight back.

"Now, that you have all had a chance to get a good look at *my* fiancé's body, you can put the image in your wank bank, men. But for now, let's get back to the issue at hand. If I demand she removes these hideous, slutty images, what do you think she should do?" he asks the room full of men who have now all turned their attention away from me and back to Grant. His little reminder to them that I am his and the best they can ever do is wank about me at night seems to spur them all into action. Desperate to show their loyalty to the psychopath again, the room fills with noise as everyone replies at once. Varying different ways of saying it, but what it boils down to is they are all saying that I have to get rid of my tattoos. Even the ones who, not even five minutes ago, were salivating over me. I keep my shoulders back and my chin jutting out so I am standing up nice and tall. My gaze is pin pointed on one particular spot on the polished wooden wall and I stare at that as though nothing in the world can touch me. I cock my hip to one side to accentuate the natural curve of my body and also show off my tattoo. If they're going to look, then I will give them something to look at. I see them all staring at me and licking their lips, but at the same time, they are agreeing with Grant, too afraid to challenge him in any way.

"Did you hear that, princess? Are you going to be a good girl and do as you are told? Are you going to get rid of your tattoos to please your future husband?" As he is asking me in a sickly sweet voice that almost rots my teeth, he is grinning at me and making sure his gaze never leaves mine. It's a challenge. He wants me to submit to him in front of them. This was his plan all along; to degrade me to the point that I feel humiliated and have no choice but to agree with him. I'm not going to lie, for a short while, it really was working, but then I got angry. Now, there is fire coursing through my veins and I will never submit to him.

"Fuck you. My tattoos stay and if you don't like them, don't marry me," I spit back at Grant, making sure I hold his gaze the entire time. I can see the hatred that flares there and it makes me wonder what is it that has him hating me so much. What did I ever do to him?

The room around that was filled with raucous laughter and snide remarks is now deathly silent. All eyes are on us and the looks of shock on everybody's faces is a great sight. I don't think anyone in this room has ever had the balls to stand up to Grant. Yet, here stands a petite female, who is supposed to be his fiancé and she isn't afraid to challenge him. I hope they are thinking about that and questioning their entire existence.

Grant's face scrunches up into revulsion and I can see how much he hates not being in control. He absolutely detests the fact I have the balls to stand up to him, especially in front of his friends. Seeing his pain gives me a sense of pride and an overwhelming feeling of strength. Out of the corner of my eye, I catch a look at Ryder. No matter what I do, no matter how hard I try, my eyes always find him. I am drawn to him, even when he is acting like a dick. We shared one night together and agreed to walk away, but I can't. I want us to both walk out of this together. This time when I look at him, instead of the look of pride I expect to see on his face to mask my own, he looks scared. His eyes are shifting around the room and he is doing that risk assessment thing that he does. This instantly sets my nerves on edge. If there is something going on that is enough to frighten my strong and stoic Ryder, then that is something we should all be worried about. But it turns out, I was not prepared for the danger quick enough.

Like a flash, I am pulled from the spot where I was standing near the door and the next thing I know, Grant is physically manhandling me and pulling me to a free arm chair. He sits down without even letting go of me and I'm pulled down on to him. My stomach is pressed against his thighs and I am lying face down with my legs dangling down. I shuffle a bit trying to get free, but it feels as though he has a thousand arms that all have a firm hold on me. All I've successfully managed to do is to wiggle into a better position for him because now, I am very clearly bent over his knee with my arse up in the air. Fearful as to why he is doing this, I writhe around in his hold as much as I can. Just as I am about to shout out a string of expletives explaining why he needs to get the fuck off me, my breath is taken when I feel a sharp slap against my arse.

Time freezes as I register the sting rippling over my arse cheek where his hand just landed. The ring of flesh on flesh filled the air and was quickly replaced by cheers and celebrations. That's when it suddenly occurs to me I'm bent over Grant's knee with my barely covered arse in the air while he spanks me like a naughty child. The moment feels almost surreal, but before I have time to even think about my next move, another stinging blow is delivered to my other cheek.

"What the fuck are you doing, you bastard? Let me down right now," I say, trying to hide the yelp I couldn't help but release when his hand connected with my skin. He is not pulling back and is hitting me with a force I have no doubt will be leaving red marks on my white skin. The thought of him and all these guys seeing me get spanked and my arse turn pink has embarrassment running through my veins. I can feel the blush creeping up my cheeks, to the tips of my ears and even down my chest.

"You know you are getting the punishment you deserve, princess," he practically sings to me before delivering two quick successive blows to each of my cheeks. I can't help it this time, the cry falls from my lips as soon as the second blow hits. I was unprepared for two at once. My humiliation continues further when Grant begins to stroke and caress my cheeks, making sure to pull the panties as far up as he can get them. This then causes the front of the panties to bunch up and slide inside my slit, leaving my pussy lips on display. Dread fills my stomach as my mind begins working overtime, wondering if this is all he is going to do or if he is going to force me to do something I don't want to do in front of these men. My brain is frantically trying to think of a way out of this, but it's cut short by more blows. Alternating between every patch of available skin on my butt, he rains down blow after blow of slaps onto my increasingly tender cheeks. The more he slaps, the more my whines become cries before moving onto full on sobs. Tears are streaming down my face and at every available opportunity, I try to move free of him, but that never works. His hold just becomes tighter and then his blows become harder or land on more sensitive areas.

I can still hear the men around the room shouting encouraging words at Grant, generally singing his praises, all the while discussing my reddening arse, my pussy being on display, my bad behaviour, and generally how much the slut in me must be enjoying this. These pathetic excuses for men actually think that despite the hysterical sobs, the tears streaming down my face, no doubt mixed in with leaking mascara and snot making me a less than desirable subject, they still think I look like I am enjoying this abuse. I have lost count of how many blows he has delivered and he only stops occasionally to rub and pinch my arse to make sure my flesh is the most sensitive it can possibly be. Although my brain isn't exactly thinking during this attack, I tried to hide deep in my mind to help me ignore this terrible situation. He can destroy my body, but he can never break my soul. Desperate to know what was happening, in between blows whilst Grant was stroking my skin and boasting to his men, I blocked them all out and searched for the one face in the crowd I needed to see.

I know you are probably thinking, why the fuck would I do that to myself? After everything he has put me through, and it's very clear that he is not going to step in to stop this, otherwise he would have done it already, I can't help the draw I feel for him. I feel a pull to him still, even now. The logical part of me remembers the conversation we had before we parted after that night. We talked about how we would need to act like strangers so Grant never suspected. Ryder told me that not only was his job very important to him, but also, because of how deeply he is in the family, there is no out for him. He knows too much, so leaving is not an option. That's where the logical part of my brain reminds me that if he tries to save me, he could get us both killed, and I understand his actions even if I don't like them. Then with every searing spank that is delivered, the less logical part of my brain rears her ugly head. This has always been the fantasy side of my brain and she is desperate. From her perspective, she can see we had a special night together and that it meant more to us both than we ever admitted. She sees the way he looks at me, the way he protects me whenever we are in a room together. She sees the way his searing hot gaze bores into me, making me feel like I'm the most beautiful woman in the world. She knows that everytime I see him, my heart speeds up and I get butterflies in my stomach. She knows that no matter how much I deny it, I'm developing strong feelings for Ryder. She completely ignores the impracticability, the fact he is clearly more interested in his job and that it would be dangerous for us. She ignores the horrendous situation we are both in. To her, it is simple. If he cares for me, he would never let this monster keep hitting me. She needs to know if he is going to save me and it's the less logical side of my brain that wins out in this debate. I turn my head slightly to try and find where Ryder is. Grant doesn't notice my movement, he is too busy alternating between smacking and stroking.

I see Ryder standing, leaning against the same wall he was before, holding the same beer bottle. The look on his face is devastating because it's like he is wearing a blank mask. It's almost as though he is trying to pretend that what is happening around him isn't actually happening, but it is and yet he still stands there. Despite the blank look on his face and almost bored looking exterior that he is giving off, there is something in my mind that makes me think it's an act. I can see the knuckles on the hand holding the beer bottle are white as though he is gripping it tightly from anger. I see that his other hand is balled up into a fist with equally white knuckles. Then when I study his face further and try to ignore the blank stare, I can see the rigidness of his jaw, almost like he is grinding his teeth. If I didn't know any better, I would think he was angry, but if he truly was, he would stop this. I'm sure it's the fantasy side of me that wants to believe Ryder is my hero, but I don't think he is, I think he's just another monster.

My arse now is so sensitive, it feels as though it is red raw and yet, Grant continues with his assault. My screams are constant now and fill the room. The tears I had tried to stop from flowing were now turning back into an even worse sob than before and I am begging him to stop. It seems like everytime I tell him how much pain I am in and beg him to stop, he hits me harder. I can feel his hard erection straining against my stomach and can feel that with every one of my yelps or cries of desperation, he gets harder. The sick bastard is getting off on this. I feel like my mind is going to explode with an overload of sensations, the pain combined with the rubbing he administers after each hit confuses me so much. The pain is becoming unbearable and I am wiggling to get free, desperate for this humiliation to end, but it feels as though the hits just keep on coming.

At first, I think he is just caressing my bruised and mottled skin for longer than normal but the hit that my body is tensed up ready to receive doesn't come. I am unsure whether I should let my guard down, but I take in some big deep breaths to try and get control over myself and to stop the sobbing and shaking. I feel him rubbing gentle circles over the skin that must now be ruby red. It feels so inflamed and sore, even such a gentle gesture causes a sting. He has spanked me literally over every surface of my arse, upper thighs, and lower back, making sure he didn't miss any area. So I'm not shocked that he is stroking in the same area, that is until it changes.

I feel Grant lift up the part of my panties that, during the beating, had made its way firmly into the crack of my arse. Just the idea of him pulling it out of my arse sends shivers of shame sweeping through my body. Just when I think that Grant isn't capable of degrading me any further, I feel his finger slide past the crack of my arse and into my slit. Instantly, I start to panic and try as hard as I can to get away, but before I have a chance to shout and tell him to stop, he slaps each arse cheek hard and in quick succession. Having a break allowed my skin to start to cool down and so the feeling this time, when he strikes, is so much more intense. I scream and flinch with the pain, but still, Grant keeps me pressed hard against him.

"Well, well, men. It looks like the princess here likes the pain. She may scream and beg to get away, but her pussy tells a different story, doesn't it, Ava? Tell my men what your pussy is telling me." As he asks me the question, I feel his finger slip back into my slit and curve right to my peak. His fingers are just millimeters away from my sensitive bud and I am internally praying to anyone that will listen, to help me make this stop. I know I don't want this and I am not getting off on the idea of this sick bastard using and humiliating me in front of his men. But I also know, the second his finger touches my clit, none of that will matter. It doesn't care who is doing the touching or whether I have consented. The pleasure and the reaction my body makes to his touch is all instinctual, I have no control over it. Not that it will matter to this room full of pervy, sick bastards. They will think I enjoy being vulgarised because that is what men like this think of women. So, I try my hardest to concentrate on anything else but Grant's finger. Of course, the fact I have retreated into my own head results in me not answering Grant's question and so he punishes me with a further spank.

"Oh, Ava, baby, are you too ashamed to admit that your greedy little cunt is dripping wet from being spanked? Admit it, princess, you love it!" As he is speaking, his finger finally makes contact with my clit and no matter how hard I try to ignore it, when his finger starts to circulate and press on my sensitive nub, I can't help the moan that escapes from my lips. I know that despite it only being a small, gentle moan, it was heard by the whole room. I feel Grant chuckle as though he has just proved his point and the rest of the room all start shouting words of encouragement or vulgar things. They call me a whore, say I'm begging for his cock, that I love the pain and humiliation. Some praise Grant on his new fiancé, telling him what a good little slut he has and how much fun he will be able to have with me. Hearing complete strangers talking about how pretty my pussy is and how they like to hear me moan and scream is so humiliating. They call me a whore and talk about how they will be wanking over this scene for a long time and that thought is heartbreaking. Not only can they see my most vulnerable area, but they will be imagining that they are in Grant's place. In their heads, each of these guys plan to use and abuse me while they whack off. My skin feels like it's crawling and I feel so small. My heart sinks at the utter humiliation that I am feeling. Then I hear them refer to me as nothing more than his sex slave, which is disgusting because I would never consent to letting this vile creature touch me. Just the very idea that his plan for this fake fucking excuse of a marriage is so that he can use and abuse me every day scares the shit out of me. I can't let him beat me. I have to keep fighting and let him know that if it's a good little submissive housewife that he is looking for, then he has definitley got the wrong fucking girl.

"Fuck you. You are forcing yourself on me and you assaulted me. There is no fucking way on earth that my pussy would get wet for you. You disgust me, now take your fucking hands off of me," I shout with as much fight as I can muster. My voice is hoarse from all of the shouting and screaming and sobbing that I did during the beating. I can tell my reaction has momentarily stunned everyone because not only does the whole room go silent, but Grant's finger stops its assault on my clit. I feel him tense up beneath me and I don't need to look at him to know I have pissed him off. I tense, waiting for the punishing spank to make contact, but it doesn't come. The eerie silence just continues and I'm not sure what to do. I try to wriggle slightly to see if he is finally going to let me get free, but all he does is tighten his hold around my waist to the point that my side will most likely be bruised. I start to obsess over what is going to happen now. I have obviously pissed him off, which he says will always lead to a punishment, but since I am already in the middle of a punishment and he hasn't hit me again, I worry he is planning something else. It's almost like I can hear the cogs in his brain ticking away while he thinks up a way to adequately punish and demean me. Hushed whispers begin to spread around the room and I'm sure they are all thinking the same things as me, 'what the hell is Grant going to do next'? Maybe I shouldn't have fought back, but I don't want him to think he has won. I have no intention of just rolling over and letting him have his way. If he wants me as his wife, then he gets me as I am; feisty, stubborn, independent, and a fucking bitch when I want to be.

"Ava, you know that type of behaviour is completely unacceptable and you will be punished for it when I feel like administering it. I need to make sure the punishment fits the crime, as all my men know." Mumbled agreements and mass nodding floods around the room as they agree with their leader. I shudder at the thought of what he plans to do to me in private.

"So, Ava, back to the matter at hand because I know my men are desperate to know. Princess, don't deny that being spanked in front of my men turns you on. I can feel that you are dripping wet." Blush floods my cheek at his vulgar words, but the deep shame I feel comes from when he places his finger back on my clit, presses hard, and a wonton moan fills the air. This time, his movements feel different. He is no longer lazily stroking up and down my slit and grazing my clit to see if I am wet. No, now he is pressing hard on my nub and drawing circles around it with his finger. In between my gasps and groans, I realise he is now trying to make me cum. He wants me to orgasm on his fingers in front of all his men and if he carries on the way he is, I won't be able to stop him.

"You like that, my dirty princess?" Grant asks as he sweeps his finger up my lips before reaching the entrance to my pussy. Every time he has done this before, he curls his finger around the hole before going back to my clit, but this time it's different. Before I have a chance to register what he is doing, I feel him slip a finger into my pussy. I try desperately not to react, but a deep moan escapes and my pussy clenches against his finger.

"You would not believe how tight her greedy snatch is, men. I can't wait to feel it stretched open with my cock." His words cause a deep disgust to thread through my veins. How can my body betray me in this way? I am repulsed by this man in every possible way, so how can he illicit this kind of response from me? That thought feels like a heavy boulder is sitting on my chest and I am overwhelmed with the loathing that I feel for myself right now. That, combined with the shame I feel from being exposed and used in front of so many people, sends me spiralling. Despite the moans coming from my lips, I have tears of sadness and despair streaming down my face. I am shaking, not with need or desire, but with fear. It finally registered with me that he plans on fucking me, probably right here, in front of all his men. The idea of people watching me like I am a prostitute participating in a live sex show is so degrading, I feel my heart start to break. My mind is whirling, trying to find a way to get out of this situation. I can't be fucked in front of everyone, in front of Ryder. Oh God, I was so busy trying to block out the situation, I forgot all about Ryder. Just as I am about to look up at him again, I feel Grant insert a second finger into my pussy.

His fingers piston in and out of my pussy with great speed, but also great accuracy. Somehow, he is able to curl his fingers to the exact angle that he is able to hit my deep spot everytime. The more he does it, the more my moans become louder and more needy. I will not beg or speak to let him know how much my body is enjoying this. I will not show him he is winning, but he is. I can feel the tell tale signs of my body getting ready to ignite. My pussy walls are clenching, my skin is heating, and it feels like flames lick inside my stomach as my body craves the release my mind is desperate not to allow. The mewls of desire that fill the room give away my true feelings and it is obvious that my body is responding. But that isn't enough for Grant. He wants to humiliate me, to torture me, and most imporantly, he wants to break me.

"Princess, you wouldn't be getting ready to cum all over my fingers, would you?" he says it with such sarcastic glee because he knows the answer. Hell, the whole room just needs to look at me and they know the answer. No, this question is for me, to degrade me even further. He can fuck off if he thinks I am going to obey him.

"Fuck... You..." I manage to scream out in between my panting. I hear an evil chuckle and he removes his fingers from my dripping wet hole. The loss and emptiness is instant and my walls try to clench against air, desperate for the help they need to meet their release. My groan at the loss of friction needed to activate my oncoming orgasm seems to please the room. The words 'whore', 'slut', 'desperate for it', float around the room and I try to block them out, but I would be lying if I said they didn't get through my walls. They penetrate my heart and soul, causing a pang of great shame and self-disgust. This worms its way through my veins and spreads all the way through my body and tears of regret fill my eyes. How the fuck did I get myself in this situation?

Before I have a chance to think about it further, I feel Grant's skillful fingers move back to my swollen pink bud and he begins lazily twirling his finger around the nub. Not enough to send me over the edge, but more than enough to continue driving me crazy. I try to restrain myself, but it's like my mind has gone completely blank and is giving into the maddening sensations. I feel Grant shift slightly beneath me and his engorged cock pokes me hard in my stomach, reminding me how much he is getting off on this vulgar act. Is this what he is like with all women, or am I just getting special treatment?

"Oh, don't you worry, princess, I have every intention of

fucking you. I am going to slam my dick so hard into that tight little pussy and stretch you open. I am going to ruin you for every other man and make you beg for me. You see, I had to give up the perfect pussy to marry you and not only will you pay dearly for that, But right now, in front of my men, all I require from you to end this punishment is for you to ask me to let you cum. That is it. No strings attached. Not only will the punishment end, but you will get the release you so desperately crave. So, what do you say, Ava?" The movement I felt before was Grant bending forward so his head was right against mine. As he whispered the words for only me to hear, his breath fanned over my ear and down my neck, causing a shiver. I want to say it was a shiver of fear over what this monster is capable of doing, but I would be lying. At this stage, I am so aroused, every little thing makes me wetter. The feel of his cock bobbing against me, the bruising grip of his hand around my hip, and the feel of his fingers in my most sensitive area, they all drive me crazy. I know in my heart that it is my body betraying me, that it is just lust and desire that is desperate for relief, but it still guts me. Even just the fact that I am considering letting this man touch me, as opposed to him just taking it, disgusts me. But my sensitive, pulsing nerves tell me I can't cope with this torture any longer, I need to find my release.

Just as I am about to say the magic words, I hear a cough in the background. I don't know why this noise, out of all the others in the room, is enough to pull me out of the lust driven haze I am currently stuck in, but it does. I look up and

I see Ryder staring straight at me. Before I have a chance to look away, Grant obviously ramps up his attempts to get me to beg by inserting his two fingers back into my pussy. The shock of the abrupt penetration makes me cry out, but as he curves his fingers into my most sensitive spot, my cries turn to wanton moans. I realised, as I moaned at being fingered by another man, I was staring straight into Ryder's eyes.

A part of me hopes he sees the situation for exactly what it is, my body responding to stimulation, that is all. This is Grant abusing me, degrading me in front of his men, and attempting to gain power over me. Surely, the gorgeous man who managed to actually make me feel things rather than just have my body respond, is able to tell the difference. Can he tell the moans he hears now are nothing compared to the primal urge just being near him created? The way I voluntarily and eagerly screamed his name and begged for more. This couldn't be more different and I am desperately hoping he can see that. I want him to realise Grant is the abuser here and that I am not, nor will I ever be interested in him.

When Grant's fingers slow down for a second during his change of pace, I force my brain to focus on the beautiful face in front of me. I want him to see the real me and to know how much I want him to help me by ending this before I have to lose myself completely. But his eyes are not heavily fixed on Grant as you would expect, they are firmly on me and that causes a sinking feeling of humiliation worse than anything Grant has done. I have spent the last hour or so with men looking at me like I'm a whore, calling me all the names under the sun and degrading me, yet I never felt it, until now.

Ryder's face is contorted into a mixture of disgust and pain. I try to focus on the fact he is in pain at seeing this, but the look of revulsion is too much to ignore. From the moment I met Ryder, he has always looked at me with an awe I had never experienced before. It was like I was the most beautiful woman in the world to him and every time his beautiful eyes sparkled just through looking at me, I felt it. I felt beautiful and sexy, but mostly, I felt like I was his. It was an instant connection, like my heart knew I was supposed to be with this man. That was emphasized even more after our night together. Maybe, if we had met under different circumstances, things would be different, but we didn't. I have ruined everything and looking into Ryder's eyes now, I know, no matter what happens in the future, this will always be what he remembers. Our beautiful night together is a distant memory. All he will see is the slut who got off on being fingered by a guy she hates in front of a room full of people. The more this sinks in, the more my heart starts to crack. I realise I can't possibly sink any lower in his eyes and that breaks me. I need to get out of here and away from his disapproving glare. I cannot see his revulsion anymore, I have to make this end and I only know one way. Looking deep into Ryder's eyes, I speak the words neither of us want to hear.

CHAPTER TWENTY-ONE
RYDER

"Please let me cum," Ava whispers the words quietly and the desperation in her voice is obvious. Although she says it so quietly half the room probably can't even make out what she said to me, she might as well have screamed it.

Her eyes bore into mine and there is so much pain and sadness engulfing her normally bright chocolate eyes. Seeing the tears as they roll down her face is heartbreaking. What hurts more is the look of disappointment I see in her eyes because that is aimed straight at me. I know she is begging for my help and all I can do is stand here. Fuck, I wish I could help her. Watching her fall apart at the hands of another man is cutting me up inside. To say that my vision is clouded with red and green mist, equal parts rage and jealousy, would be an understatement. I know logically that Ava is not mine, but fuck, do I wish she was.

Her moans fill the room and it's like a knife directly into my heart, but no matter how hard I try, I can't look away from her. Having elicited more than one orgasm from her beautiful body the other night, I have the noises she makes committed to memory. These sound different, there is not as much passion in them. With me, she screamed, begged for more, and she called out my name as though I was a God. There is none of that here and my heart holds on to that and tries to remind my stubborn brain that there's no way she wants this.

As she is about to fall apart, the jeers from around the room increase. Calls for the slut to cum echo around me and I see the moment Ava hears them because her eyes become dead. She is looking at me and the hope I initially saw there dies. I see a small tear escape her eyes and I feel myself moving closer to her. My instinct is to stop this and get her out of here. Grant has some sick plan for her and I am starting to think this isn't the worst of it. My mind feels as though it is at war with itself and I am pulling myself in two. There is a part of me that desperately has to save a girl that I haven't known for very long, but I can feel in my soul that she should be in my life. Ava is my girl and I need to make that happen. Then there's the other side of me, the one who remembers why I am here. This is my job. I have spent two years working my way to the top of this empire and I have to get there. My father has expectations for me and I feel the weight of them heavily on my shoulders. This is the job I have always wanted to do. I have lived and breathed the

Blakeman family for the past two years. I don't even remember the last time I saw my family or my friends. This has become my life and if I were to give it up now it would be disastrous. I can't even begin to imagine what my father would say. I know I can't stop this, but I can be there for her.

I look deep into her eyes and give her a smile. I know it's forced and not the brightest smile I've ever managed, but I want her to know this is alright. She has been forced into a difficult position and she has to end it somehow. The strength she has shown in fighting for this long is amazing and it does warm my heart to know that my little vixen is still in there.

I can tell the moment she sees my smile because she returns it with one of her own. I see a flicker of light appear in her eyes but then Grant obviously changes technique and she falls over the edge. Her beautiful body shakes and her lust filled sounds fill the room. Despite the situation and the resentment I feel that it is Grant who made her body sing like that, I can't deny her beauty. The way her teeth catch her plump red lower lip as her face contorts into pleasure and when her body writhes around as she rides out the waves, it's almost as though her skin sparkles. I can't stop my cock from getting harder. I try to block everyone else out and imagine I am the one causing her to make those sounds, that it's my hand causing her to orgasm. That way I won't feel as disgusted with myself over the fact my cock is so hard, it is straining painfully against my jeans, desperate for relief.

Once Ava has finished, things seem to move so quickly, I

struggle to keep up. Grant stands up with a floppy Ava still in his arms, and as he stands to the side, he drops Ava back onto the seat. The impact, although soft and non-harmful, is enough to startle her out of the trance she appears to be in and she sits up. She folds her knees up to her chest and wraps her arms securely around them. She has curled up into a ball, making herself as small as she can. Obviously, she is trying to hide away as much of her body as she can to regain some of the dignity she has lost over the last couple of hours.

All I can see is the look of pain in Ava's eyes when she looks around and realises what happened. There are perverts all around the room stroking their dicks, some even outside their trousers, not bothering to hide their actions. As she looks around, she sees them all, she hears the words they call her, and her face contorts into pain. It looks like she is going to burst into tears right there on the seat, but then her face changes. She becomes blank and distant, almost as though she is wearing a mask to hide her real feelings, but it's the look in her eyes that bothers me the most. They are vacant and don't hold even a flicker of fire that I am used to seeing in her beautiful brown eyes. It worries me that a part of Ava will never be the same again after this and I'm not sure I can blame her.

"Well now, gentlemen, that was quite a show, wasn't it? Now that my beautiful bride-to-be has learnt some respect, I feel confident that this marriage will be very useful. But, I want you all to heed this warning. I brought you here because you are my closest allies, you are the men who have shown me the most loyalty and respect over the years and for that, I thank you. Tonight, you helped me discipline Ava. But from the moment you walk out of this door, tonight will not have happened. As far as everyone else in the world is concerned, Ava has always been the beautiful, obedient woman that I feel sure she will be from now on. She is not a slut or a whore, she will be my wife. You will not degrade or humiliate her in any way, doing so would be a direct insult to me. Tonight, I allowed you to see Ava's beauty and what I have to look forward to, but she is all mine. From the moment she begged me to make her cum, she agreed to be mine. You will all do well to remember that. Is that understood?" Shouts of agreement fill the room and suddenly there are no cocks swinging around or men leering at Ava. They are all sitting upright as though someone shoved a rod up their arse, while they look anywhere but at the beautiful, broken girl in the middle of the room.

"Ava, baby, please confirm to my men you have learnt your lesson so we can go on with the evening. There is a party going on, after all." Grant's request is like the final nail in Ava's coffin and I can see her cheeks fill with shame. She bows her head into her knees and speaks out with the tiniest voice.

"I'm sorry I disrespected you. I've learnt my lesson. I am your… yours." Although Ava's voice is tiny, it is also monotone. She sounds like a robot, just relaying the information that she has been told to. Well, right up until the end that is.

When she gets to the part where she has to confirm to Grant that she belongs to him, she stutters over the words. She looks up at me and with her vacant eyes boring into mine, it's clear what she means. She is talking to me and not him.

It doesn't mean much to anyone else in the room, and I don't even think it registered to Grant what she did, but I heard it. It was her way of saying she will be his wife, but she will never be his. She wants to be mine. A spark of hope ignites in my chest and I think that the feisty Ava I love so much is still in there. Her flame may be dimmed right now, but it is not out completely. I just wish she wasn't looking at me like I am just another one of the perverts here in the room. Because that is exactly what is happening. When she walked in, she looked at me with lust and seduction as she remembered the night she bared herself to me, exposing her beautiful tattoo. She looked at me like she wanted to climb me in front of everyone. Now that spark has gone. Instead, she looks at me with a mostly vacant expression due to the mask she is wearing, but when the mask slips, I get to see her real feelings. The pain, the shame, the disgust, the anger that are all bubbling under the surface. Then when she looks at me with disappointment and regret, I can feel tears start to fill my eyes. She may want to be mine, but that causes her pain because I let her down. I stood here and let it happen. She has every right to feel those things, but fuck, are they like a knife to the chest.

Grant seems satisfied by Ava's response as he calls for everyone in the room to go back down to the party. As the sick freaks go to leave the room, they are back to wearing the gentleman facades they had when this night started. Before they behaved like a hyped up mob and degraded a beautiful girl into nothing more than a slut. I feel the urge to punch each and every one of them grow as they walk up to Ava to say goodbye. They have the nerve to pretend like this was a social gathering. They say how lovely she is, how much of a pleasure it was to meet her, and how happy they are for the couple. When they tell her how much of a beautiful bride she will be, I see her shoulders sag. She does her best to nod at them from her scrunched up position on the chair. The first one offered her his hand and she ignored it, so the others learnt from that and didn't offer. But the whole time they are interacting with her, despite her nods, she never makes eye contact. Her gaze remains fixed on her knees and it's like she is a vacant shell of herself.

The room clears except for Grant, Ava, myself, and Vic. Since we are his security team, it only makes sense that we would remain with him, but I have another idea. Before Grant has a chance to give any orders, I decide to step in. I have become an expert at making him think they are his ideas and I hope it will work now.

"So, Grant, I take it you are planning to go back to the party?" I ask and as he confirms, I swiftly continue to avoid him interrupting. "I think Vic should go with you to the party, he knows all the security plans. Ava, here, is in no fit state to meet the rest of your guests like this. Maybe it would be better for them to meet her another time, when she is at her best? I could take her upstairs and guard her up there. I will make sure she has all the necessary first aid things she needs and secure her in her room. How does that sound?" When I speak, I try to make it sound like he is the one in charge and that I am desperately trying to please him. Grant responds best when he thinks that people are obeying him. He has a craving for power and control, most likely because he has never had that around his father.

Grant smiles and walks towards me. At first I'm a little hesitant, he has been harder to read lately and his unpredictability is a whole other factor to consider when I am looking for danger. But I know that no matter how he comes at me, I could take him easily, so I wait it out to see what he is planning. When he is in front of me, he reaches up and pats me on the arm in what I am assuming is a friendly gesture. Fuck, that is freaking me out.

"Ryder, I'm so glad I have you. Always one step ahead, thinking about what I need to do. You are right, of course. I can't show my bride off in this current state. Take her upstairs and guard her. My men saw more tonight than I intended and I don't want anyone getting any grand ideas thinking that they can touch what is mine. You, I trust completely, to guard her as though she were me." I gulp as he speaks, wondering if he knows, but there is no way he does. We were far too careful. I school my features so he doesn't know what I am thinking, I also have to hide the insurmountable anger I feel at him referring to Ava as his.

"Of course, I will," I reply. With that, he flashes his freaky grin at me to let me know he is pleased with my response. Then without any further fuss or even looking in Ava's direction, he leaves the room and Vic follows like the good little lap dog he is trained to be. I realise then, it is just me and Ava in the room now and she still looks just as vacant and terrified as she did when it was full of people. She doesn't see me as any better than them any more and I feel my heart crack. I kneel down in front of her, making sure I am at her level, but I'm far enough away to give her space. I have dealt with victims before, and if you rush in, you lose them. I need to build the trust back up with her and I'm not even sure it's possible.

"Ava, I'm going to take you upstairs away from everyone. You will be safe in your room, I promise. Do you feel able to walk?" I speak in the gentlest tone I can so as not to scare her. She looks like a frightened little mouse right now, and at any moment, she can bolt. She looks up at me with her vacant eyes, but doesn't say a word. Her silence speaks volumes because she knows I'm lying. I can't promise her safety and I have no right to act like her rescuer because I am a little late to that party. Fuck, I can't deny the burning need I have sizzling over my skin, screaming at me that I need to take care of her. He wasn't gentle with his beatings and I need to make sure she is not hurt physically. With her silence, I'm at a loss for what to do. I know what I want to do, but I better ask first, so she doesn't hit me.

"Ava, please will you let me carry you upstairs, away from this room?" I ask gently and I see her glance her eyes around the room. She is obviously remembering it full of men because her eyes start to fill with tears again, but she refuses to let them fall. When she gives a small but definite nod, I feel like my chest is going to explode and I spring into action.

Scooping up this tiny girl should be easy. Hell, I did it the other night when I threw her onto my bed, but this time is different. I need to be tender and aware of the mottled skin that adorns most of her thighs, arse, and back. Before I reach to pick her up, I take off the shirt I am wearing. At first, her gaze flashes with undeniable heat at seeing my bare chest and fuck, does that not make me feel like a lucky son of a bitch. Then it all comes crashing down when just as quickly fear reaches her eyes. Her brain obviously overthinking has brought the whole situation into focus. She was just assaulted in front of a room full of men and now she sees me removing my clothes. She starts to panic and scrambles in on herself. Fuck, doesn't she know that I would never hurt her?

"No… no, Ava, please. You don't have to be afraid, I would never hurt you. I just wanted to give you my shirt to cover you up." Ava looks down, almost like she had forgotten she was almost naked. She holds her hand out for me to give her the shirt, which I do straight away. She shuffles about as she pulls the shirt on around her back, placing her arms inside. As she moves, I see that she winces and tries her best to make no sound, it's obvious she is in pain and that sinking feeling I've had all night in my gut returns. Why didn't I stop him?

BROKEN

My mind is stuck in a self deprecating loop as I berate myself for allowing this gorgeous girl to be hurt in such a way. No matter how rational my brain is, I cannot deny my heart wanted to do the right thing and the fact I didn't, kills me. I make sure I look down at the ground to give her some privacy as she buttons up the shirt, she has been exposed enough for one day and I don't want to make it worse. But when I look up, I see her hands are no longer tucked around her knees, they are holding onto both sides of the collar. Her knees are relaxed a little more now that she knows her body is covered. Then I see her take a deep breath and I realise she is inhaling my scent from the shirt collar. The way her body responds as her shoulders sag and her muscles relax, the barest hint of a smile on one corner of her lips, they all give me hope. Hope that my Ava, my feisty vixen, is still in there and I haven't lost her yet. I try to pretend the thought of my smell giving her reassurance and safety doesn't give me the biggest head alive and a smile adorns my lips for the first time on this shit hole of a night.

Once Ava is covered fully with my shirt, I move towards her slowly, my eyes seeking the consent my lips are too scared to voice. Her nod is so small, if my vision had not been tuned into every single flex her body makes, I might have missed it, but I didn't. It was there, clear as day and as though she weighs nothing, which, of course, to me, she doesn't, I scoop her up into my arms. My brain flashes to an image of what this could have been like if we had met under different circumstances. Maybe if we had met without all of this bullshit, then one day I would be carrying her over the threshold as my wife, not his. But I put that out of my mind and try to take what little pleasure I can from the here and now.

It doesn't take long for my fantasy to blow up into a puff of smoke. Even just the slightest touch of my skin against hers has Ava hissing and jumping from the pain. It's a stark reminder of the damage that has been inflicted on her poor petite body. But when she willingly wraps her arms around my neck, it feels right again. Except it's clear she isn't holding on for comfort, instead it feels as though she is digging her fingers and hands into my skin, desperate for me to never let her go. To show her she is safe, I pull her in tighter, almost squeezing her to let her feel the warmth of my whole body. I hate the initial wince in pain when I pull her tight, but then, when she nestles her face into the crook of my neck and closes her eyes, I know she feels safe.

I practically run upstairs to the floor we share, not wanting anyone from that hideous party downstairs to see us. Once we reach her room, I all but kick the door down to get her inside before closing it again with my foot once we are on the other side. I walk straight over to the bed and lay her down on it. Her breathing has slowed down, but I can tell she isn't asleep. She is merely vacant and statuelike, as she has been since her ordeal ended.

She obviously feels the moment her back connects with the softness of the bed because instead of relaxing into it as you would expect, she freezes and grips tighter onto me. Her eyes fly open and are as wide as saucers as she surveys the room. When she realises she is in her own room and she is safe, she slowly lets go. It's almost like there's a war going on behind those pretty brown eyes. She isn't sure if she wants to let go of me, but then she remembers what happened and she drops me like I'm on fire. She rolls over into a ball and just lays there. I know this is my cue to leave, but obviously I'm either a dumb motherfucker or a glutton for punishment because I don't leave. I know she is trying to hide it, but I can hear the tears falling from her eyes. She is quiet and they are probably a lot fewer than she has every right to shed, but just seeing one of them fall is my undoing.

I reach over and touch Ava's forehead, I begin stroking her face and wrapping her sweat matted hair behind her ears. Even when she looks like this, she is beautiful. The sweet gesture seems to be too much for Ava because it causes her to cry further. This was not my intention and it's like a fucking knife to the heart. I didn't want to cause her more pain, I would never want that.

"Ssh, little vixen, you don't need to cry. I've got you. You're back in your room and you are safe with me. I've got you." As I softly mutter the words into her ear, the second lot of repetition is more for myself than her. It's my way of telling myself this cannot happen again. I need to figure out a plan. But it would seem Ava doesn't take my kind words the way she should, instead they light a fire in her eyes. She swats my hand out of the way before firmly pushing against my chest. Her tiny strength isn't enough to actually do anything to me, but I'm not that much of an idiot that I don't know when I'm not wanted. So I allow her to push me off the bed. What surprises me is that she then follows, but gone is the vacant shell of a girl I carried up here. This girl is different. She may have the fire of my old Ava, but she has the hurt and the pain of the Ava from tonight. It's a painful combination to witness, but fuck, if just seeing her filled with fire in her eyes again doesn't cause my cock to twitch. I'm so busy thinking about my bloody dick that when she pushes me with both hands against my chest, she actually manages to catch me off guard and I stumble backwards.

"Did you really just say that you've got me? What a sack of shit. The time for you to have my back passed hours ago and instead you stood there with the rest of the pathetic excuse for the male species and you did nothing. Tell me, Ryder, were you one of the one's calling me a slut? Did you encourage that piece of shit to hit me harder? Or maybe you were there stroking your dick and getting off on my pain? So which was it?" The venom in her voice as she speaks are like spikes being stuck into my body. Every accusation that she throws at me wounds me a little bit more. Does she really think that just because I didn't stop it, that must be because I was enjoying it?

"Ava, you know I would never do that. I wish to God I could have stepped in to stop it, but I couldn't. There's more at stake here than you know about and doing so could have put us both at risk." I try to explain as much as I can, but I know she will never get it. All she sees is a guy who let her down.

"I don't give a shit about your excuses, get the fuck out. NOW!" Her voice cracks as she shouts out the command. I move towards the door, trying to show her with my expressions how sorry I am. I know that hearing the words right now is not what she wants to hear, but I will say it anyway. As I open the door and step outside into the hall, I turn back to Ava. She is wiping away silent tears that are falling as though she doesn't want me to know they are there.

"I'm sorry," I say the words I need her to hear even if she doesn't want to. I speak quietly but try to push as much emotion into those two little words as I'm capable of getting.

"So am I," she whispers back before slamming the door in my face. I'm too stunned to move and that's when I hear it. My beautiful, strong Ava begins to sob. It is an ugly, hysterical cry that she has clearly been holding inside from the minute this whole thing ended. Of course, she would be the type of person that wouldn't want them to see her real pain. Then I hear what sounds like her slumping against the other side of the supposedly soundproof door before scraping down to the floor and I just know that she is sitting on the other side of this door, on the floor, alone and in pain. I cannot hold it back, and for the first time in a very long time, I feel tears coming to the surface. I've always been raised by my dad to believe that real men don't cry or show any real type of emotion. We get the job done, no matter what. But in this moment, the pain I feel at the part I played in Ava's ordeal is too much. She is the only girl I have ever really had feelings for, and no matter how hard I try to pretend they don't exist, they do. I know that some of the tears she is currently shedding are because of me and that rips my soul into pieces. I sit on the opposite side of the door, hoping that my presence can act as some kind of support. Who am I kidding? It's me who needs to be close to her. I need to hear her pain, no matter how much it kills me. I have to remember this moment, the pain it caused me when I made the wrong choice. Hopefully, this moment is all I will need to remind myself this is what will happen, or worse, if I choose this job over Ava again. Fuck, I still don't know if I could make a different decision.

The next morning, after a night of tossing and turning, I head downstairs. My body is coiled up with anxiety. A night of dreaming about Ava's haunted eyes, her hateful words and hearing her desolate sobs will do that to a guy. Knowing exactly where I need to go, I make my way through the enormous house towards the little room Grant uses for his breakfast. It's less ornate than the grand dining room, but just as pompous. It's still covered in flashy expensive artwork and big handcrafted wooden furniture. Before I go bursting in there, I stop myself and take a deep breath. I have to remember where I am and who I'm dealing with. I can't forget every piece of information I have aquired about Grant over the last two years just because I am raging over a girl. Taking a few deep breaths and controlling my features to present the serious yet fun Ryder that he has grown close to, I knock on the door.

"Enter," he bellows like he is a fucking king. God, he really is a cuntwaffle. I walk through the door and smile, waiting for him to speak first. He likes to think this is his show and right now, I need him to believe it is.

"Ryder, hello, please sit down. Would you like some coffee or breakfast?" Before he has even had a chance to finish the sentence, another house girl enters the room. They are nothing but well trained here. Initially, I wonder where Trixie is, but it's not unusual for there to be new staff wandering around. Grant isn't the easiest to work for, but he is careful. They never see or hear anything they shouldn't do. Anyone who even comes into contact with him, his business associates, or his father are subject to a rigid selection process including a less than legal deep dive background check. One of the things I pride myself on is the fact my team is good. Nobody gets within a mile of this house or Grant without my team knowing everything about them. He also has a very expensive lawyer, who, along with Vic's threats, gets them to agree to the strictest non-disclosure agreement I have ever seen. There's a reason that the Blakeman family has ruled London for four generations, five if Grant takes power. They have this town and everyone they need firmly in their pocket. But I'm not like everyone else because I'm not afraid of him, which is how I'm able to join him for breakfast and not get shot for disturbing him. He thinks I'm his friend and I intend to use that to my advantage.

"Coffee, please, and a bacon sandwich if we have some?" I ask politely to the house girl who is obediently staring at the floor.

She is clearly terrified because when she says, "of course," it comes out in a very squeaky voice and she scurries off. They aren't usually that terrified, even the newbies know what to expect. I turn to look at Grant, who is eating his full English breakfast like there was nothing remotely abnormal by her behaviour. In fact, he's so fucking pompous, I question whether he even knew she was in the same room.

"Wow, she's a bit skittish, isn't she?" I ask him and the menacing smile he returns with, chills my bones. When I first started working for Grant, he had a reputation for being a psychopath, he acts without thinking and he is all about not giving a shit about others, acting without reason or emotion. Then I got to know him and I realised that's not completely true. He does have emotions and he is capable of caring, he just *chooses* not to. He wasn't born this way, he was created. The product of years and years of abuse and poor upbringing at the hands of his father. I realise that's not an excuse, but during the time we have worked together, I have seen him lose control lots of times, yet every time he has, he's been enforcing a rule that his father taught him. Then there's times like right now when all of that sympathy for a poor broken little boy goes flying out of the window and all I'm left with is the man sitting in front of me, smiling like a maniac.

"She was slow with my morning juice. I showed her my gun and now she moves a lot faster," he says with a chuckle before he continues eating like what he just said is perfectly normal. I shake my head in disbelief.

"What have I told you about scaring the shit out of your employees? At least try and keep them for a whole week, if you can." Grant tuts at me, having heard the same speech numerous times and it falls on deaf ears, once again.

"Grant, about last night…" I start to say before he cuts me off.

"I know, what a party. It was an amazing night, wasn't it? Everyone seemed to have had a great time," Grant says, acting as though the main part of the evening didn't happen.

"Look, you are my friend and you know I respect the hell out of you, but you also know I have to speak my mind with you," I say and he nods in confirmation, placing his utensils down to give me his full attention. "Do you not think you went a bit far with Ava last night? To do that to her, in front of all of those people, just didn't seem right to me. I know you want her to agree to be your wife and to conform to being the girl your father wants her to be, but I'm just not sure this is the best way to do that. You know any one of those arseholes could have reported this back to your father and then what?" I ask and I can see him processing everything I have just said.

"Of course, I know they will tell my father. Hell, I chose a couple of them for that very reason. I've told you before, Ryder, there's a bigger plan at work here and the less you know about it, the better. My father is protective over Ava and I need to see how far he is willing to go with that. The family will collapse without a Blakeman running things and he knows it. The reason we hold our position of power is through fear and image. If someone else takes control over me, it will show weakness. Yet, he is still threatening to do just that if I marry Ava. I need to push him and I need to do it now. I have lost so much already to make my play now, but the timing has to be now, I have to see it through," he says with great determination and my brain is buzzing.

"Why the hell would the old man risk everything to protect Ava? Who is she to him?" I ask and I don't miss the flash of rage that shines across Grants features.

"She is from his past and I don't even think she knows why, but I do. What I don't know is how far he will go for her. I need to find out because she could be the key to getting everything," he says with a look of pure malice in his eyes. I knew that he hated his father, I mean who wouldn't? He was abused by him his whole life, yet he still followed him. I know he had his rebellious moments, but he still trained and has been on track to take over the business. That is what we have been working for, but now, I'm not so sure we are on the same page.

"Grant, are you trying to bring down your father so you can take over from him now, or are you trying to bring down your father's entire empire?" I inquire, since it's clear I don't have a fucking clue what he is up to anymore. That thought alone chills me to the bone. I have a plan and he is ruining it.

"Like I said, the less you know, the better. But, don't you worry. There will always be a job for you with me." He looks at me with a genuine smile like he is trying to express he is doing me a favour by granting me job security, but he isn't. I know exactly what job I joined this business to do and he is interfering with it. It's then that it dawns on me that I let Ava get hurt, I chose my job over her, all because of that dream of getting to the top. A dream that might never come true and that causes a sinking feeling in the pit of my stomach. My mind is working a mile a minute, trying to think of what to do about this, how to get things back on track, but I'm interrupted by a call from Grant's phone. The serene look on his face morphs from one of concern to anger in a flash and I'm instantly alert.

"I have to go. I may be gone for a couple of days. You stay here and make sure nothing happens to Ava. I wouldn't put it past my father to try and spring her free. I need her to be here when I get back. I will take Vic with me." Grant issues the orders as he kicks his chair back and stands from the table, his half eaten breakfast long forgotten. I'm torn because, of course, I want to stay here and keep Ava safe, but I also need to know what Grant is up to.

"What's going on? Are you sure you don't need me with you?" I ask in panic, trying to show how much I care about his sudden unrest, when really I just need information.

"I will tell you when I return. Vic is capable of looking

out for me by himself and I need you here. She has to be here when I get back, do you understand?" He glares at me as he questions me. For a split second, it's like he could see the thoughts running through my mind. I was thinking of all the different ways I could help Ava escape and hope he wouldn't realise it was me, but, of course, he would.

"She will be here, you have my word," I say through gritted teeth. He nods in affirmation before marching off through the door. Fuck, whatever is going on here is not good.

CHAPTER TWENTY-TWO
AVA

Waking up surrounded by plush, luxurious cushions and soft silky sheets, for just a moment, makes me think I am somewhere like a posh hotel. I know it's my brain's way of giving me a moments reprieve from where I actually am. I roll over and wince as my whole body aches. I feel sore all along my back and my arse feels so sensitive, I know I won't be able to sit down properly today without feeling pain. Then again, I think that was the point. Grant wanted to mark me and give me a constant reminder of what happens when I don't follow the rules. The more I move, the more throbs I feel coating my skin. It brings the whole night flashing back, but my brain isn't focusing on what I expect. Obviously, being finger fucked by a lunatic in front of a bunch of perverts is at the top of my list of most awful things that have ever happened to me, but that's not the memory

I'm thinking of. I can see the blank and vacant look on Ryder's face when he stood and watched Grant strip me, he stared at his beer bottle like it held the answers to life while that monster slapped every part of my thighs, back, and arse. Then he stood there, looked me in the eye and watched as I begged to cum on another guy's fingers like a performing whore. The whole time he just stood there, he made no effort at all to save me. Then he had the nerve last night to tell me I was safe with him, so I yelled and I kicked off, but I didn't do it because I was mad at him. I did it because he was right. Despite all of those visuals floating around my brain, showing me he had no intention of helping me, I knew I was safe. From the moment he covered me with his shirt, picked me up and held me in his big strong arms, nestled me tight against his rock hard chest, I knew the truth. He did want to keep me safe and as I snuggled up to his neck and felt the soothing touch of his body against my inflamed skin, I listened to the soothing beat of his heart and I felt safe. That's why I got angry and some of my sobs were for Ryder because I realised, despite all the good sense my brain was speaking, my heart was yelling louder. I am falling in love with Ryder and I have no idea why. That thought alone is enough for the tears to start up again and I begin to sob. I cry for the life I will never have, the dignity I can never get back, and the pain that wracks my body. But mostly, I cry for the love I want but will never have.

As soon as I begin to cry, I feel the bed dip down at the side of me and fear captures my body. I roll over quickly to see who the person in my bedroom is, silently praying it isn't the monster coming for round two because I really need a break to build my strength up again enough to fight. Rolling causes a loud gasp followed by a low moan to escape my lips, as I rolled without thinking about the pain. The nerves in my arse feel like they are flaming hot and are tingling and rippling with pain. But laying on my back gives me a better view of who is in my personal space.

"Sssh, Ava. It's ok, it's only me. I'm not here to fight, I just want to see how you are doing and if I need to get you any kind of medical attention. Grant has gone away for a couple of days and has left you here to heal, with me to help you. Please, just let me check you over," Ryder whispers so softly into my ear, shivers run down my back from the feel of his breath hitting my face. Despite how mad and disappointed I am with him over last night, I can't deny that my body reacts to his. Looking into his beautiful green eyes, they look like sparkling emeralds as they shine bright looking at me. He is looking at me in the same way he always does, with passion and lust in his eyes, but this confuses me. How can he look at me the same when nothing is the same? Not only is my skin covered in marks from the torturous abuse he stood by and watched be inflicted on me, but I am also wrapped in a layer of shame. I feel disgusting and like every one of my nerves prickle and remind me of what I lowered myself to, the things I said and the noises I made. Rationally, I know I had no control, but that doesn't stop the sickening feeling I have right now. I don't understand why Ryder isn't looking and seeing the disgusting whore from last night, because that's who I feel that I am. I want to argue with him, to tell him to leave me alone, to tell him he is too late to look after me because he should have done that yesterday instead. But, I am in pain and I need someone to check and make sure I'm not as broken as I feel.

Ryder stands and I hate how much his absence affects me, I feel like a piece of myself is missing, but luckily, he returns quickly. I released the breath I didn't even realise I was holding. I lay on my side slightly, trying to face him whilst also allowing him to be able to see my skin once it is exposed. His eyes never leave mine and there is a serene calm in his glistening green orbs that helps me find peace. Slowly, he unbuttons the shirt of his I am still wearing from last night. I hate to admit how much comfort I felt being draped in his scent. As he peels the bed sheets and the shirt away, leaving me completely naked, his gaze remains on my eyes. I can see he is tempted to look. The fire he felt during the night we shared is still very much alive, but he also knows that right now, it's the last thing I need. He gives me his cheeky crooked smile and although it doesn't quite meet his eyes and isn't as big as normal, it still causes my heart to flutter and my lips to raise into my own smile.

"Can I look?" he asks with a deep husky voice that causes my thighs to clench. I know he is asking to look at my wounds, but fuck, did he make that sound dirty. Then it hits me that the me before last night would have replied with some feisty comment like 'I will show you mine, if you show me yours', but that's not what happens. Instead, I'm overwhelmed by shame that he's going to look at my body and see reminders of what happened that night, of the slut Grant turned me into. This just confirms it because yesterday, I was begging to cum in front of a room full of people and today, I'm exposing myself and thinking of mounting someone else. But it's not someone else, it's Ryder. My Ryder. My brain feels like it might explode from the confusion. I need to get this over with so I can get some clothes on and try to get back to normal. So, I nod my consent.

Ryder leans over to look at my back and I hear him gasp. The hand I hadn't even realised was laced with my own suddenly tightens, almost to the point of pain and it's obvious Ryder is furious. He begins running his finger over the most tender areas and from the way they feel, I'm sure it's only bruised, nothing that will leave a permanent reminder. I will have enough of those in my head. He trails his fingers all across my back, my lower thighs, and my arse. He is very careful not to go anywhere too inappropriate and I'm glad because there's always going to be a part of me that wants that from Ryder, who craves it, but now is not the time. The electric sensation I feel as the warmth of his fingertips trail over my skin begins to feel soothing and soon the sting from the bruise is eradicated and all I feel is Ryder. I don't know how long he does it for, but my body hums in a gentle appreciation. He has brought a calmness over my body that I didn't think was possible in this state. The more he continues his beautiful trail, the more it reminds me of the first night his fingers touched mine and the jolts of passion that spread through them, as memories of that night enter my mind, I'm so grateful for the relief from the haunting visions of the night before, that I let out a small content moan.

Ryder's fingers freeze and he pulls back away from me. Before I even know what's happening he stands up, doesn't even look at me before saying, "I'm going to run you a nice relaxing bath. I will add some aromatherapy oils and things that should help with the aches and the stings. Nothing there is permanent, just some bruises. Some have already started to fade but others are more… severe."

Before I even have a chance to thank him or say anything, he walks off into the ensuite and I hear the bath beginning to fill. He walks out several minutes later and motions for me to follow him in. The bathroom is still one of my favourite places in this whole house. The bath is giant and has a jacuzzi function, which I can't wait to try. Right now, the bath is filled with an array of different colours, presumably from different bath bombs. There are bubbles all over and a beautiful floral scent, but it is the lavender that draws me in. At the back of the tub, on the ledge, Ryder has lit some scented candles and despite there being several different scents flying around, they all seem to compliment each other. They are so inviting and I completely forget Ryder is standing in the doorway, waiting for me to say something, I have to get in this bath. So, I move as quickly as my sore body will allow and drop the shirt I was holding closed and quickly climb into the gorgeous, hot water. As I submerge under the bubbles, I feel amazing and can feel the small bath salts evaporating around my body. The smells ensnare my senses and I relax further into the bath, letting out a deep moan of appreciation for the way the water feels against my sore, broken body. It's not just me who feels as though I have released a breath I have been holding, it feels like my skin breaths too. Wow, Ryder can really draw up a bath, I think to myself. In fact, he is going to be in charge of getting all my baths ready for all eternity, my body replies happily. That's when the reality side of my brain kicks in and I look over at the real Ryder, the one who can't run my baths forever because he chose his work over me.

His gaze is one of pure fire and although he tries to hide it with the mask of indifference that he has perfected so perfectly, I saw the truth. And he may be able to hide the desire in his eyes, but no matter how much he shuffles around, the bulge in his jeans is more than obvious. He sees where my eyes are and turns to leave.

"I'm gonna leave you to soak out your muscles. I will be back soon with breakfast. There's a towel on the counter and I left out some shorts and a t-shirt of mine if you want to wear them. You don't have to, I know you have your own clothes, but before..." he stumbles, unsure of how to finish.

"Thank you," I reply simply. It's the only answer I have at the moment because I don't know what I want to do.

I soak there in the bath for what feels like ages. My skin begins to look wrinkled, the bubbles have all evaporated, and the water is turning chilly. So, I know that it's time to get out. After wrapping myself in the fluffy towel Ryder left out, I stare at the clothes he brought me. I know he was trying to say that after what happened, I might not want to wear his clothes and he would be right. But my only other option is the clothes that arsehole Grant picked out for me, so I go with the lesser of two evils and put on Ryder's clothes. This is the argument I tell myself, but as I pull the clothes on and feel my body being enveloped by every scent that is Ryder's, my heart skips a beat, telling me that maybe there's another reason I chose his clothes.

Trying to put all of my confusing thoughts about Ryder out of my head, I walk back into the bedroom after brushing my teeth and hair. I wouldn't say I feel back together, but at least I look presentable. All plans of not thinking about Ryder go out of the window when I walk back into the bedroom to see him lying on his back on the bed. His arms are folded behind his head, acting as a cushion and that act has caused his t-shirt to ride up, exposing a small patch of skin. It just so happens to be my favourite patch, as it contains the gorgeous V shaped muscles and that little happy trail of hair, which leads to something amazing. The rest of him is all tight, lean muscles and just general perfection. No matter how hard I try, I can't deny I'm so fucking attracted to this man, it's unreal. But that's never been the problem. The problem is that the man inside the very pretty package is a fucking enigma. The man I met and shared a beautiful night with was fierce, caring, and protective. I got the feeling that although he didn't trust or care for people easily, if he did, then he would burn the world for them. Then there's the Ryder I see when he is with Grant. The cold, merciless, obedient, little lap dog who follows Grant's orders and seems perfectly content in his job. I just don't understand why this job means so much to him. The guy I spent the night with doesn't belong working for a crime family, so why is he?

My thoughts are broken when Ryder abruptly sits up on the bed. He looks at me with a small smile when he sees I'm drowning in his t-shirt and I have had to tie a knot in his shorts just to get them to stay up. There's a moment of awkward silence as we both stare at each other before Ryder breaks it by pointing to the vast array of foods that are on the table. There are fruits, cereals, pancakes, toast, even some fried food, like sausages and bacon. There is so much food, no way will we both be able to eat all of these. As I think that, my belly starts to rumble and I let out a small giggle. Obviously, I am hungry.

"Shall we eat?" Ryder says and I nod in confirmation as we both take our seats at the table. We eat in comfortable silence, not feeling the need to say anything. I expected our silence to be weird and awkward like earlier, but it's not and rather than dwelling on that, I tuck into some more food. Just as I am getting ready to demolish my third pancake with bacon and sausage, not to mention all the other bits I have picked at, Ryder finally speaks.

"I love a girl with a hearty appetite and you look like you are definitely enjoying the food. I'm glad to see it hasn't put you off your food." I can tell he is nervous breaking the silence and that as he is speaking, it finally dawns on him what he actually said.

"What, so normally after a girl is abused they don't like to eat? It's good to know that me eating is an obvious sign that what that bastard did to me last night didn't really bother me," I spit back in disgust and see his face fall.

"Ava, look, I erm... I want to say that I'm-"

"No, Ryder, don't. I don't want to hear it. There is nothing you can say, no apology you can give that can erase last night. Out of everything that happened, the thing that hurt me the most was you. You just stood there and let it happen. You looked into my eyes and did nothing as I fell apart. Grant may have been the one who abused me, but you are the one who hurt me. Why didn't you help me? Why didn't you save me?" I cry out to Ryder, desperate for the answers that have plagued me. I feel my eyes begin to fill with tears, but I push them back. I can't show weakness during this. I need the truth.

"Ava, I'm so sorry. You know I had no choice, if I would have stepped in and stopped things, Grant would have known about us and we would have been in great danger. I have been covering our tracks with the security cameras to protect us. Plus, this is my job and I cannot afford to lose it. I have a goal that I am so close to reaching and I can't jeopardise that. It's important. But you have to know that every second I was inside that room, it felt like my skin was crawling. I felt like a ball of pent up energy and I was desperate to release it and to help you, but I couldn't. So, I stood there, trying not to listen to the sounds of your pain."

"So, you chose your job and then for good measure, you looked into my eyes as I begged for that monster to make me cum. Wow, you are not the man I thought you were at all. The man I spent the night with was kind and beautiful, I had more feelings for him than I should have after just one night, but I felt like I was drawn to him. My body called to him and I thought he answered. I had visions of him saving me and us going off to a better life, finding out if the feelings actually mean anything. If away from this bullshit, did we actually stand a chance at a life together? But then I realised, he didn't exist because you were selfish and spineless, caring only about you and your career." I don't know why I am telling him all this, why I am confessing the feeling I had, well I do still have some of them, but he doesn't need to know that. They will go away soon enough, hopefully. I can see my words have affected him because his shoulders are sagged and his face appears cracked, he looks so sad. He even seems like his eyes are misting over and he is trying to hold them back.

"You have feelings for me?" he whispers. Out of everything I said, I should have known that would be the part he caught.

"Had, dickead. You ruined it. You give me whiplash, it's like there's two of you and one I hate. I can't cope. Please, just go." My voice breaks at the end because throwing Ryder out doesn't feel like the right thing to do, but being near him right now doesn't either. All it does is remind me I don't know who he is. His eyes are downcast and I can see he looks broken, but I don't know what else to do. He gives me a half smile and turns to leave. Before he reaches the door, without turning to look at me, I hear him speak faintly.

"I wish I could make you understand. I really like you, Ava, and I'm sorry." His words gut me as the door to the room closes behind him, I suddenly feel very empty.

I SPEND THE DAY LOUNGING AROUND IN THE ROOM I REFUSE TO think of as mine. I don't bother venturing out because I know it leads to Ryder's room before I can get anywhere else and I can't face that. So, I alternate between sleeping, showering to try and feel less sleazy, and relaxing in the jacuzzi bath as that really helps with my tense muscles. There's barely any visible marks on my back or arse that indicate last night even happened, but there is no explaining away the giant black eye or the split lip. Those will fade with time. It's not the physical wounds I worry about, it's the mental ones. The hatred, and if I'm being honest, the fear I feel for Grant has gone through the roof. I am constantly on edge, waiting for him to come back and start an argument with me so he can punish me because that's exactly how it feels. For some reason, he doesn't just inflict pain in a cruel way, he has to have some justification, which for a supposed psychopath, I find very bizarre. I also think he is a lot more clever than anyone has ever given him credit for because he has a plan for me and nobody seems to know what that is; not his expert risk analysis manager who should be able to see every possible scenario, or his crime boss father who says Grant isn't capable of organising a piss-up in a brewery, yet here we are. He was able to bring me here, he planned it all and not only did nobody know what he was doing, nobody knows why he is doing it. So, to me, that makes him really fucking dangerous.

I feel on edge all day, waiting to get summoned to another meeting with Grant but it doesn't happen. I know Ryder said he was gone, but I thought that was too good to be true. The more time that passes does nothing but worsen my frying nerves. So, when there is a knock on the door, I yelp out a terrified sounding hello, making it obvious who I thought was at the door and that I was scared.

"It's me, Ryder. I just came to reassure you he won't be back tonight. I thought you would wanna know. Also, I'm having some beer and pizza in the movie room next door. You are welcome to come and join me," he asks hopefully. How could he know how on edge I am about Grant and that just hearing he is gone for the night could relax me enough to get some semblance of sleep? I want to throw my arms around him in thanks, but instead, I sit there, not quite knowing what to do.

After a while, I hear Ryder stalk off to the cinema room

next door, his personal space. He told me the other night about how he has pretty much stolen it from Grant and everyone knows it's his sanctuary. It's where he comes to unwind and now he has opened up to let me in too. It takes me a good half an hour before I get up to go. If anyone asks, it is the draw of delicious pizza that pulls me, not the delicious man.

I walk into the giant cinema style living room and I'm in awe. The screen looks exactly like in a cinema, but there's two and three seater sofas thrown in amongst the arms chairs. Ryder is relaxing on one of the large sofas with a giant pizza box in the middle. He is chowing down on the pizza without even looking at it because his eyes are firmly glued to the screen in front of him. When it dawns on me what movie he's watching, I can't help but smile. The idea that this tough, gorgeous man is engrossed in a film like 10 Things I Hate About You, is absolutely hilarious and so endearing. But it's the laughing that wins out and my chuckles from the doorway give away my position. The look he gives me sends ripples down to my core. He always manages to look at me with sheer heat.

"What are you laughing at, little vixen?" he asks with an eyebrow raised in challenge.

"A chick flick? Really?" I ask in mock exaggeration and he just laughs.

"Now you know my secret. I have an obsessive love of chick flicks and this is one of the best." He speaks with such a straight face, I can't tell if he is lying or not. I can't help the full smile that spreads across my face, reaching my eyes.

"Really?"

"Hell yes. Guys can like chick flicks too. Now sit down and eat some pizza or you will miss all the good bits." I laugh, but I do as I'm told, feeling as though I am walking into an alternative reality. I tell myself I chose to sit on the same sofa as Ryder because it was closest to the pizza. Honestly. That's when I first get a look at him. He is wearing relaxed, baggy grey sweatpants and a tight black t-shirt that shows off every bit of definition. His relaxed position has caused the shirt to ride up, exposing his curved hips and the defined V shape that leads to heaven. Sitting there, he looks like he belongs in a male fitness model shoot and he looks good enough to eat. Forget the fucking pizza, I want him, but we can't. That thought hits me like a tonne of bricks, bringing me back to this moment. I decide not to focus on the bad side of things just for one night and instead, I lounge around with Ryder, eating junk food, talking crap, and watching his favourite chick flicks. It's the perfect night and that's the excuse I give for why I allow myself to fall asleep, curled up with my head on Ryder's lap and his arm tucked securely around my body.

Some time later, I feel my weightless body being lifted and carried, I know by the scent and protectiveness I feel surrounding me, it's still Ryder. He is carrying me to bed and I really hope it's his, but when I open my eyes slightly and recognise the familiar decor, I know we are in my room. He puts me in the bed and tucks me in tightly, it's such a sweet gesture and so like Ryder from the other night. A tired smile creeps across my lips. "Stay with me, Ryder, please," I say, as I tuck up further into the covers trying to get comfortable. He doesn't respond initially and I listen intently for sounds that he is moving to get into his side of the bed, but none come. Instead, I feel a featherlight kiss on my forehead. There's nothing sexy about it, but the heat from that light touch explodes all over my body, heating me up.

"I'm sorry," Ryder whispers into my ear. Even in my exhausted state, I know what that means. He is saying no to me again and it hurts.

"You are always saying that to me." I don't wait for him to answer, instead I fall back into the most blissful, undisturbed, and peaceful sleep I've had in a long time.

CHAPTER TWENTY-THREE
GRANT

Walking into the same old familiar shit hole makes my stomach crawl. I'm parked in a part of town where I'm pretty sure, if it wasn't for the fact I left Vic out there with his gun, we would come back to find our car missing, or at best, just the tires. This is one of the worst areas in the city and as I walk up to the fifteenth floor of the high rise, because the lift is fucking broke again, I feel that tell tale shiver of disgust.

The further up I go, the more depravity I discover. I pass a whore blowing a John in the corridor while her pimp looks on, I pass needles on the floor that hold God knows how many diseases, and I pass children as young as ten smoking and swearing, pretending like they are gangsters. Even though this area is gang territory and belongs to the 49er's, I know they are only pretending and aren't really a part of the gang. I'm not worried about being seen in gang territory because the Blakeman family are not a gang, we do not need to squabble over territories because it is all ours. Every area the gangs fight over belongs to us. Every drug they sell in their territory was bought from us. Every gun they shoot and every hooker they sell, they all came from us. That's how I know the children are pretending to be gangsters. We have a no under the age of fourteen rule and everyone sticks to it. We all know that living in this area doesn't give them many life options and the gang life is where they will end up, but at least our way gives them a chance. I expect no trouble while I'm here, but it's always best to be prepared.

Walking down the corridor to what in any other building would be considered a penthouse suite, makes me laugh because there's no way that term could be applied here. It is simply a shining star placed on top of a steaming pile of shit, no matter how you dress it up, it's still shit. Everytime I walk down this corridor and shiver at all the possible diseases I could be catching by just being here, I wish that Eli would take me up on my offer to buy him a new place, but he always declines.

Eli Sanders is a twenty-three year old tech genius and he works for me as a hacker. He doesn't work for the family, he works directly for me, and I hope to fuck that Father knows nothing about Eli, because his life is safer that way. Eli is the best investment I have ever made. I bailed the kid out of a pretty serious situation a few years back that would have seen him do a considerable amount of jail time. In exchange for me getting the charges on Eli dropped, he agreed to work for me. He probably worked off his debt a long time ago, but he keeps on working for me. To be honest, I would be lost without him and he knows it. The kid is a walking contradiction. To look at him, at first with his typical sweet, boyish good looks, floppy brown hair and glasses he looks like your standard geek, but underestimating Eli Sanders is the first mistake people make, and their last. Beneath his clothing, he is covered in tattoos, most that he has drawn himself, he is also covered in scars from being in more fights than I'm sure even I know about and he's a cocky son of a bitch. But I don't have him out in the field, he's too valuable to me, and I can't risk my father finding out about him. Obviously, he has his own hackers, but they are nowhere near Eli's level.

As I approach the door at the end of the corridor, I begin to notice the tell tale signs that someone not to be messed with lives here. This floor is the quietest of all that I have walked through, there's no drugs or whores and I don't feel like my shoes are sticking to the floor. As I approach the white wooden door at the end, I see the security camera above. Looking up to it and giving my best smug grin that I know pisses Eli off, I hear the clicking that tells me the bolts on the door are now unlocked. This may look like your ordinary run down flat, but with the security system that Eli and Ryder setup here, it's harder to break into than Fort Knox. I don't wait for him to open the door because he never does, instead, I let myself in.

Eli lives in a bright, airy open plan apartment that was

probably three of the shit ones below but knocked through to make one large flat. This place looks like an expensive bachelor pad that you would find in the more upscale parts of London, but Eli insisted on building his here. All I know is that he used to live in this building with his mother before she died and his life went to shit. Growing up with an abusive father is something we have in common, and just like me, Eli never talks about his childhood, so I don't ask.

Walking into a room off the bright white and airy living room, it's obvious that, just like Eli, this room could not be more different. It is dark, windowless, and filled with technology. There are computers and screens all over the place, I don't even pretend to know what all the stuff is or what he does with them. All I care about is that he produces results.

"All right, Boss." Eli swings around on his chair and flashes me his cocky lopsided smirk that, according to him, is a big hit with the ladies. He's lounged back in his leather desk chair and he looks so relaxed, like all the equipment is an extension of him. His dark, low slung jeans and tight white t-shirt that shows off not only his tattoos, but also the hard muscles underneath are not exactly the normal clothes I would choose for one of my employees, but he doesn't listen.

"Eli, for God's sake, sit up straight. You look like trash." He chuckles at my comment but makes no effort to do as I instructed. I grip my hands together and grind my teeth. This boy is infuriating, but he is also irreplaceable and the cocky twat knows it.

"I need an update, Eli. Things are taking too long and I need to make my move soon. What do you have?" I take a seat in one of the other desk chairs that are in the room and focus my intense gaze on the guy sitting in front of me. He's only a couple of years younger than me, but we couldn't look more different.

"I have a lot of the information we need about your father's operation, but nowhere near enough. I have managed to trace some of the money exchanges and the contacts here in the UK, based on the people you have already dealt with, but the major issue is the importing. So far, it is impossible to tell how the old man is importing anything, who he is using, or how he is moving the money. What we need is an in, like with the girls. When you went to that auction, I was able to use facial recognition to track down a couple of Alan's overseas contacts and that helped me work out who he uses to import the girls. I have a programme running currently that is trying to expose the money trail. What I need is the same insight. When will you be going to the next stage meetup?" Eli asks and I try to hold back the groan. I had hoped he would be able to expose my father's business dealings without me needing to be exposed to them.

"So, we have a problem with that. My father has said that I will not be involved in his business dealings unless I agree to call off my marriage. Stubborn old fool knows he needs me as the face of the business, but he has to fight for control in some way," I explain to Eli and I watch as his eyes widen and he runs his fingers through his floppy hair, the frustration clear.

"What the fuck? You are marrying Katyia?" he asks in a stunned voice that sounds strained like he is holding back.

"Erm... no. I'm marrying Ava Delgado and my father is not happy about it. He doesn't want me to marry her and so in retaliation, he is making me choose between her and the company," I explain.

"So why the fuck would you not choose the company? We have been working for years to bring down this fucking organisation and now your throwing it all away for a bit of pussy?" he snaps. I grind my teeth and take deep breaths as I try to get a hold on my anger. Him and Ryder are the only people that get away with talking to me like this and if I'm being honest, I like that they challenge me. I like that they aren't afraid of saying what they think around me. But, obviously, because Eli has no idea about my plans, he doesn't have a clue what's going on and so I think it's time to share my plans with someone.

"Of course, I want to bring down the company," I explain to Eli but before I have a chance to continue, he stops me and starts talking to himself.

"Wait a minute. Ava Delgado, I knew I had heard that name before. She is the chick who I practically online stalked for months, her and her father. You got him set up by the 49er's, they agreed to a bet that you authorised but knew he couldn't pay for and they said they were going to kill him. She's the one who is under the protection of your father, isn't she?" he rants while running his fingers through his hair again. Before I can answer, he begins tapping away at the keyboard in front of him, and the next thing I know, he is pointing to a picture of Ava on his computer screen. I nod in confirmation and he growls in frustration.

"What the fuck, boss? What are you doing? I thought we had a plan!" He shouts.

"We did... I mean, we still do. But we both know that she is his weakness and if I'm going to bring down his company, then I need to have him at his weakest. I thought that when he found out I was marrying her, he would do whatever it took to stop me, and he is, but I also know he is trying not to let on how much Ava means to him. She has no fucking idea he is even part of her life, I don't think. As far as she is concerned, he has bailed Manny out a few times and that's it," I reply, trying to calm Eli down as much as possible.

"So, what you are saying is that your spontanous plan you have undertaken without discussing with me, was intended to weaken your father in an attempt to make it easier to fulfil our ultimate goal of taking down his enterprise and surprisingly, it has fucking backfired? What the hell were you thinking? He has hidden his past with this girl for her entire life, did you really think that he was going to just fold once you used her as leverage?" As he finishes, he gives an evil laugh and is looking at me like he can't believe how stupid I am, and for the first time in far too long, a blush spreads across my cheeks and embarrassment causes my stomach to flip nervously. But I don't have to worry about Eli because he is back to typing on his many computers and when he is in this mood, it's best not to disturb him.

A short while later, probably not even five minutes has passed, I'm getting ready to look at my phone for a distraction, but before I'm able to, I hear Eli start to groan and he's back to running his fingers through his hair in his usual nervous mannerism. However, this time he doesn't look like he is nervous, now he looks furious.

"Please, tell me you didn't spank and finger fuck this girl in your office in front of a group of dickheads that you call followers?" he asks, sounding exacerbated. I may sound like I'm shocked, but I knew those idiots wouldn't keep their mouths shut. In fact, I counted on that.

"How the fuck did you find that out? They were all told to keep quiet." His response is a dark chuckle and it grates at my skin. My instinct is to lash out at his utter disrespect, but I need him and there's a part of me that knows deep down, I need his honesty too.

"You're seriously asking me how I found it? I hacked their phone records, of course. You have two men in particular who are very chatty about it with other members of their little group. Typically, it's two of your rich CEO buddies who probably think they are exempt from any of your little instructions. I also believe that one of them has employed a hacker to try and get the footage from the security cameras in your office, which is fucking laughable. As if anyone could hack a system I created. But, you think you have control over these dicks and you don't. Within the last hour or so, word of this encounter reached your father. He has gone radio silent and now I have no idea what he is thinking, but if this girl means as much to him as we think, then he is going to move against you. He could throw you out of the company and we could lose everything, you dumb prick. All because you wanted to wind him up about Ava. Fuck!" he shouts before standing up and pacing around the tiny room and I have to admit that my brain is working a mile a minute right now. He is right that when I went down this route to get revenge against Father using Ava, I did throw all my plans to bring his company down out of the window. But this became so much more because it's personal. The moment I found out about the existence of Ava and her link to Father, I was fuming. I needed to know why he would care for an unknown, poor little girl from the wrong side of the tracks more than he does his own son and heir. So, I started digging and it consumed me. I have to admit that initially, I expected to find that she is my illegitimate sister, but computer records and an illegally performed DNA test confirm that she has, in fact, no relation to either of us, which is why I decided to use this plan to find out just how much she means to him.

My whole life it has been carved into me that a Blakeman must run the family business, without having our face and notoriety at the center, there would be potential for the whole enterprise to crumble. So, when I found out about Ava, I realised there have been times when he has made himself look weak to his opponents by paying off Manny's debts, all for Ava.

I wanted to know what makes her more important than the rules that he has quite literally beat into me from an early age, which is how this plan came about. If he wants me to rule the Blakeman family, then he has to let me marry Ava, or I walk away. Of course, he knows I don't actually want to marry Ava. Sure, she is gorgeous but the very sight of her is a constant reminder of how much he cares for her. This is when my plan changed and I decided I needed to really test how much my father cares. I am going to slowly break Ava until she is a shadow of the girl he likes so much, and I will mould her into the perfect wife if I have to be married to her, but really, I'm just trying to work out how far I have to push him. How much do I have to break Ava before my father breaks and gives me what I want? Hopefully, it doesn't take too long because I am on a very tight deadline with a very sensitive anniversary approaching. Hope that I will have vengeance for them drives me forward.

So in this little room with Eli, I play the part and pretend to be outraged that those two men would share the information after being threatened. But, I knew when I invited them into the room, they were secretly working with Father. Ryder is fucking good at his job. So, I let them in and made sure they got an encrypted copy of the security footage. Using a programme Eli had shown me how to work for a previous task, I made sure the video would only open on a phone attached to those two idiots and my father. So the video of Ava cannot be shared with anyone except my father, and it did not take them long to get it back to him. What I need to know now is what he plans to do about it. So, I tell Eli what he needs to know and set him up some more tasks before I head out.

Before I even know what I'm doing, I find myself outside Katyia's apartment. I know that I can't go in there, not with the way we left things. But it's more than that. I know that Katyia would hate this plan, the way I'm using Ava. The idea that I would use a woman and break her spirit for the sole purpose of exposing my father and manipulating him to get my revenge, that would appall her. As far as my beautiful Katyia is concerned, there is nothing more disgusting than men who abuse women and I know she is right, but I feel like I have this tunnel vision. It's like nothing matters except bringing down Father. I had a way of doing it and a plan, it was a long game but I was committed and I knew it would work. Then Eli discovered Ava and I became obsessed. The little boy in me that Katyia slowly brought back to life is crying out to know what it is about this particular girl that he can care about when he is incapable of showing that same feeling to his son. I know that it was jealousy and envy that were initially driving my plans, until I discovered the reason behind his behaviour. Jealousy was replaced by hatred and anger. I know the only logical source of these emotions is my father, but every time I see Ava, I see my father's betrayal and my skin glows hot with the need for revenge.

Katyia would tell me that there are other ways to do this. That Ava is innocent and probably has no idea Alan Blakeman even knows her family, let alone their sordid past. But I don't care. I need to get revenge and not just for myself. My mother deserves to have her revenge too. Her anniversary is fast approaching and she needs closure.

As I'm looking into the apartment window, I see Katyia look out, like she senses I'm here and just catching sight of her silhouette, hitches my breath. She truly is beautiful and that is why I won't be near her whilst I'm going through with this plan. She deserves better. Maybe when all is said and done, I will go back and seek forgiveness, but who knows the person I will become after going down this road. For now, my beautiful Katyia is lost to me. I just hope that it is not forever.

I spend a week in a hotel, just lazing around and generally escaping from the world. I indulge in massages, room service, and lots of alcohol. My phone is on, but on silent and I completely ignore it. I check in regularly with Ryder, who is taking care of Ava. Man, was he pissed about the office incident! But I've always said that Ryder is the better side of my conscience and he would never have let me go through with the plan if he had known in advance, but he would never challenge me in front of people. He knows better than that. Truth is, I never intended on taking it that far at all. I was just going to strip her to her underwear in front of everyone to humiliate her, but the problem is that she really knows exactly how to fucking push my buttons. Ryder says she is fine physically, but may need some time mentally and he advised some space while she recovers. I know he is right and I did push Ava too far, I let my anger get on top of me, but just looking at her sets off my rage, so when she then starts with that fucking mouth of hers, I have no chance of staying calm.

Ava isn't the only reason I'm staying away. As soon as word reached my father, he demanded an audience with me the next day. That's when I decided to push him. I checked into the hotel under both my name and Ava's. I paid the staff to tell anyone who enquires that there is a man and a woman matching Ava's description staying in the room. I know that he cannot get close to the real Ava with Ryder guarding her. The longer I do not message him back and he thinks that I am holed up in a room with Ava, doing God knows what to her, the crazier it will be driving him. He stopped attempting to make contact over twenty-four hours ago and all my staff have been put on alert in case he tries anything. But rather than waiting for him to act, I decide to keep him on his toes even further and make the first move. I turn my phone on and dial the one number that always sets my nerves on edge.

"Where the fuck have you been, you little shit?" my father screeches down the phone at me after just two rings. I have to hold back the little giggle that is threatening to ripple out.

"Me and my fiancé decided we needed some special time together. So, we checked into a lovely spa and have been having a great time. Word just reached me that you have been trying to get in touch." My reply is full of fake courtesy and respect. I sound like I am playing dumb and trying to kiss his arse to anyone who knows me, but that is exactly why Alan Blakeman has no idea I am lying to him, because he doesn't know me.

"Bullshit. When I call, you answer. You don't get to take fucking personal days. I have important things I need to discuss with you. Both you and Ava will report here for breakfast tomorrow morning. Is that clear?" I can hear the venom in his voice as he speaks.

"Father, if it's me that you need to speak to, why do I need to drag Ava away from this beautiful spa? We are booked for longer and she really doesn't need to be there to talk business. Besides, I thought you didn't want me to be part of the business any more." I know I'm winding him up right now, but he gives away more clues than he intends to when he's annoyed.

"You are still part of this family, even if you have chosen some pussy over your birthright. I still expect you to report to me when I ask you to. As for Ava, I have heard some quite disgusting stories about how she is being treated and quite frankly, I want to see with my own two eyes that she is well." I feel like whooping in celebration because this is a massive slip up for him. Not only has he exposed he has a mole in my team, he has also shown his true colours for how he feels about Ava. Now, I just need to pull more out of him.

"Who exactly have you been hearing these stories from?

BROKEN

We both know the story you are referring to was a very private event and I would like to know who felt the need to betray my trust. And as for Ava, what do you care? She is my fiancé and I can do as I please. So why would it matter to you what goes on in my relationship with Ava? You have taught me everything I know about how to be in control in the relationship." I spit out the last point because he most definitely did spend years teaching me that I should always have dominance over the women in my life. That I should show them who's boss and break them to make them the perfect obedient partner. So, all I'm doing with Ava is exactly what he taught me. What is really pathetic is that for years, I thought this was all true. I thought it was my responsibility to let the woman know that I'm in charge and she is less than me. So, I used women for sex and threw them away, not letting anyone get close because none of them deserved it. They talked back, they got put in their place. Then I met Katyia and she told me that is how men have treated her throughout her whole life. She has always felt like a second class citizen, if she felt like one at all. Hearing her say this broke a wall in me my father had spent years carefully constructing. The idea that any man would dominate, abuse, or belittle this gorgeous, fragile angel is a fucking mystery. There's no way she is a second class citizen, she's so far out of all our leagues, it's unreal. She helped me see the way my father had raised me to feel is wrong and with her help, I started to heal.

But right now, I need my father to believe I'm just doing

what he taught me was right. He has to believe it's real. Given the growl at the end of the phone as I speak, he knows that he will struggle to argue back, given that he is arguing his own teachings, but this is my father and I know he will find a way.

"Don't bring up irrelevant shit from the past. You will be here at nine in the morning and you will have Ava." With that, he instantly hangs up, allowing no room for argument. I can't help but laugh because this reckless behaviour is exactly what I want to see from him. I need him off his game.

I call Ryder to update him and inform him to have Ava ready tomorrow morning. I haven't given any instructions regarding clothing, but I know that she won't let me down. I need her to keep pushing me because that's what triggers my rage and I feel the overwhelming desire to make her pay and punish her.

CHAPTER TWENTY-FOUR
GRANT

I get back to the house early to make sure Ava and Ryder are ready to go on time. I just have visions of her arguing and making us late. Whilst you would think the idea of pissing my father off and keeping him waiting would be amusing to me, it is so ingrained in me that I am required to show up on time when he calls, that I can't even imagine anything else. I still have the scars from other times I have challenged him on this issue.

When I arrive at the house, I ping Ryder a text, telling him to get Ava's arse downstairs. She will be more amenable for him, he is the nice guy after all. It's not long before Ryder is walking down the curved wooden staircase, dressed in his typical black suit with black tie. My father believes that if you want to be a success, you need to dress like it and for Ryder, he says that everyone should know his roll in security, but I know that he fucking hates dressing in the suit, which is why his top button is undone. The perfectionist side of me is desperate to button it up, but I lost that battle a long time ago. My eyes are not on Ryder long before the beauty behind him with the jet back hair begins her descent. She could not look more different from the clothes she usually chooses. She's wearing a cream pencil skirt that falls just below the knee and clings to all of her curves. Matching that is a cream tweed suit jacket with three quarter length sleeves that sits elegantly over a pale, dusty pink t-shirt. Ava has no skin on display and looks like your typical rich society housewife, exactly what I told her that I wanted, but there is no denying that the edge that makes her Ava is still there. I could dress her in a paper bag and you would still be able to see her sexy body and curves, but it's her attitude that gives her away. Her hair is worn loose in curls and the jet black colour shines in the sunlight, like a beacon that she was instructed to wear her hair up and didn't. Normally, she does not wear much make-up I have noticed, but that just won't do around my father and whatever whore he brings to breakfast, which is why I instructed her to wear make-up, but not much and nude tones. So, the bright red colour she's wearing that makes her lips look plump and like they are sending a personal invitation out to any nearby cocks, is definitely breaking the rules. Given the little glint in her eye and the small cocky smirk, she has had time to forget about the rules she was taught at her last encounter and that makes me sneer at her as I watch her travel down the staircase. Seeing the look on my face has her momentarily stalling, I guess she hasn't completely forgotten the lesson.

She makes it to the last step and Ryder holds out a hand to help her down, even though these disgusting pink pump heels are the lowest I have seen her wearing yet. Like I said, he's the gentleman here, not me. She takes his hand somewhat reluctantly, almost as though she isn't sure if she is allowed to touch him or if he is allowed to help her. I'm glad she has a healthy suspicion of Ryder. I want her to feel comfortable enough with him that she lets him look after her when I'm gone, but I need her to remember Ryder works for me. The sweet little smile she gives him in thanks does not go unnoticed. Apparently, my fiancé is still attracted to my security manager, but his steel face remains unchanged, like he hasn't even noticed she was looking at him. His eyes are too busy focused on the job, exactly where they should be. Fuck, it never occured to me until now that Ava and Ryder spending so much time together could, potentially, be problematic. I mean, I'm not blind, they are both ridiculously good looking people, but in the two years I've known Ryder, I haven't seen him with a woman. He has always been all focused on the work and his career, which is what I have loved about him. He is always there and never let's me down, which is why I never saw a problem between him and Ava. Ryder is probably the most professional member of staff that I have. So what if she has a crush on him? He will never let it effect his ability to do his job and thank fuck for that, because I would be seriously lost without him.

The drive over to the Blakeman residence is filled with awkward silence and tension. I talk to Ryder and Vic, who both sit in the front seats, about some up and coming work that we have. Ava just sits there, staring at the window, not saying a word. This is exactly how I need her to behave, but it's infuriating me because I can feel that it's all an act, one that I don't need her to let slip at the big house.

"I expect you will be able to remember how to behave appropriately when we get to my fathers?" I ask Ava and her back straightens at the fact I'm talking to her.

"Of course. I would never forget how to be your good little wife." Her tone to anyone else would sound serious, but I can hear the mocking behind it.

"Should my father question you about our engagement party the other night, how will you respond?" This is not the first time we have rehearsed this question and every time her shoulders tense and her jaw tightens. She looks physically uncomfortable about the reminder of what happened and that brings a little smirk to my face.

"I had a lovely night. It was so nice to meet so many new people. I hope I made a good impression with them." As she grits the final line out, I chuckle. I may have added that last part to wind her up and I'm loving the fact it's working.

"Good girl," I say patronisingly as we pull up the long driveway towards the main house. Ava scowls at me and looks like she is going to say something before thinking better of it. I feel her taking deep meditating breaths beside me, like she is trying to calm herself down and that sadistic side of me smiles at how easy it is to wind her up. I'm just hoping she snaps in front of my father.

We are all out of the car and the door to the main house springs open before we have even had the chance to ring the doorbell. That isn't even the most confusing thing, the fact it's my father who answers the door, personally, is truly baffling. I don't think I can ever remember a time when he has opened the door to company by himself and looking around at Hilda, the maid, I see she's in just as much shock as me.

"Grant, you finally made it," he grinds out to me and I know it is not a comment about us being late for breakfast as we are actually ten minutes early. It's more of a comment about the length of time it took to get in contact with me. He is shooting daggers at me and if looks could kill, I would have been dead the second he opened the door. But then he notices Ava standing next to me and he stares at her like he is trying to bore a hole through her, but I know he is assessing her for any signs of damage, which he will not find. Her body stiffens up and who can blame her with the way the crazy old guy is staring at her. His eyes assess her and I notice just for a fleeting second that a flash of what looks to be pain or sadness fills his eyes and vanishes just as quickly. It's only because I have spent years looking into those shallow, vacant orbs, desperately seeking some semblance of emotion other than anger or shame to be aimed my way, but it never came. Yet, this very clearly is emotion and it is aimed at Ava, making my blood start to boil and I can feel my cheeks start to redden with fury.

"Ava, beautiful girl, how lovely to see you again. Tell me you are well." He leans in and kisses both of her cheeks, giving her the high society version of a hug where there is no actual touching involved, just the way my father likes it. He hates when people touch him, but I think right now, he looks like he wants Ava to return it with an actual hug, a word I was not sure my father even knew. Ava's body is tight and rigid, with a smile so fake, it looks to be almost painted on her face. But her eyes give everything away, her smile doesn't reach that far and her eyes look empty, like Ava checked out back in the car.

Ava answers Father exactly as we rehearsed. He leads us through to the breakfast room whilst she continues telling him all about the beautiful couple's massage we enjoyed together last night. I mean let's be honest, the girl isn't going to win any bloody Oscars with this performance, but that's the point. I want him to know how much I have her under my spell. I want him to see how much she's changed to be married to me. I also want the old man to realise he has run out of options.

Sitting at the table when we arrive in the large bright conservatory is my most recent stepmother Mindy. As I'm sure you can tell by the name, she is not with my father for his looks. Although Alan Blakeman is in his early sixties, he doesn't look particularly old. His once sandy blonde hair is now a gray colour. His chiseled jaw and angular features that replicate my own are covered in short stubble, which is most unusual as my father shaves daily. His eyes are the type of blue that should shine bright, but the darkness within his soul takes the edge off them, dimming their colour. He is as tall as me, at just over six feet, and despite his age, he continues to exercise regularly, which is why he is still muscular. So, while he isn't bad to look at and I'm sure that does help Mindy slightly when she has to suck his wrinkly cock, clearly there are other reasons why this blonde Barbie, in her early twenties, with severely surgically enhanced breasts, is with my father. The notoriety of being a crime lord, the power, and the money bring in the stupid women, because let's be honest, clever women would run as far away from this life as they possibly can, but sadly, money can be a dreadful motivator.

"Ava, come sit. I don't think you have met my wife yet. This is Mindy. Mindy, this is Grant's fiancé, Ava. Please, everyone, have a seat. You too, Ryder." Despite the fact Ryder has always been made to feel more included in this household than even I have, he still always hesitates. He knows my father can be unpredictable and that at the end of the day, he will always be an employee. I also think it's Ryder's way of showing the old man that he still respects him enough to get his permission to join the table again, each time. Arse kisser!

"Oh, how wonderful that you are getting married. I am so excited for you both. Have you set a date yet?" Mindy gushes and Ava looks stunned, like she has no idea what to say. We did not rehearse this part and she is looking at me like a deer in headlights. But it is my father's expression of fury that is spurring me on.

"Well, no official date yet, but I have hired us a wedding planner who will get everything sorted for us. We are just so in love that we don't want to wait. We are hoping, if we can get a good enough venue, for it to be in the next couple of weeks." I don't know who my statement shocks more. Ryder starts to choke on the mouthful of water he had just taken an unlucky sip from. Ava's already ramrod straight back gets impossibly firmer and her gaze turns towards me. I don't even need to look at her to know that her eyes are burning a hole in the side of my head. Mindy probably has the same vacant expression as always, but it's not their reactions that I care about. It's his.

"Like hell! You are not getting married that soon," he screams, causing both Mindy and Ava to jump as his fist smacks down onto the wooden breakfast table, causing all of the tableware to shake. Me and Ryder don't even blink, clearly we are used to his outbursts. I'm about to return his argument with one of my own when a flurry of staff enter the room, carrying all of the breakfast foods and begin to place it on the table. I take a huff because there were many things I had ingrained into me as a child and one of those was that meal times were protected from any bullshit arguments, it is our fake family time, but the most important one is that our family image, the idea that we are a perfect family unit, must always be preserved. This means no arguing or backchat in front of the staff. I know that if I want to unravel him over this Ava thing, then I have to play by his rules, for now.

Breakfast at the Blakeman residence looks like it has been filmed for a bloody soap opera. Everyone is dressed immaculately, women with their perfect hair and make-up, men with their smart business suits. Your typical rich, high-society family getting ready to start their day. There's a vast array of food from cereal and pastries, to hot cooked meat, such as sausage and bacon. It looks more like the type of breakfast that you would get if you were staying in a hotel rather than the everyday breakfast you get in your own home. Don't be mistaken to think that this is only put on as a special occasion because we are visiting, this is how my father has always started his day, whether he is alone or with company, the only thing that differs is the amount of food. You see, it's all about the perfect image he has been trying to burn into my soul since I was born, and I know it was burnt into him by his father. But it all just seems so false. We talk about the weather, whatever surgical enhancement Father is paying for Mindy to get, and how lovely the food is. But we never discuss any real issues and despite the light and friendly conversation that we are trying to maintain, I can see that the longer this farce continues, the more agitated everyone is getting. Well, everyone but Mindy, who has no idea what is going on and I don't know whether that's a blessing in disguise or not.

Once everyone is finished with the food, the waiting staff enter the room and clear the table away just as quickly as when they first came in. The most senior member of staff asks my father if we would like another cup of coffee. He asks him on all of our behalf because he has been trained that way. To know that Father is the most important person in the room. But when I look at the young wait staff, who I haven't seen before, his gaze is not on the floor like it should be, like he has been trained to do. Instead, his eyes are roaming all over Ava's body like he is imagining what she looks like under her clothes and I can already tell he knows about what happened the other night. The way he leers at her disgusts me, but what really catches me by surprise is the growl that erupts from Ryder.

"Show her some fucking respect, or I will personally remove your eyeballs with an ice cream scoop," Ryder barks at the waiter and the whole room looks at him in shock. His face is a purple fury and I have never seen him struggling to hold back his rage like this before. I know he can tell the same as me about what that pervert was thinking and it obviously pissed Ryder off, but still, he is not normally the type to lose control the way he does. I don't know what it is, but this starts my brain ticking, like I'm trying to work out a really hard math equation. But before I have a chance to question Ryder's motives, he speaks again.

"She is engaged to your boss' son, who happens to be sitting right here. Do you like playing Russian roulette with your life?" he asks, a lot more casually this time. Gone is the emotional Ryder from earlier who lost control, this is the cold, calculated Ryder I'm used to. I don't know why I questioned his motives. Of course, he was thinking about how that dickwad's behaviour reflected on me.

The employee begins to bumble through an apology, talking about how he meant no disrespect and was simply admiring her beautiful ring and that he was so happy for the family. He apologised profusely for forgetting his training, but before he could get through a second round of whimpering sorry's, a hand clasps firmly on his shoulder, interrupting his word vomit. Standing behind him is my father's right hand man, Bullet, and now the waiter looks like he is about to piss himself, but he stays silent.

"Mindy, baby, why don't you take Ava on a tour of the gardens? She has never been before and I'm sure with you as a guide, she will love them." He makes it clear with the tone of his voice that this is an instruction and Mindy quickly agrees, taking ahold of Ava's hand to lead her away. Mindy talks animatedly about how it will be so much fun and the wedding plans they can discuss, and I think, for a second, Ava considers making a run for it before shaking her head and taking some deep breaths. I'm glad she is thinking clearly because my father wanting to be left alone with me while he is in this type of mood is dangerous, but that's kinda the point. Push him until he breaks.

Once the girls are firmly out of earshot, Father stands and addresses the waiter, but makes it clear to me and Ryder that we are to remain seated.

"I am about to ask you a question, and I'm sure you have worked out that the conclusion is not going to go well for you, but I am a fair man. If you answer me truthfully, then I am prepared to go easier on you. Do you understand?" Father says in his cold, hard tone that he always uses for his business transactions. The man responds with a silent nod, showing a healthy amount of fear and the side of my mouth curves up into a grin.

"When you were looking at my daughter-in-law-to-be, what were you thinking about?" He asks the waiter, who audibly gulps and I can see beads of sweat starting to form on his brow. In my head, I am silently egging him on to confirm to my father what he already knows.

"Well, Sir, erm…,there's a rumour going around and some of the other employees are talking about their engagement party the other night." The waiter is mumbling, but you can just make out his words. If he thinks he's getting away with just saying that, he is sorely mistaken. Father growls at him.

"And?" he asks sarcastically, but before the waiter has a chance to answer, Father continues. "And for fuck's sake, speak clearly." As he finishes the sentence, he takes a step toward the waiter and without even blinking, he slaps him hard across the face. The crack of skin hitting skin reverborates around the room, followed by the waiter's yelp and scream. Father looks as calm and composed as always, if it not for the giant red hand print that is starting to occur on the boy's face, one would think that nothing had even happened.

"Yes, Sir. Sorry, Sir. At the engagement party, everyone is

talking about the private performance that was given. Miss Ava did not attend the full party, but rather a special one with just Mr. Grant and his associates. From what I have heard, she displayed her body, including her gorgeous tattoo, then took a very thorough spanking for some bad behavior, before she begged to cum with everyone watching. When I heard this I, erm… I thought it sounded hot. But after meeting her… erm… I mean, Miss Ava. Sorry, Sir. When I saw Miss Ava, she was even better looking than I could have imagined, making the situation even hotter and that's why I was staring. I'm so very sorry. It will not happen again. I'm sorry, Sir. Mister Grant, Sir, please forgive me and take it as a compliment that you have such a beautiful fiancé." He stutters and fumbles his words as he gets what passes for an apology out. I continue to hold the cocky smirk on my face, but I do acknowledge his apology with a nod of my head. Very non-committal. I want to see how my father responds.

My father's face begins to scrunch up into a ball of rage. His eyes are squinted, with the almost black fire within aimed directly at me now instead of the waiter. His fists are balled up tightly and his whole body looks like a coiled up spring, or more accurately, a coiled up viper that is getting ready to launch out at their victims.

"Bullet, get him out of here now," he demands in a hiss through his clenched teeth. I can tell the guy wants to ask what is going to happen to him, but then he thinks better of it and allows Bullet to drag him out by the scruff of his crisp white shirt. His yelp and the footsteps are the only sound left in the room.

Father turns to me with a murderous expression on his face and despite the fact he has been looking at me with murderous intent for my entire twenty-seven years of existence, this is the first time I have looked in his eyes and felt that he truly could go through with it.

"Tell me you didn't debase that beautiful girl in front of a room full of scumbags," he spits the command at me, but I can tell by the casual way he is stalking towards me, he knows my answer. Ryder and I are on our feet, standing close together from the moment Bullet entered the room. That guy is unpredictable and Ryder takes his job of protecting me very seriously. But as my father stalks towards me like the devil stalking his next victim, Ryder doesn't move closer to me as he would with anybody else, instead he remains frozen. I can see his muscles twitch as it goes against his natural instincts to ignore danger, but we both know he has to. I might be his boss, but Alan Blakeman is the big boss, no matter how much we might hate that. Plus, I know I am trying to push him to his limit and I don't want Ryder to have to be punished for something I'm doing. But his hero complex is threatening to come out and I shoot him a firm glance that tells him everything he needs to know. He relaxes his posture and with a huff that is so typically Ryder, he takes a big step back.

"She is my fiancé and she disrespected me, so I taught her not to do it again. As you can see, there's a big difference between the girl you first met and now. Ava knows she has to learn how to become a lady and is taking my lessons very seriously," I reply as politely and as plainly as I can. I need to make it seem like my treatment of Ava is the most normal thing in the world and growing up with him, it may well be.

"You worthless piece of shit. How can you humiliate your future wife in such a way?" As he says the words, I feel a sharp crack across my cheek as his hand connects in a fierce slap. Initially, I'm in a state of shock, normally I can tell when the arsehole is going to lash out, but not this time. I feel my face begin to sting and pulse with pain as the nerve endings feel like they are on fire and have no doubt flushed into a bright red colour to match. My instinct is to move my hand to my cheek to try and stroke away the sting, but I stopped reacting normally to his acts of violence many years ago. I didn't even yelp or make a sound when his hand connected, I learnt that he hates it more if he thinks he isn't hurting me and so I trained my body to pretend like it isn't happening. So I ignore his pointless act of violence and focus on the words he just said to me and as they register in my brain, a sadistic sounding cackle rips from my lips. I can see my father continuing to leer at me with disgust, except now he is looking like I might be a bit insane.

"Are you kidding me? Do you not remember your very first lesson to me about how to make women know their place in this world? I was fucking eight years old and I can still remember it now," I scream at him, because I still remember that day like it was yesterday. It was supposed to be his way of teaching me the correct way to treat women, but all it did was teach me how a woman should never be treated. Ava flashes into my head for a brief second as I remember the vow I made as an eight year old and for the first time since I started this plan, I start to ask myself, do the ends really justify the means?

I'm eight years old and curled up on a hard, leather sofa in our library, my favourite room in the house. Surrounded by all of these books and no people is my dream place. I am reading a first edition copy of Fairy Tales by The Brothers Grimm and the version I am holding in my hand was published in 1900. There is a newer edition, which is the one I'm supposed to read, but I don't get the same sensation as I do holding the original and reading the words. I love reading stories that everybody knows, but this tells us as it really is complete with the darkness. Even at the tender age of eight, I know all about the darkness of the world because I'm being raised right in the middle. To the world, my life looks like a fairy tale. I have the big house, the money, and a father that everyone fears enough to make sure I'm never messed with. But in true Grimm style, that's just what's on the surface. In reality, my life is darkness, pain, and fear.

As if to confirm these very thoughts, the shouting that before sounded further away is now right outside the library and I quickly hide the book I'm reading and pick up the version I am supposed to read. Getting punished by my father is never fun, but he has just spent the last hour having a screaming match with his new wife,

BROKEN

Sandy. She hasn't been around that long, they never are. My mother died when I was four years old and since then, our house has been a revolving door for girlfriends and wives. In fact, it wouldn't surprise me if that wasn't the case before my mum died. My father is no saint and doesn't care about people's feelings. The only reason I can tell why my father has anything to do with me is because he wants me to take over the family business one day. Most eight year olds are out playing with their friends or having fun, but I'm not allowed to do that. Instead, I have just spent the morning learning how to shoot a gun and defend myself from a knife attack. I didn't do as well as I should have and Bullet, my father's friend who trains me, got too close and cut my arm. Sandy patched up my arm and I came into the library to read and escape from the world, but the arguing has been happening since then.

It's nice of Sandy to feel like she has to stand up for me with my father, but she needs to learn fast that it's a waste of time. All this is going to do is increase the severity or duration of her punishment. All of a sudden, the argument stops and I feel like I have just entered the eye of a tornado. The books I have read describe it as like a calm and stillness before the storm really kicks in and that is how I feel, on edge and anticipating what comes next.

The door to the library slams open and bangs hard against the wall. My father enters and he is pulling Sandy behind him by her curly brown hair. It looks like at the start of the day it had been styled and perfectly put together, a bit like her make-up, but now her hair is in total disarray and her make-up is running down her face, mixed in with snot and tears as she sobs hysterically. She has a cut above her eyes that is slowly trickling blood down her cheek to mix in with the tears. She looks up at me with pleading eyes and I just look away. A pang of regret settles in my stomach and there is a part of me that wants to help Sandy, but I'm a small, weak little boy who knows better than to challenge my father and he knows that, which is why he has brought her in here. She stood up for me against him and now we are both going to be taught a lesson.

My father throws Sandy and she stumbles into a heap right in front of the sofa that I am still curled up on. My knees are up against my chest with my arms wrapped tightly around them and my chin tucked against my chest to ensure I keep as small as possible and look like I am not involved with this. As I tighten my arm around my legs, I feel the sting from the cut on my right upper arm from where Bullet slashed me earlier. Luckily, I didn't need to have stitches, just those butterfly strips that pull the skin together. Those I can deal with, but stitches hurt worse than the injury usually. This is by no means the worst injury I have sustained in this house and I wish Sandy had known that so she could have picked her battles a bit better. She's arguing for a lost cause.

"Grant, Sandy here seems to think I shouldn't have allowed Bullet to cut you in the way he did today. Do you agree?" His cold, hard gaze bores into me with great intensity and I know this is a test, just like all of the others. So I drop my legs and pull my shoulders back so I am now sitting up straight. It's important to remember that my father is not just the leader of our family, but also the Blakeman crime family and how to address him with respect has been drilled into me already. I know the answer he wants me to give. I cast a glance over to Sandy, who is silently sobbing on her knees in front of me. Her scared eyes are begging me to side with her, to speak up, but that would be pointless and despite the fact I feel a weird ache in the pit of my stomach, I ignore it and do what I have been trained to do.

"No, Sir. I lost focus and didn't do the drill as well as I am capable of. Bullet cut me because I allowed him to and that is my fault." I sound like a robot rather than an eight year old boy. There's no emotion or feeling in my voice, I'm simply repeating what I have been taught and I see out of the corner of my eye Sandy's head drop.

"Thank you, Grant. So, do you think Sandy was right to shout at me and question how I parent you?" My heart sinks because I realise now what he is doing. He wants me to tell him to punish Sandy.

"No, Sir. She should respect your authority as the leader of this family." The grin that spreads across his face looks manic, but it stopped looking scary to me ages ago.

"You see, Sandy. Even my ten year old child knows how to behave better than you do." I heard his mistake, but I'm not stupid enough to correct him. Sadly, Sandy has not been here long enough to learn her lesson and she laughs.

"You don't even know how old your own son is. He is eight years old and even if he was ten, that is still too young to be involved in this shit," she shouts up at my father and I wince away from the inevitable. He grabs hold of her by the hair again and pulls her up so she is sitting up on her knees. Sandy yelps as my father manhandles her and looks down at her with venom in his eyes. I have a strong suspicion their marriage is not going to last much longer, I just hope that Sandy manages to walk away with her life, because I'm almost certain there are some who haven't been so lucky.

"Grant, would you agree when I say that Sandy here has a big, dirty mouth and that she is using it to talk rubbish rather than doing as she is told?" he asks me and I mumble a yes in confirmation. My hands begin to shake because I don't know where he is going with this. Normally, I can tell his punishment routines, we have been through them many times, but this is new and I am terrified that I don't know the rules.

"You see, Sandy, women in this house play a certain role and you need to learn it. I expect my women to look good and to only speak when necessary. You will never disagree with me or argue with me about anything because I am always right. I am the leader of this family and you should show me that respect. Do you agree that you have disrespected me?" he asks Sandy. She is no longer crying but it's not difficult to see the fear radiating from her. Her whole body is shaking and she is breathing so fast, I'm sure if she doesn't start breathing normally soon, she will go dizzy. I know that because it's happened to me. I bet her pulse is beating so fast, she can hear it whooshing through her head. It's a really strange feeling. I use it to distract me and pull myself away from whatever punishment I am about to receive, but Sandy doesn't look like she is calming down to embrace the panic, she looks like she is going to start freaking out.

Right on cue, Sandy starts throwing her hands all over the place, trying to get free from my father's tight grip on her. It's a waste of time and energy because he just pulls up harder with one hand and slaps her hard across the face with the next. I see her momentarily stunned by the impact and as she raises her hand to her lip and blots away the tiny droplets of crimson blood that have started to form from the split in her lip, she begins to cry. It's a soft, internal cry and I know it well. She has given up, just what my father wants and the smile on his face tells me that he can see it too.

"Grant, there will come a time in your life when you will have a girlfriend and eventually a wife. You can take this as your first lesson in how to make sure that they behave and respect you as their superior. Sandy has been using her mouth as a weapon, so I am going to teach her to use it for something good. Do you think that is fair?" he asks me and of course, I say yes. I have no idea where he is going with this, but all I can do is sit on the sofa and hope that he doesn't decide to take any of his anger out on me.

"Well, Sandy, looks like I can teach my son a lesson in how to treat women at the same time that I teach you a lesson about how you should really use your mouth." Her eyes go wide as flying saucers and they flick over to me in a panic. It looks like Sandy has worked out what my father's punishment is going to be before I have and for some reason, she is concerned for me. Even as she stares down, I can see in her eyes that she is genuinely worried about me and my heart starts to ache. I think I might be staring at the only person, other than my now dead mother, who has ever cared about me. She doesn't even know me and yet she is fighting for my right to be a normal kid. What she doesn't know is that I lost that battle a long time ago. I also learnt that caring about *someone else can only lead to pain, which is why I turn to look away from Sandy's pleading eyes.*

"Please, Alan, you can punish me, but don't make Grant watch. He's just a boy," she pleads and my father just laughs. He doesn't even bother to respond to her, instead, using the hand that is not still gripping tightly onto Sandy's hair, he begins to unfasten the button of his trousers.

"Let this be a lesson to you, Grant. Women should show you respect at all times. If they start mouthing off at you or arguing with you, then it is your job to show them who is in control. Remind them that this is all their mouth is good for. Sucking cock like good little whores. Now get the fuck out of here and close the door." I'm making a run for it before he even finishes his sentence. Before I manage to get the door closed, I hear the sound of Sandy choking and my father saying something about her taking his cock and putting her mouth to use. My brain is spinning as I make my way up to my bedroom and all I keep thinking is that a willy, or a cock as I now know it's called, can be used for so much more than just to wee and that's such a baffling thought for my eight year old brain to take in. Then again, I never really had a childhood anyway.

As I am recounting my horrific childhood memory back to my father, all he does is sneer. Normal children would have been taken away by children's social services. They would have recognised the highly damaging physical, emotional, and sexual abuse that I was put through. Don't get me wrong, I was never touched or molested by anyone as a child, but being taught to use a blow job as a weapon against women at the age of eight probably does come under the realm of sexual abuse. But Alan Blakeman isn't just above the law, he owns the law. He has judges, lawyers, and police chiefs in his pocket, but I have yet to find out who. It's one of the things Eli is trying to find out for me. I wasn't particularly interested, but Ryder says knowing who the bent cops are will give us good leverage when we need it, so we have set Eli on it.

A growl from my father brings me back to the present, he's standing directly in front of me now in an act of power, but he forgets I'm taller than him now and when I stand up straighter, it's very noticeable.

"This is a completely different scenario and you know it," he screeches and genuinely sounds like he can't explain why Ava is different, but I know he can and that is what I am pushing him for.

"How is Ava any different? You taught me that it was all women who needed to be punished and reminded of their place," I reply calmly in an attempt to wind him up further.

"Bullshit! You know that women who really matter, who are better than that or you love, like you say you love Ava; of course they aren't included in that." He starts to get more frustrated with his hands tightly clenched into fists and the vein on his forehead pulsing an angry purple colour. That just makes me laugh even more.

"How the fuck would I know that? I saw you beat up

every woman who stepped foot into our house, including my mum. How would I know Ava is any different to Mum?" I ask, goading him and leading him down the track where I want him.

"Your mother was a whore, just like all the others. Ava is special and you will not touch her like that." Hearing him talk about my mother in that way, the only woman who has ever truly loved me, cracks my calmness as I close the gap between us and we are nose to nose. I growl straight into his face.

"My mother was not a whore!" I shout in his face, spittle flying everywhere because of my rage. My father places both hands on my chest and pushes as he starts to laugh. I stumble back a couple of steps, but make sure I don't fall over and give him the advantage.

"Boy, of course your mother was a whore. The only reason I kept her around was because of you. Well, that and the men needed a pussy on hand to bang after a rough assignment. Your mother knew that if she wanted to be part of your life, then she had to play her part and I'm sure if you ask any of the men who were around at that time, she played her part real well." I'm about to lunge for my father when I think better of it, he thinks that he can win by talking shit, but two can play at that game.

"Was Marianne a whore too?" I say softly and the expression on his face shifts to one of confusion. He looks like he has been slapped and I can't help but smile.

"What... how?" He is incapable of forming full sentences, but I know what he is trying to say.

"Marianne was the whore you were with while my mother lay dying, wasn't she? She was probably riding your pathetic shriveled cock while my mother was by herself in a hospital bed. I know the hospital rang you. They told you about Mum's accident and of her critical condition. She didn't die until nearly six hours later, yet you told nobody. I could have been with her and said goodbye, even at the age of four, I deserved that. But instead, you told nobody and went back to banging your whore, didn't you?" For the first time in my life, he actually looks stunned, like he doesn't know what to say and so I take advantage of the situation and throw him completely off balance.

"I read the letter you wrote her. You were begging for her not to finish things with you. You said that you couldn't abandon me, no matter how much you wanted to because you needed an heir, but if she produced one, then I wouldn't be a problem anymore. You promised to make sure my mother would not get in the way of your relationship. All she had to do was agree to stay with you. But she didn't, did she? Instead, she went off and lived her own life. She was dirt poor and lived on the wrong side of the tracks, but she had a nice house because of the money you kept sending her. Even after she met and married Manny Delgado, you continued to send her money. Then little Ava was born, just a year later. At first, I thought you had carried on banging the slut and that she had given birth to your bastard, but obviously that's not the case. She didn't want to see you again, did she? Well, not until she found out she was dying from advanced stage cervical cancer. That was when she called you, isn't it? Manny hadn't coped with her diagnosis well, he lost his job and went off the rails slightly. Marianne was worried about what would happen when she kicked the bucket. So, you agreed to look after the drunk husband and random child of your old whore. When I got involved in the business, I always wondered what made Manny so special. Why is he exempt from the same forms of punishments that you teach us to give out to everyone else? What made him so special? That's when I looked into it and the whole story unfolded. It was all because you fell in love with a whore who didn't want you. I didn't believe it at first, mainly because I didn't think you were capable of love, but I can see that you did. I've seen pictures and I know that Ava looks a lot like Marianne did when she was younger. Do you see her when you look at Ava?" I ask and his eyes glaze over with fire. He looks menacing and cold, but this is a side I am very used to. Before I even know what is happening, I feel a punch land on the crease of my nose and onto my cheek. It whacks my head back and I can't help the groan of pain that releases as my cheek begins to throb. I move my hand to my nose to check for blood, but I come up dry.

"Are you fucking telling me this whole farce with Ava is because I knew Marianne?" he shouts like he can't quite believe it and I can't help but laugh.

"No, you stupid fuck. I am going to marry Ava, but that's

just the start. I'm going to use her, abuse her, ruin her for every other man, and then I'm going to break her; mind, body, and soul. You made a promise to someone you love and I'm going to make sure that you can't keep that promise. But I'm not doing all of this just so that you can break a promise to a dead whore you once loved, I'm doing it for revenge. You chose that whore over my dying mother. You robbed me of the chance to say goodbye and you forced her to die scared and alone. I loved her and you ruined her, so that is why I am returning the favour. The anniversary of her death is coming up soon and I decided that your downfall would be the perfect way to honour it," I spit at him and for the first time since we got in the room, I hear a noise other than ours. As I talk about my plans for revenge, I hear Ryder begin to growl. I don't know what has caused him to get worked up all of a sudden, most likely it's the fact I have made a plan without him. He likes to go through all my plans and risk assessing them so he can be prepared for every possible eventuality, but I don't need him to with this one. I don't care what my father does to me, I don't care what he says, I will not stop until he is broken. My plan was to just make him into a shell of the man he is now, but Eli made me see I can have so much more. I thought that by following this path to revenge, I would have to give up the desire I have to bring down my father's company. The plan with Ryder has always been to work my way to the top, but only Eli knows the real reason I need that is because that is where all the knowledge is hidden.

Bringing the entire Blakeman enterprise crashing down has always been my focus, particularly since I met Katyia and saw the depraved side of human trafficking that is being performed in my name. This had been my driving force until Eli unearthed the information about Ava, then revenge for my mother became key. Thinking of her dying all alone because he wanted to spend more time cheating on her just makes me sick. I didn't think I could hate my father more, until I learned this. So I planned to break him, but Eli made me see that if I make him vulnerable enough, then I can get him to give me what I really need, the key to his kingdom. But I know it's not going to be as easy as throwing a few words at him, but now he knows that I will walk out of here with Ava and she is mine until he stops it.

"I will stop, you know. If you want me to walk away from Ava at any point, then I will, but you will have to be prepared to give me exactly what I want. And trust me, it will be something that I get before Ava is set free, just in case you try to shaft me. So, it's all on you now, old man," I sneer out the nickname that I know his workers use for him in an affectionate way, but mine is full of malice. I'm reminding him he is old and that it's time for a regime change.

"That will never happen, you little shit. You need a lesson in respect and then you will let Ava go. If you do, we can put this whole fucking mess behind us. There are no other options here and you do not want to test me on that." I start to laugh at his audacity, he actually thinks, despite me having all the information and power, that he has the upper hand.

But before I can finish contemplating that, I feel a blinding pain and a crunch slice through my nose. I scream as blood begins to spurt out of what I'm sure is now a broken nose. I look up and see my father's hand travelling towards me to deliver another explosively painful shot and that explains why his punches hurt more than they should. Sick fucker is wearing a pair of brass knuckles. He must have had them in his pocket and slipped them on. After a third blow to the head my vision is blurry and I begin to sway as I see dark spots in my vision. Falling to the floor, I hear Ryder call out my name, but that's the last thing I recall before the world goes black.

I wake up sometime later and I know instantly I am fucked. I can feel that I am strapped to a smooth wooden surface and as I open my eyes, it all becomes too real. I have been here before many times, but I never anticipated that this was going to happen. Fuck, I thought I was stronger than this now.

I am lying face down across my father's mahogany desk in his office. I have been stripped of my t-shirt as my chest feels cold against the smooth surface. My legs also have a similar sensation, but thankfully, my balls are not freezing, so he had the decency to leave my boxers on this time. My arms are tied down on either side of the desk at one end and my legs are the same at the other end. I wriggle at the restraints, but know it is no use. These are properly installed bondage equipment. The wrist and ankle restraints are custom made to go with the desk and they bite tightly against my skin. Thankfully, my father did not have this desk custom made with the soul purpose of torturing his child, although I wouldn't have put it past him. Instead, this was more of a happy coincidence, particularly when I got older and started getting stronger. At the tender age of eight, I would stand there and accept my punishment, fully believing the shit that he spouted about me needing to be punished, or that he was teaching me a valuable life lesson. But, by the age of fifteen, I knew the truth. My father is just an abusive arsehole who likes to throw his power and authority around, and it was around that time I started fighting back. At first, it was things like not letting him beat me or constantly challenging him, particularly in public, but I soon learnt that all that got me was more rage from him and a bad reputation. The more I kicked off, the more people thought I was unruly and that he should be able to discipline me. In fact, not just should he be allowed, he should do more because I was a danger. My father is great at painting the narrative that he needs people to believe. So, when I started fighting back, he needed to restrain me and this became his preferred place of punishment. I think he knew how much I hated the idea that I was in the exact same position all of his whores have been. That thought alone is just as humiliating as this whole fucking experience.

I look around the room to try and see where he is standing, it helps just a little to know where the blow will come from. But I am strapped so tightly, I cannot lift my head. All I know is that he is not in my line of sight, but just out of the corner of my eye, I see Ryder sitting in a chair in the corner of the room. He has a face like thunder and I can tell he is not at all happy with this situation.

"Oh good, you are finally awake. I can see you looking at Ryder over there. No point asking him to help you, we have already had a little discussion about it. He knows you need to accept your punishment and he will not interfere. Don't you, Ryder?" His voice is back to that sadistic almost sing song quality, the one he uses when he thinks he has all the power, and right now, he most definitely does.

"You told me, if I interfered in any way, you would put a bullet between my eyes. That's what I know!" Ryder states. It almost makes me smile that he is still willing to stand up to him, even just a little. I stare at Ryder, giving him a look that I hope lets him know it's fine. I have been in this position before and survived, so I will do it again.

"Grant, do you know why you are being punished?" he asks condescendingly and it grates on me so much, I know I'm going to get myself into even worse trouble.

"Erm... was it because I finger fucked Ava in front of a room full of my men and made her beg to cum, or was it because I found out all about your sordid little affair and called her a whore?" Silence fills the room and I lay as relaxed as I possibly can. I know all of his techniques by now and I can hear the sharp increase in his breathing. He is fuming at my words, but he is waiting for the right time to retaliate and catch me off guard.

CRACK!

The whip of the belt connects with the skin on my lower back and the sting of the impact spreads across my skin, heating it up, but I remain still. Silent. I never give him the satisfaction of hearing me scream. The next one lands harder still on my upper back and the impact causes me to jolt out, but again, I don't make a sound. This is what he wants and I will be damned if I let him break me.

Several more whips from the belt cascade across my upper and lower back, and my upper thighs, they get harder and more frenzied as my father really gets into the punishment. For him, it doesn't matter who he punishes, he loves exerting the power and the dominance over people and it is always the same. He starts off slow and not putting too much bite behind the belt, hoping that he can see how easily they will break, but after a while, it stops being a game for him and the lust he has for it takes over. He becomes more frenzied with his attack, hitting harder, like a starved man desperate to hear the cries of his victims and to see them break. This is always the hardest part for me because no matter how much I try to train my mind to ignore the pain, it becomes overwhelming with no respite in between. The blows keep on coming and I can't catch my breath in between them. All of my back feels as though it is on fire and I can feel that there are tiny areas of my skin that are starting to split under his impact. I have been through this so many times before, my whole back is just a myriad of scar tissue, making it tough and fibrous, and harder to cut open, but I know he still will because that's the ending he loves.

"Did you really think that you could get away with plotting and trying to manipulate me, you little cum stain? This stops now. Ava goes home to Manny tonight and we forget this whole shit show ever happened. Do I make myself clear?" he grinds out through exhausted breath, his voice low and gravely to match the obvious turn on that he feels at the power trip. Hearing him speak just disgusts me even more and I can't help the very slight chuckle that leaves my lips. I too am panting hard and bordering on going into shock as even the slightest little jostle from my laugh causes intense pain to radiate all over my body. Fuck, it's going to take some time to recover from this.

"Sorry, Father, no can do. We have a wedding booked in two weeks time. You should be receiving your invitation in the post in the next day or so. I really do hope you can make it." The sharp intake of breath above me is my father's shock at my utter lack of respect because we both know that by now, I would normally have broken. But it's Ryder's exacerbated groan that fills the room and I look over at him. He is running his hands through his hair in his usual stressed manner. He's staring at me with fire in his eyes and also a helplessness that I'm not used to seeing there. He genuinely wants to help me and he hates seeing this, he really is too good for this job. I have often thought Ryder was more of a good guy than this family has ever deserved. I give him a little cocky wink to let him know that I'm fine, but we both know that it's got none of my normal swagger behind it. I don't want him risking his life for me and that is exactly what he would be doing. I know this will be over soon, I just hope I'm not too damaged at the end of it.

CRACK! CRACK! CRACK!

Before I even have time to think about the searing pain from the first hit, the rest just keeps coming, but this time it's different. As the belt makes contact with my skin, I feel the fire of the leather making contact with my already inflamed, sore skin, but then I feel the coldness of the belt buckle as it connects and slices through my flesh. I cannot contain my screams now as he continues to rain heavy blows down onto my back using the buckle side of his belt. My flesh rips open and I can feel the warm ooze of blood seeping from the wounds as the belt pulls out, tearing pieces of me with it. Hearing my screams and watching me flail about against my restraints, desperately trying to get free is exactly what my father has been waiting for. He shouts loudly and incoherently about how he will be respected and that he's the boss. His words flit in and out of my brain as I struggle to understand what he's trying to say. The room is full of guttural moans and screams, both from me and my father. His breathing is coming in deep grunts and heavy inhales. I hear the sound of the leather snapping before I feel it's bitter impact. My screams become more uncontrollable and I know that I'm no longer just screaming with each blow. I am sobbing hysterically, begging for this cruel torture to be over and as the snot and tears run down my face, it finally hits me that this might be how I die.

I have always suspected that my death would come at the

hands of my father and that he would relish the opportunity to end my life. He has always had such clear goals for me and expectations for my life, and I have always known I have no intention of being anything like him. I hate who he is and everything he represents. The entire Blakeman crime organisation and every evil deed that we have committed feels like it is a black mark upon my soul. I know I will have to pay for the blood that runs in my veins, but I have always vowed, from a young age, this family would end with me. I have spent my entire life doing what I can to bring down my father and to ensure that the pain and hurt our family causes people stops with me. Once Alan worked out what I was trying to do, he would have no choice but to kill me, but that's where my plan will always succeed. Even with me dead, I will still win. There will be no Blakeman standing by to take over as the head of this family. What there will be is people waiting in the wings, people who are ready to take advantage of there being no Blakeman and to take this family apart, piece by piece. Eli has everything he needs to make sure that it happens in the event of my death at any time. So, laying here and facing the possibility of death, I feel a strange blanket of peace fall over me.

My whole body begins to feel cold, but it is a nice sensation to cool the fire that had been burning on my back. My eyes are closed now and the darkness that brings feels so inviting. My body is violently shaking, but I don't feel as though I am moving at all, instead I just feel light. I can hear a commotion in the distance but soon the noise starts to fade out completely and for the first time in a long time, I feel numb. Then, like a vision straight from heaven, an image of Katyia flashes onto the back of my eyelids and my peace is tainted. I want to leave everything behind, but I know I can't leave her. She is the person who I have hurt the most and she doesn't even know why I have done it. I wish I had explained everything to her and gotten the chance to apologise. I have done so much bad in this world, but loving her will always have been my greatest achievement. I drift further into the darkness, filled with the love I feel for Katyia and trying to forget all the wrong that I have done.

My eyes begin to flutter open and the first thing I notice is that the room is too bright, the lights are blindingly painful, so I quickly close them again. The room feels as though it is spinning around me but I can feel that I am lying flat on my stomach. There's a strange warm sensation along with a sharp pain on the back of my hand that tells me I currently have an IV drip running into my arm, probably administering some pretty decent pain killers. The bed feels soft under my bare skin and I try to move slightly to see what the damage is, but I know that was a bad idea straight away.

My back feels as though it has been sliced to pieces and then glued back together, but that it's only just holding. It feels raw and inflamed and I'm sure without the painkillers, even just a breeze from the wind would cause it to sting. This is the worst pain my father has ever inflicted on me and it gives me a sick sense of joy to know I pissed him off so badly.

"Try to stay still. Doctor Landers has been here regularly to check on you. You have a fluid drip going into your arm and you are receiving regular doses of morphine. But, you have to tell us if you are uncomfortable. Landers has brought his nurse, Debra, over and she has been here the whole time, caring for you. You just have to say if you need anything, ok?" It's Ryder's voice I hear and given the direction his voice is coming from, it sounds as though he is sitting right next to the bed. Of course, he wouldn't take me to a generic hospital, he knows better than that and we pay Doctor Landers a healthy retainer to ensure he comes when he is called.

I open my eyes slowly and as my vision starts to straighten, then I can make out Ryder. His face has a couple of days of stubble on it and he looks tired with dark rings around his eyes. I try to speak but my mouth is so dry, it feels like it is full of cotton and as I move my tongue around, it feels like it sticks to everything.

Suddenly, Ryder is gone, replaced by a redheaded woman who gently places a straw into my mouth and that is all the encouragement I need. The cold liquid feels like Heaven as it touches my dry mouth. My throat feels like razor blades as I swallow, which means I have probably been asleep for a while. I swallow the fluid and start to take larger gulps through the straw, desperate for more, but that's when the redhead takes away the straw. Before I even have time to protest, she interrupts me.

"You cannot take in too much fluid because you are on a drip and we are concerned there may have been damage to your kidneys. Until we get the blood results back, you are fluid restricted," she gently explains, while still crouched down in front of me to give me eye contact as she speaks. I instantly like that about her, she really does care.

"My kidneys? How? What other damage?" I manage to croak out and I see her eyes become downcast and a sad look passes over her face. She clearly feels sorry for me and doesn't want to answer my questions, but she does anyway.

"You have several large, deep cuts to your back that have been sutured. There appears to have been a lot of impact to your kidney area, which has potentially caused internal bruising. You have blood in your urine and we are regularly monitoring your kidney function to make sure it doesn't worsen. It has been stable so far, but we expected the blood to have stopped by now. Ideally, you need an MRI scan, but since that is not going to be possible, Doctor Landon is working on getting an ultrasonographer to scan you and check for any internal damage. Other than that, all the damage is superficial. You will have scars, but that's nothing new for you by the looks of it." Her candidness makes me smile and I trust in her and Doctor Landon. I chose him because he's the best trauma surgeon in the city, so I know that whatever staff he brings in will work to the same standards that he does. I also know that they will abide by the same confidentiality rules that come with any patients, but even more so when you treat a member of a crime family in their bedroom.

"Thank you. How many days has it been?" The young nurse stands up to begin checking out the bandages on my back as Ryder leans forward to answer.

"Three days," he says with a solemn expression and that explains his stubble. He has obviously been sitting here, worrying about me and that is quite surprising to me. I guess Ryder really is my friend after all. Then I remember the reason for my current state and my mind turns to anger. As Debra pulls at one of the bandages and cleans my wound with an antiseptic, the sting causes me to hiss out, further fueling my anger.

"Where's Ava?" I hiss through gritted teeth. I'm really hoping Ryder did as I instructed and kept her here rather than obeying my father. I better not have taken this beating for nothing.

"She is in her room. The old man keeps getting in touch every day to find out why she is not home yet. We have been shielding his calls, but there are rumours he is getting ready to send people over. There's a chance we could be going to war here, Grant. I didn't let Ava go because you made it clear that wasn't what you wanted, but I really hope you have reconsidered." I can see the pleading look in his eyes. Ryder is the risk assessor and he knows that keeping Ava around is the most risky option, but I need to see this through.

"She stays. End of discussion. Tell her to be ready in the

morning to meet with Daphne. Call Eli and he can get everything set up. No arguments, Ryder." I hear him huff, but he doesn't fight me. It was hard enough to strain and get those sentences out through my morphine muddled brain and the pain. I don't have the energy to argue and Ryder knows this.

"I'm not arguing, Boss. But I think this is a fucking bad idea. Keeping Ava will ruin all the plans we have ever had for taking over this family together. We have spent two years talking about making it to the top and taking over from your father. Now you want to throw it all away for revenge. I heard what you said about Ava's mother and yours, and I am sorry about what your father did. But why should Ava be punished for choices that were made before she was even born? Do you really want to hurt her and throw away the business all at the same time?" Ryder's voice is calm and logical as it always is, but I can hear the passion behind it. I also heard what he said about *we* were going to take over the company. I knew Ryder wanted to climb all the way to the top, but it always baffled me because he is the least power hungry person I know. The only thing I can think of is the knowledge. Ryder likes to know everything that is going on, how everything operates, so he can accurately do what he does. So getting to the top of the Blakeman family means getting inside access to how the business operates, something that, no matter how hard I try, has eluded me. The only way to find it out is to be told it by my father, which is why we planned to play his little game and let him tell us what we need to know. But my father loves to play games and I got sick of being his fucking puppet on a string. In two years, he has told us about the human trafficking and sex slavery operation only, and even that he only told us bits. Luckily, it was enough for Eli to fill in the blanks. But I still need to learn about the drugs and the guns, and I was starting to get frustrated about how long it was taking. So when Eli told me about Ava, that's when I decided to speed things along.

"No, Ryder, I don't care about the business. I never have. The only reason I am working my way up to the top is so that I can tear it down. I need to know everything about the girls, drugs, and guns before I can bring down his empire, so that is what I have been doing. But it was taking forever. So when I found out about Ava, I decided to use her to speed my father up a bit. I want him to know what it feels like to lose everything. I want him to watch as the world around him burns. I plan on getting him right to the edge, to be really desperate, and then he will have to give me what I want. If he does it in time, then maybe he can save Ava, but to be honest, I don't really care. I just want to see him burn." I can see the fury in Ryder's eyes as I speak. I'm in pain now from my little rant, I can feel the tell tale itch from the stitches where I have been pulling them with my sharp breaths.

"So, all this time, you have never wanted to be part of the business, you have wanted to destroy it?" Ryder asks me, more confused than ever. I guess I played my part well if he never even suspected.

"I have always wanted to bring him down. I hate everything the Blakeman name stands for and there's no fucking way I will be associated with it." I seethe at him, letting him finally see my true intentions.

"Fuck, then why not carry on with your plan? Get all of the information we need from the old man and bring him down that way. He said there's that big shipment in a month and he can tell us everything. You don't need to hurt Ava." He's angry with me now. I know he has never liked me involving her, but he doesn't get it.

"I have always wanted to bring down my father's enterprise because I thought that was the only thing he has ever cared about, ever loved. Until I found out about Marianne. About Ava. She is nothing to him and yet he cares for her just because some dead woman asked him to. My mother was his wife and she told him to care for me. When she realised that nobody was coming to be with her, she asked the nurse to write me a note and make sure that it was given to her lawyer to get it to me on my eighteenth birthday. She talked about how much she loved me and all the dreams she has for me. About how she hopes I have a good and happy life. How she told my father about her hopes and dreams for me and she can die happy knowing that he will raise me right. He shit all over the memory of my mother and ignored everything she said on her deathbed. She wanted me to lead a normal life, away from all this shit and I intend to honor that. But first, he has to pay. If he cares about Ava, then she is exactly what I need to break him. He has to pay," I shout with all the passion and focus I feel and I know my eyes are wet with the tears I refuse to properly shed. I can cry for my mother's memory when I have avenged her death.

All the talking has put massive stress on my body and I can feel I'm breathing heavier and my heart is racing. With each breath I take, the pain in my back becomes unbearable and I start to wince. My eyes crinkle shut and I hold my hands tight into fists. I wait for the comeback from Ryder that I know will come. He will never get on board with my plan of using Ava. Like I said, he has always been too good for this family. But it is happening, so he either gets on board or he gets out of the way. Vic has his instructions. If anyone at all tries to remove Ava from the property, they get a bullet to the head and he will do that to anyone. The reason we hired him is because he is a sick son of a bitch who has no emotions. He shoots who I tell him and doesn't care. The fact that he has worked with Ryder for two years, they have shared drinks together, I think he has even managed to make the surly fucker laugh, yet none of that matters when it comes to the job. Ryder knows it too.

"No more! Out!" I hear a soft voice with a slight northern accent shout. I open my eyes to find the tiny redhead nurse going toe to toe with Ryder. He is almost a good foot taller than her, yet she stands her ground, pointing to the door, making her feelings perfectly clear. Ryder goes to speak and I can't see the look she gives him because all I can see is the back of her head, but it must have been one scary face on such a small woman because he stops whatever he was about to say.

"He needs rest. You can come back when you have both calmed down. There will be no arguing while I am here. Now I have to change his bandages again because you getting him all agitated and worked up has caused some to start to weep." Before Ryder even has a chance to reply, she is frog marching him out of the room. For a tiny woman, she has some fight behind her and she just earned herself one hell of a bonus. I hear the door slam and then feel her perch on the other side of the bed. I'm tempted to turn my head to look at her but I'm comfy like this and I think it will just hurt like a bitch.

"Now, you need to rest. Stop getting yourself so worked up. Plenty of time for arguing when you are back to full fitness. I am going to give you something to help you sleep. You will heal better and faster while you are asleep, plus you won't have to deal with the pain. Is that ok?" she asks gently. She has a kindness about her that I'm sure I don't deserve. I don't like the idea of her essentially drugging me to sleep until I'm healed, but I do know it's the fastest option, and the most painless.

"I agree, but only if you pass on these messages to people for me first. I have to keep things running while you make me into sleeping beauty after all." She chuckles at my comment but agrees. It's not long before everything is fading into black.

CHAPTER TWENTY-FIVE
AVA

Over a week has passed since I travelled home in a car with an unconscious and bleeding Grant. When Ryder found me after I had been for a walk with Mindy, I couldn't be more glad to get away. She was so delusional and fake, going on and on about what a beautiful wedding I would have and how happy I will be. Like I don't see the excessive amount of concealer she is wearing on her right cheek, or that her eyes look sunken and dark, like the colour has been dimmed from them completely. She looks like a doll because that's how she has been taught to be and she behaves exactly how is expected. All I can think when she speaks is that this is what Grant expects from me. This is what he wants to make me into and the thought repulses me. She is so scared, she has thrown away the person she used to be and now just exists, I don't want that. This is like seeing a glimpse into my future and all it has done is made me more determined than ever to get the fuck away from Grant Blakeman.

When Ryder finds me, he is covered in blood and I start to panic, my eyes roam over his whole body to see where his injury has come from, but I find nothing. He grabs hold of my hand and flutters travel through my heart. Has he finally fought for me? Here I am, dreaming about wanting to get free, has he done it for me?

He politely says goodbye to Mindy and I do the same as he drags me quickly towards the front door. The car is already waiting with Vic on the driver's side. Ryder opens the car door and I see Grant, laying across the seats on his stomach, covered in blood. All the blood makes my stomach turn and I find myself feeling worry on his behalf before I push that away. How can I feel sorry for a man who has made no effort to hide his desire to hurt me?

"Please just get in the car, Ava. We have to leave right now." The urgency in Ryder's voice snaps me out of the trance I seem to have found myself in. But as I move towards the entrance, I don't know where to sit as Grant is taking up the whole of the back seat.

"I will lift him slightly for you to slide in and he will have to lay with his head against your leg. I'm sorry, Ava. I have to sit up front, on guard." He moves his hand towards his gun as he says this and I know that I have no room to argue. The idea of having this man's bloody head in my lap is pure torture.

I do as Ryder says and once Grant's head is rested in my lap, I feel a whole range of emotions. I look down at his mottled body and what I see horrifies me. His back is almost shredded to pieces. It looks like someone has clawed at it and pulled away at the edges of skin. There is blood seeping out and Grant appears to have passed out. Maybe he's even in shock, which wouldn't be surprising with these injuries.

I can see a very ragged and sparse rise and fall of his chest, so he is breathing, even if he is struggling and it's not as often as it should be. I am no nurse, but I am guessing that he has lost a lot of blood, the pain will have been too much for his body to cope with and he will have passed out from shock or pain.

I don't need Ryder to tell me that Grant was beaten with a belt by his father, that much was obvious, but what I don't understand is why. Looking down at Grant laying in my lap, he looks so small. All I can see is a little boy who has been beaten half to death by his father. It's not hard to miss the excessive amount of old scars littered across Grant's body and I know that this is not the first time this has happened to him. None of this excuses what he has done to me and I will never forgive him, but staring at him now, I think I understand him a little more. My heart bleeds for the little abused boy who should never have known this much pain and suffering at the hands of a man who should have loved him. I can't imagine my papa ever laying a hand on me. I wouldn't wish this on my worst enemy.

The drive back to the house is long and I keep telling

Ryder he needs to go to a hospital and he keeps telling me we can't. Once we arrive at the house, there are men waiting with a stretcher and medical equipment, they lift him out and a man, whom I assume to be a doctor, with a stethoscope around his neck, shouts orders at everyone as he instructs them to lead him quickly into the office. I sat there shaking, covered in Grant's blood and frozen to the spot. I hate what happened to him and I hate that I feel any kind of sorrow for the shit who hurt me. Then, as I see Ryder crouch down in front of the car, just the two of us as everyone else has taken Grant in, it hits me like a lightning bolt and a smile spreads across my lips. My heart starts to race and I take hold of one of Ryder's hands with my own, which is shaking from adrenaline.

"This is it, Ryder. This is our opportunity. You have to let me go now. I can drive off in the car and be free. You can come with me. We can get far away from this place and be together. Please, Ryder. Help me." I plead with him, laying my soul bare and showing him how desperately I need to get out of this situation. His gaze drops from mine and he stares at the ground. His mouth is not turned into a smile that matches my own, instead he's grimacing. He looks to be in pain, but I know what he is going to say. I drop his hand and my heart breaks.

"I'm sorry, Ava. I have orders. I will keep you safe, but you have to come inside." He looks up at me now with pleading eyes. He is asking me to walk into Hell with him just because he has orders to follow. He can fuck off if he thinks I am going that easy.

I lash out at him with a war cry, kicking and punching in an effort to get Ryder far enough away that I can close the car door and scramble into the front seat. The engine is still running. Vic is obviously expecting someone to move the car, but it's perfect for my getaway. All I have to do is get Ryder away. If he won't let me leave, I have to make him. My initial punches and kicks catch him off guard and he refuses to fight back, instead shouting and trying to reason with me. But he has no good explanation as to why I would willingly go back into that Hell hole and he knows it. He ends up restraining me, throwing me over his shoulder, and carrying me to my room, where he locked me in.

Every day since then, Ryder has brought me food and tried to get me to talk, and every day I have ignored him. I stay in my room, talking to no one and enjoying the fully stocked Kindle that he gave me on the first day. I may not want to talk to him, but I would be bored stupid sitting here all the time by myself. Of course, I wasn't going to throw that back in his face.

The third day was different because Ryder was firmer. He came into the room and he stood differently. I could tell that this time he was talking to me as Grant's employee, not as my Ryder. Not that there was a *my* Ryder anymore. That ship sailed when he refused to free me. He instructs me I'm needed down in the dining room on Grant's orders. I'm tense and not afraid to admit I'm more than a little scared of facing Grant. I know there is no way he can have recovered from that beating this quickly, so he will be weak, but I'm also sure he will blame me for his father beating him. He always seems to blame me.

Walking into the dining room, I'm shocked to see it's not Grant sitting there, but instead it's an older lady with a bright grey perm. She looks to be in her late sixties and is dressed in an outfit that looks exactly like those that the queen wears, she even has a matching handbag. Looking at her smiling at me, she actually does look like a younger version of the Queen of England and I can't help but smile.

"Hello, Ava. Please come and sit, my name is Daphne. I am here to go over the plans for the wedding with you." Just like that, any like I might have had for this woman flew out of the window. I hear a groan from Ryder over in the corner of the room and I shoot him an evil look. He doesn't get to be pissed off about this, he's the reason I am still here. I am the one who gets to be pissed off.

"I'm sorry, Daphne. You have travelled all this way for nothing. I am not getting married," I explain to the sweet old lady who is smiling at me like this should be one of the happiest events ever. But then her face changes and it contorts into something ugly. Her sweet, queen-like smile is replaced with a sneer as she looks down her nose at me. The change is such that she honestly looks like a different person and I have flashes in my head as I think about the Evil Queen who turns into the old hag in Snow White and that is exactly what has happened here. I should have known that nobody good would ever work for the Blakeman's.

"Well, dear, if that is the case then Mr. Blakeman has told me that we should instead plan your father's funeral." This time it's my turn to growl and I hear Ryder take steps towards us. No doubt he thinks that I am about to launch myself at this old hag, and I have to admit, the thought did cross my mind. I try to calm my breathing down but my heart won't be slowed down. This is what I agreed to. If I don't marry Grant, Papa will die. I have seen so much death and destruction whilst I have been with Grant, that I know he will not hesitate to go through with it. But when I said yes originally, there was always a part of me that thought it would never happen for real. That something would stop it. I hoped that my knight in shining armour would ride in and rescue me, but that's never going to happen. Instead, the knight is the one holding me prisoner. I sigh deeply, resigning myself to my fate. I feel a numbness settle over me as I lock away everything that makes me Ava. All my quirks, all my fight, and I lock it into a box. I vow that one day, I will set old Ava free, but for now, I have to switch off if I want to survive. I realise now why Mindy acts like the perfect doll, it's so she doesn't have to think or feel. In her mind, she is probably somewhere else, living the life she has always wanted to lead and that is exactly what I plan to do. Grant can marry my body, but my mind and soul will be locked far away from him.

The days pass in a blur. I spend time with Daphne, planning the wedding, talking about flower arrangements and cake like it is the most exciting thing in the world. Because it is, in the little world I have created for myself. I continue to be pleasant to everyone and act like the lady of the house would be expected to behave. I exercise, I read my Kindle and the days pass just fine.

Every day, Ryder tries to talk to me and every day, he gets more exacerbated by my response. Apparently, he wants to talk to Ava, not the robot version he is presented with. My heart that is firmly caged away still aches for Ryder. I can't deny that when his fingers touch my skin, it feels like electricity and my heart starts to race. In the darkness of the night, when the whole world is sleeping, that's when I allow my fantasies to take over. I allow my brain a small time to travel back to that night, the best one of my entire life. I remember the way he touched me and the way my body responded. I basked in the words he spoke to me when he made me feel beautiful or when he was talking dirty to me. I allow my stomach to cramp, my thighs to clench and my core to heat up. It feels like he is really here with me and for that short amount of time, my body feels alive. My nerves are crackling and I feel like all of my skin is on fire as I let my thoughts return to the way he made my body come to life. He played me like I was an antique instrument that only he knew how to make sing. I gently allow my fingers to slide between my folds and as I circle my clit, I imagine it's him. I call out his name in my head as I crumble into oblivion in the same way that he made me do several times over. Then I allow myself to fall apart for just one moment and I silently sob. Pleasure still hums in my veins, but it is being forced out by the pain and sadness. I long for a better life, one far away from here, but I don't allow myself to hope. That died the night I realised Ryder would never choose me over his orders.

The next morning I wake up the same as always, but something feels different. Ryder is not in my room that morning. Normally, he comes in every morning when I wake up to try and get me to talk to him, but not today. This instantly sets my nerves on edge and I dress quickly to go down for breakfast. As soon as I enter the dining room, I know why Ryder didn't come to my room, he is already seated at the dining table next to Grant.

Grant looks pale and has dark circles around his eyes, his movements seem slower and more reserved than normal, but his face is still the same. He still wears the same sadistic sneer that he always seems to have when he looks at me. Ryder has tried over the last week to tell me Grant isn't really a bad guy, that he has reasons for acting the way that he does, but it's all just a fucking excuse. I know that I have never done anything to hurt him and therefore, he should have no reason to want to hurt me. That's what it boils down to for me. Simple. Black and white.

"Morning, Ava. How are you today?" Grant taunts at me.

He gets pleasure in tormenting me, but what he doesn't realise is that things have changed. He is no longer dealing with Ava, instead it's who Ryder has so eloquently named, Robot Ava. If Grant brought me here to play a role, then I damn well am going to play it good.

"Oh, Grant, darling, I am so glad to see that you are up and about. I have been so worried about you. Haven't I, Ryder?" I say in the most cheery fifties housewife style that I can muster up. As I practically run over to him and kiss him on the cheek before I take my seat next to him, opposite Ryder at the table.

I can see the matching look of shock on both Ryder and Grant's face, and inside, I am laughing. When I was coming towards him, I saw Grant tense up and Ryder shifted forward, they genuinely both thought I was going to attack him. They never expected this, but this is exactly what Grant wanted. Ryder mutters some confirmation at my question whilst still staring at me like I have two heads. So, I carry on.

"I'm so very pleased you are looking more like yourself. Hopefully, a couple more weeks of rest and you will look like your usual handsome self in our wedding pictures. I'm so excited." My voice has reached strange squeaky levels that I have never heard it do before, and I do a very girly little clap to show I really am playing the part. They both look confused.

"What is the matter with you? What kinda game are you playing?" Grant asks with distrust lacing his voice. Normally, he would be right to distrust me, but I have resigned myself to this life. I just hope that if I give him a little of what he wants, then maybe for the rest of the time I can be left alone, like I have been this last few weeks. That, I can live with.

"No game, darling. I'm just excited for our wedding day to come. I have been planning it with Daphne for the last couple of days and now that you are better, it would be great to get your input," I say cheerfully.

He looks over at Ryder, who just shrugs and begins helping himself to the food on the table. I follow his lead and do the same. Grant doesn't move. Instead, his eyes flick to me like I'm a wild animal that he has yet to decide is dangerous or not. He still thinks I'm a threat to him, but I'm not. I don't have the energy to be.

I spend the rest of the morning babbling politely about the wedding plans. My mouth is moving but my mind is somewhere far away from this place. Somewhere where I might actually stand a chance at being happy. Ryder doesn't even look at me. His eyes flit everywhere but at me. I know that if his eyes did land on me it would hurt him because he knows the girl sitting in front of him is like this because of him. Not because Grant tried to break her, but because he refused to free her. He didn't choose me and that broke me. It's always the heart that breaks the worst. My body will heal long before my heart ever will.

The days pass by in a blur as we prepare for the wedding, but things with Grant are getting more tense. He is still nervous about this new amenable version of me. This is exactly what he wanted, and yet now that he has it, he doesn't believe it's real. He thinks it is too good to be true and he doesn't trust me. Even though I stay calm and never argue back, he always resorts to violence. A slap to the face, a punch to the stomach, a spank on my arse. I am starting to think that it doesn't even matter to him what version of Ava he has in front of him, he will always hate me, and that scares me.

I have tried to do everything I can to lessen the punishments. I don't argue back, I do as I'm told, I even behave in a loving way towards him. Even with my emotions closed off, there's no way to stop the way each nicety makes me sick to my stomach. But still, I keep being nice and yet the beatings don't stop. He finds any excuse and gets more creative every day. Yesterday, he even whipped me on my bare arse with his leather belt. I cried and sobbed hysterically every time the belt connected with my skin and yet, he still stood there with the same look of disgust on his face. I wanted to ask him how he could do it to me when his father had abused him so cruelly in this way, but I know that will only result in another punishment.

Last night, I lay in bed, on my side, feeling the heat and burn ripple across my arse and I let myself cry. Not just crying, I sobbed. I think that was when I realised Grant doesn't want to keep me as his wife, he wants to hurt me. He is punishing me for something and I have to know what. I can't survive unless I know what I am fighting.

When I hear Ryder let himself into my room and sit on the bed beside me, I don't say anything. I know it's him, not just because of the smell that is so very Ryder, but I can feel him. It's like our souls are connected and we could always find each other. He lays down behind me, careful not to make contact with my arse, and he lays his arm over my chest tentatively. He is expecting for me to throw him out, but I am too far gone in my hysterics to even think about getting rid of him. I have bared my soul in this moment, let it feel everything that I keep hidden and there's no denying that what my soul craves the most is him. No matter how much I deny it, or wish it wasn't true, no matter how much he lets me down, it can't be denied. I am in love with Ryder. So, I allow him to hold me, I even snuggle in and bask in his warmth. Even though he always chooses his job, and he leaves me here at the hands of my tormentor, when he holds me like this, I know he loves me too. What a fucked up situation we are in. Two souls desperate to be together, forced apart by obligation.

Waking up this morning felt different. Ryder was gone, no sign that he was ever here except for the warmth I feel in my soul. After my revelation last night, not just about how I truly feel about Ryder, but also about the fucked up situation I am in with Grant, I know I need to act. I need to find out why I really am here and what Grant wants with me.

The morning passes as it has every day; breakfast with Grant and Ryder, followed by time planning the wedding with Daphne. She keeps trying to convince me that today is the day we need to try on wedding dresses, but I keep refusing. I know it's stupid but I have always been raised slightly superstitious. I have always believed you should only ever put on a wedding dress for the man you love, or your love life will forever be impacted. I'm sure it is just a silly superstition passed down through families that no other family has ever even heard of, but I have always lived by it. Not that I have ever been a wedding kinda girl, but when I did allow myself to dream, this was not the scenario. I dreamt of going to dress shops with my mum, trying on beautiful dresses and watching her tear up as she tells me how beautiful I am. Even though my mum will never be here to experience it with me, I still imagine the dress shops. Never in my wildest dreams did I think that a crazy old lady who styles herself based on the queen would come to the house where I'm essentially being held hostage to help me plan my wedding and bring dresses for me to try on. I know that she has turned one of the rooms past Grant's office into a makeshift bridal salon and there are more dresses in there than some dress shops have.

I agree that we will do it tomorrow and instead, we discuss wedding favours for the hundreds of guests that will be coming, not one of them I know. We will be having the event at a hall just outside of the city. I have seen pictures and Daphne has run down the itinerary for the day, but I could hear what she was really saying. With each step, she explained the security protocols that would be put in place by Ryder. She was basically saying 'don't even think about running', but what she doesn't realise is that I never will. I love my papa too much to ever risk his life. Without Ryder's help to free me and keep us both safe, I would stand no chance, so I don't even bother.

Grant only lasts about ten minutes into the wedding talk and both he and Ryder leave. Ryder never stays for long while this is going on, it's like he can't listen to the planning. I know he uses this time to go for his run because I have seen him come back, he looks hot and sweaty, and my sex starved brain just wants to lick him. I try not to run into him after that little embarrassing episode.

Today, Daphne finishes early as she has an appointment with the venue and I realise this is my moment. Ryder is still on his run and Grant is alone in his office, I need answers. Knocking on the office door and waiting for him to let me in sets my nerves on edge. My heart is racing and my palms are sweating. In fact, I am sweating everywhere because he is so unpredictable and I just have no idea how this will unfold. He calls me in and I tentatively walk in with a smile, I want to show him I'm not a threat, but I see the distrust and loathing cross his face the minute he sees it's me. He stands from his seat and walks around to lean against the front of his desk as I take a few steps forward further into the room. He just stares at me and I know he is trying to intimidate me.

"I'm sorry to bother you, Grant. I need to talk to you." His eyebrow quirks up and I know he can hear the difference in my voice. He is no longer talking to bubblegum, robot Ava. No, right now, standing in front of him ready to bare her soul is the real me. He remains silent, so I carry on.

"For the last few days, I have tried to be the person you

told me you wanted me to be. I have taken all your punishments, even when they have not been deserved. I have thrown myself into the wedding plans because you promised to save my papa. You said that you wanted to break me and make me into your perfect wife, I let you do that. Yet still you hate me. Still you punish me and I need to know why. I need to know what I can do to get you to stop hating me. I know we will never have a real relationship, but when I agreed to marry you, you told me exactly what you wanted and I am giving you that. If that's not enough, then what do I do? I can't live my life on edge, knowing you are going to attack me at any moment for no reason. I don't deserve that. I have done nothing to you," I say softly, trying to be honest and beg for the chance at a normal life.

Grant's face shifts into one of fury and he closes the gap between us instantly. He fists my hair into his hands and tugs my head as I cry out in pain. My eyes were downcast, refusing to make eye contact for fear of provoking him, but that was pointless. Now, he pulls my hair so my eyes make contact with his and I can see the fire burning there.

"You do deserve it. You deserve this and so much more. I am punishing you because I can't punish your mother," he spits at me, tugging further on my hair. Hearing Grant mention my mum is like being hit by a brick. How can he want to punish my mother? He must have only been about twelve when my mum died, he couldn't possibly have known her.

"My mum... how do you even know my mum?" I stutter

and I feel him tug harder on my hair at just the mere mention of my mum.

"Haven't you ever wondered why my father is constantly bailing your father out of shit? You should have lost your house and drowned in poverty years ago, yet he kept bailing your pathetic arses out of shit. Everytime your father pissed away your inheritance, mine replaced it for you so you would never know. He has basically been funding your father's lifestyle for years. Had he not, I'm sure he would have got himself killed a long time ago," he growls at me, releasing my hair. As he does, I feel my legs give way and I fall to the floor. My brain is spinning and it is making me feel so dizzy. I know there have been occasions when I have questioned how we had not fallen into the shit, but I guess I didn't want to look too closely. I never even imagined it was all because we were under the protection of the biggest crime boss in London.

"Why is he protecting us? I didn't even know your father before I met him with you," I say from my heap on the floor.

"You may not have met him, but your mother did."

"What?... I... When?" I stutter and just the thought of my sweet school teacher mum having anything to do with a crime boss is baffling.

"She was his whore!" he spits out and that spurs me into action. I leap off the ground as fast as I can and push Grant as hard as I can. Whilst he is off his guard, I pull my hand back and punch him in the nose as hard as I can. The crack as my knuckles connect and the bridge of his nose shatters fills the room and a pain shoots up my arm, but I take pleasure in knowing that his pain is worse. Grant's roar fills the room and he clutches his hand to his nose and as soon as he feels the warm blood trickling from his nose he lashes out.

His hand connects with my cheek in a loud crack and I'm stunned even though I had seen his hand coming towards me, almost as though in slow motion. My skin prickles and then starts to burn as my head is knocked to the side. Black spots swamp into my vision and the dizziness causes me to stumble backwards until I find my feet again.

"How fucking dare you call my mum a whore!" I shout once I have gotten my bearings back and Grant's laughter fills the room.

"You have no idea, do you? Your mother and my father were fucking for years before you were born. They were at school together, childhood sweethearts. She wanted to settle down with him, but only if he left this life. He refused, but she still couldn't let him go. They were young lovers who wanted different things. My father met my mother, someone who wasn't afraid to stand by his side and rule this kingdom, but still your mother refused to let go. Even when I was born, that wasn't enough for her to close her fucking legs." I stand there completely stunned, not quite knowing what to do. Part of me wants to rage at him and beat the shit out of him for saying crap about my mum, but then the other part of me feels so incredibly broken that this might be true. I don't know anything about my mum's life when she was younger. She didn't live long enough for us to be able to become friends and talk about boys or past loves, and obviously, it's not something Papa would ever talk about. I don't know if it's that I don't believe him or that I don't want to.

"You're lying," I mutter, but we both can hear there's no conviction behind my words and the evil chuckle that passes his lips is infuriating. He seems to have given up trying to clean the blood off his nose and it is slowly trickling and spread across his face where he has tried to wipe it, but he is too far gone to care.

"Why the fuck would I lie? Do you think I would make up the worst story of my life? I know you know that my mother is also dead, but do you know anything about it?" I am shocked by the pain I hear in his voice and I feel an emptiness in the pit of my stomach as my brain is telling me I don't want to know the answer to his questions, so I just shake my head.

"My mother was in a car accident and if you ask anyone, they will tell you she died at the scene, that's even what was reported in the news, but of course, that's just the version my father insisted be told. Instead, she was taken to hospital in a critical condition and my father was called. He was informed of her condition and the fact that she would die soon. They told him to come and say goodbye and that during her lucid moments she asked for me. But he never took me to say goodbye, do you know why?" he asks whilst staring at me with tears in his eyes. I ignore them because I can already feel the exact same tears flowing down my cheeks. I don't answer him because I know he doesn't need me to.

"He was with your mother. They were having sex as my mother lay dying. Your mum had called to break up with him for real this time. She had met someone that she really liked, someone she thought might be able to give her a good life; your father. Naturally, Alan tried to talk her out of it and they decided to part ways on a high. But, by the time they finished with each other, my mother was already dead and I was robbed of my chance to say goodbye. The hospital rang him numerous times but he never answered. If your mother had just kicked him out instead of dropping to her fucking knees for him, then my mother wouldn't have died alone." We are both full on sobbing now at the pain of reliving his worst experience. The thought of his mother dying alone whilst mine was sleeping with her husband truly disgusts me. I can't even bear to think of my mum that way, he is ruining the memory I have of her and I don't want that to happen. But then I remember I got to say goodbye to my mum and he never will. It doesn't make what he is doing right, but I can understand his pain.

"I'm sorry you never got to say goodbye to your mum, I truly am. But that was a choice your father made. I'm not saying my mum was completely innocent, but she is dead and can't answer you as to her motives. But to blame me for something that my mum did is wrong and you know it. How would you feel if you were punished for something your father was responsible for?" I say softly. I don't want to make him angry but at the same time, I have to make him see that this is ridiculous. He is acting out of grief and revenge, not logic.

"Don't you see, with you I don't just get to punish her, but I am punishing my father too. He feels some strange kind of love for you, one that he has never shown me, his actual child. It turns out that he visited your mother on her deathbed. From what I have found out, they had had no contact since she had married Manny, but he did carry on paying a large sum of money into your family account every month. An amount that continued up until a couple of months ago when I stopped it. Your mother reached out to Alan and asked him to watch out for you. She was concerned that your father's drinking and gambling had gotten out of hand in the last few months as he struggled to cope with her cancer diagnosis. She knew it would only get worse and she was worried for you, so she sought help with the most powerful person that she knew. So all of this, is all because of your mother. My father is threatening to go to war with me, to remove me from the family and risk the collapse of his entire enterprise, all because of a promise he made to your mother. I genuinely never believed he would go this far, but your mother must have had one magic pussy," he says scornfully.

A rage like no other fills my veins and I feel a roar in my head that propels my body forward as I charge at Grant. Hearing his total disrespect for my mum when I have shown his mother nothing but kindness and understanding is disgusting and it heats a fire in me. My fists are raised and I go to attack without thought of the consequences. But Grant is quicker than me and he grabs me before spinning us around. Before I know it, he has me bent over his desk with my breast squashed against the cold mahogany. His body is plastered against my back and he has one hand gripping my neck and pressing tightly, limiting my air supply. Breathing becomes harder and short sharp gasps escape me as I throw my body weight around as much as I can to try and get free. I scream at the top of my lungs, hoping that someone, anyone can hear me. But in my head, I know I'm shouting for Ryder.

"What's the matter? Don't like hearing about how magical your mother's cunt was? I mean, it must have been like gold because I worked out that my father paid her over a quarter of a million pounds in total. That's some really tight snatch. Or maybe he was getting some of yours too?" he breaths into my ear and I shiver with disgust. I can feel bile rising in my stomach and do everything I can to stop myself from being sick.

"You are disgusting. Having lost your own mother, you should know how massively hurtful it is to hear someone say that about my mum. What the fuck is wrong with you?" I shout back and he presses harder into my neck.

"What is wrong with me? Oh, sweetheart, the list is too fucking long. Let's start with the fact I am twisted up over not being able to say goodbye to my mother because of yours. Then I spent my whole life being abused by my arsehole father, convinced he was just not capable of love, only to find that actually it's just that I was the wrong kid. He wanted you. He wanted to have kids with your mother, not mine. You got the love of my father and to grow up with a mother, then when she died, you got to say goodbye. You got my fucking life!" he screams, pressing down harder on my neck, causing pain to shoot down my spine and my vision to blur. Then I feel him pull up the short black skirt I am wearing and my eyes fly open as I desperately try to get free again. He begins spanking my bare flesh, exposed by the thong I put on this morning. The blow hits me at full force and I am pushed even further into the desk. His chest is still pressing hard against my back and his other arm is still pressing around my neck, but not as tightly. He is allowing me to scream between blows. He strikes repetitively one side after the other with no rest in between and my screams fill the room along with his madness.

"I have given up everything for this revenge. Did you know I gave up the only woman who has ever cared for me so I can do this?" he screams at me and I am shaking in fear.

"Nobody asked you to do that, did they? You choose to give her up, you stupid son of a bitch. Obviously, she didn't have a magic fucking pussy or you wouldn't have been stupid enough to walk away," I shout with venom. After everything that he has said, I could understand all of it. I could understand him wanting to get revenge on his father. I could understand him wanting to avenge his mother's death and make up for the goodbye he never got. But letting go of someone that loves him because of his need for revenge feels like utter bullshit. If I could walk away from this place with

Ryder and pretend that it never happened, I would do it. Even if we lived in poverty, or on the run for the rest of our lives. All I ever wanted from the moment I met him was for him to choose me, but he didn't and now it's too late. I will never get to experience his love and that kills me. Yet this stupid fucker is just willing to walk away from his.

"Fuck you, bitch," he spits and continues to strike my arse and thighs with all the force he has and I can't stop the tears from streaming down my face and the screams from erupting from my lips. Grant only stops to catch his breath and all of my lower back, arse, and thighs are burning with pain. My brain is struggling to keep up with what is happening and I must be losing the plot because once the screams finish, I can't help the manic laughter that escapes me. I sound just like Grant and that is a fucking scary thought.

"What? So now you have ditched the saggy cunt, you want access to mine instead? Talk about fucking desperation. You can marry me, but you will never really have me." I shout and he roars. I feel his fingers dig into the edge of my thong and he rips it off, exposing me to the world. I feel the coldness hit me and fear ripples through me causing me to freeze.

SMACK!

I feel his hand connect with the sensitive flesh of my core and a high pitch scream erupts from me.

"Trust me, bitch, your cunt is nothing special and after I destroy it, it never will be. That will be your lesson for talking shit about Katyia," he says before roughly pushing a finger into my dry, unprepared vagina. I am pinned down by Grant's body, incapable of moving, so I cry out begging him to stop. The pain as he pushes his finger inside, scraping along my tight, dry walls is excruciating. He is not even bothered that I'm not wet, he just keeps going and thrusts another finger deep inside.

My mind is reeling from the invasion and I know he isn't going to stop with his fingers this time. I can feel his hard length pressed against the side of my thigh and the mere thought of it has bile rising in my stomach. My whole body is shaking and it feels like a drum is pounding in my head. There's no erotic or sexual feelings for me from what he is doing, all I feel is pain and disgusted.

"Please… stop… I don't want this. You are hurting me. Please… Grant… stop this. You don't even like me, how can you be hard for me?" I sob as I feel him grind his cloth covered cock against my arse.

"You don't get it, princess. We are going to be married. There's no other way to truly destroy my father and that means you will be mine. I have no interest in your cunt, but I do want to ruin you. That thought is what gets me hard." As he talks, I hear him pulling the zipper down on his trousers and they fall to the floor. I feel soft, slightly wet skin pressing and wiping all across my arse cheek and I realise that he is smearing me with his pre-cum. As he uses his body and hips to keep me pinned down, I can hear him fisting his cock with one and and roughly finger fucking my pussy with the other.

His moans and my screams intermingle and fill the air, depravity hanging around like a thick smoke. Luckily, my pussy has started to generate some wetness so his rough, thick fingers are not causing too much pain anymore, but the problem is that my body is responding naturally. So the more he thrusts deep inside, the more my walls clench with need. My body doesn't recognise that inside I am desperately shouting "NO!", all it is responding to is the feelings and whether I want to admit it or not, Grant has talented fingers.

When he started fucking me, it was about trying to cause me as much pain as possible, but then his cock got involved and from the minute he started fisting his hard length, all he was thinking about was having sex with a girl. My brain is shutting down because I know he is going to do this and there is going to be no coming back for me. I have been screaming for help for what feels like forever and nobody is coming. This is going to happen and I have to work out a way to get out of this intact. Do I keep fighting right until I can't fight anymore, or do I close off my mind and just let it happen? Which one will leave me the most whole at the end?

After a few seconds, I decide that I am not the sort of girl who gives up. I tried playing the perfect wife to Grant and that isn't what he wants. He wants to destroy me, that's how he wins. If I just lay here and let him do what he wants to me, that would be him winning and he can fuck right off if he thinks that is the case. As I am making this realisation, I can feel the wet tip of his penis sliding up and down the length of my folds and circling around my clit. I bite down on my tongue to stop the instinctual moan that is desperately trying to break free. I bite down so hard, the familiar coppery taste of blood fills my mouth but I feel a sense of confidence because I am fighting.

"FUCK... OFF!!!" I scream at the top of my lungs and when I have finished with the words, I just scream incoherently, begging for someone to help me, just trying to get the attention of anyone who might help me. I already know it's a lost cause because everyone in this house is paid to ignore what they hear, they know what Grant is capable of and they are paid to ignore it, but not everyone. The one person I am screaming for is off God knows where on his run and I have no idea when he will be back. Then there's the small part of my brain, the section that has already given up, that reminds me that there's a good chance that even if Ryder does find me, he won't help. He will always choose Grant and his work.

Grant's manic laugh fills the room along with my screaming and I can feel the soft skin of his cock parting my folds and running along them slowly but harder each time. When he reaches my clit, he slaps the tip of his cock against it hard and we both cry out in a sex filled squeal that causes tears of shame to roll down my cheeks. I am yelling both in my head and out loud that I don't want this and yet my body is still responding. I feel disgusted with myself and it hurts my heart.

"You are wet, princess? It sounds like you are enjoying it. Do you get off on guys forcing you? You really are a whore!"

he spits the words into my ear and each word is like a knife to my chest. I can feel my soul cracking and a darkness overtaking me. My brain is thinking he must be right because I am getting wet. My pussy walls are clenching with anticipation of being filled by a big cock, even though my brain and body feels revolted by it. I always thought it wasn't possible to get turned on unless you were really into the guy, that is why I never had an orgasm with anyone but Ryder. Yet here I am, getting wet for a man that is planning to rape me. Who has degraded me and plummeted me into true depths of depravity using his fingers, and yet my body is waiting for more. I don't feel anywhere close to orgasm, thank fuck. He doesn't give me those sort of feelings and I'm fairly sure that he never will. But that doesn't mean that my body isn't going to respond when he shoves his cock inside, and that thought is too much for my mind to take. I can feel the shattered pieces of my soul float away and I close my mind off to what is going to happen. My cunt may be a whore who responds to his abuse, but he will never have the rest of me. I summon a darkness to fill my body, to become numb from it all and it feels as though I am floating away from the situation. Like I can see what is happening but that my brain knows it's not really happening to me.

I watch as Grant slowly starts to put the tip of his cock against my opening, taunting me with what he is about to do. But there is nothing to taunt because I am not really there, he is going to fuck an empty vessel and I am going to float away. As I am preparing myself to fully block the world out, I feel something strange tugging on my heart. I didn't think it was possible because I had encased it in so many walls of protection that it can never be reached, but something is touching it. As Grant slowly pushes his long hard length into my pussy, scraping along my tight walls and stretching them fully, I scream one final time before I float away into the darkness I have created in my mind. I pull on that imaginary string that goes from my heart to his and I pray to anyone who is listening that he hears my cry for help. I am scared that Grant is going to hurt me, but mostly I am scared that after I retreat fully into the darkness in my mind, I will never be the same again. I know I have no choice. Grant can have my body, he can have the moans and the groans that break through as he thrusts, but he will never have me. So, in one final desperate act, I call out to the one person I need right now, the only person I have ever been in love with, the guy I have always dreamt of being my knight in shining armour.

"RYDER!"

CHAPTER TWENTY-SIX
RYDER

I jog back into the house and I'm covered in sweat, my heart is racing. I ran for well over an hour and it still hasn't stopped the itchy feeling I have that something is not right. My whole body feels like I am on edge. Part of me thought it was hearing all the talk about the fucking wedding, I can't listen to that shit anymore, but I know that's not it. I know it's the fact that Grant has ruined everything. I have been working for two fucking years on this plan. To get to the very top of the Blakeman crime family, to learn how they operate and how their business survives. They are the biggest crime family in London and I needed to be a part of it. My dad has been drumming it into me for years that this family is my destiny and I truly believed it. Because when I have a plan, I go through with it and it's so well thought out, there are no other options but to succeed. I thought I had

Grant worked out, I thought we were on the same page. Well, we were until that little shit Eli gave him the information about Ava. Then he became so fueled by revenge, nothing else mattered. But it does to me and now I have to find a way to get what I have worked for. I will not have wasted the last two years of my life.

I wandered through the entrance hall and removed my ear phones, the loud rock music I was pounding into my skull did nothing to dull the thoughts. I put them into my pocket and look around, constantly assessing. It's not unusual to find nobody around and the house quiet, but still I have an aching feeling that something is not right. My nerves are prickling like pins and needles and my heart is still racing. I take some big deep breaths to calm myself and that's when I hear a sound that strikes fear straight into my heart.

"RYDER!!" There's no mistaking that the pain-filled cry belongs to Ava and that it is coming from Grant's office. I have stood by these past few weeks and watched as he has continuously hurt Ava in numerous different ways. With every bruise, every cut, every soul shattering cry, my heart breaks a little more. So many times I have been tempted to say fuck it to the job and to walk away with her, to save her from this bullshit, but something stops me. I have spoken with my dad a couple of times and he just keeps telling me that things will sort themselves out. That my plans to get to the top will be realised, but I can't risk everything for a girl. So I listen to him because he's my dad, but he is wrong. Ava is not just a girl, she is *my* girl. This time I cannot turn away and pretend it isn't happening. This cry was different. Not only did she sound in pain and desperate, she also sounded like she was giving in. All of the fight I normally hear in my little vixen's war cries are gone, she sounds hollow and that scares me more than the cry itself.

I reach the door and it is locked. I can hear Grant on the other side of the door making weird grunt sounds in between manic bouts of laughter, but I can't hear Ava. My heart races and I can feel sweat pouring down my body as I begin to shake, not just with rage, but also with pure fear. Using my fists, I pound against the thick mahogany door, but there's no reply. Neither Ava nor Grant acknowledge they can hear me, that sets my nerves on edge. Fuck, if I wasn't in my running gear, I would have the master key with me. Instead, we are going to have to go old school.

I take a few steps back and then shoulder charge at the large, thick door with a bit of a run. I threw all my weight into my shoulder and onto the door. Cracks of wood can be heard but the door itself doesn't move. I ignore the shooting pain that is crackling down my arm and the painful ache that is sitting over my shoulder. It doesn't matter if I have to dislocate both of my shoulders and bruise every part of my body, I'm getting that door open.

Next, I try a strong kick to the lower part of the door using the sole of my trainer covered foot. Not as effective as if I was wearing my biker boots, but I still throw my full weight behind it and a satisfactory crack and creak can be heard, but it's not enough.

I alternate between shoulder barges and kicks a few times, the entire time I scream to let Ava know that I am here and that I will save her, no matter what I have to do.

I finally break the door open on a shoulder charge that sends a roaring pain across my whole left arm and I know that it is dislocated. My left shoulder is burning and shifted at an odd angle causing a blinding pain, but that pales in comparison to the pain I feel when I finally understand what is happening in front of me. My beautiful Ava lays pinned over the desk, limp, almost lifeless, while Grant impales her from behind with his cock.

A red mist descends across my vision and I can feel the blood in my veins beginning to boil. A fury like I have never felt before hums all across my skin and I launch myself at Grant. Ignoring the pain I feel in my body, I pull Grant away from Ava and catch him unaware, I hit him as hard as I can with my right fist. I pour every emotion that has built up in me for the last couple of weeks, every time I have wanted to fight back for Ava, I pull all of that to the surface and I let it soar free. I pounce onto him, raining blow after blow onto any part of his body that I can find. When it becomes impossible to move my left arm because I have worsened the dislocation, resulting in loss of feeling, I ignore it and continue with just my right. We are on the floor, Grant attempting to cover his face as I kneel on his chest as hard as I can. Blood spurts from all angles and covers both of our bodies. The cast off spray that flies off my fist covers the walls and furniture around us and I get a sick pleasure at knowing I am painting the walls with Grant's blood, just for Ava. When he goes limp, I'm frantically panting for breath and the knuckles on my right hand are cracked to pieces. I press down harder with my knee against his ribs and he doesn't cry out in pain because he has passed out. But that is not good enough for me. I want him to suffer, so I slap him until he wakes back up. His frenzied blue eyes are staring up at me and I know he won't be able to see my usual green orbs, they will be replaced by the fire I feel when I look at him. My lip sneers up in disgust and as he tries to talk to me, I place my hand on his neck and press down hard on his neck. He gasps frantically for breath as his arms and legs try to flail around, desperately trying to get free. Never in my life have I ever wanted to take a life. I have only ever done it if it has been a life and death situation and I have had no other choice but this is different. This is a rage that is consuming me and taking over me in a way I have never felt before. I don't even feel like myself. My head is pounding, my blood is pumping furiously and my breath is panting desperately as my ears ring and try to block out the world. I don't want to hear Grant's futile cries for help or his worthless sobs.

That's when I hear it, one small sound that breaks through the wall of noise and chaos. A soft, scared voice saying my name. "Ryder." It's like a plea for me to hear her and, of course, I do. I let go of Grant's throat and turn toward the voice. Curled up on the floor with her knees against her chest and tears cascading down her face, there's a light shining on her small frame that makes her glow like an angel. Then when you look in her eyes, you see the emptiness and a pain that was never there before. She looks at me like she has never seen me before and I know she is scared of the Ryder she just saw, so I put away the rage I feel, the desperate need for vengeance, as that can wait. Right now, I need to take care of the beautiful girl in front of me.

I walk towards Ava at a very slow pace, careful not to spook the scared girl in front of me. As she sees me striding closer, her eyes widen and her whole body starts to shake. I stop further away from her than I would like to be, but recognising it has to be her decision to close the gap. My heart is breaking as I watch the most amazing woman I have ever met fall apart in front of me. She is crippled by fear and there's a blankness to her eyes that I have never seen before. I have a sinking feeling that the old Ava that I now know I am hopelessly in love with, may never be the same again. But I don't care. I know this is all my fault and I will burn in Hell for this and never forgive myself. I could have, no I should have saved her a long time ago but I didn't. I rationalised it in my head that I needed to be here, to do my job, but all of that seems so small now. I know I don't deserve her, but I do know that she is stuck with me from now on. I failed to protect her, but that will not happen again. I am going to spend every day for the rest of my life showing her how much I love her and how sorry I am, even if she never returns the feelings. Even if in her eyes, it's too late. I gave up on us once and that was the biggest mistake of my life, one that I won't make again.

"Ava, baby, are you injured anywhere?" I ask gently. No point asking if she is ok because it's obvious that she is not. She shakes her head and I breathe out a sigh of relief.

"It's all over now, ok. I'm so sorry I couldn't get in sooner. Fuck, I tried. Please believe me, Ava. I tried to save you and I'm so sorry." My voice cracks as my heartfelt apology floods out of me. The tears I was fiercely trying to hold back whilst I looked at Ava are now streaming down my cheeks. I cry for all the pain that she has endured and all the ways I could have saved her and didn't. I cry for the life we could have had.

She looks up at me and I see her tears are flowing a little more now too. Her chocolate eyes bore into mine and we both share the pain together, but I have no right to feel anything. Feeling sorry for myself is not an option and disgust ripples through me that I even thought about myself as Ava sits there broken. Ever in tune with my emotions, she sees the change on my face and she thinks the disgust that is etched on my face is aimed at her. I quickly shake it away and give her a small smile.

"Ava, please don't think that this makes me feel any less about you. He's the fucking monster and he will pay. You will always be my little vixen and yes, you are a little battered, bruised, and lost right now, but I am here. I will help you get through this. You are strong, and you will be ok. Do you hear me?" As soon as I finish the words, she launches herself into my lap, knocking us both over so I am sitting on my arse instead of kneeling. She wraps her arms and legs around my back and clings on. I can feel her fingers clawing at the t-shirt on my back, making sure she has a good enough grip and that I'm real. She snuggles her head up against the crook of my neck, laying her head on my mangled shoulder, but of course, I don't complain. As her jet black hair wafts around my nose, filling me with the delicious lavender scent that is all Ava, I feel a sense of calm take over.

She continues to sob against my neck and I know she is listening to my breathing and trying to make hers match. It doesn't take long for us to become in sync and I try to slow my breathing down to help Ava, but the pain that is radiating around my body will not be quietened. I push it down, I can deal with all of that later, right now it's all Ava.

Out of the corner of my eye, I see Grant's foot begin to twitch and I know it won't be long before Grant wakes up and I need to have a plan in place for when that happens, but before that I need to get Ava as far away as I can. I stand up, lifting her with me as she continues to cling to my body like a spider monkey clings to a tree. I don't mind, my body feels a sense of belonging when it is wrapped up with hers.

"I need to get you out of here, ok?" I whisper in her ear and she nods, letting me know that she is on board. I walk her up to her room and I curse the fact that it is not as far away as I would like it to be. When I sit down on the bed, Ava feels the dip and opens her eyes frantically. She pushes away from me and crawls back up onto the bed, hugging herself into the protective ball again. The look of regret and sorrow in Ava's eyes kills me.

"You... you said... you said we are getting out of here?" she asks in between her shaky breaths. The pain in her eyes is something I wish I never had to witness.

"Ava, I'm sorry..." I try to apologise, to explain I need to take care of Grant before I can get her away safely, but she interrupts me. She holds her hand out and, of course, I listen.

"Don't apologise. You don't need to. Ryder, I know you made your choice a long time ago and it's my own stupid fault that I didn't accept that. I allowed my feelings for you to grow, built them up from fantasies and dreams, but that doesn't make how I feel any less real. I fell in love with you the night we had sex. You changed me irrevocably and for that, I will always be grateful. I can say I did know real love in my life, even if just for a short time. But this life is something I can't carry on living. The pain, the uncertainty, and the anxiety of living with Grant has been slowly chipping away at me, and each punishment took more chunks. But after tonight, there is nothing left of me. I know after every punishment, I normally beg for you to save me and you say you can't, but tonight I'm not going to say that. Instead, Ryder, I'm going to ask you something else and I need you to promise me that you will do it. Do you?" Her words shatter me and I feel about one centimeter tall. I feel like a complete piece of shit, because after every punishment when I came into her room to check on her, she did ask me to save her and everytime I said I couldn't. I promised myself that I would make sure it never happened again, but it did, and it carried on happening. I will never let her down again.

"Ava, I love you too, and I will do anything for you." I shove as much passion and honesty into my words and bare my soul to her. I want her to know how I really feel, but the expression on her face doesn't change. That vacant, determined stare remains the same.

"I know I will never be saved now. So, I need you to kill me." Ava says the words that shatter my heart as though she is asking me to go to the shop for her. The words have no emotion, no pain, it's like she is nothing and that scares me more than anything. Like a cloud of hopelessness and depression has taken her over and she cannot see any way out. So much so that she doesn't realise this is me saving her. I look at her with fire in my eyes and ignore the distance I have been trying to respectfully maintain. I crawl across the bed towards her as fast as I can and take her face gently between my arms. I don't miss the fear that flashes across her face followed by the repulsion she clearly feels at being touched, but I have to make her see how I feel. She has to be able to see the passion in my eyes, and the love in my touch.

"Ava, I never want to hear you say that again. This is me saving you. This is me taking you far away from this place, but before I do, I have to go and take care of Grant. If I don't, we'll always have a target on our backs and I don't want that for you. I know you can't ever forgive me and that it is probably too late for us, but I will make sure that you are safe." For the first time since I barged down the door to the study and saw the worst thing I have ever seen, I looked into Ava's eyes and I can see she believes me. She breathes a quick breath but her darkness remains. That is not going to disappear with kind words alone, but at least she believes me, that is a start. I explain I am going to leave her here, but that I will be back as soon as Grant is sorted. She nods her head I'm still holding between my hands. I know I shouldn't but I can't help myself. I lean forward and gently touch my lips to hers. It's quick and chaste but it tells her everything she needs to know. I try to ignore the way her body becomes stiff and the way she shudders as our lips touch. I know after what she has been through, doing anything remotely sexual is the wrong move but that was not how I intended it. I wanted her lips to feel my warmth, to feel the tingle under her skin that I know floods her the second our flesh connects. I want to remind her that she can still feel and that closing off everything might sound like the best thing, letting the darkness consume her will definitely take away the pain, but it will also take away the good and I don't want that for her.

I stand up and go to leave, every part of me is pulling me back to the girl in the bed, but I have to make things safe for her. I have to do my job. But before I can reach the door, her words ring out around the room and cause my heart to race with excitement.

"Please, come back, Ryder. You promised," she says softly and my heart swells. The darkness hasn't completely consumed her yet.

BROKEN

When Grant wakes up a short while later, I have placed him on his chair and I'm perched on the end of the desk. His hands are in handcuffs and his flesh is covered in cuts and the purplish colours that will inevitably result in bruises. It takes him a while to fully come around and he blinks his eyes several times trying to focus them. No doubt his vision, and brain in general, is a little messed up, I hit him quite a lot of times. I see the moment that Grant take's everything in and not only remembers, but fully recognises the situation. At first, there's a look of confusion because he can't understand what is happening, then his face locks on mine and it is full of rage.

"Ryder, what did you do?" he screams at me, but I just hold my arms up because the longer I spend dealing with his bullshit, the longer I am away from Ava.

"Grant, you have crossed a line this time and I had no choice. You went too fucking far," I explain to him, but he is shaking with rage and doesn't want to hear what I have to say, but I know he will soon.

"What I do is none of your business. You work for me! You do as I tell you! Now get these fucking cuffs off me and we can forget that this happened." He still acts like he is in control and I keep my face neutral and emotionless, like I have been trained to do. The more emotion I show, the less likely he will be to listen to what I have to say.

"No can do, I'm afraid. You are under arrest, so the cuffs

have to stay on," I explain and his face contorts into a murderous rage.

"You called the fucking police on me? All for some girl?" he screams and I grip my hands into fists, closing my eyes to take deep breaths. I need to remain calm and professional.

"No, Grant. I am the police and I have placed you under arrest. I have been working undercover for the last two years. My assignment was to work my way up to the top of the Blakeman crime family and learn how it operates. The Met and Scotland Yard have numerous task forces whose only job is to try and work out how your father brings in the guns, drugs, and girls. But they got nowhere and so I was ordered to go undercover. Up until recently, I thought that my job was to bring both you and your father down and that you would help me to do that without even realising, but then you started to piss about. You went off script and brought in Ava. You followed your own path of revenge and vengeance and instead of punishing the people who really deserved it, you aimed it at a young girl who is now curled up in bed, a fragile, broken version of her former self. I can't let you continue to destroy her, I won't.

"I have spent the last few weeks watching you hurt that beautiful girl and wishing I could stop it, wishing I could take her away from you. But not only would I put a target on my back from you, I would also be failing the mission I came here to do, flushing two years worth of undercover work down the shitter. Believe me, though, it was not an easy decision to make. Every time you hurt her, I came closer to ending it all and just arresting you, but tonight, you left me with no choice. I want to see your arse rot in prison, but apparently, you must have a guardian angel because my superior officer seems to think you have a use. You do, after all, want to bring down your father, don't you? So, we are offering you a once in a lifetime olive branch. If you work with us to expose the inner workings of every single aspect of the Blakeman organisation, and ensure your father spends the rest of his life behind bars, along with every other head of his operation, then we will give you a free pass. You will be on our radar for the rest of your life, obviously, and one slip up will see the offer revoked. But if you do everything that we ask and keep your nose clean, then you will be free. What do you say, Grant, will you help me bring down the entire Blakeman organisation or am I arresting you?"

EPILOGUE
AVA

I stay sat curled up tight on the bed, but on high alert waiting for Ryder for what feels like ages. My breathing has finally calmed down and my tears have stopped falling. Hearing from his lips that he is going to save me, set off a tiny light inside my soul. It isn't much but it's a little bit of hope that I haven't allowed myself to properly feel since this whole thing began. I focus on that light, making sure it doesn't get any bigger, but also that it doesn't go out. This is exactly the type of task that I need, something to keep my brain from thinking about the horrors I faced in that office.

The bedroom door opens and I jump as the noise startles me out of my thoughts, I tremble with the fear that it is anybody but Ryder. When I see his beautiful face appear around the door, for the first time all day, I feel a genuine smile of relief spread across my face. As soon as he sees it, his typical cocky smile hits his face, but I can see the shadow that it's not quite the same as it once was. He strides over and as he walks, I notice that he is holding his left arm at a strange angle, and that he is covered in blood. Then something in my brain flashes back to the room and I remember that he was like that when I jumped into his lap. His shoulder was hurt even then and yet he let me cling to it and cause more pain without saying anything. My heart pounds at the thought of that, it reminds me of the man I met that night. Not the one that works for a crime family, but the sweet, sexy guy who always put me first.

He is on the bed instantly and I don't even think, I lean over and I capture his lips with mine. It's a brief kiss, but it's full of passion and hope. It's also my way of showing him how thankful I am he came back for me. We don't need words, instead we just hug. Ryder settles down with his back against the pillows on the bed and I lay my head on his right shoulder, careful to avoid his left. He wraps his arm around me and I lock my leg tightly around his. We are wrapped together in peaceful harmony and I hope this is the start of something new. I know we both have so much to talk about and to work through, but I want to and I'm sure he does too. I think we might actually get a chance to see if we can be together like I always dreamt about.

We lay like this for what feels like forever, wrapped up in each other, holding hands and synchronising our heart rates. He provides me with a calmness I desperately need to chase away the darkness. It almost feels like I might relax enough to fall asleep when the door to the room opens and in walks an older man I have never seen before, but Ryder startles. He sits us up, puts me on his lap and sits us over the edge of the bed so we are facing him. Ryder's body is stiff as a board, yet the hand that is gripping mine, the thumb is gently drawing circles across my skin to calm me. Whoever this man is, Ryder knows him.

Looking over the strange man, there's something about him that seems familiar, but I have no idea what it is. I don't think I have ever seen him before. His dark suit gives off an air of authority and it's not hard to miss that Ryder respects his authority, given the way he is sitting and making eye contact, despite the fact the man looks like he wants to chastise Ryder. He takes a deep breath and his face changes, it morphs into one that is completely professional.

"Miss Delgado, it's a pleasure to meet you and I'm sorry it has to be under these circumstances. My name is Superintendent Richard Williams and we do not have long to talk I am afraid. I was hoping that my son here would be the one to tell you this, but it appears that he is sticking with his guns. I, however, am here to do a job. Ryder is a police officer, a detective inspector, who has been undercover for the last two years. His job has always been to learn everything he can about the Blakeman crime family so we can bring the entire operation down. He has been on track to achieve this until Grant Blakeman went haywire by focusing on you. That's when it all turned to shit and we thought that the investigation was over for good. You have no idea how many times I had to remind my son of his job when he wanted to pull you out. I insisted that you stay in play and after what happened today, I will apologise for that. But, now an opportunity has presented itself and it requires you. We heard only an hour or so ago that Alan Blakeman is willing to give Grant everything he wants. He has agreed to teach him the whole business and hand it all over to him in six months time, on the proviso that as soon as it is exactly six months after your wedding, you get divorced." His words hit me like a million little needles and in just one short conversation, my body has been through a roller coaster of emotions and I am stunned. Ryder is a cop. He wanted to help me but couldn't. Now I know why I felt like I was dealing with two different Ryders and that thought makes my heart race. But I don't have time to focus on that because the rest of his words finally sink in and I start to shake. Ryder holds me tighter and growls.

"No, she is not doing it," he shouts at his father with a passion.

"I'm sorry, Ryder, and you too, Ava. If there was any other way, I would never ask you to do this," he apologises and now I know why I thought I recognised him earlier. When he relaxes his face and doesn't look as professional, I can see an older version of Ryder. They share the same eyes and mouth, it's sweet to see their similarities. I don't know why because I don't know him, but I trust Ryder and that seems to have passed a little over to his father.

"What exactly are you asking me to do?" I whisper and am already shaking because I think I know the answer.

Ryder seems to grip me that little bit tighter and I let his warmth give me strength.

"I need you to stay here. Earlier on, we offered Grant a deal, which he has accepted. He will be working with us to bring down the organisation. We will learn how they find, important and finance the drugs, girls, and guns. If we can bring this operation crumbling down, it will be the biggest bust in UK history and will make London an awful lot safer. If we were to pull you out now, and Grant goes back to wanting to learn the business, forgetting all about his revenge, then that would send up a red flag for Alan. He would become suspicious. We put feelers out to find out what kind of deal he would be interested in and it turns out he has a lot of love for you because he is willing to hand over his entire enterprise to his son. He was always going to do it because the Blakeman family must be run by a Blakeman and he is getting on a bit now, but he has been dragging his heels. Now, he has set a deadline. He will teach Grant and Ryder every rope that there is to the business and in six months time, he will hand over the operation, sign everything over to Grant. At that point, we will have everything that we need to take him down. But he will only hand over the final piece at the six month mark once you have signed your divorce papers and are free and clear." His explanation is calm and rational, but I had already worked all of this out for myself. I need to hear the word from him.

"So, you want me to marry Grant and stay with him for six months so you can bring his organisation down?" I mutter as I feel Ryder go rigid at the side of me. Richard drops his head like he is genuinely ashamed he's even asking me. He looks over at his son and at our joined hands with a sadness in his eyes before his gaze captures mine. He looks at me with confidence, like he is asking me to do that because he knows that I can. My heart is racing when he speaks.

"Yes, that is what I am asking you to do."

Well, fuck me!

To be continued...

AUTHOR NOTE

So what about that ending, huh? I know a few of you probably want to kill me and I feel your pain, but I trust you, it will all be worth it. Book two will be with you soon.

Broken really was a labour of love and took over my life so completely. Ava, Ryder, and Grant have become a massive part of my life and I'm so pleased I now get to share it with you. They have taken me on a rollercoaster ride and I hope I was able to do the start of their story justice.

Reviewing is the best way for you to help any author and I would be very grateful if you could leave me a review. Any feedback will help me to grow so much as a new author and be much appreciated.

I love talking with readers and if you would like to talk to me about Broken, that would be great. Use any of my stalk me links below.

ACKNOWLEDGMENTS

Thank you to my gorgeous boyfriend for all the love and support that you have given me. Sorry for all the nights where I spent more time with my laptop than you. But even then, you have always encouraged me and helped me. You are my rock and my soulmate, I love you!

Amanda - Queen of Smut - Thank you for all your help and support over the last few months. For listening to me rant, encouraging me to buy lots of sexy covers, and sharing all the hot me with me.

Dani - my Knight in Shining Armour - Thank you for coming through for me at the last minute and helping me out so much. You are amazing and I'm so grateful for you.

Carol and Robin - Thank you for being such amazing Betas. Your help has been enormous and I couldn't have done it without you.

Scarlett - my Slothical PA - I knew that me and Amanda could train you up to be an awesome PA. Thank you!

Claire, Kira, and Alex - my Misfits - I am so honoured to have worked with all of you. You are great writers and I can't wait to watch you take the author world by storm.

LUNAtics - You are the greatest group of people I could ever ask for as readers. Thanks for always participating and being the crazy active group I love. Your support is always appreciated and I will continue to keep the Asylum fully stocked with chaos.

Finally, a big thanks to you, all of the people who took a chance on reading Broken. You are the reason I write and I am so humbled you even picked up my book. I hope the words affect you as much as they did me.

ABOUT EMMA LUNA

Emma Luna is a midwife and lecturer who lives in Cambridgeshire, UK, despite her heart still very much being Northern. She lives surrounded by her crazy family; her Mum who is her best friend and biggest fan, her Dad who helps her remember to always laugh, her Grandparents and Brother who can never read what she writes, her gorgeous Nephew who lights up her world, and her long suffering man-child Boyfriend who she couldn't live without (but don't tell him that!).

In her spare time she likes to create new worlds and tell the stories of the characters that are constantly shouting in her head. She also loves falling into the worlds created by other authors and escaping for a while through reading.

When she's not adulting or chasing her writing dream, she loves dog-napping her Mums shih-tzu Hector, chilling curled up on the sofa with her Boyfriend binge watching the latest series or movie, drinking too much Diet Coke (it's her drug of choice), buying too many novelty notebooks, and completing adult colouring books as a form of relaxation. Oh, and she is a massive hardcore Harry Potter geek. Ravenclaw for life!

Thank you for taking a chance on a newbie author - hope you enjoy and come back for more!

FOLLOW ME LINKS

If you want to know more about all things Emma Luna, you can stalk me here:

Website and Newsletter -
   http://www.emmalunaauthor.com

Join The Asylum - My Facebook group -
   http://www.facebook.com/groups/EmmasLUNatics/

OTHER BOOKS BY EMMA LUNA

Living in the Shadows: Legacies Series (first published as a preview as part of the Draiochta Academy Anthology) - Full Length Novel Coming Late 2020

Printed in Great Britain
by Amazon